W9-BXQ-916

THE BELOVED
CHRISTMAS QUILT

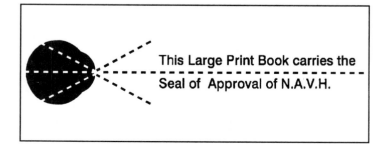
This Large Print Book carries the
Seal of Approval of N.A.V.H.

THE BELOVED CHRISTMAS QUILT

THREE STORIES OF FAMILY, ROMANCE, AND AMISH FAITH

WANDA E. BRUNSTETTER, JEAN BRUNSTETTER & RICHELLE BRUNSTETTER

THORNDIKE PRESS
A part of Gale, a Cengage Company

Farmington Hills, Mich • San Francisco • New York • Waterville, Maine
Meriden, Conn • Mason, Ohio • Chicago

Luella's Promise © 2017 by Wanda E. Brunstetter.
Karen's Gift © 2017 by Jean Brunstetter.
Roseanna's Groom © 2017 by Richelle Brunstetter.
All scripture quotations are taken from the King James Version of the Bible.
All German-Dutch words are taken from the *Revised Pennsylvania German Dictionary* found in Lancaster County, Pennsylvania.
Thorndike Press, a part of Gale, a Cengage Company.

LIBRARY OF CONGRESS CIP DATA ON FILE.
CATALOGUING IN PUBLICATION FOR THIS BOOK
IS AVAILABLE FROM THE LIBRARY OF CONGRESS.

ISBN-13: 978-1-4328-4208-6 (hardcover)
ISBN-10: 1-4328-4208-0 (hardcover)

Published in 2017 by arrangement with Barbour Publishing, Inc.

Printed in the United States of America
1 2 3 4 5 6 7 21 20 19 18 17

CONTENTS

■ ■ ■ ■

LUELLA'S PROMISE

BY WANDA E. BRUNSTETTER

■ ■ ■ ■

CHAPTER 1

Bird-in-Hand, Pennsylvania

Luella Ebersol had never been lazy, but this morning it was all she could do to push the covers aside and pull herself out of bed. She'd put in long hours yesterday, taking care of Atlee Zook's wife, Dena, and their son, Daryl. When Dena's health declined a few months ago, Luella had been hired as her caregiver while Atlee was at work in his shop or had to be away from home for other reasons. Atlee usually stayed home from their biweekly church services on Sundays, so Luella could go with her family, but sometimes she sat with Dena, allowing Atlee to attend the service.

It was not easy leaving the warm confines of her blankets this morning, and Luella cringed when her bare feet touched the cold wooden floor. The late November weather had turned chilly, and snow was in the forecast. The dull light coming into her room was an indication of how dreary it was outdoors. The Indian-summer days of autumn were gone, and she already missed having the windows open at night. "I'll never complain about hot summer days again," Luella mumbled as she slipped into her robe and fuzzy slippers.

Quickly making the bed, she shivered, guiding her hands over the sheets and covers to smooth them out. Mama was probably downstairs scurrying around the kitchen; which prompted Luella to close her eyes and inhale deeply. Tantalizing aromas drifting up from the kitchen made her stomach gurgle in protest.

Walking over to the window, Luella ran her fingers down the moisture on the glass. Looking toward the barn, she saw the door was open. Dad had most likely been there awhile, getting his morning chores done.

Forcing herself away from the view, Luella needed to hurry and dress so she could help get breakfast on the table. Surely, her full-of-energy, twelve-year-old sister, Sara, would already be there. Luella and Sara were ten years apart, so with the exception of their easygoing personalities, they had little in common. Sara liked to be outdoors with the animals, whereas Luella enjoyed indoor things like embroidery work, reading, and cooking. One of her favorite things to make this time of year was apple butter bars. She'd baked a batch of them last night to take over to the Zooks' this morning.

"And I'd better get dressed or I'll never get there." Luella washed her face and hands with water from the basin on her dresser then chose a plain, dark blue dress to wear. Once she'd gotten dressed and put on her shoes, she secured her hair in a bun and put her heart-shaped white head covering on.

Downstairs in the kitchen, the first thing she did was slip her black apron on. "What's for *friehschtick,* and what can I do to help you?" she asked her mother.

Mom turned from where she stood at the stove. "Thought we'd have *pannekuche* for our breakfast this morning."

Luella grinned. "Pancakes sound good to me. Shall I mix up the batter?"

"Already done." Mom stepped aside and pointed to the griddle on the stove, where bubbles formed on the surface of four nice-sized pancakes. "Sara set the table, and now she's outside helping your *daed* in the barn."

Luella's brows furrowed. "How come Samuel's not helping Dad feed the animals? Did my little *bruder* sleep in this morning?"

11

"Your brother came down with the flu during the night. He's resting in bed."

"I'm sorry to hear it. Sure hope he feels better soon and no one else gets it." Luella especially didn't want to get sick. It would mean not being able to take care of Dena, and Luella certainly didn't want her dear friend to get the flu. It was bad enough Dena's heart was failing. Atlee's wife was pure sweetness, and although her heart had weakened, she never complained. According to what the doctor had told Atlee, Dena would not live to see their young son become a man.

"Daughter, did you hear what I said?" Mom tapped Luella's shoulder, halting her contemplations.

Luella turned around. "*Ach.* Sorry, Mom. I was deep in thought."

Mom gave a nod. "It looked as if you were."

"What did you say to me?"

"I asked what time you need to be at the Zooks'."

Luella glanced at the battery-operated clock. "I should leave within the hour."

"Then we'd best eat soon. Why don't you run out to the barn and tell your daed and *schweschder* to stop what they're doing and come in for breakfast? If they're not done,

12

they can finish up when the meal is over."

"Okay, Mom." Luella pulled her woolen shawl from the wall peg and slipped out the back door.

Pulling the shawl tighter around her shoulders as she approached the barn, Luella heard Dad whistling. He always made music when he fed the livestock. Luella felt blessed to have such a cheerful father. For that matter, both of her parents had positive attitudes, even when faced with trials. Luella hoped someday, when she was married and had children, that she could set a good example for them as well.

Upon entering the barn, Luella spotted her sister down on her knees, petting one of the barn cats.

Luella cleared her throat real loud and, with a jerk of her head, Sara looked up. "You shouldn't sneak up on a person like that. Almost gave me a *hatzschlack.*"

Hearing her sister say "heart attack" caused Luella to think about poor Dena again. Ever since she had begun working for Atlee, she thought about him and his wife's situation. How sad it would be to marry someone and then a few years later learn they were gravely ill.

In an effort to redirect her thoughts, Luella knelt beside Sara and reached out to

13

stroke the cat. "I thought you were supposed to be helping Dad feed the animals." She wagged her finger.

Sara's pale brows lowered, and she pushed a lock of silky blond hair back under the head scarf she wore to do chores. "For your information, I've already fed the *katze* and the *hund,* so now I'm just takin' a little time to pet Cloud."

Luella snickered. Her sister loved animals and had named every one of their cats. This one she called Cloud because of its fluffy white fur. "Okay, Sara, I understand, but Mom sent me out here to fetch you and Dad so we could eat breakfast."

Sara rose to her feet. "Oh, good 'cause I'm *hungerich.*"

Luella smiled. "You go ahead to the house, and I'll get Dad."

"All right. See you up in the kitchen." Her sister scampered out the door with Cloud following close behind.

First, Luella paused to check on Buttercup, the Nubian goat her parents got for her sixteenth birthday. The floppy-eared goat came to the front of the stall and bleated, most likely hoping Luella would follow through with the normal ear scratching. "Don't worry, I didn't forget you, Buttercup." Luella had to giggle when the goat leaned into her hand as she scratched behind its ears. "Why, I believe you are actually smiling."

After fussing with Buttercup, Luella followed Dad's whistles to the back of the barn. She found him inside the stall of Mom's buggy horse.

Seemingly engrossed in his chore of spreading fresh straw, Dad didn't notice her at first. It wasn't easy running a farm, but somehow he put enjoyment behind the hardest of work. Even now, as her father followed his normal routine of freshening the stall, one would never know he'd been up before daybreak, putting in a few hours before breakfast.

She stood watching him a few seconds longer, until he paused to wipe his forehead. "*Ach,* Luella! I didn't hear you come in. How long have you been standing there?"

"Not long at all. I've enjoyed the tune you've been whistling, while watching you work." With tender emotions, she looked at her dad. "You know what I always say, Dad. 'Keep your happiness in circulation.' "

He grinned, giving his full dark beard a tug. "You know me . . . always singin' or whistlin' when I have chores to do."

She nodded. "The reason I came out is to tell you breakfast is about ready. Since I

15

have to leave for the Zooks' house soon, Mom said I should call you in to eat."

He gestured to the pile of straw yet to be spread. "I still have a little more work here."

"I know, but Mom thought you could finish up after breakfast."

He reached under his straw hat and scratched his head. "*Jah,* I suppose I could do that all right. Who knows, I might be able to work a lot harder once my belly is full." Dad winked at Luella. "Agreed?"

She grinned up at him. "Jah, Dad, I agree. But ya better not eat too much, or it'll make you sleepy."

"I've never looked at it that way," her father said with a chuckle, as he put his arm around Luella's shoulder and they walked out of the barn together.

"How is Dena doing today?" Luella asked when Atlee let her into his house.

"Not well." Atlee slowly shook his head, glancing toward their bedroom, which was on the first floor. "She didn't sleep well last night, so I insisted she stay in bed this morning and rest." He reached up to rub his neck. The poor man's somber expression said it all; he was worried about his wife.

Luella wanted to offer him comfort but

wasn't sure how. She certainly couldn't give Atlee a hug, like she did whenever Dad was troubled about something. That would be inappropriate. "I'm sorry, Atlee. I'll keep Daryl entertained today and make sure Dena's needs are met."

His shoulders drooped, and he rubbed the heel of his palm against his chest. Luella saw only sadness in Atlee's brown eyes. His thick, dark brows, matching the color of his hair and beard, pulled downward. He looked so defeated. "According to the doctor, short of a miracle, my *fraa* doesn't have long to live."

Luella's heart went out to him. Although Atlee tried to stay strong for his wife and son, she could see the stress was wearing on him. Dark circles under his eyes suggested he'd gotten very little sleep last night. She'd been praying and praying for Dena, but the dear woman seemed to be getting weaker every day. How would Atlee cope when she was gone? How would their son manage without a mother? At times such as now, Luella couldn't help but question God. Why did He call some people home in the prime of their life, while others got to live to a ripe old age? It didn't seem fair, but it wasn't her place to question God. As their bishop had said in a sermon lately, "God's ways are not our ways, and He has a plan for every one of His people, even if we can't see or understand it."

Luella tilted her head toward the stairs but heard no noise coming from up there. The Zooks' house was a large two-story, with one bedroom down, and the other four bedrooms on the second floor. "Is Daryl still in bed?" she asked, feeling the need to talk about something else — something that didn't speak of death.

"Jah." Atlee ambled over to the woodstove and picked up the coffeepot. "Would you like a cup of *kaffi,* Luella?"

"No, thank you. I'll fix you some friehschtick, though."

He shook his head. "I've already had breakfast."

Luella glanced at the table, where only Atlee's empty cup set. No sign of any plates having been out, nor was there a frying pan or kettle on the stove. "What did you have?"

"I ate a piece of that tasty shoofly pie you made yesterday, to go with my coffee."

"I see." She glanced at the kitchen sink, but it was empty.

As if he could read her thoughts, Atlee quickly said, "I didn't use a *deller.* I put the pie on a napkin and ate it with my fingers." He held up his hand and wiggled his fingers.

18

"It got kind of sticky, but that's what soap and *wasser* are for."

She resisted the urge to laugh, certain that he didn't mean it to be funny. Truthfully, the only time Luella saw Atlee laugh, or even smile, was when he took time out from his job to play with his son. Atlee had a woodworking shop in a separate building on his property, where he made doghouses, birdhouses, picnic tables, lawn chairs, and some small storage sheds. He did most of the work himself, but one of the young Amish men in the area came to help when Atlee had too many orders to fill. At noon-time and at least once more during the day, Atlee came into the house to check on Dena and spend a little time with Daryl. If Luella had learned one thing about Atlee since she'd been working for him, it was that he was a devoted husband and father. She hoped to find a man someday who would be equally devoted to her. For now, though, her only goal in life was to be a good care-giver for Dena and see that Daryl had everything he needed. That's what Atlee had hired her for, and she wouldn't let him down.

CHAPTER 2

Luella took a seat in the chair beside Dena's bed, while Daryl played with his wooden horse on the floor nearby. Luella had brought the boy into the bedroom with her, partly so she could keep an eye on him and also to give Dena a chance to be with her son.

"You don't have to sit here with me." Dena's brown eyes closed then fluttered open. It was an obvious struggle for her to stay awake. "I'm sure you have other things to do."

Luella shook her head. "The lunch dishes are done, and the laundry is hanging on the line outside, so there isn't much I need to do till it's time to bring the clothes in and start supper." She touched Dena's pale hand. "Besides, I enjoy talking with you. But if you're too tired to visit, I can come back later to check on you and see if there's anything you need."

"What I need is to get up and do something meaningful. I don't know why Atlee insisted I stay in bed all day." Dena released a lingering sigh. "I feel so useless."

"Would you like me to bring your basket of yarn so you can sit up in bed and knit or crochet?"

"I suppose I could do that, but it's not the same as cooking for my family, cleaning house, or going for a walk with my precious little *bu.*" When Dena turned her head to look at Daryl, tears gathered in the corner of her eyes. "I'm missing so much not being able to care for him like I should, and . . ." Her voice lowered. "It breaks my heart to think that I won't be around to see him start school."

Luella gently squeezed her friend's fingers. "Please don't talk like that, Dena. You must not give up hope."

Dena lifted a shaky hand to push a wisp of auburn hair away from her colorless cheek. "My hope lies in Jesus, but I have to face reality. My heart's not getting any stronger, and it's only a matter of time until . . ." Her voice trailed off as several tears seeped out from under her lashes. "There's so much I want to tell you, Luella, but I can barely keep my eyes open. We can talk later. But for now, why don't you take

Daryl outside to play while I take a nap?"

Luella nodded. "I can do that. Is there anything I can do or get for you before we head outdoors?"

"No, I'm fine. I just need to sleep for a while."

Luella patted Dena's arm then tucked the lovely quilt covering her bed up under her chin. "I'll be in to check on you after we come back inside."

"Danki." Dena closed her eyes.

Luella continued to sit a few more minutes, until she was sure Dena had fallen asleep. Then she left her chair, took Daryl's hand, and led him silently from the room.

"Why can't *Mammi* come outside with us?" Daryl's innocence tugged at Luella's heart.

"Your mamma is a little tired still, and she needs her rest."

With no more questions, Daryl stretched out each arm while Luella slipped his jacket on, then put her heavy woolen shawl around her shoulders.

As they stepped off the porch, Luella stopped. In certain spots, sunlight glistened on the grass, making dewdrops sparkle like tiny diamonds. But in other shaded areas, yet untouched by the warmth of the afternoon sun, frosty patterns coated the still-frozen blades of grass. Luella was glad they both wore heavier attire, as she blew air from her mouth and watched the vapor dissolve into the cold, nippy air.

"*Schnee!* Schnee!" Daryl pointed to the thin layer of sparkling ice lingering on the trees in the Zooks' backyard.

"No, Daryl, it's frost, not snow," Luella said in Pennsylvania Dutch. At the age of four, he was still too young to understand most English words, but that would change when he turned six and went to school.

The boy tipped his auburn head back, looked up at her curiously, and repeated the word *schnee.*

She didn't correct him this time. He'd learn the difference between snow and frost eventually. As chilly as it was, all too soon Daryl would be correct in yelling, "Schnee."

Luella watched as the young lad ran through the yard, making a matted-down trail in the frost as he went. While Daryl was content amusing himself, she turned and looked back at the large, five-bedroom house. How exciting it must have been when the Zooks were first married and moved into this place.

She wiped the tears that had escaped her eyes. No doubt they'd planned for a big family with plenty of children to fill all those bedrooms — hopes and dreams that would never be fulfilled.

Continuing to study the house, Luella couldn't help noticing all the beautiful shrubbery planted here and there. In between the bushes, and along the fence line surrounding their property, were remnants of late summer and autumn flowers, now blackened or lifeless by the brutal cold frost. Dena must have felt such joy when planting those flowers and watching them bloom, adding color to the landscape. Tending the house, cooking, cleaning, and taking care of her husband and son — it would be hard to give it all up.

As Luella looked around the rest of the property toward the barn, and then back to Daryl, the ache inside her grew deeper, knowing what all three of these good people would be losing. It was a horrible situation, no matter from whose perspective she looked at it. Dena was losing out on all the hopes and dreams she would have shared growing old with her husband.

I can't even think what will happen to Atlee and Daryl once Dena is gone. Will Atlee stay here, or will it be too hard to be reminded daily of the precious memories he and Dena made inside and outside this home? Will this land and house be too big for just him and his son?

Luella knew when the time came, only Atlee could decide what would work best for him and the boy. Oh, how her heart ached for them, though.

Startling Luella out of her thoughts, Daryl ran up to her and pointed to the frosty designs in the grass. "Look what I did." He giggled as the sun went behind a cloud.

"Now that is quite pretty, isn't it?" Luella had to chuckle at Daryl's pleasure, even with the foreboding going through her mind. Taking a deep breath, she reached for the boy's hand. "Why don't we go for a walk?"

"*Daadi!* Daadi!" Daryl pointed across the way to his father's woodshop.

Atlee would be busy, but to deny his son the right to say hello wouldn't be right, either. "Okay, we'll go see your daddy. But only for a little while, because he has work to do."

Luella thought about the shoofly pie Atlee had eaten for breakfast this morning, and wondered if he'd like another piece. Or maybe he would enjoy some of the apple butter bars she'd brought from home.

"Let's go inside for a minute and get a treat for your daed." She guided Daryl toward the house. "Would you like some dessert, Daryl?"

The boy's round face broke into a wide smile as he bobbed his head. *"Kichlin."*

She smiled. They weren't cookies, but it was all the same to Daryl. *Maybe along with the bars, I'll take a Thermos of coffee out to Atlee.*

Atlee's stomach growled. It had only been a few hours since lunch, but for some reason he was hungry. *Guess I should have had a second sandwich when Luella offered it to me. That's what I get for bein' polite.* Atlee appreciated Luella's willingness to help out. Of course, she was being paid for her work. But he had a hunch the young woman would have done it without any pay.

It amazed him how quickly his wife and her caregiver had become friends. Even though they were more than ten years apart, Dena and Luella always seemed to have something to talk about. In addition to keeping Dena company and Daryl entertained, Luella was an excellent cook, and they were all well fed. She also did the laundry, cleaning, and other household chores, all without the slightest complaint. Luella was patient and kind, and most always had a smile on her face. Hiring Luella had been the best medicine he could have given his precious Dena.

When the door to his shop opened, Atlee's musings came to a halt. Seeing Luella and Daryl come in, he dropped what he was doing and went over to greet them.

"Daryl wanted to visit his daadi," Luella explained. She held out the plate, along with Atlee's old Thermos. "And I thought you might enjoy these apple butter bars and some coffee."

Grinning, he ruffled his son's wavy hair. "You bet I would."

Daryl stood close to Atlee. While the two of them ate their share, Luella remained off to one side, watching them.

"Aren't you gonna join us?" Atlee gestured to a chair near his workbench. "Why don't you have a seat?"

"I ate a bar before we came out of the house."

"Well, there's no reason you can't have another. After all, you're the one who made them."

A light in Luella's blue eyes shone when she smiled and nodded. "True. All right, I'll eat another one, but then Daryl and I need to go back in the house so I can check on Dena."

"How's she doing this afternoon?" He poured himself some coffee and waited for her reply.

"Dena seems quite tired today. She was sleeping when I left her."

Atlee gave his full beard a tug. "She didn't sleep well last night, so I told her to stay in bed today."

"Jah, that's what Dena said."

He set his coffee down and crossed his arms. "My wife would like to be up and around, doing all the things she used to do, but she's not up for that anymore." He paused, reaching around to rub a sore spot on his lower back. "I don't know how we'll get along without Dena. This may be our last Christmas together." He paused, and glanced down at Daryl, glad his son couldn't understand much English yet.

"You mustn't think that." Luella tipped her blond head to one side. "Your wife may be here for a good many months yet."

Atlee groaned. "I hope so, Luella. Jah, I truly do. If only God would give us a Christmas miracle."

Back in the house, Luella put Daryl down for a nap. He didn't want to rest, of course, but after she read him a story, he fell asleep on the sofa. Now it was time to see how Daryl's mother was doing.

Luella peeked through the small opening in Dena's door and was surprised to see her sitting up in bed. She poked her head into the room. "I see you're awake now. Would you like some dessert and hot chocolate?"

"Maybe after a while." Dena glanced toward the door. "Where's Daryl?"

"He's asleep on the living-room sofa."

"I'm glad. Some *kinner* his age don't take naps anymore, but my son does better when he's had one." Dena offered Luella a weak smile. "He will be in a good mood during supper."

"Would you like to get up for a bit, and sit in your rocking chair?" Luella asked.

"Maybe later. Right now, I need to talk to you about something."

Luella felt concern, seeing Dena's serious expression. "What is it?" Biting her lip, she pulled the rocking chair next to the bed.

Dena picked up one corner of the lovely quilt on her bed and held it close to her heart. "The pattern for this is called 'Country Patch,' but I call it my beloved Christmas quilt, because my mother, who made the covering, gave it to me and Atlee for Christmas the first year we were married."

"It is a lovely quilt. Your *mamm* was a talented quilter."

Dena got a faraway look in her eyes. "Jah, she certainly was. I miss my mamm and wish she was still alive to take care of Daryl when I'm gone."

Luella's throat felt swollen, and it was difficult to swallow. She wished Dena would stop talking about her imminent death.

"Would you do me a favor, Luella?"

"Jah. What do you need?"

"I'd like you to take this quilt home with you, as an early Christmas present."

"Ach, no, I could never accept such a gift." Luella's fingers touched her parted lips. "It should remain in your family; especially with it being a present from your mother. Besides, it's not even Christmas yet."

Dena shook her head. "I may not be here to give it to you on Christmas Day. Please, Luella, I want you to have this beloved quilt. It would mean a lot to me, knowing you will someday pass the quilt on to your eldest daughter."

"But I'm not even married, and I may never find a husband, so really, you should reconsider."

Dena shook her head. "I have no sisters, and since my parents have both passed on, I have no family to give the quilt to. Please, Luella, I insist that you take it."

"Oh, okay. Danki, Dena. I will treasure it always."

Dena breathed in and out slowly. "I have

another favor to ask."

Luella was hesitant to even ask what. She hoped her dear friend didn't want to give her some other family heirloom. "What other favor?"

"I want you to promise that after I'm gone, you will take care of Atlee and Daryl."

"Well, of course, I will come over and check on them regularly, but I really wish you wouldn't talk of such things."

"It's important that I say all this now." Dena stroked the quilt lovingly. "My son will still need someone to care for him while Atlee's working in his shop. And Atlee — well, he's not good in the kitchen, and he won't have time to clean house or do laundry. Won't you please agree to keep working for him after I'm gone, as you are now? It would give me a sense of peace to know that my family will be taken care of after I die."

Luella had to force a smile as she nodded and said, "Jah, Dena, I will take care of the household and watch your son."

"Be a friend to Atlee, too." Dena lowered her head. "Please . . . I know it won't be easy for him, but he will need someone to talk to."

Luella squeezed her friend's hand. "Jah, Dena, I will."

"My husband is trying to stay strong for

31

me and our son, but I feel his sadness and the concern he has for me." Tears welled up in Dena's dark eyes as she released a sigh. "Danki, Luella. This means so much to me. I feel such a relief knowing you'll be here for them."

Although she kept her thoughts to herself, Luella realized the decision of whether she would continue to work here or not would be up to Dena's husband. She would only be able to keep her promise to Dena if Atlee agreed.

CHAPTER 3

Tears stung Atlee's eyes as he stood beside his wife's simple coffin, made of poplar wood. Staring at her lifeless body, he swallowed several times, hoping for some sort of control. The last thing he needed was to break down in front of his son. He had to be strong, if only for Daryl's sake, but oh, he couldn't imagine spending the rest of his days without the love of his life. Dena was only thirty-five — just three years younger than him. She was too young to die. His beautiful wife should have had many good years ahead of her. It was hard not to feel bitter, even in his state of shock.

Since Dena's passing, Atlee had felt like he was in a fog, unable to think clearly or even process his thoughts. It was almost as though he were walking through a long dark tunnel with no end.

Dena had breathed her last breath three days ago, but the truth of it hadn't fully set in until her funeral service today. It simply didn't seem possible that his precious wife was gone, and yet here he stood, viewing her body one final time. Soon, the lid on her coffin would be screwed down, and then Atlee, along with all the other mourners who'd come to pay their respects, would follow the enclosed, horse-drawn hearse to the Amish cemetery for the graveside service.

Dena's funeral service had been a somber occasion, as two ministers spoke, offering various scriptures about death and the resurrection of the dead. The event concluded with a reading of Dena's obituary, followed by the closing prayer and benediction.

Atlee glanced back at his son, who stood with his uncles — Dena's two brothers from Ephrata. They lived thirty minutes from Bird-in-Hand, and over the years had come to visit with their wives and children for special occasions and other family gatherings. Daryl was used to his uncles and enjoyed being around them. Atlee appreciated them keeping his son by them right now, as he struggled to keep his emotions in check.

Just as his parents approached their daughter-in-law's casket, Atlee reached out to touch his wife's white cape and apron. They were the same ones she had worn the day they were married. It seemed like only yesterday, instead of eight years ago that their wedding took place. They'd been disappointed during those first few years of marriage when Dena did not get pregnant. They'd both wanted children and had purchased a house large enough for a growing family. Then, when they'd all but given up hope, God gave them a son. How happy they were when Daryl was born. But a year later, they'd learned that Dena's heart had been weakened because of having rheumatic fever as a girl. The doctor advised them not to have any more children, as childbirth would be a strain on Dena's heart. They'd known even then that she might not have long to live, but Dena kept a positive attitude and enjoyed the time she'd been given with Atlee and their son.

Atlee's mother, who'd been stricken with Parkinson's disease seven years ago, reached out a shaky hand and touched his arm. "I — I wish I could trade places with Dena. I wish God had taken me and given your fraa a new heart."

Before Atlee could form a response, his father stepped forward. "I'm sure you mean well, but you must not talk that way, Sadie.

Your purpose on earth isn't over, and we are not to question God. Everyone has an appointment with death, and this was Dena's time."

Was it? Atlee swallowed against the burning sensation in his throat, trying to come to grips with Dad's statement. The Bible clearly stated that everyone had an appointed time to die, but didn't God sometimes change His mind and allow a person to live when someone prayed hard enough for them? Well, maybe not. Perhaps it was futile to pray and plead with God on someone's behalf. When a person's time was up, that was it — plain and simple.

Atlee rocked back and forth on his heels, remembering his and Dena's last conversation, the day before she died. Dena had told Atlee she'd given Luella her Country Patch quilt as a Christmas present. At first, it hurt him to know she'd given it to someone outside their family, but then he reasoned that there would be no daughter to pass the heirloom on to, and the quilt was Dena's, to do with as she chose. Of course, if Dena hadn't given the quilt away, Atlee would have saved it to give to Daryl's wife when he got married someday. *Guess it's too late to worry about that. What's done is done. Besides, Luella might appreciate having the quilt more than anyone else, and it will be something she can have to help her remember Dena and the friendship they once shared.*

Atlee shuddered, reflecting on his wife's final request, as she lay gasping for air. Dena had made him promise to take another wife after she was gone. He could still hear her pleading words: "Daryl will need a *mudder,* and you'll need a fraa. Please don't close yourself off to the idea, Husband."

Another wife? Atlee shook his head. *No one could ever replace my sweet fraa. I wish she hadn't asked that of me. Don't see how I can keep such a promise. The only woman I will ever love is Dena. If I married again, it would only be for convenience's sake.*

Luella shivered against the cold as she stood beside her parents inside the cemetery enclosure, watching two of Atlee's cousins, who'd been asked to be pallbearers, shovel dirt into the grave. When they became tired, two other pallbearers took over.

As gray clouds, shot through with glimpses of blue, drifted overhead, a chilly wind blew the remaining leaves off the trees outside the cemetery. It seemed the weather was undecided what to do, but at least the rain that had been forecast for today held off. Being wet and cold would not be a good combination for the mourners at Dena's grave.

It was difficult to watch young Daryl standing beside his father as the boy's mother was laid to rest. What a brave little lad he was today, shivering and holding hands with his father. Atlee should be pleased with his son, as he stood as tall as his little frame would allow.

Luella's feet remained firmly planted, although she struggled with the desire to go to the trembling child and wrap him in her arms. But that would be inappropriate. She would comfort Daryl once they were back at Atlee's house, where a simple meal would be served.

Luella tried to concentrate on the words of the hymn their bishop had begun to read when the grave became half full of dirt. Following their usual custom, he would continue to read until the job had been finished.

At the conclusion of the graveside service, the bishop asked the congregation to pray the Lord's Prayer silently. Luella bowed her head, along with the others. *Our Father which art in heaven, hallowed be thy name. Thy kingdom come, Thy will be done in earth, as it is in heaven. Give us this day our daily bread. And forgive us our debts, as we forgive our debtors. And lead us not into temptation, but deliver us from evil: for thine is the kingdom, and the power, and the glory, for ever. Amen.*

Luella had memorized these verses from Matthew 6, verses 9–13, when she was a young girl. It had brought her comfort during sad times, as it did now. She hoped the same was true for Atlee today. He would most certainly need to seek God's Word many times in the days ahead.

Looking up after the prayer was said, her gaze came to rest on Eugene Lapp, a friend of hers since childhood. Eugene had been looking at her and nodded when their gazes met. Luella acknowledged him with a slight smile but then turned her attention back to Atlee and Daryl.

Luella thought about her promise to Dena. She wanted to keep her word about caring for Daryl and continuing to work for Atlee. But what if he wanted someone else to watch his son while he was at work or away from the house? Perhaps Atlee had only hired Luella to care for Dena because he knew they were friends. Since Dena's parents were deceased, and Atlee's mother, Sadie, had some health issues of her own, no family members were available to take care of Daryl or keep house for Atlee.

He lived near two single Amish women,

both close to his age. After a reasonable time, he might decide to marry one of them. That wouldn't solve his immediate problem of needing someone to manage the house and provide for his son's needs while he was unavailable. Atlee surely couldn't take Daryl to his woodshop every day and try to keep an eye on him. It would be difficult, if not impossible, for him to do all the cooking, cleaning, and other household chores while running a successful business.

Taking a calming breath, Luella put these worries out of her mind. She would speak to Atlee later today — perhaps after mourners had eaten the meal at his house. Luella just needed to think of the best way to ask her question. She didn't want Atlee to feel obligated or keep her working for him because he thought she needed the money. While the extra income had given her the opportunity to help her parents with expenses, it was not the reason she'd agreed to work for Atlee in the first place. Hopefully when Luella broached the subject, she would make that clear to him.

That evening, after Luella got ready for bed, she picked up the lovely quilt Dena had given her, which she had draped over the back of a chair, and held it snuggly against her chest. *Oh Dena, my dear friend, I already miss you so much.*

Christmas was only a few weeks away, but this special quilt with Christmas colors would be Luella's most cherished gift. She took a seat on the end of the bed and closed her eyes, visualizing her friend singing with the angels in heaven. This thought alone gave Luella some measure of comfort. She felt certain that Dena was in a place where there was no pain or suffering. She had been a good Christian woman, and her sweet spirit was a testimony to others. Surely she was welcomed into heaven when she breathed her last breath.

When Luella opened her eyes again, a thought popped into her head. *I should place Dena's quilt on my bed and put my old covering away. Then every time I come into my room I'll be reminded of the special friendship Dena and I shared and be thankful.*

Earlier that evening, she had spoken with Atlee after most of the people had finished their meal at his home and left. Before she could ask about caring for Daryl, Atlee had approached her, saying he hoped she would continue working for him. He also said he appreciated everything Luella had done for his wife and mentioned how well Daryl got along with her. Of course, Luella had agreed to take care of Atlee's little boy and provide their meals, in addition to doing all the household chores. So tomorrow morning, at Atlee's request, Luella would return to his house. With the exception of caring for Dena's needs, her duties would be the same. It would be bittersweet, however. She would miss seeing Dena's sweet face and their long talks. On the other hand, Daryl needed Luella now more than ever. It would be a difficult adjustment for the boy to not have a mother to tuck him in at night, read him a bedtime story, and hold him in her arms when he needed comfort and nurturing. Luella hoped to provide Daryl with all those things, although she would never try to replace his mother. She felt sure Atlee would do all he could to raise his son in a pleasant environment, but he would need to deal with his own grief before he could bring joy and laughter into their house.

Luella drew in her bottom lip. *It will be my job to find things for Daryl to laugh about. And hopefully, when the time is right, Atlee will be able to smile and laugh again.*

When she lifted the lid of her cedar chest to tuck her old bed covering away, she noticed one of her childhood storybooks. Sitting on the floor, Luella laid the covering aside and reached for the small, hard-covered book. As she ran her fingers over the front that illustrated two little fawns in the company of a Dalmatian, she noticed the cover was a bit worn.

When Luella fanned through the pages, it pleased her to see the entire book was still intact. "This was my favorite story, growing up." Luella spoke quietly, remembering all the times her mother had read about the talking animals to her. She stopped at the page where the two orphaned fawns were being scolded by the dog, who'd actually taken on the role of their mother, when the mother deer died. It was a cute story, centered around the fawns, their antics and adventures, and how they adapted to new surroundings. *Think I'll keep it out so I can share it with Daryl. Maybe it will bring him a little joy, like the story did for me when Mom read it out loud.*

Sighing, she folded her old bed covering and placed it inside the cedar chest, where she'd put several other items in anticipation of someday getting married. Then, spreading Dena's quilt out over her bed, she noticed something on one corner of the backing she hadn't seen before. A scripture had been embroidered there, possibly by Dena, or maybe Dena's mother.

Luella's fingers trailed along the precise

stitching as she read the verse out loud. " 'For thou art my rock and my fortress; therefore for thy name's sake lead me, and guide me' — Psalm 31:3."

Her eyes teared up. *What a wonderful scripture and reminder for me when doubts fill my mind and I don't know what path to take.* Luella closed her eyes once again. *Thank You, Lord, for being my rock and my fortress. May I always remember to seek Your will in all things and follow the right path, as You lead and guide me. Amen.*

CHAPTER 4

Snow storms had been moving in and out since Luella left Atlee's house with Daryl. But after each burst of snow, which lasted fifteen minutes or so, the sun would break through, the skies would clear, and the roads remained only wet.

Looking out the front of the buggy window, Luella glanced at the sky, watching another line of clouds approaching. *Hopefully the sun will come out after this one, too,* she thought, clucking to Dixie to keep her moving. Luella never had any problems with her horse. Even in heavy traffic, Dixie usually remained calm and under control.

Luella could hardly believe tomorrow was Christmas, but here she was, out shopping with Atlee's son on a cold snowy day. She'd been busy with all her responsibilities at Atlee's place and hadn't found the time to buy any gifts for her family. They'd gone to a few stores so far, and she had bought some gifts, but she also wanted to find something for Daryl. Luella had become quite fond of the boy and enjoyed the opportunity to spend time with him. But having Daryl along made it difficult to buy anything without him seeing it. She wished now she'd thought to invite her mother along. At least Mom could have kept the boy occupied while Luella picked something out and paid for her purchases.

"I'm hungerich." Daryl reached across the buggy seat and tugged on Luella's shawl, as a few snowflakes started to fall.

Glancing at one of her father's old pocket watches, which she'd put in her purse this morning, Luella realized it was half-past noon. No wonder the boy was hungry. Now that Luella thought about it, she could probably eat something, too. She squeezed Daryl's cold fingers. *Maybe a pair of gloves would be a good gift to get Daryl for Christmas.* "Well then, let's go get something to eat." Luella snapped the reins and directed her horse onto the road leading to the Bird-in-Hand Family Restaurant.

When they entered the building a short time later and were waiting to be shown to a table, Daryl shouted, *"Sandi Klaas!"*

Luella turned to look at the door where the boy pointed. Sure enough, there stood a

46

large man dressed in a red suit and hat, both trimmed with white fur. He wore shiny black boots with large gold buckles, and his curly snow-white beard hung down to his chest. He was obviously one of the local English men dressed up like Santa Claus.

Before Luella had a chance to say anything to Daryl, the man marched right over to him, reached into his cloth satchel, and pulled out a candy cane. "Here ya go, little fella. Merry Christmas!"

Luella wasn't sure if Daryl understood what the pretend Santa had said, but with no hesitation, the boy took the offered candy, his eyes full of wonderment and a smile stretching wide across his face.

"Say thank you to the nice man," Luella prompted.

"Danki." The boy offered a shy toothy grin.

The would-be Santa gave a nod and hurried into the restaurant, where he proceeded to hand out candy canes to all the children who were seated at tables with their parents.

"Will Santa come to my house?" Daryl asked.

Oh, dear. Luella sucked in her lower lip. *Now how should I respond to that?* She was well aware that the Amish didn't teach their children about Santa Claus, Christmas trees, or colored lights. Christmas was a time to focus on the birth of Christ, and celebrations were centered around family time and reading the Bible story of how the baby Jesus was born in a stable. How much Atlee and Dena had told their son about Santa Claus, she didn't know, but Luella felt since the boy was in her charge, she should at least explain it in the way that she knew.

She leaned close to his ear and spoke to him in Pennsylvania Dutch. "Daryl, we don't celebrate Christmas because of Sandi Klaas. It's Jesus we think about, and how much God loved us when He sent His Son to earth as a baby."

Daryl tipped his head. "Does Jesus bring the presents?"

"No, but neither does Santa Claus."

The boy's lower lip jutted out. Luella wondered if he was going to cry.

She gave his hand a gentle squeeze. "After we eat, you can enjoy the candy cane the nice man gave you."

The hostess approached and led them to a table by the window. By this time it was snowing steadily, and Luella could hardly see across the road. Looking up at the sky, she just made out a dim, milky sun struggling to break through the swirling snow. It almost made her dizzy, watching all the tiny flakes, resembling millions of white bugs flying in every direction. She quickly looked away.

Luella felt relieved when Daryl climbed onto a chair and began playing with his spoon as though it were a train. *"Choo-choo . . . Choo-choo . . ."* Well, at least his mind was on something else. Hopefully the subject of Santa Claus would not be brought up again. When they finished eating their lunch, Luella would stop by her parents' house and see if Mom was willing to watch Daryl for a few hours this afternoon. This would allow Luella the chance to finish her shopping without the boy seeing what she'd bought.

"Look, it's snowing!" Luella's sister pointed out the kitchen window. "I was hoping we'd get schnee on Christmas Day."

Luella joined her sister at the window, gazing at the lacey flakes drifting out of the sky. Unlike yesterday's intermittent bursts of snow, this was more like a normal snow event. "It is beautiful. If the snow keeps up, the grass and trees will soon be white."

Flashing Luella a grin, Sara clapped her hands. "Maybe we can go outside after dinner and catch snowflakes on our tongues."

Luella chuckled. "I'm sure Daryl will be excited to see the snow. If the wind doesn't pick up, and it's not too cold, we can take him outside after our meal, and we'll all catch snowflakes and let 'em melt on our tongues."

"I hope it snows really hard so we can build a snowman. Bet Daryl would like that." Sara's eyes shone with the enthusiasm of an eager twelve-year-old.

"Jah, maybe so." Luella glanced at the battery-operated clock across the room. "I wonder what's keeping Atlee. Sure hope he didn't change his mind about joining us for Christmas dinner. It wouldn't be good for him and Daryl to spend the holiday alone."

"I wouldn't worry, Luella. I'm sure they'll be here soon." Mom stepped between Luella and Sara, peering out the window. "You're right. The snow is beautiful. If the sun comes out later, it'll be even prettier." She tapped Luella's shoulder. "Would you mind checking on the ham, while I go down to the cellar to get a few jars of green beans?"

Luella smiled. "Certainly, I can do that."

"And Sara," Mom added, "would you please finish setting the table?"

Sara's eyebrows lowered. "I did that already."

"The plates, glasses, and silverware are on the dining-room table, but you forgot the *bauchduchdicher.*"

"Oops, sorry. I'll get them now." Sara grabbed several napkins and hurried from the room.

Shaking her head, Mom looked at Luella. "That girl can be so forgetful at times."

"I think she's just excited because it's Christmas Day."

"Jah. This is a day when we should all be excited." Mom pointed up. "As we celebrate the birth of Christ, it's a reminder of how much God loves us."

Luella nodded. She hoped Atlee would be able to experience the joy of today, too.

As Luella watched Atlee from across the table, where he sat between Daryl and her brother Samuel, she could almost read the man's thoughts. Atlee had come here for his son's sake, but his heart wasn't in it. Even though she'd hoped it would be different, Atlee's placid expression let her know he felt no joy in celebrating Christmas this year. How could he, when his wife had died a few short weeks ago? It would be some time before Atlee could smile or laugh again. But Luella would keep praying for him and do everything she could to keep his household running smoothly so he'd have less to worry about.

Several family members, including Luella's father and older brother, Matthew, had tried to engage Atlee in conversation, but he'd only responded with a few words. Luella noticed that he hadn't eaten much, either.

When the meal was over and the table had been cleared, Atlee entered the kitchen, where Luella and her mother had begun doing the dishes. "Think I'm gonna head for home now, before the snow gets any worse."

Luella glanced out the window. Seeing the thick layers of white accumulating on the barn roof and all over the yard, she nodded. "Before you leave, though, I have a gift for Daryl."

Looking steadily at Luella, Atlee placed one hand against his heart. "Danki for thinking of my boy. This is a difficult time for me, and the only gift I have for Daryl is a little wooden carriage I made for him a few months ago. Since Dena's death, I haven't felt like shopping for gifts."

"It's understandable." Mom set her dish towel aside and placed her hands on Atlee's arm. "We will keep you in our prayers, and if there's anything we can do for you or Daryl, please let us know. You are always welcome here."

Ducking his head slightly, Atlee murmured, "I appreciate that."

Luella dried her hands. "I'll go get Daryl's gift now."

"And while my *dochder* is doing that, I'll cut a few pieces of pie for you to take home."

"That would be nice. And danki for inviting Daryl and me to share your Christmas dinner, Esther. Everything I ate was good. Sorry I didn't feel up to eating more."

As Luella slipped out of the room, she heard Mom say, "I'll give you some slices of ham, too, Atlee. You can eat them later this evening or maybe tomorrow for breakfast. It'll make good sandwiches for your lunch, as well."

Luella smiled. She felt thankful to have a mother who was so thoughtful of others. When Luella went to Atlee's house in the morning, she would fix him and Daryl ham and eggs for breakfast.

Boldness was not in Eugene Lapp's nature, but dropping hints and stopping by the Ebersols' on occasion wasn't getting him anywhere with Luella. So today, he'd decided to come right out and ask if he could court her. He knew when he pulled his horse and buggy into their yard that they had company, but hopefully he could speak to Luella alone for a few minutes. He certainly couldn't ask her in front of everyone. It would be embarrassing for him, as well as to her.

As Eugene guided his horse up to the hitching rail, he saw Atlee Zook taking his horse out of the barn, while Daryl waited close by near the fence. *I'll bet the Ebersols invited the Zooks to join them for Christmas dinner. Guess that makes sense, since Luella works for Atlee and they live just a mile from each other.* Eugene reached under his hat and scratched his head. *It seems strange, though, that Atlee wouldn't be at his folks' house today.*

Eugene got out of his rig and secured his horse, Chip, at the rail. Since he wouldn't be here that long, even though it was snowing pretty hard, he saw no point in putting Chip in Owen Ebersol's barn.

"En hallicher Grischrdaag!" Eugene gave Atlee a friendly wave.

"A Merry Christmas to you, too." Atlee began hitching his horse. "Did you come for a slice of *pei*?"

Eugene shook his head. "Came by to bring Luella a Christmas gift, but if I'm offered some pie, I sure won't turn it down.

How about you, Atlee? Did you have dessert?"

"No. We'll have it later this evening." Atlee held up and pointed to the paper sack Luella's mother had packed for them. Then he helped Daryl into the carriage. "My son and I were here for supper, but we'll be heading for home now."

"I see. I'm surprised you're not at your folks' house today."

"Mom and Dad went to my brother Dewayne's place today. Since it's fifteen miles from here, they hired a driver to take them there. My boy and I were invited, but I decided it'd be best to stick close to home. I'm glad we did, since it's snowing like this."

"Guess that makes sense." Eugene shuffled his boots in the snow. "How ya gettin' along these days?"

"Doing the best I can." Atlee stood by his rig. "I've been trying to remember that where God leads, He will light the way." He dropped his gaze. "I just never expected He'd be leading me down a path without a helpmate."

Since Eugene had never been married, he wasn't sure what to say. "Sorry for your loss," he mumbled.

"Danki." Atlee took off his hat, shook the snow off it, then stepped into his buggy.

"See you around, Eugene."

Eugene lifted his hand in a wave then reached into his buggy and retrieved Luella's gift. He glanced back, watching Atlee guide his horse toward the road and disappear into the veil of snow. Sprinting through the powdery build-up, Eugene felt giddy in the pit of his stomach. Was it the snow giving him so much delight, or the fact he'd be seeing Luella as he knocked on the Ebersols' back door? A few seconds later, the door opened. Luella stood in front of him. His mouth became dry, and his cold hands felt clammy.

"Oh, Eugene, it's you. I thought maybe Atlee had forgotten something."

"Nope, it's me all right. Came by to give you this." He handed Luella the gift. "Merry Christmas."

"Ach, I didn't expect you to give me a present." Luella's face turned a light shade of pink as she took the package. "Sorry, but I don't have anything for you."

"Aw, that's okay." Eugene brushed some snow off his sleeve. "Your friendship is gift enough for me."

The color in her cheeks deepened. "I . . . I appreciate your friendship, too."

Eugene cleared his throat while shuffling his feet. "Enough to let me court you?"

There, it was out, and he'd said it without any of Luella's family hearing. Of course, he had to stand out here in the cold in order to do it. He was sure if she'd invited him inside there would have been someone within earshot.

But then, why hasn't Luella asked me to come in? he wondered. *A good friend wouldn't let someone remain in the cold.*

As if she could tell what he was thinking, Luella opened the door wider. "Why don't you come inside out of the cold? Maybe you'd like to join us for some dessert."

"Okay, I will, but you haven't answered my question. Are you willing to let me court you, Luella?"

"Well, I — uh . . ." The flush on Luella's cheeks had crept down to her neck. "I'm flattered that you'd want to court me, Eugene, but the truth is, I don't have time for courting right now."

"You mean because of your job working for Atlee?"

"Jah. I go there five days a week to watch Daryl and help out around the house. On Saturdays, when I'm here at home, I keep busy helping my mamm."

"I understand that, but what about on *Sunndaag?* Couldn't we go for a buggy ride after church, or maybe I could come by here

some evenings so we could spend time together?"

Luella blinked rapidly, as she leaned
against the door casing. "I'd rather not
make any kind of commitment right now,
Eugene. I hope you understand."

*No, I don't. I don't understand at all. If you
care about me, then you oughta want us to
begin courting.* Eugene reached out and
placed his hand on her arm. "Would you at
least give it more thought? Maybe sometime
next year Atlee will decide to court another
woman, and then you won't have so many
responsibilities to worry about."

She nodded. "All right, Eugene. We can
talk about this some other time." Luella
stepped aside. "Now, please come in and
have a piece of pumpkin or apple pie."

"Okay." He stomped the snow off his
boots and stepped inside. Well, at least
Luella hadn't completely shut the door on
him or the idea of them courting. As soon
as Eugene heard anything about Atlee
courting another woman, he would approach Luella again.

After Atlee read Daryl a bedtime story from
the new book Luella had given him for
Christmas, he tucked the boy in and gave
him a hug. "Sleep well, Son. I'll see you in

the morning." Atlee had to smile when he noticed the pair of gloves she'd also given Daryl lying right next to his pillow. Luella was a thoughtful young woman.

"Wait, Daadi." Daryl pulled his hands out from under the covers. "When will Mammi come home?"

Atlee crossed his arms, holding them tightly to his shoulders so they wouldn't shake. Even though he'd explained the day of Dena's death that she'd gone to heaven, he'd been afraid his son might ask him this question. He swallowed hard and took a seat in the chair beside Daryl's bed. "Your mamm is in heaven with Jesus."

"But she's coming back, right, Daadi?"

Atlee shook his head. "She won't be coming back, Son. We won't see your mamm again till it's our turn to go to heaven."

The boy's blue eyes filled with tears. "Then I wanna go to heaven now."

Atlee was at a loss for words. Truth was, he wished he could be with Dena in heaven, too. But it wasn't his or Daryl's time yet. And until God called him to his heavenly home, Atlee would do the best he could to make it through and be a good dad to his son. That's what Dena would have wanted.

CHAPTER 5

Luella smiled. Since she'd first come to the kitchen to prepare lunch, Daryl had been sitting on the braided throw rug near the warmth of the woodstove, looking at the pictures inside her old storybook about the dog and twin fawns. It had been two weeks since Luella gave Daryl a book about a family of horses for Christmas, but he still preferred the book from her childhood. The boy liked the story so much, Luella had decided to keep it at Atlee's house so she could read it to Daryl as often as he requested. When he grew older and lost interest in the book, she would return it to her cedar chest to read to her own children someday.

"If I ever get married," Luella whispered, as she stood in front of Atlee's woodstove, stirring a pot of chicken noodle soup. She thought about Eugene's desire to court her. *If I were free to let him court me, would our relationship eventually lead to marriage?* Her forehead wrinkled. *Eugene will probably find someone else before I'm free for courting.*

"Ha! Ha! Ha!"

Luella's thoughts were pushed aside when Daryl started laughing. She figured he must be looking at the picture of the dog holding his paw on top of the one fawn's head. That part always made him giggle, and her, too, recalling what it was like when she was a little girl. It was good to see the child's happiness. He'd been so sad since his mother passed away.

"My mamm's in *himmel.*"

Turning from the stove, Luella knelt on the rug beside him. "Yes, Daryl, your mother's in heaven."

"I'm goin' there, too." He lifted his chin. "I'm gonna tell Mammi she needs to come home. I want her to read me this book, too."

Luella rubbed the little boy's back. It wasn't her place to tell Daryl his mother wouldn't be coming home, so she quickly changed the subject. "How would you like to help me build a snowman after lunch?"

Eyes shining, he bobbed his head. "Can we put a *gehlrieb* in his *naas?*"

Luella bit back a chuckle. "Yes, we'll give him a nose made out of a carrot." She stood and went back to the stove to check on the soup. The chicken and vegetables seemed tender, so she pushed the kettle to the back of the stove to keep it warm. "I'm going out to your daed's shop to call him for lunch. Can you sit there and read your book while I'm gone?"

Daryl's head moved up and down.

"Okay then, I'll be right back." Luella took her woolen shawl down from the wall peg and wrapped it around her shoulders. Then she slipped on a pair of boots and scooted out the back door.

When Luella entered Atlee's shop, a blast of warm air greeted her. The small woodstove in one corner of the room kept the building well heated. "I came out to tell you that lunch is ready," she hollered against the steady *Bang! Bang!* of Atlee's hammer.

He stopped working and turned to look at her. "I'm not really hungerich."

"Oh, but it's important for you to eat. I made a pot of soup, and it'll warm your insides."

Atlee said nothing; just looked down at his boots.

"You know, Daryl probably won't eat, either, if you're not there to share the meal."

After a yielding sigh, he nodded. "You're right, and I don't want to disappoint my boy." Atlee set the hammer down, grabbed his jacket, and followed Luella out the door.

When Atlee entered the kitchen, he was greeted by a tantalizing aroma. He hung up his jacket and sniffed the air. "Chicken noodle soup — jah?"

Luella nodded. "And I made a loaf of wheat bread to go with it."

Grinning up at his father, Daryl held up Luella's storybook. *"Sehne die buch?"*

"Jah, Son, I see the book." Atlee leaned over and ruffled the boy's thick auburn hair. "Are ya ready to sit at the table and eat lunch now?"

Daryl clambered to his feet, but before he reached the table, Luella pointed to the sink. "You and your daed should wash your hands first."

Atlee stiffened. Who did Luella think she was, telling him what to do? The only person he'd ever allowed to boss him around was Dena; but that was because he knew she loved him, and he did what she asked because he loved her. However, Atlee couldn't deny that his hands were dirty and Daryl's probably were, too. So without a word of protest, he pulled out a chair and set it in front of the sink. Then he picked up his son and stood him on the chair. Standing beside Daryl, Atlee turned on the water, grabbed a bar of soap, and proceeded to wash his hands as well as the boy's. By the time their hands were dry and the chair was in its proper place, Luella had set the soup and bread on the table.

They all took seats and bowed heads for silent prayer. When they finished praying, Luella handed Atlee the bread basket and a jar of apple butter. He stared at the jar several seconds, blinking rapidly. "Dena and I made this apple butter before you came to work for us. It was a fun time, and we enjoyed being in the kitchen together."

"It's good, too." Luella spread some on a piece of bread and gave it to Daryl. "I tasted a spoonful when I first opened the jar."

Atlee sat, staring at his bowl of soup, as memories washed over him like waves lapping against the shore. *Oh, my precious Dena, how I wish you were sitting here at the table with us.* He blinked again, hoping he wouldn't give in to the tears threatening to spill over. He needed to be strong for Daryl's sake.

"I hope you like the soup," Luella said. "It's the same recipe my mamm uses — plenty of chicken pieces cooked in the broth, along with diced carrots, onion, celery, noodles, and just the right amount of spices." She snickered. "My daed always says my mamm's chicken noodle soup tastes like heaven."

Daryl tipped his head in Luella's direction. "My mamm's eatin' soup in himmel?"

"It's hard to say, but maybe so, Son." Smiling ever so slightly, Atlee looked at Luella and winked. It was the first time since Dena's death that he'd felt even a tinge of humor. *What would I do without my boy?* Atlee wondered. *He's the one bright spot in my life right now.*

After lunch, Luella left the dishes on the table and read the fawn story to Daryl again. By the time she'd finished, he was fast asleep on the living-room sofa.

Luella slipped back into the kitchen and attacked the dirty dishes. As her hands soaked in the sudsy water, she thought about Atlee. He was still somewhat subdued, and Luella could always tell he was thinking about Dena. But there were also times she'd witnessed in the last two weeks when he'd been trying to work his way out of depression.

Her mind drifted back to Christmas and the gift Eugene had given her. It had been difficult to thank him for the rabbit fur she'd discovered inside the package, when she wasn't even sure what to do with it.

Luella had to admit it was soft when she rubbed her cheek against it. Until she found a better place for the hide, she'd placed it on top of her cedar chest. She was thankful, at least, that Eugene hadn't killed the rabbit. He said he'd found it dead in the woods behind their place, and rather than tossing it away, he'd skinned and preserved it, the way he'd learned from a book on taxidermy he'd gotten from the library. It certainly wasn't the kind of gift Luella had expected, but it was the thought that counted.

"Sure wish I didn't have to clean this barn all the time," Eugene mumbled, following his father past a stack of straw.

"What was that?"

"Nothing, Dad."

"You weren't complaining, I hope." Dad stopped walking and turned to face Eugene. "The barn needs to be cleaned, and it won't get that way by itself."

"Jah, I know." Eugene paused at the door of his horse's stall, leaning on the gate. "It's just that sometimes I wish I could do something else besides farming in the warmer months and spending the winter helping out in here."

"The barn is not the only place that needs work in the winter." Dad nudged Eugene's arm with his elbow. "Besides, what other work would you want to do? I thought you enjoyed farming with me."

Eugene shrugged. "It's okay, I guess, but sometimes I think about how nice it would be to learn some other kind of work."

"Like what?"

"Oh, I don't know. Maybe horseshoeing, harness repair, or even taxidermy."

"Those are all good professions, but so is raising hogs and farming."

"I suppose." Eugene's gaze dropped to the floor.

"Is there something else bothering you, Son?"

"Jah."

"Want to talk about it?"

"Sure, if you don't mind taking the time to listen."

"I always have time to listen to one of my kinner." Dad gestured to a nearby bale of straw. "Let's take a seat, and we can talk about whatever's bothering you."

Eugene drew in a breath and released it slowly. "Well, as you know, I've been friends with Luella Ebersol ever since we were kinner."

Dad nodded.

"I've developed feelings for her, and when I stopped by her folks' place on Christmas

Day, I asked Luella if I could court her."

"What'd she say?"

"Said she didn't have time for courting. She's too busy helping out at Atlee Zook's place." Eugene groaned. "If she's too busy to let me court her, then I don't see how things can ever work out for us."

Dad quirked an eyebrow. "You thinkin' of asking Luella to marry you?"

"I want to, but not till we've courted awhile. I'm frustrated and just not sure what I should do."

"My advice is to be patient and wait awhile before you approach her again. For now, just be a friend to Luella."

"I've been her friend since we were children, and where has it gotten me? I have to wonder if she'll ever see me as anything more than a friend. I even gave her a soft rabbit skin for Christmas, but she didn't seem to like it that much." Eugene lifted his hat and pushed a lock of hair back under. "You don't suppose she'll end up marrying Atlee Zook, do you?"

Dad raised his eyebrows. "Now where'd ya get such a silly notion? Why, Atlee's sixteen years older than Luella — almost old enough to be her daed."

Eugene nodded. He hadn't even thought about that. "You have a point. Guess maybe

I'm worried for nothing."

"There are a few widowed ladies in our church district, plus a couple of single women in their early thirties. Bet it won't be long till Atlee asks one of them to be his fraa."

Eugene plucked out a piece of straw from the bale they sat on and stuck it between his teeth. "But what if Atlee never remarries and expects Luella to work for him till Daryl's in school and old enough to do things on his own?"

Dad shook his head. "I've never known anyone who could worry so much about nothing." He stood and handed Eugene a pitchfork. "Now let's get back to work. When we're done here, we still have some hogs to feed."

Eugene opened the bale of straw and began spreading it inside his horse's stall. *Think I'll drop by Luella's house some evening next week — just to see how she's doing. If I stay in touch with her, she's less likely to forget about me. And who knows — maybe she'll get tired of working for Atlee and feel ready to become a wife.*

CHAPTER 6

By the middle of February, Luella had developed an even stronger bond with Daryl. She didn't mind getting up early each day to head over to their place and loved spending time with the boy, while caring for his needs. It made her long to get married and have a child of her own.

As she took a shoofly pie out of the oven, her thoughts went to Eugene. He'd dropped by her parents' house to visit with her a few times in January and again last night. Although he hadn't mentioned courting, she could see the look of longing on his face. While Luella cared for Eugene, she didn't think it was love she felt for him. Now that she thought about it, Eugene seemed more like a brother than a potential husband.

But would it be so bad to be married to someone you only liked and not loved? She'd heard that when Great-Grandma

Ebersol married Grandpa, they'd barely known each other, since the marriage had been arranged by their fathers. Love came later, as time went on and their relationship developed into a devoted bond. Perhaps that would be the case if Luella married Eugene, even though they already knew each other quite well.

I'd feel more love for Atlee if I married him than I would Eugene. Luella slapped her forehead. *Now where did that thought come from?* Feeling her cheeks grow warm, she fanned her face. In addition to their age difference, Atlee had shown no signs of caring for Luella in any way other than as his employee. And truthfully, she didn't expect him to.

Maybe my feelings for Atlee are admiration and not love, Luella told herself. *He's a kind, gentle man — so patient with his son. Atlee is also hardworking, strong, and mature. Not like Eugene, who sometimes acts like a teenager instead of a twenty-four-year-old man. Besides, Atlee's still grieving for Dena, and I'm certain he would never be interested in anyone as young as me. He probably sees me as a girl, not a woman. I'm just a person he hired to cook, clean, and take care of his son.*

"Is that a shoofly pie I spy there on the counter?"

Luella jumped at the sound of Atlee's voice. How long had he been standing there? When had he come in from his shop? "Umm . . . jah, I took the pie out of the oven a few minutes ago, so it's still quite warm."

He smiled, although it didn't quite reach his eyes. "That's okay. It'll be a treat to have later in the day. I don't believe I've had shoofly pie since the last one you made when Dena was still here." Atlee paused, stroking his beard. Then he added, "Did ya know it was Dena's favorite pie, too?"

"I don't think she ever told me that. I'm sorry if it stirs up sad memories for you. I would have made another kind if I'd known." Luella could hardly look at him.

"No, no, it's fine. As hard as it is, I have to teach myself to think of these remembrances as a good thing and not have them bring me down. So I'm glad you made shoofly pie. Lately, I've had a hankering for some." Atlee took a few steps closer. "Oh, I almost forgot. I came in to let you know I'm going out to run a few errands and wondered if there's anything you need me to get."

"Maybe. Let me see." Luella went to the desk, where she kept the grocery list.

Atlee glanced around. "Where's that son

of mine? I thought he might like to go along for the ride."

"He's upstairs in his room playing." Luella was pleased Atlee wanted to spend time with Daryl, but she felt a little hurt that she'd been excluded. It would have been nice to get out of the house for a while on this cold but sunny day. It was wrong to be selfish, though. *Atlee probably figured I have plenty of work to do here. Besides, he's under no obligation to take me anywhere, much less a shopping trip with Daryl.*

Luella smiled and handed Atlee the grocery list. "I'm sure Daryl will be excited to go with you. And by the time you get back, I'll have supper started." Normally, Luella joined Atlee and Daryl for the evening meal, and then after she got the dishes done, she would head for home. Sometimes, however, like yesterday, Atlee would offer to do the dishes, saying Luella was free to go home and join her family for supper.

Atlee started out of the kitchen but turned back to face Luella. "You know, now that I think about it, maybe you'd like to go with us. I can run a few errands of my own while you do some shopping. When we're done we can stop by a restaurant for supper, and afterward I'll drop you off at your place."

"That sounds nice, but what about my

horse and buggy? If I leave them here overnight, I'll have to walk to work in the morning."

Atlee tipped his head, looking at her strangely. "As I recall, you walked here this morning, and since I don't think it's a good idea for you to walk home in the dark, I was planning to give you a ride home after supper."

Luella's cheeks warmed, and she brought her hands up to touch them. "Ach, how silly of me to forget such a thing. I walked here this morning because my horse is getting shod today." Luella didn't know why she felt so jittery all of a sudden. Was it the concern she saw on Atlee's face, or the fact that he'd invited her to join him and Daryl for shopping and then eating a meal out afterward?

"That's okay. We all forget things sometimes." Atlee pointed to himself. "I'm sure guilty of it, and especially so since Dena died."

Luella nodded. "I would enjoy a little shopping for a while, and eating supper out sounds real nice."

"Okay then, I'll go round up my boy, and while I'm doing that, you can get your things ready." Atlee paused near the kitchen door. "Don't think I've ever said this before,

Luella, but I want you to know how much I appreciate everything you've been doing to help around here." He turned and quickly left the room.

Luella smiled as she heard Atlee's boots clomping up the stairs to his son's room. It was nice to be appreciated, and even nicer to be asked to join them for shopping and supper this evening. Her grin grew even wider when the sound of Atlee's laughter and Daryl's giggles echoed down from upstairs.

As Atlee sat across the table from Luella at the Bird-in-Hand Family Restaurant, a lump formed in his throat. The last time he'd eaten here, Dena was with him. They'd stopped for lunch after her doctor's appointment. Dena hadn't felt well that day, but she'd put up a good front, no doubt for his sake. Her favorite meal was fried chicken, with a side dish of pickled beets. Even when she'd felt poorly, she had managed to eat them.

Sitting across from Luella as she ate that same special meal was particularly difficult. All he could think about was the void in his life left by his wife's untimely departure. *Life isn't fair,* Atlee thought for the hundredth time. *What good could come from De-*

na's death? I'm missing a wife and Daryl has to grow up without a mother. Where's the fairness in that?

Atlee took a deep breath, trying to think his way through all this. Didn't he tell Luella earlier that these precious memories, such as Dena enjoying fried chicken, were the little things that summed up who she was?

"You're not eating much. Don't you care for the *hinkle*?" Luella's question pulled Atlee's thoughts aside.

He glanced down at his half-eaten meal but couldn't tell Luella the real reason his appetite had left him. "The roast chicken's good. I'm saving room for that piece of pie we'll have when we get home. I'll ask our waitress to box up the rest of my meal. It'll be enough to heat up for my lunch tomorrow or the next day." Atlee looked over at Daryl's plate, noting that it was almost empty. "Guess my son's eating his share and mine."

Luella smiled. "Daryl's a growing boy. I've noticed his pant legs are getting shorter."

"I'm a growing boy," Daryl repeated, grinning at Luella.

"I'll bring my mending basket with me tomorrow and let the hem down on all of his trousers that are too short."

Atlee shook his head. "You don't have to do that, Luella."

Tiny wrinkles formed across her forehead. "You don't want me to let the hem down on Daryl's trousers?"

"No, no, I have no problem with that. I meant you don't have to bring your sewing basket. You can use Dena's sewing supplies."

"Oh, okay." Luella picked up the crunchy chicken leg and took a bite.

Atlee reached forward then quickly pulled his hand back before he flicked a crumb of chicken coating that was stuck on Luella's face. Many times he and Dena did that for each other, and he recalled fondly how Dena would joke and say, "I'm saving that crumb for later."

This was Luella, though, not his wife. *Whatever was I thinking?* Atlee sat quietly, watching as Luella took a napkin to wipe her mouth and fingers.

"This fried chicken is so good, and there's just no easy way to eat it, except with your fingers." Luella giggled, looking over at Daryl, who was licking his fingers clean after eating a drumstick.

That's how Dena used to eat her chicken, too. Atlee had to look away so Luella wouldn't think he'd been watching her and be embarrassed.

They ate in silence the rest of the meal, until Daryl asked if he could have a dish of ice cream for dessert.

"I don't see why not." Atlee poked his son's belly. "After all, a growing boy needs a little ice cream once in a while to help him grow even more."

Daryl giggled, and Atlee even managed a smile.

As Eugene approached the Ebersols' house, he began to have second thoughts. He'd come here to give Luella a Valentine's card, since tomorrow was Valentine's Day, and he knew he wouldn't see her then because he had to go out of town with his dad. But now he wondered if the card was too mushy or if Luella might think he was being too forward.

"Well, I'm here now," Eugene said aloud. "So I may as well go through with it."

He guided Chip up the driveway and to the hitching rail. After securing the horse, he stuck the card inside his jacket and sprinted for the house. Every time Eugene visited the Ebersols', his hope for more than just a friendly relationship with Luella was reenergized. He knocked only twice when Luella's mother answered the door.

"Is Luella here?" Eugene shifted from one foot to the other.

"Sorry, she's not home from Atlee's yet."

"Oh. I was hoping she would be here by now." He tried to give Esther a smile, but he couldn't get his lips to move.

"I'd invite you to wait for her, but I'm not sure what time she'll be home." Esther shivered. "Luella walked to Atlee's this morning, so he'll probably give her a ride home after supper and the dishes have been done."

Eugene frowned. "She works too many long hours."

"I agree, but Luella enjoys her job, and she feels it's important to keep the promise she made to Atlee's wife before she died."

"What promise was that?"

"To take care of Daryl and to keep helping Atlee. He has a lot more responsibility now, when it comes to raising his son."

Eugene nodded. Then, remembering the card, he reached inside his jacket and pulled out the envelope, which ended up being a bit crinkled. Running it through his fingers to get the wrinkle out, he handed it to her mom. "Will you please give this to Luella when she gets home? I'd planned to give it to her tomorrow, but my daed needs me to go out of town with him. We'll be looking at buying some more hogs."

Esther took the card. "I'll make sure Luella gets this. Have a nice evening and a safe trip tomorrow."

"Danki." Hope deflated, Eugene headed back to his buggy. *Maybe it's a good thing Luella wasn't home this evening. If she didn't like my card, I'd feel even worse right now.*

Eugene's horse trotted as soon as they started down the main road, no doubt eager to get home. As they approached the Bird-in-Hand Family Restaurant, Eugene did a double take. Was that Atlee Zook coming out of the restaurant with his son and Luella?

Eugene gripped the reins tighter, slowing his horse so he could get a better look. Sure enough, it was them, and they were headed toward the line of buggies at the hitching rail.

Now why would Atlee take Luella out for supper? Could he be interested in her? Eugene's jaw clenched. *Luella's not free to let me court her, but she can go out to eat with him? What's going on here, anyway?*

When Luella stepped into the house, she was greeted by her mother, who sat reading a book in the living room.

"Where is everyone?" Luella asked.

"They all went to bed." Mom gestured to the grandfather clock on the other side of the room. "It's late, Luella, and you're home later than usual. I stayed up because I was worried about you."

"I'm fine, Mom. I went shopping with Atlee and Daryl this afternoon, and then we had supper at the Bird-in-Hand Family Restaurant. Afterward, we went back to his place to eat some of the shoofly pie I made earlier today, and then Atlee brought me home."

Mom gestured to the envelope lying on the coffee table. "Eugene came by earlier and left this envelope for you. He was disappointed that you weren't here."

Seeing the red envelope, Luella put both hands on her head. "Ach, I'd forgotten all about tomorrow being Valentine's Day. I'll have to do something special for Daryl."

"I'm sure he'll like whatever you do." Mom set her book aside. "I hope you going out with Atlee for supper doesn't happen again, Luella."

"What do you mean? Why would you say that?"

"If people see you and Atlee out in public together — especially having a meal at a restaurant — they might get the wrong idea."

Luella pursed her lips. "Wrong idea about what?"

"They might think . . . Oh, well, never mind." Mom started to get up.

"No, wait. What were you going to say?"

"Well, some folks might think he's set his cap for you." Mom's shoulders lifted. "But then, that would be ridiculous. Atlee's way too old for a young woman like you."

"Not to worry," Luella said with a shake of her head. "Atlee's still in love with Dena, and he may never get over her death."

"And what about you, Daughter? Are you interested in him?"

"Course not, Mom. Why would you even ask me such a question?"

Mom gestured to the card, still lying on the table. "You haven't bothered to open Eugene's valentine. I figured you'd be eager to read the card."

Luella reached for the envelope. "You're right. I'll take it up to my room and read it before I go to bed." She yawned. "It's been a long day, and I'm tired. *Gut nacht,* Mom. See you in the morning."

"Good night, Luella."

As Luella left the room, she couldn't help but wonder if her mother could see into her soul. *Does Mom have an inkling of the way I've begun to feel about Atlee? If she knew for sure, what would she say? Probably nothing in a good way.*

Luella thought back to earlier this evening, while sitting at the restaurant with Atlee and Daryl. She'd forgotten something until now. Halfway through the meal, she'd looked toward the restaurant's exit in time to see her friend, Ruth Yoder, about to leave the building. But what Luella noticed most was the backward glance her friend gave her before going out the door. *I wonder why Ruth didn't come over to our table and say hello? Especially when we haven't visited in a while. Maybe Mom's right. I should have thought everything through before I accepted Atlee's offer to join him and Daryl for supper.* She released a heavy sigh. *I don't want to be the cause of any gossip or bring embarrassment to Atlee, so maybe it would be best if we weren't seen together in public anymore.*

Chapter 7

Luella had finished doing the lunch dishes, when Daryl tugged on her apron. "Let's go outside and play in the schnee."

She looked down and tweaked his freckled nose. "I guess we can do that. A little fresh air will do us both good." Luella led the way to the utility room, where jackets, hats, and boots were kept. After she helped Daryl into his outer garments, she put on hers as well.

When they stepped out the door, a cold blast of air hit her face. With all the snow still covering the ground, it was hard to believe spring was only a month away. While the snow was pretty, Luella was eager for warmer weather.

Except for Saturdays, when Atlee closed his shop and stayed home with Daryl, Luella would have no time to help her mother plant a garden. Sara would have to take over that job this year. Luella wondered if she should ask Atlee if he'd like her to plant a garden here once the weather warmed. It would be nice to have fresh vegetables and herbs to use for meal preparations. While she worked in the garden, Daryl could run around and play in the yard.

Luella had begun to think of Atlee's place as her second home; especially since she spent more time here than she did at her parents' house these days. She watched Daryl romping in the snow and smiled. The boy was good-natured and easy to please. He had quite an imagination, as well, and because of that had no problem entertaining himself. Atlee was fortunate to have the child. Once more Luella found herself wishing she had children of her own.

Splat! Luella's thoughts took another direction when Daryl tossed a snowball that hit her arm. "Why, you little dickens . . ." She scooped up some snow, formed it into a ball, and threw it at the boy's leg.

Daryl squealed with glee and tossed more snow her way. This time it hit her foot.

"You'd better run, because here I come!" Luella formed another snowball and took off in hot pursuit.

Slipping and sliding, the boy hurried across the yard and ducked behind the trunk of a tree. Luella snuck up on him and touched his face with her cold hands. As expected, he took off in another direction, laughing all the way.

"Hey, what's goin' on out here?"

At the sound of Atlee's voice, Luella stepped back, slipped on a patch of ice, and landed flat on her back.

"Are you okay? Did ya hurt yourself?" Atlee came racing toward her.

"I don't think so." Luella moved her arms and legs back and forth. "Nothing seems to be broken. She could only imagine how foolish she must look.

Atlee pointed to her and chuckled. "Well, would ya look at that? You've just made a snow angel."

As he held out his hand and helped Luella to her feet, she had a sudden urge to throw some snow at him. Acting on her impulse, she stepped back, scooped up some snow, and tossed it at Atlee. At first, he stood looking at her with a dazed expression, but then he took a handful and chucked it at her. After it hit her square in the shoulder, a sly thought came to mind as Luella's gaze went upward. *Time for me to get serious now.* Carefully forming another snowball, then throwing it higher this time, she held her breath, watching Atlee as he followed her aim then paused looking right above his head. Quickly his gaze shot back to Luella, as though contemplating what was about to happen. Seeing his eyes grow large, Luella's hands instinctively covered her mouth just as the snowball connected with her intended mark — a snow-laden branch precariously bobbing up and down from the weight of the snow.

Before Atlee could react, the snow was released and showered down over him. Atlee's shoulders hunched from the frozen spray, and Daryl squealed, "Daadi, you look like a snowman."

Luella tried to cover her giggles, but the hysterics of the moment kicked in. Holding her stomach, she laughed even more and pointed to Atlee's head when he removed his hat and whacked it against his leg. His brown hair was a sharp contrast with the white of his beard, now stuck fast with snow. To prolong any retaliation before Atlee could put his hat back on, Luella quickly scooped up more snow and aimed it toward the top of his head. *Splat!* Snickering, Luella pointed again. "Now your hair matches your beard."

Soon Daryl got into the act, as all three of them enjoyed a snowball battle with one another. Time flew by as they laughed and frolicked in the snow. Luella laughed so hard her sides ached, and she could hardly catch her breath. The lower half of her dress was thoroughly drenched, but she didn't care. It felt so good to have a little fun like this, and hearing Atlee's laughter made it all worthwhile. It was good for him to unwind and not be working all the time. His laughter was contagious.

At one point, Daryl was chasing Atlee, and Atlee chased Luella, each trying their best to out weave another snowball. Short of breath and getting played out, Luella lost her footing and landed in the snow again. Atlee couldn't stop himself in time and ended up falling next to her, with Daryl landing on top of him. Daryl was still laughing, but Atlee and Luella grew quiet when their gazes locked and their labored breath mingled.

Then with the speed of lightning, Atlee jumped up and suggested they go into the house to warm up. Looking at Luella, Atlee sobered. "Your *frack* is sopping wet. You need to go inside and change." He looked at his son. "For that matter, we all need to warm up by the fire."

"But I don't have a dry dress." Luella's cheeks warmed, despite the cold.

"You can wear one of Dena's." As if the

issue was settled, Atlee turned and headed for the house.

Luella took Daryl by the hand and followed. The idea of wearing one of his wife's dresses made her feel a bit strange, but what other choice did she have?

When Luella entered the living room a short time later, Atlee's breath caught in his throat. He inhaled deeply and tried to swallow. He felt a heavy sensation in his chest and limbs.

In some ways Luella reminded him of Dena, when she was a young woman and they'd been courting. She was a petite, pretty woman, with a smile that could melt anyone's heart. Luella was like Dena in other ways, too. She could laugh at herself, had a nurturing spirit, and put other people's needs before her own. The trouble was, she wasn't Dena and never could replace her. No one could.

Atlee stared at the flickering flames lapping at the fireplace logs. He couldn't deny that he'd had fun out there in snow with Luella and Daryl, but he wouldn't let it happen again. If there was any romping in the snow to be done, it would only be with him and his son from now on.

Atlee hunkered down beside Daryl and

held the boy's hands out to the fire. *It should be Dena wearing that dress, not Luella. It's my fault for suggesting it, but I hope Luella never has occasion to wear any of my wife's clothes again.*

Luella stood near the fire, a safe distance from Atlee. As soon as she'd come into the room wearing Dena's dress, she had sensed Atlee's displeasure. No doubt seeing her in his wife's dress was a painful reminder that Dena wasn't coming back.

When I come here tomorrow, I'll bring a few of my own dresses to have on hand in case something else unexpected happens and I need another change of clothes. I should have thought of it sooner, since my work could at any moment require me to change into something different. Atlee had been through enough, and Luella didn't want to put him through the anguish of seeing her in Dena's dress ever again. For that matter, frolicking in the snow with Atlee probably wasn't a good idea, either. It had been so much fun at the time, she hadn't given it any thought. From now on she would be more careful to keep to her place as Atlee's employee.

CHAPTER 8

When Luella awoke the following day, it was all she could do to get out of bed. Her muscles and head ached like she'd been kicked by a mule, and the simple act of swallowing made her wince. *Guess that's what I get for romping around in the snow yesterday with Daryl and Atlee. The chill I got from wearing a wet dress probably set things in motion for me to get sick. Well, I can't let it stop me from going to Atlee's today. He needs me to take care of Daryl.*

Plodding across the room to get out a dress, Luella inhaled deeply through her nose then exhaled from her mouth. *I can do this. Atlee's counting on me.* She had to pause, letting a dizzy spell pass.

By the time Luella got dressed and made her way downstairs, spots formed before her eyes and she feared she might faint. It had been a long time since she'd felt so ill, but determination kept Luella on her feet.

"What do you need me to do?" she asked her mother.

Mom turned from her task at the stove. "Ach, Luella, your face is flushed. Are you feeling *grank* this morning?"

"Jah, a bit." Feeling woozier by the minute, Luella took a seat at the table and shielded her eyes from the brightness pouring in the kitchen window.

Mom pushed the kettle of oatmeal she'd been stirring to the back of the stove and hurried over to Luella. When she placed her hand on Luella's forehead, her eyes widened. "You have a *fiewer*, and you should be upstairs in bed."

Luella shook her head. "I can't, Mom. Atlee's expecting me to watch Daryl today."

Mom planted both hands against her hips. "Well, he's either going to have to close his shop and stay home with the boy or find someone to take your place." She pointed toward the door leading to the upstairs. "Go on back to bed now. I'll bring you some herbal tea and a bowl of oatmeal as soon as it's ready."

"But what about Atlee? He'll be expecting me."

"I'll call and leave him a message." Mom pointed to the stairs once more. "Go on with you, now. Get back to bed and close your eyes. Rest and plenty of liquids are what you need today, Daughter."

With a heavy sigh, Luella grasped the arms of her chair and pulled herself up. "You're right, Mom. I barely have the strength to stand up, much less make it to Atlee's house. I only hope he can find someone to watch Daryl today."

"I'm sure he will manage until you're back on your feet and feeling better."

Luella shuffled out of the room and, holding on to the rail tightly, made her way upstairs. By the time she'd climbed into her bed, Luella's ears were ringing, and the bedroom seemed to be spinning in circles. Luella pulled Dena's quilt up to her chin. She snuggled into the warmth of the flannel sheets and closed her eyes. *Oh, Dena, I'm sorry I could not take care of Daryl today. Maybe tomorrow I'll be better.*

Atlee went to the living-room window and peered out. There was no sign of Luella, and she should have been here half an hour ago. He scratched his head. *She's never been late. I wonder what could be keeping her.*

He had several projects he needed to work on in the shop, but until Luella came to watch Daryl, his work would have to wait.

It wasn't a good idea to take Daryl to the shop with him, and he sure couldn't leave the boy in the house by himself.

Atlee glanced over his shoulder, where Daryl sat on the sofa, looking at Luella's storybook. "Luella *kumme?*" the boy asked, tipping his head.

"I don't know if she's coming, Son. She was supposed to, but maybe something happened and she couldn't make it." Atlee moved toward the dining room and plucked his jacket off the back of the chair where he had hung it last night after he'd done his chores. "I'm going out to the phone shed to see if she called and left me a message." He pointed at Daryl. "I want you to stay right where you are till I get back. Understood?"

"Jah, Daadi."

Atlee smiled. Daryl was such a good boy. He was always eager to please and usually did what he was told.

As Atlee stepped outside, a blast of frigid air hit him in the face. It seemed even colder than it had when he'd done his barn chores early this morning before Daryl was awake. *Sure hope Luella didn't decide to walk here this morning. That could be why she's so late.*

He opened the door of the phone shed and shivered when he stepped inside. It wasn't much warmer in the small wooden building than it was outside. Atlee noticed the light flickering on the answering machine and knew he had at least one message. He clicked the button and waited for it to play. The first message was from a customer, asking about the storage shed he'd ordered. The second one was from Luella's mother, Esther, saying Luella had come down with some kind of a virus or flu bug and wouldn't be able to work for him today and possibly not for the rest of the week. Esther suggested Atlee find someone else to take Luella's place until further notice.

Atlee's brows furrowed. *Luella seemed fine yesterday. I wonder what happened to cause her to get sick between then and now.* He rubbed his forehead. *Well, I'd better make a few calls and see if I can find someone else to fill in till she's feeling better.*

Luella lay in bed, staring at the ceiling and feeling sorry for herself. She didn't know what made her feel worse — the pounding headache, her sore throat, or the guilt she felt for not going to help out at Atlee's today. She would miss seeing Daryl, and Atlee, too, for that matter. Yesterday had been so much fun when they'd played in the snow together. Atlee had almost seemed like a different person when he'd been tossing snowballs and cavorting around the yard. Luella figured that was probably the way he used to be before Dena's heart became so weak and her health declined.

Luella sat up and reached for the cup of herbal tea Mom had given her awhile ago. Although it hurt to swallow, the warm tea felt soothing as it bathed her throat. She hated being sick, and especially now, when others were dependent on her.

Tap! Tap! Tap!

Luella turned her head toward the door. "Come in," she rasped. She wondered if she might end up losing her voice. *I'll bet my sister and brother would like that.*

Luella's bedroom door opened, and Mom stepped in. "How are you feeling?"

"About the same." Luella lifted her cup. "The tea's good, though."

Mom gave a nod. "I wanted you to know that I'm going into town for a while. I need a few things and thought I'd stop by the pharmacy, and maybe the health food store, to pick up some items that will hopefully make you feel better — especially something to soothe your throat."

"Okay, I appreciate that." Luella took a drink and set her cup on the bedside table. "Did you leave a message for Atlee?"

96

"Jah. I suggested he find a replacement for you until further notice."

Luella moaned. "I hope it won't be too long. Dena asked me to take care of her family after she was gone, not someone else, so I need to get back to work as soon as I can."

Mom pursed her lips. "I don't think she meant forever, Luella. Eventually Atlee will take another wife, and then you'll be free to begin a relationship with Eugene, and hopefully get married and start your own family."

"My future may not be with Eugene, Mom." Luella winced when she swallowed.

"What do you mean? Why, the way that fellow looks at you, I'm surprised he hasn't already asked you to marry him."

"It wouldn't matter if he had. I'm not free to marry anyone right now." Luella closed her eyes. "Can we discuss this some other time? I'm tired and it hurts to talk."

"Of course. You get some sleep, and when I get back from town, I'll have some throat lozenges for you to suck on, as well as a few other things." Mom slipped quietly out of the room.

Luella rested her head on the pillow and closed her eyes. *Mom doesn't understand the importance of the promise I made to Dena.*

When Esther entered the pharmacy, she spotted her friend, Myrna Lapp, picking up a prescription.

"Is someone at your house sick, too?" Esther asked, joining her friend at the counter.

Myrna sighed. "Jah, my daughter, Anna. She has a sore throat, fever, and chills."

"There must be something going around, because Luella is sick with similar symptoms." Esther frowned.

Before Esther could add any more, Myrna relayed some things she'd heard recently. "Did you know the Beachys from our district are expecting their first child?"

"No, I hadn't heard."

"Jah, sometime in October the baby is due."

"Bet her parents are happy, since this will be their first grandchild."

"Oh, and Pauline King almost knocked me down as I was coming into the pharmacy."

"Is that so? What was her hurry?" Esther half listened, running through her mind the items she didn't want to forget to purchase. She really wasn't interested in this idle chit-chat.

"I did speak to her briefly, but Pauline said she was in a rush. Something about having to drop her daughter, Mary Jane, off at Atlee Zook's to help him out and watch his son." Myrna paused. "I didn't see Mary Jane, though. Guess she was waiting in the buggy."

"Since Luella is sick in bed, I'm glad to hear he found someone to watch his little boy. As you know, my dochder's been working for Atlee and was determined to go there this morning until she admitted how bad she felt. I had a time convincing her to stay put in bed. Why, the poor thing could hardly walk up the stairs to get back to her room."

"Sorry to hear your daughter is sick." Myrna leaned closer to Esther and whispered, "Aren't you a bit concerned about Luella being around Atlee so much?"

"What do you mean? She has to see him every day, since she takes care of his son and does all the cooking and cleaning for them."

"I understand, but word has it that Luella and Atlee were seen eating together at the Bird-in-Hand Restaurant." Myrna blinked several times. "And then my son Eugene said he was driving by Atlee's place yesterday, on the way to pick up some supplies for his daed, when he saw Atlee in the yard, throwing snowballs at Luella. Now, I ask you, does that sound like something a grown man should be doing with his hired help? To say the least, Eugene was a bit disappointed."

Esther cringed. *Myrna is right — Atlee should not be running around like a schoolboy with my daughter. I'm just not sure what I can do about it.*

It was way past lunchtime when Atlee came in to the sound of Daryl crying. He quickly washed his hands and walked into the living room, where he found his son sitting in the middle of the braided throw rug.

Hurrying across the room, Atlee picked Daryl up, took a seat on the sofa, and sat the boy on his lap. "Hey now, what has these tears falling from your eyes? And where's Mary Jane?"

"Upstairs, cleanin' my room. She told me to stay down here till she was done." Daryl sniffed. "Daadi, I don't like her. I want Luella back."

"Now, now. It's Mary Jane's first day here, and we have to give her a chance." Atlee tried to sooth Daryl by rubbing his back. "Did she make you some lunch?"

"Jah, she made soup, but I wanted a

peanut butter and jelly sandwich." Daryl hiccupped a few times, and just that quickly, like turning off a faucet, his hiccups subsided. "Mary Jane's not like Luella. Luella fixes whatever I want."

"Everyone is different, Son." Atlee leaned back as Daryl laid against his chest. "Soup is good for a growing boy. It sticks to your ribs." Atlee poked his son's side and grinned when Daryl giggled.

"That tickles, Daadi." The boy jumped off Atlee's lap and picked up the book Luella had given him. "Would ya read this to me?"

"How 'bout we save it for this evening, after I tuck you in bed for the night?" Atlee smiled at Daryl, who now stood leaning against his leg. Then he glanced toward the stairs when he heard movement coming from his son's room. "There's something else I want to say before Mary Jane comes down."

"What, Daadi?"

"Let's try to make it work for however long she's here. It's only temporary, until Luella returns, and we should be grateful Mary Jane was able to come on such short notice." Atlee ruffled Daryl's auburn hair. "So what do you think, buddy? Is it a deal?"

"Deal." Daryl giggled more when Atlee shook hands with him. Then he pulled him close and gave him a big hug. "I love you, Son."

"Love you, too." Atlee's heart swelled when Daryl returned the hug.

"Ach, Mr. Zook! I didn't hear you come in." Mary Jane stammered when she came down the stairs. "I was straightening up Daryl's room. Can I fix you something to eat? There is still some soup left from our lunch."

"That will be fine." Atlee stood. "Once it's heated, I'll eat it in here, so I can spend some time with Daryl before I go back out to work. By the way, when I came in the living room I found my son in tears. Did you know he was crying?"

Mary Jane pursed her lips. "I did, but at my house, whenever my little sister cries for no reason, my mamm lets her cry it out."

Atlee tapped his foot. "Daryl has a good reason to cry. Losing his mamm is still fresh in his mind, plus he misses Luella because he's used to her caring for him."

"I understand." She gave a quick nod. "I have a lot of cleaning to do here today, but I'll try to be more sensitive to his needs."

"Danki."

When Mary Jane retreated to the kitchen, Atlee sat back down and sighed. *I hope Luella gets better soon.* It surprised him how in one short day, things weren't the same around here without Luella.

CHAPTER 9

"How are you feeling now?" Atlee asked when Luella returned to work a week after she'd taken sick.

"Much better. I've missed being here to help out. Although I was anxious to come back, I needed to make sure I wasn't contagious." Luella placed her hand on top of Daryl's head as he looked up at her with a look of adoration. "I certainly wouldn't have wanted this little fellow, or you either, Atlee, to get what I had. For the first several days I felt miserable."

"Well, we're glad to have you back." Atlee leaned closer to Luella and whispered, "My boy didn't cooperate with Mary Jane the way he does with you. He kept asking and asking when you were coming back. But this morning, because he knew you'd be here, I had no trouble getting him out of bed."

Luella couldn't help but smile. It was nice to be appreciated. She'd missed Daryl and his father more than she dared to admit. During the week she'd spent recuperating from the flu, she'd come to realize how much they both meant to her. She thought about her mother's comment this morning before she left. *"Why don't you quit working for Atlee and find another job?"* Luella had reminded Mom of the promise she'd made to Dena, but even now, it bothered her to think her mother didn't understand.

"Well, now." Luella turned toward the kitchen. "I'd best get some breakfast made for the two of you."

Atlee shook his head. "No need to bother with that. I fixed us some oatmeal before you got here. Figured it would be one less thing you'd have to worry about today."

"Danki, but I wouldn't have minded. After all, part of what you're paying me for is to cook three meals a day for you and Daryl."

"I know, but it's your first day back, and I don't want you getting overworked. Having the flu is nothing to fool around with."

Atlee sounded genuinely concerned, and it touched Luella's soul. "What would you like me to do today?" she asked.

"If you only keep Daryl occupied, that'd suit me just fine." Atlee grabbed his jacket from where it hung on a peg near the door. "You can make something simple like sandwiches for lunch, and for supper, there's leftover chicken in the refrigerator from the meal Mary Jane fixed for us before she went home last evening."

"What about laundry or cleaning the house?"

"No need to do either of those today. Mary Jane made sure those chores were caught up, too." Atlee slapped his hat on his head. "I'm heading out to my shop now, so all you need to do is relax and spend time with my boy." Before Luella could offer a response, he opened the door and stepped out, closing it behind him.

As nice as it was to be told she didn't have to do much today, Luella would feel worthless if she did nothing but occupy Daryl all day. No, she would find something constructive to do, even though Atlee had said otherwise. She turned toward the kitchen, calling over her shoulder, "Kumme, Daryl. You can help me bake some peanut butter cookies."

Grinning, the boy clapped his hands. "Kichlin! Kichlin!"

Stepping lightly, Luella opened the kitchen door. She knew better than to allow herself such fanciful thoughts, but being here in this house felt like she'd come home.

Eugene was fit to be tied. He had heard from his mother this morning that Luella would be going back to work for Atlee today. He'd hoped the young woman Atlee hired in Luella's absence might still be working for him and end up staying on permanently. Then Luella would finally be free to begin courting. It still irked him to think of seeing her with Atlee fooling around in the snow like a couple of kids. At his age Atlee should have known better, and for that matter, so should Luella.

"I can't be expected to wait for Luella forever," he muttered, throwing food into one of the hog troughs. A couple of noisy sows came pushing, grunting, and sticking their snouts into the trough. "You greedy old pigs. I can think of lots better things I'd like to be doin' today. Sure wish I didn't have to take care of you swine."

"You talkin' to yourself again, Son?"

Eugene jerked at the sound of his dad's voice. "Uh, no. I was talking to the pigs."

Dad chuckled and thumped Eugene's back. "Guess I'd be more worried if they started talkin' back."

Eugene said nothing. To his way of thinking, there was nothing funny about a bunch of hungry, selfish hogs. *I wonder what Dad would say if I told him I'd like to quit hog farming. He'd probably be upset.*

Dad bumped Eugene's arm. "Your mamm wanted me to remind you about your dental appointment this morning."

Eugene groaned. Going to the dentist was the last thing he wanted to do, but he'd had a toothache for the last three days, so it was time to get the tooth looked at.

"Mom doesn't need to worry. I'll get there on time." He reached up and rubbed his jaw. *Sure will be glad when the dentist fixes my tooth.*

"Okay, Son. I hope everything goes well in the dentist's chair." Dad turned and started to walk away, but Eugene called out to him.

"Say, Dad, if you have a few minutes, I'd like to say something that's been on my mind."

"Sure, go ahead." Dad turned to face Eugene.

Eugene rubbed his hands down the sides of his trousers. This was going to be harder than he thought.

"Well, speak up, boy. What'd ya want to tell me?"

"The things is . . ." Eugene closed his eyes

briefly and took a calming breath. "I don't like hog farming much, and I was wondering if you'd be okay if I tried my hand at something else."

Dad tipped his head, looking at Eugene curiously. "What else would you do?"

Eugene moistened his lips with the tip of his tongue, his courage rising a bit. "I was thinkin' about becoming a taxidermist."

"What?" Dad's bushy eyebrows rose high on his forehead. "Don't see how you can make a living doin' something like that. You're not thinking straight, Son."

"I figured you wouldn't approve. You're stuck on the idea of me raising hogs the rest of my life, so I may as well accept it." Eugene threw the last of the hog slop into the trough and walked off. He felt worthless right now. Like his wants didn't matter one little bit. "Nothin' ever goes right for me," Eugene muttered as he made his way to the house. "I'll probably never get Luella to let me court her, either."

Atlee whistled as he kept busy in his shop. He felt a sense of relief knowing Luella was in the house with Daryl. The boy sure had missed her when she was sick and would no doubt be a lot happier now that she was watching him again. He was pleased with how his son had cooperated with Mary Jane after the little talk they'd had. Daryl might only be four years old, but he was learning how life doesn't always go as people would like sometimes.

Atlee grabbed a can of nails from the shelf overhead. *My fraa was right in asking Luella to keep working for me after she was gone. For a young woman her age, Luella is more responsible than many women in our community who are much older.*

Atlee's thoughts came to a halt when his friend Henry Riehl entered the shop.

"Wie geht's?" Henry asked, stepping up to Atlee's workbench.

"I'm getting by. How are things with you?"

"Good as rain, which, by the way, I wish we'd get more of instead of snow." Henry snickered. "I never have liked winter that much. How about you?"

Atlee shrugged. "It's okay, but I'm looking forward to spring and warmer days."

"Jah, you're right. Then, all too soon, we'll be complaining about the heat and humidity of summer." Henry leaned against the workbench with arms folded. "Ah, besides the weather, there's something I need to talk to you about."

"Sure, what is it?"

"Well," Henry rubbed his forehead. "It

may not be my place to say anything, but I wonder if you realize you're the topic of some gossip going around."

"What do you mean? What kind of gossip?" Atlee eyed his friend with furrowed brows.

"Well, according to my wife, Fannie, someone told her you were seen with Luella eating supper at the Bird-in-Hand Restaurant a few weeks ago." Henry leaned forward. "Is it true?"

Atlee's jaw clenched, and he set his can of nails down so hard, several popped out. "I don't know why anyone would gossip about that. It was just a meal, and Daryl was with us." His pulse quickened. "It's not like Luella and I are courting, for goodness' sake."

Henry lifted both hands. "Whoa now, Atlee. I wasn't insinuating anything. Just wanted you to be aware that a few tongues have been wagging."

"Well, let 'em wag. There's nothing going on between me and Luella. I hired her before Dena died, and she's doing a good job taking care of Daryl, as well as cooking and cleaning for me." Atlee stared straight at his friend. "That's all there is to it."

Henry nodded. "Okay, but there is one other thing."

"What's that?"

"I also heard you were seen frolicking in the snow with Luella a week or so ago."

Atlee's eyes blinked uncontrollably. It was difficult to hold his temper right now. "So what? We were playing with Daryl and tossing snowballs at one another. Is there anything wrong with me and the boy having a little fun — especially after all we've been through? Or is that against some law or church rule?"

Henry reached out and touched Atlee's shoulder. "You'd better calm down. You're getting worked up over nothing."

"It's not nothing. If people are saying things about me behind my back — and Luella's for that matter — they oughta come talk to me face-to-face." Atlee planted his feet in a wide stance. "Then I could set them straight about their suspicions and how ridiculous they are."

Henry turned his hands palms up. "You know how it goes. Most people would rather talk about someone than talk to them, when it comes to something that is really none of their business."

"Jah." Atlee rubbed the back of his neck. The gossiping needed to stop. If he got wind of any more of it, he'd nip it in the bud real fast. He and Luella had done nothing wrong and didn't deserve to be the discussion of wagging tongues.

CHAPTER 10

By the middle of May, Atlee was slowly coming to grips with Dena's death. He also felt more comfortable around Luella. In fact, he sometimes struggled with guilt because feelings of happiness were slowly coming back to him. It helped to see Daryl reacting positively to Luella. The other day, he'd overheard her putting Daryl down for a nap, and just as the boy was drifting off to sleep, he mumbled, "I love you, Mammi." It had been difficult to hear, but Atlee understood Daryl's need for a mother, so he couldn't fault him for that.

Shaking his thoughts aside, Atlee stamped the mud off his boots and stepped into the house. "Daryl, are ya ready to go?"

No response.

Atlee went to the kitchen, where he found his son sitting at the table staring at his bowl of cereal. "You need to hurry and finish your breakfast so we can go to the bakery

114

and run a few errands."

Daryl's eyes lit up. *"Beckerei?"*

"Jah. Thought I'd buy us some kichlin and maybe a shoofly pie."

"Luella bakes good pies."

"You're right she does, but this is Saturday, and it's her day off, so she won't be baking any pies for us today."

Atlee took out a drinking glass, filled it with water, and put the tulips he'd clipped from the flower bed, in it. He then centered the arrangement on the kitchen table and leaned down to inhale the fragrance. The pink, yellow, purple, and red blooms gave the kitchen some much-needed color.

"Aren't these flowers pretty?" Atlee looked down at Daryl.

The boy's lip protruded. "Wish Luella could stay here all the time. I miss her, and I love her, too."

Atlee blinked rapidly, forgetting the flowers. He hadn't expected such a bold statement from his son and wasn't sure how to respond. "Um, well, that's not possible, Daryl. Luella lives with her parents."

"But if she was my mamm, she could live here with us." Daryl's comment was so innocent. He clearly didn't understand.

Atlee thumped the boy's shoulder. "Enough talk now. Finish your breakfast so we can go."

With no argument, Daryl picked up his spoon and started eating.

Atlee moved over to the stove to pour himself a cup of coffee. *If Luella were a few years older, there might be a chance for a future with her, but she's not much more than a girl. I'm sure she would never consider marrying someone as old as me.*

Luella enjoyed her time off, but on the weekends she missed being with Daryl. He was such a sweet child and had recently begun calling her Mammi. *I hope Atlee doesn't hear his son say that,* Luella thought as she hitched Dixie to her carriage. *It would probably upset him.* She'd promised her mother she would run a few errands for her this morning and would be on her way to town as soon as the horse was ready.

Luella stood for a moment and looked toward the clear blue sky. Rubbing Dixie's nose, she spoke out loud. "Oh, what a beautiful morning this is." The spring warmth filled her soul with energy, and she was actually anxious to do a little shopping.

Dixie nickered and twitched her ears. Luella ran her fingers through the horse's long mane. "I'll bet you are raring to go, too, aren't ya?" As if she understood, Dixie's head bobbed up and down, while she snorted.

As Luella climbed in the buggy, Sara, ran outside, waving her arms. "Wait up, sister! You forgot Mom's list."

Luella opened the carriage door and took the piece of paper from her sister. "Guess I was in such a hurry to get going, I forgot about the list."

Sara's shoulders drooped. "Wish I could go with you today, but Mom wants me to help plant more vegetable seeds in the garden. Don't see why you always get to have fun and I get stuck here doin' all the work."

Luella shook her head. "You're exaggerating. I do more than my share of work around here. And don't forget, when I am not working at home I'm at Atlee's working for him."

"But you get paid for that. Besides, you like goin' over there so you can pretend you're Daryl's mudder and Atlee's fraa."

"I–I am doing no such thing," Luella stammered. "Where did you ever get such an idea?"

Sara shrugged. "I hear you talkin' about them all the time. Atlee said this, and Daryl did that. You talk more about them than you do any of us."

Luella bristled. "I do not."

"Jah, you do."

"Well, if it seems that way, it's only because I'm there five days a week, from early morning till after supper usually. And for your information, I don't pretend I'm anyone's mother or wife." Luella clutched the reins. "I'm going now. Have a nice day." She got Dixie moving down the driveway and didn't bother to look back to see if her sister was watching. *The nerve of Sara, talking to me like that!*

As Luella guided her horse and buggy down the road toward town, she passed the Lapps' place and spotted Eugene out in the field with his brothers, Amos and Dan. Eugene must have seen her, too, for he lifted his straw hat from his head and waved at her with it. Luella waved back and kept on going. If she stopped to say hello, she'd never get those errands for Mom run. Besides, Eugene might pressure her to let him court her, and that was still out of the question. The truth was, Luella might never feel ready to be courted by Eugene, because she only saw him as a friend, not a suitor.

Is my sister right? Do I have some silly notion about being Daryl's mother and Atlee's wife? Luella shook her head. *I can't even allow myself to think such thoughts.*

Concentrating on the road, Luella still admired the rainbow of colors from budding trees, and blooming flowers. The air filled with sweet fragrances caused her to relax. *Monday when I go to Atlee's, I'll have to clip some posies from one of his flower beds and put them on the kitchen table.*

Luella was just a mile or so from town, when a horn blared from behind. A truck roared past so close that it rocked the buggy. Dixie snorted and reared up.

"Whoa, girl, settle down." Luella spoke softly as she tugged on the reins.

The usually calm horse thrashed her head side to side then took off like a flash. Luella held on tightly and pulled back, but Dixie kept running, zigzagging back and forth from one lane to the other.

Luella wrapped the reins around her hands a second time, so she would not lose her grip. Fortunately, the road was clear of other vehicles, but Luella knew if she didn't get the horse under control soon, it could be disastrous.

"Whoa, Dixie! Whoa!"

Dixie veered to the right and went into the ditch, taking the buggy right with her. It rocked back and forth then flipped onto its side. Luella screamed. Her consciousness faded.

"We'll be at the bakery soon. What kind of kichlin would you like?" Atlee looked over at Daryl and smiled.

"Peanut butter!"

Atlee chuckled. "You're stuck on those cookies, aren't you?"

Daryl nodded. "Luella's makes good kichlin."

"I know. You've mentioned that a time or two."

Atlee clucked to his horse to get him moving faster. Smokey was taking his good ole sweet time today.

Atlee took a deep breath, inhaling the warmth of the air. *No wonder Smokey was poking along.* Even with his thoughts drifting to Dena, life was starting to feel right again. His wife loved spring and working in the flower beds. She certainly had a way with those flowers, too. Everything she planted grew under her tender care, even the wildflowers that came up from where she'd scattered seeds along the fence row. Every year Dena was tickled to no end when she saw how those wildflowers had spread. A few times he'd even caught her talking to the flowers, as if they were a close friend.

Since April, Dena's flowers had opened up with beautiful fragrant blooms, and each day a different one appeared. Could it be his wife's whispers from heaven were even now keeping them alive and healthy? Or was it that Luella cared for them as if they were her own?

Passing by a few houses, their landscapes bursting with color, Atlee felt a tinge of giddiness. The air was warm and filled with fragrance from all that was in bloom. *How could a person not feel heady on a day such as today?*

Smokey whinnied as a field came into view. A few mares were grazing and whinnied in response as the buggy rode by. With head held higher, Smokey pranced with a bit more spirit.

"You're feeling it, too, huh, ole boy?" Atlee relaxed and enjoyed the scenery.

"Look, Daadi." Daryl pointed in the opposite direction. "There's a baby deer like the one in the story Luella reads to me."

Atlee looked toward where his son was pointing. On the edge of a field, near a grove of trees, stood a doe with a tiny fawn nursing.

Springtime is so wonderful, Atlee thought. *Nature brings new life into this world.* A new sensation surrounded him with a feeling of hope.

"Did you see its tail wagging?" Daryl giggled as they started up a small hill.

"Jah, I saw it. That little baby sure was hungerich." Atlee glanced at his son, remembering how it seemed like only yesterday when he was born.

A little farther, Atlee spotted a buggy tipped on its side in a ditch alongside the road. He glanced quickly around but saw no sign of a horse. He guided Smokey off the road, jumped out, and tied the horse to a fence post. "Stay put, Daryl. I'll be right back."

Atlee approached the buggy. Luella was inside. His heart leaped into his throat. He called out to her, but she gave no response and didn't appear to be moving. "Oh, no! Dear Lord, please let her be all right." If Luella died, it would be like losing Dena all over again. *Only it's not Dena, it's Luella, and I don't know what I would do without her.*

A shock of realization hit Atlee. He didn't know exactly when or how it had happened, but like Daryl, Atlee loved Luella — but in a much different way.

Lord, help me, he silently prayed. *I never should have let this happen, but it has, and I'm begging You not to take her from me.*

CHAPTER 11

Lancaster, Pennsylvania

Atlee sat in one of the hospital waiting-room chairs, twisting the brim of his hat. Luella had been in the examining room over an hour, and still no word on her condition. Her parents had been notified, but they were down the hall filling out paperwork. He was thankful an English driver had come along soon after he'd arrived at the accident, and gone to a local business to make the call for help. After the ambulance came and transported Luella to the hospital, Atlee took his horse and buggy home and called one of his drivers. Then, not wanting to upset his son any further, he'd asked the driver to drop Daryl off at Mary Jane's house so she could watch him until Atlee came home from the hospital. The boy had been in tears when he'd seen Luella's buggy on its side in the ditch. Now all Atlee could do was sit here by himself and pray.

Atlee had known for several weeks that his affection for Luella was growing, but he'd been fighting it, even to the point of trying to avoid her as much as he could. Some days he would take his lunch in the shop so he'd have an excuse not to visit with her. But after seeing her today, lying in her buggy unconscious, Atlee could not deny his feelings any longer. He had no idea how Luella felt about him, but if she recovered from her injuries, he planned to open up to her and express his feelings. The worst that could happen would be rejection on her part. He placed his hat over one knee and clasped his hands together. Living with Luella's rejection would be better than losing her altogether. He could endure that, as long as God allowed her to live.

Atlee's attention was drawn to the door when Luella's father entered the room. Seeing her father's placid expression, it was hard to tell if he had good news or bad. As Owen approached, Atlee got out of his chair. "Any word on Luella yet?"

Owen shook his head. "Nothing definite. They are still running tests to see if she has a concussion or any broken bones." He motioned for Atlee to sit, and he took the chair beside him. "Sure wish we knew what caused the accident. My daughter's *gaul* is usually easygoing, and Luella's a good driver. It doesn't make sense that the buggy tipped over and went into a ditch." He frowned. "The shaft was broken in two, and we found Dixie down the road. If only she could talk to us, we'd know for sure how the accident happened."

"Luella can tell us when she wakes up." Atlee's throat constricted. *She has to wake up. Dear Lord, please let her wake up.*

A few minutes later, Luella's mother entered the room and rushed over to Owen. "I just spoke with the doctor, and our daughter has a slight concussion, some bruises, and a nasty cut on one hand, but otherwise, she's going to be okay."

Breathing a sigh of relief, Atlee bowed his head. *Thank You, Lord.*

"When can we see her?" Owen rose to his feet.

Esther placed her hand on his arm. "She's being admitted and will soon be taken to a room. Once she's settled we can see her."

Owen's forehead wrinkled. "But if she isn't seriously hurt, why can't we take her home with us?"

"Since she was unconscious for a while, the doctor wants to keep her overnight for observation," Esther explained. She looked over at Atlee. "We appreciate you being here, but there's really no reason for you to stay. I'm sure you would rather be home with your boy."

"Actually, Daryl's with Mary Jane and her family, and I'd rather stay awhile so I can see for myself how Luella's doing."

Esther glanced at Owen then back at Atlee. "We're glad you came along when you did. No telling how long our daughter would have been trapped in her buggy if you hadn't found her."

"I was sure glad an English driver came along and went to call for help." Atlee sagged against the back of his chair, pressing his elbows into his sides. "It nearly scared the life out of me when I came upon her rig in the ditch. Your dochder means a lot to me." His mouth felt dry and he swallowed a couple of times. "Truth is, I'm in love with Luella."

Owen's eyes widened, and Esther touched her throat as she let out a little gasp. "You can't be serious," she said with a shake of her head.

"I am completely serious. In fact, if she'll have me, I'd like to marry Luella."

Before Esther could respond, Owen asked, "Does Luella know how you feel about her?"

"No, not yet. I am hoping she feels the

same way about me." Atlee breathed deeply and lifted his chin, trying to gain a sense of calm. His declaration of love for Luella had no doubt shocked her parents, but it actually felt good to admit the truth.

Esther brought a shaky hand to her forehead. "Do you realize that our daughter is only twenty-two?"

Atlee nodded.

"And that doesn't bother you?" Esther's voice rose.

"Well, it did at first, but a couple's age difference shouldn't matter if there is love between them."

Esther folded her arms, staring hard at Atlee. "Luella is almost young enough to be your daughter. What in all the world are you thinking, Atlee? If you must replace your wife, don't you at least have the decency to find someone closer to your age?"

"I understand your concerns, Esther, but —"

Owen held up his hand. "I think we should put this discussion on hold. Now's not the time or place to be talkin' about this." He looked at his wife. "Don't you agree?"

Pressing her lips together she slowly nodded.

"Good. Then we can talk about this some

other time."

Atlee had a feeling that no matter when the discussion came up again, he wasn't going to win Esther over. But before he even tried, the first order of business would be to speak to Luella.

As Esther made her way down the hospital corridor toward Luella's room, her stomach quivered. Her suspicions about Atlee were not unfounded. She had every right to be concerned. She wished now that Luella had never accepted Atlee's invitation to take care of his wife or to keep working for him after Dena died. It was not a good situation. Luella was young and impressionable. She was probably flattered by an older man's attention.

I wish my husband would have put that man in his place, once and for all. Atlee has no right to expect our daughter to become his wife. Doesn't he care what a sacrifice she would be making?

Esther was glad Atlee had gone home without seeing Luella today. Just waking up and finding out she was in an accident would be enough for her to handle, and she didn't need Atlee going into her room and proclaiming his love.

Esther bit her lip so hard she tasted blood.

128

If he truly feels love for my daughter. Most likely Atlee wants a young wife so she can keep up with all the cooking, cleaning, and taking care of his son — all the things that an older woman might not be able to handle.

As Esther approached Luella's door, she paused to take a deep breath and collect her thoughts. One thing was certain: she was not about to mention what Atlee had said to her and Owen. With any luck, her husband could talk Atlee out of the silly notion of asking Luella to marry him, and then Luella would be none the wiser.

Squaring her shoulders, Esther opened the hospital-room door and stepped in. Luella was lying in the bed with her eyes closed.

Esther took a seat in the chair near the bed and reached out to touch Luella's hand. "Daughter, are you awake?"

Luella opened her eyes slowly, blinking as she looked at Esther. "Where am I, Mama, and why does my head hurt so much?"

"You're in the hospital. Atlee found your buggy on its side in a ditch."

"Atlee?" Luella rubbed her eyes. "I don't remember seeing his horse and buggy." Her chin quivered. "I'm sorry, Mama. I never got to run any of your errands."

Esther shook her head. "Never mind about that. Your daed and I are just glad you weren't seriously injured."

"Where is Dad?"

"He's in the waiting room. Said I should come in and see you first and then he'd take his turn." Esther patted Luella's uninjured hand. "You have a nasty cut on your other hand, as well as a slight concussion. So the doctor wants to keep you overnight, and then tomorrow you can go home."

Luella rubbed her temples and winced. "No wonder I have such a horrible *kopp-weh*. It feels like my head's going to explode."

"Hopefully the pain will subside soon. Do you remember how the accident happened, Luella?"

"Jah. A truck blew its horn and passed a little too close. Dixie got spooked, probably because the horn was extra loud. The next thing I knew, she was running down the road for all she was worth, zigzagging from one side of the road to the other."

"Do you remember the buggy flipping onto its side?"

"I do, but that's the last thing I remember. What about Dixie?" Luella closed her eyes and winced. "Is she okay?"

"Dixie is fine. She's at a farm near where we found her." Esther gave her daughter's hand another gentle pat. "We'll get her on the way home."

"Oh, thank goodness." Luella sighed. "I'm glad she wasn't hurt."

Esther didn't want to, but the words came flowing out. "So you don't have any recollection of Atlee showing up?"

"No, none at all. Is he here now?"

Esther shook her head. "He was for a little while, but he went home after we learned that you were going to be okay."

"I wish he could have stayed. I would like to thank him."

"Your daed and I told Atlee we appreciated him finding you."

Luella smiled, although Esther could tell her daughter was in pain.

"I'll tell Atlee thank you when I go to work for him tomorrow."

"I don't think so." Esther put both hands on her hips. "Remember I just said the doctor won't release you until tomorrow, and when he does, you'll be doing nothing but resting for at least a week or so. Even if you didn't have a concussion, with the cut on your hand, it would be difficult to do any chores."

Groaning, Luella lifted her arm and looked at the large bandage on her hand. "I lost a lot of time not going to Atlee's during the days I was sick with the flu, and I sure don't want to lose any more. Daryl would miss me, and I'd be yearning to see him, too."

"What about Atlee? Would you miss him also?" Esther couldn't help herself. She needed to know how Luella felt about Atlee, and she couldn't wait to find out.

"Jah. The truth is . . . Well, Mama, I . . . I'm in love with Atlee, but please don't say anything, because he doesn't know." Luella grimaced. "It would be embarrassing for him to find out. I'm almost certain he doesn't have such feelings for me."

Esther sat quietly. She was tempted to tell Luella what Atlee had said and caution her against accepting a marriage proposal from him, but that could wait until Luella felt better. This was not a good time to say anything that might upset her daughter. Esther squeezed her eyes shut. *I just hope when she does find out, I can talk her out of accepting his marriage proposal.*

CHAPTER 12

Bird-in-Hand

"I don't think you should go to work for Atlee today."

Forehead wrinkling, Luella looked across the breakfast table at her mother. "Why not, Mom? It's been a whole week since my accident, and I'm feeling fine." She lifted her hand, where only a small bandage remained. "Even my cut doesn't hurt anymore."

Mom glanced at Dad, as though hoping he might say something, but he merely shrugged and picked up his cup of coffee.

"What's going on here?" Luella touched her mother's arm. "Don't you realize I'm needed at Atlee's?"

Mom blew out a quick breath. "I think it would be best if you quit working for him."

"You mean for always?" Luella could hardly believe her mother would suggest such a thing.

"Jah."

"But why?" Luella's neck bent forward.

"This is not the time to be talking about this," Dad spoke up. "It can wait until the kinner have gone to school."

Luella glanced at her younger sister and brother; they both sat staring at her. "But, Dad, if we wait till then, I'll be late getting to Atlee's to fix his and Daryl's breakfast."

"I'm sure Atlee can manage the meal without you," Mom interjected. "After all, he does so on the weekends when you're not working for him."

Luella could see by the stubborn set of her father's jaw, and the way Mom's lips were pressed together, that they were determined to discuss this with her, but not in front of Sara and Samuel. Not wishing to create a scene or disrespect her parents' wishes, she slowly nodded. She would head for Atlee's place as soon as they talked this out.

Atlee glanced at the battery-operated clock on the kitchen wall, wondering what could be keeping Luella. She should have been here an hour ago. When he'd spoken to her after church yesterday, she had assured him she would be here this morning at the usual time. He'd been relieved to see that the cut on her hand was healing nicely. When Luella said she felt well enough to return to work, Atlee had been pleased. He hadn't said anything to her yesterday, with all the other people around, but today, if he could work up the courage, he planned to tell Luella that he'd fallen in love with her.

"Daadi, I'm hungerich." Daryl pointed to the back door. "Where's Luella? You said she'd come today and would fix our breakfast."

"I know, Son, and I'm sure she's still coming. Something probably came up to cause her to be late." Atlee took out a bowl and a box of cold cereal and placed them on the table. "I'll fix your breakfast, and then when Luella gets here, she'll have one less thing to do."

Daryl made a face. "I don't want cereal. I want pannekuche."

"I'm not good at making pancakes." Atlee poured cereal into the boy's bowl and added some milk. "Now eat your breakfast. Maybe by the time Luella gets here you'll be done and ready for her to read your favorite story." He tweaked Daryl's nose. "And I'm sure if you ask her nicely, Luella might make those pannekuche for your lunch. Nothing says pancakes can only be eaten at breakfast. Right?"

"Right!" Daryl grabbed his spoon and

started eating.

Atlee smiled. *My son is just as excited to see Luella this morning as I am.*

As soon as Samuel and Sara were out the door, Luella turned to her mother. "Can we finish our conversation from earlier now? Atlee and Daryl probably think I'm not coming."

Dad went over to the stove and retrieved the coffeepot. "Let's us three sit at the table and drink some hot kaffi while we discuss a few things."

"I'll listen to whatever you and Mom have to say, but I don't care for any coffee." Luella took a seat and waited for Dad and Mom to join her at the table. Absentmindedly, she rubbed the bandage that covered the cut on her hand. It sure was itchy, and Luella couldn't wait to have the dressing off for good.

Once they were both seated, Mom was the first to speak. "Your daed and I think it's time for you to stop working for Atlee. It's not a good situation, and people are beginning to talk."

Luella shifted in her chair. "But, Mom, I —"

"You may think you're in love with Atlee," Mom interrupted, "but it's just a silly infatuation. You are way too young for him, and it would never work out between you."

"I don't expect anything to work out." Luella's gaze darted to her father then back to her mother. "Although I am in love with Atlee, he's never said anything about loving me, so you and Dad have nothing to worry about. I'll go on working for Atlee and taking care of Daryl, and Atlee will never know the way I feel about him."

Dad shook his head. "It's too late for that."

"What do you mean?" Luella looked at her father again and waited while he took a sip of coffee.

"When you were in the hospital and your mamm and I were sitting in the waiting room with Atlee, he confessed that he's fallen in love with you."

Barely able to comprehend what her father had said, Luella's fingers touched her parted lips. "Atlee really told you that?"

"Jah, and I don't think it'll be long till he tells you the same thing."

"Ach, my!" Luella clasped her hands to her chest, barely able to remain in her chair. "This is certainly a surprise. I never dreamed Atlee felt the same way about me."

Mom leaned forward, looking right at Luella. "Do you understand now why we want you to quit working for him?"

137

Luella shook her head vigorously. "No, I don't. I love Atlee, and if he loves me, then I would think you would be happy for both of us — Daryl, too, for that matter. The boy needs a mother, and I've grown very fond of him. In fact I love Atlee's child as if he were my own."

"While that may be true, it doesn't make up for the fact that you and Atlee are sixteen years apart. Compared to you, he's an old man." Dad took another drink of coffee and set his cup down so hard some spilled out on the table. He turned to face Luella. "You're too young to know what you're doing, and Atlee's old enough to know better."

Tears sprang to Luella's eyes. Didn't her parents even care how she felt? Couldn't they remember what it was like to be in love? Didn't Luella's happiness mean anything to them?

She pushed her chair back and stood. "I promised Atlee when I spoke to him after church yesterday that I'd be at his house this morning, and I can't go back on my word."

"All right." Mom gave a slow nod. "But please think about all that we've said, and don't let your emotions overshadow good common sense."

Luella grabbed her things and hurried out the door. She didn't know what would happen when she got to Atlee's house this morning, but she hoped if he truly loved her, he would say so. Then they could talk about the things Mom and Dad said.

Eugene flicked the reins, anxious to go a little faster. "Let's go fella. You can move quicker than this." Eugene smiled when Chip's ears swiveled forward and he picked his feet up in a fanciful trot. "Atta boy. Now you're talkin'."

As if the horse understood, he whinnied.

This morning, Eugene had taken extra care in brushing Chip's coat. Very quickly, he'd transformed it from a dull brown to a shiny chestnut. He'd also taken a few minutes more to comb out his flaxen mane and tail. Chip was the one thing Eugene could admit to loving about living on a farm, since he'd raised his horse from a colt.

As Eugene looked out over the back of his horse, he couldn't blame Chip for meandering and poking along. The stretch of nice warm weather they'd had lately would make anyone want to slow down and take it all in. This morning, however, Eugene was eager to see Luella, especially since he hadn't talked with her since the accident.

After church yesterday he'd been about to approach her, but then he realized she was conversing with Atlee. Eugene got annoyed and walked away.

After he'd thought about it awhile, he decided he'd much rather visit Luella on a more personal level, and hopefully without so many others around. Maybe this morning he'd get to actually appreciate this weather, if Luella agreed to go for a buggy ride with him. It would be all too perfect, since he couldn't remember the last time he'd been able to take part in anything gratifying. All Eugene seemed to do was help his dad around the farm, and his heart just wasn't in it. He still yearned to train in taxidermy.

As they rode along, Eugene noticed some wildflowers growing along a fence row. *Think I'll stop and pick some of those for Luella.*

Hopping out of the buggy, he secured Chip to one of the posts and began picking a few flowers in shades of pink, purple, and yellow. He even found smaller blue ones he could add to the bunch he'd tied together with twine.

Satisfied, he drove on to the Ebersols', and as he pulled into their yard, he waved at Luella's father, who was just coming out of the barn.

"Good morning, Eugene." Owen took hold of the horse's bridal as he pulled up to the hitching post.

"Nice weather we're having, isn't it?" Eugene grabbed the flowers and came around to where Owen stood. He handed the colorful arrangement to Owen then secured Chip to the post.

"Aw, shucks," Owen teased, holding the flowers like a baby. "You shouldn't have."

Eugene laughed and pointed to the flowers. "Thought I'd come by and see how Luella is doing. I was hoping these might cheer her up."

"She's doing pretty well, but sorry, you just missed her."

"Will she be back soon?"

"No, she won't be home till this evening, after she fixes Atlee and Daryl's supper."

"Oh, I see." Eugene gulped, trying to swallow his annoyance. "Guess she's feeling a lot better, if she's working again." *It figures she's with Atlee.* "Well, I didn't get a chance to talk with her yesterday after church, and before I help Dad around the farm today, I was hoping I could see her this morning. Maybe take her for a ride — that is, if she was feeling up to it."

"I'm sure Luella will be glad to hear you stopped by. Oh, and before you go, I have a favor to ask."

"What's that?"

"I have a bunch of rotten fence posts in my back field, and I've put the word out to a few men, asking for help replacing them. If you have some time on Saturday, do you think you could come by to give us a hand?"

"Sure, I'd be glad to." *Maybe I'll get to see Luella then.*

"Danki. I appreciate your willingness to help." Owen turned to go back to the barn. "I'll see you around 9:00 a.m.," he called over his shoulder.

"That works for me. See you at nine." Eugene unhitched his horse and climbed back into the buggy. As he was backing up, Luella's mom came running out with a plate.

"Good morning, Eugene." Esther smiled. "I just took my first batch of oatmeal raisin cookies out of the oven and thought you might like some."

"I certainly would. In fact, I'll have one on the way home." Eugene was pleased Luella's parents seemed to like him. Now if only he could get Luella to like him, too.

Atlee had just finished washing the breakfast dishes when he looked out the kitchen window and spotted Luella coming up the driveway in one of her father's open buggies, perfect for the warmer weather.

As he watched Luella pull up to the hitching rail, Atlee's fingers and toes began to tingle. *Should I say something to her today, or wait for another time? If I asked Luella to marry me, would she reject my proposal? Will Luella say she's too young for me?*

He smiled when she entered through the back doorway, but felt disappointed that she didn't smile in return. From the red in her eyes, Atlee guessed Luella may have been crying.

After she'd greeted Daryl, Atlee asked his son to go into the living room and play with his toys, saying Luella would be in later to read from his book. Daryl left the kitchen without an argument, and Atlee suggested Luella have a seat at the table. Before he had a chance to say anything, she spoke.

"I'm sorry for being late this morning. My parents wanted to talk to me, but they wouldn't do it in front of my sister and brother." Luella paused and drew a quick breath. "They want me to quit working for you."

Atlee's stomach clenched. "It's because of what I told your daed the day of your accident, isn't it?"

She dropped her gaze to the table. "What

143

exactly did you say, Atlee?"

Throwing caution to the wind, Atlee lifted Luella's chin and looked directly into her shimmering eyes. "I told your folks that I'm in love with you, Luella. I understand if you don't have those same feelings for me, but you need to know, and I wanted them to know, too."

Luella's eyes swam with tears. "Oh, Atlee, I love you, too, but my folks think you're —"

"Too old for you?"

"Jah." Her voice quavered. "To me, our age difference doesn't matter, but if Mom and Dad don't approve, I would feel like a disobedient daughter if I went against their wishes."

Atlee reached across the table and placed his hand over hers. "Let me talk to your daed again and see if I can make him understand. I am not the kind of man who would take a daughter from her parents without their blessing."

CHAPTER 13

Saturday morning Luella woke up and was pleased to see the sun streaming in through the crack in her window shade. Right after breakfast a few men from their community would be coming to help her father replace fence posts around the property, and this was good weather for the project.

With the exception of Eugene and a couple of other men who lived close, Dad hadn't asked for anyone's help. However, word spread quickly around here, so Luella wouldn't be surprised if several other men showed up, as well. Yesterday, she'd mentioned her dad's plans to Atlee, but with him taking care of Daryl on Saturdays, it wasn't likely he would show up.

Luella had been thinking and praying about her situation with Atlee, as Mom had asked her to do when Luella insisted on continuing to work for him this week. Luella had also reflected on her promise to Dena.

Would her friend approve of her becoming Atlee's wife?

Swinging her legs out from under the covers, she ran her hand over the quilt. *Oh, Dena, what should I do?* Luella sat, staring at the floor and wiggling her toes. *It hasn't even been six months since Atlee lost you. Is it too soon for him to be thinking of another?*

Well, I can't take time to think about all this right now. I need to help get breakfast on the table. Luella took out her clothes and hurried to get dressed. They'd be busy preparing food for the hungry men, and she needed to help her mom as much as she could.

"I thought you were going over to the Ebersols' place to help put in new fence posts," Eugene's mother remarked when she came into the living room where he sat on the sofa. "Did you forget?"

"No, I didn't forget. My back's acting up, and I decided to stay home and rest it today."

"I'm sorry to hear that. Did you call and leave a message for Owen so he'd know you weren't coming?"

Eugene shook his head. "I'm sure he'll figure it out. Besides, lots of others from our community will be there to help out.

He won't miss me."

Mom clucked her tongue. "That's not the point. The polite thing to do is let someone know when you're not coming; especially since you agreed when Owen asked for your help. We taught you better manners, I hope."

"Jah, you're right. I'll take care of doin' that soon." Eugene leaned back against the sofa cushion, trying to find a comfortable position. *I'd much rather have to deal with a toothache than with this horrible back pain.*

"Would you like me to make the call for you?"

"No, that's okay. I'll phone him soon. I need to stretch out for a while yet."

"All right then. I'll be in the kitchen if you need me."

After Eugene's mother left the room, he tipped his head back and closed his eyes. In one way he'd looked forward to going to the Ebersols', hoping to see Luella. But pulling out fence posts and replacing them would require bending over, which would only aggravate Eugene's back. He'd see her some other time when he wasn't hurting.

Luella was bringing out the paper plates and plasticware to the two tables set up in the yard, when her friend Ruth Yoder approached.

"Hi, Ruth." Luella walked over and gave her friend a hug. "It's good to see you."

"I'm glad to see you, too. It's been awhile, but then you've been rather busy lately." Ruth looked down at the ground.

"Yes, ever since I started helping at the Zooks', my days seem to fly by." Luella shook her head. "Then on Saturdays, I try to help Mom as much as I can, but that's still no excuse. I've missed talking with you."

"I wanted to come by after your accident, but then my mom slipped and fell and ended up with a sprained ankle, so I needed to keep close to home until she was up and around again."

"Well, I'm glad you're here now. What brings you by today?" Luella asked, walking with her friend toward the house.

"Thought I'd come by and see if you and your mamm needed help with anything." Ruth looked out toward the field. "We'd heard several men from the community would be here helping your dad, and we sure know how these men like to eat. I figured I could visit with you while helping serve lunch or anything else you need me to do."

"We certainly can use an extra set of hands." Luella held the door open as they walked into the kitchen. "Look who's here to help us, Mom."

Mom turned from the stove where she was stirring a large pot of chicken corn soup. "Why hello, Ruth." She walked over and gave Luella's friend a hug. "Thank you for offering to help."

"No problem. I'm happy to be here."

"What's next, Mom?" Luella asked.

"The bread will be done in about fifteen minutes, and the soup can simmer until it's time to eat." Mom wiped her hands on her apron. "Sara is going to make a chocolate cake as soon as the bread comes out of the oven. For now, though, you and Ruth can get out the lunchmeat and cheese then arrange it on the platter over on the table."

"Sounds good, Mom. Where is Sara?"

"She went to feed some scraps to your goat." Mom grinned. "You know how Buttercup eats anything."

Luella looked at her friend and laughed. Ruth giggled, too, and Mom chimed in. "Yep, it's like having our own little garbage container."

As Luella and Ruth got the platter ready, Luella told her friend about the accident and how she was healing. "I was only laid up for a week. My scar is healing nicely, too, from where I got cut. See — no more bandage." Luella held up her hand.

"That's good. So, you're still working for Atlee, huh?" Ruth asked, right out of the blue.

"Jah."

"Oh, I see. I figured he might have found someone else by now or asked one of the older single ladies to marry him." With a slight frown, she tilted her chin toward the floor.

Luella remembered back to the evening she had seen her friend at the Bird-in-Hand Restaurant, but remained quiet, not wanting to put Ruth on the spot. There must have been a reason her friend hadn't spoken to her that night. Perhaps Ruth had her own opinion where Luella and Atlee were concerned. But Luella didn't want any tension between her and Ruth. So unless Ruth pursued this conversion about Atlee, she would change the subject and talk about something else.

After the meat and cheese platter was prepared, Ruth sealed it with plastic wrap. Luella got out the mustard, mayonnaise, and pickles.

"Well, it looks like everything is ready." Esther put the lid on the pot of soup. "All we need to do is take the rest of these things out, and by that time the men should be coming in from the field to eat."

As Luella held the door for her mom and Ruth, she glanced down the driveway toward the road. Deep down, she had hoped Atlee would show up, but maybe it was for the better that he hadn't — especially since Ruth was here. She suspected soon enough her friend would be asking questions.

"Where's Eugene?" Esther asked when she handed her husband a cup of cold water. "I thought he was coming to help with the fence posts today."

"Said he was." Owen gulped the water then wiped his mouth on his shirtsleeve. "Something must have come up."

"Did you check the phone shack for messages? I'm sure he would have called if he couldn't be here."

Owen nodded. "I did check before the other men and I got started, but there were no messages from anyone."

"Hmm, that's strange." Esther pursed her lips, glancing toward Luella where she was dipping soup into one of the worker's bowls. "If Eugene came today, I was going to make sure Luella brought him water."

"You'd like to see the two of them get together, am I right?"

"Jah. Wouldn't you?"

Owen shrugged. "I would if it's what our

151

daughter wants."

Esther poured him another cup of water. "You know who she wants, and neither of us approves of her choice. It would help if Luella weren't working for Atlee. Being with him every day is what created the problem in the first place. We should have put our foot down after Dena died and Luella wanted to continue working for him."

Owen shook his head. "If we had done so, she would have resented us."

"Well, Atlee should have had better sense and hired someone else."

"I agree, but what's done is done." Owen motioned to the horse and buggy coming up the driveway. "Speaking of Atlee, that's his rig coming in."

Esther grimaced. "I wonder what he wants."

"I don't know. Maybe he came to help with the fence posts."

"Did you ask for his help?"

"No, but then some of the men who showed up here today weren't invited, either. They heard I needed help and came on their own." Owen handed his empty cup to Esther. "I'll go see what Atlee wants."

Atlee had no more than tied his horse to the hitching rail, when Owen stepped up to him. "I heard you needed some help replacing fence posts today, but before I start working, I'd like to speak to you about Luella."

Owen frowned. "I believe I made myself clear that day at the hospital. Luella is too young for you, and I can't offer my blessing."

"You're right, she probably is, but it doesn't change the fact that I've fallen in love with her." Atlee dropped his gaze to the ground then looked up again. He noticed all the helpers were in the yard, eating lunch, and hoped not to cause a scene. "That being said, I will honor your wishes and do nothing that would come between you and your daughter."

"I appreciate that. My fraa will be glad to hear it, too. As you may know, Eugene is interested in Luella, and we feel he'd be a better choice for her."

"I understand." Atlee could barely get the words out. What a predicament he'd gotten himself into. If Dena hadn't died, he wouldn't even be in this position. He looked right at Owen. "Would it be all right if I speak to Luella a few minutes before I begin helping with the posts? I owe her a word of explanation."

Owen nodded. "The last time I saw Luella, she was heading into the house."

"Danki." With a heavy heart, Atlee made his way up the path and stepped onto the porch. He knocked on the door, and a few seconds later, Luella's sister, Sara, opened it. "Is Luella inside? I need to speak to her."

"Jah, sure. I'll go get her." Sara didn't invite him in, but she did leave the door open.

Atlee shifted from one foot to the other, wondering if he should go in or wait here on the porch. *Probably better to wait here,* he decided, even though it felt like all eyes were on him.

A few minutes later, Luella came to the door. Her expression was unreadable.

"I need to talk to you. Can we go somewhere private?"

She nodded. "Follow me."

Atlee stepped off the porch behind Luella and followed her around the side of the house, out of sight from everyone else.

Luella stopped in the shade of a large maple tree. "What did you wish to speak to me about?"

"I came here to say that even though my feelings for you are strong, I won't go against your parents' wishes." Atlee paused and drew a quick breath. "I can't change how old I am, but I can set you free to

154

marry someone closer to your age."

Luella's chin trembled. "I don't want anyone else."

"Nor do I, but we cannot go against your parents' wishes." It was all Atlee could do not to touch Luella. His arms ached to hold her, to wipe away the tears streaming down her cheeks. But he held himself in check. To prolong this would only bring misery to both of them. He had to sever all ties with Luella. "There's one more thing I have to say."

"What?" Her single word was barely a whisper.

"I've found someone else to care for Daryl."

"Oh, no, please, Atlee. I love that little boy as though he were my own."

"He loves you, too, but under the circumstances, it would not be good for any of us if you kept working for me. Daryl would become more attached to you, and so would I." He gave his beard a tug. "It's best if we don't see each other anymore."

"But that's not possible," she argued. "We'll see each other every other week during church services, and we might run into each other in town."

Atlee shook his head. "I'll be putting my house up for sale soon and moving to another location."

Luella's eyes widened. "But Bird-in-Hand is your home, and your business is here."

"I can begin again someplace else." He folded his arms. "I need to start fresh, and so do you. Until my house sells and I'm ready to move, Mary Jane will be watching Daryl. We will attend church in a neighboring district." Atlee took a step back, afraid if he didn't, he might succumb to his desire to hold Luella in his arms for the first — and last — time. "Someday you will look back and be thankful for the way things turned out."

"No, I won't." Luella shook her head. "I will never love anyone but you."

Atlee stood silently, wondering if he and Luella could be happy if they got married against her parents' wishes. No, that would not be the right thing to do. Having such a conflict surrounding a marriage would put strain on the marriage itself.

"I'll go inside and get Dena's quilt. It's not right that I should keep it."

"No, Luella. Dena wanted you to have the quilt. Please keep it as a remembrance of the friendship you and she had." He turned, unable to endure the pain written on her lovely face. "Good-bye, Luella. May God bless you in the days ahead."

CHAPTER 14

Throughout the month of June, Luella could barely function. She was crushed beyond measure and could not come to grips with Atlee's decision to ask Mary Jane to watch Daryl. Worse yet was knowing he planned to pack up and leave Bird-in-Hand. How could he declare his love for her one day and less than a week later, set her free to be courted by someone else? It was a bitter pill to swallow, and Luella was at loose ends about what to do. She had no appetite and only slept a few hours every night.

Feeling as though she were in a fog, Luella helped her mother with chores around the house and in the yard, but her heart wasn't in it. It was difficult to go to church, with Atlee and Daryl no longer attending their own district's services. She'd heard Atlee had put his house up for sale, but to her knowledge he hadn't yet moved. Luella hoped Dena couldn't look down from heaven and see that she wasn't able to keep the promise she'd made to her.

At her mother's request, Luella had gone a few places with Eugene, but it was only to please Mom. Last Sunday night he was supposed to pick her up for a young people's singing, but he never showed up. She remembered back to the day he hadn't come to help with Dad's new fence posts and concluded that Eugene was unreliable. Even if he wasn't unreliable, Luella felt no more than friendship for him. Mom said love could come later, but Luella doubted it.

"Are you going to kneel there in the garden all day with your eyes closed, or did you plan to pull a few weeds?"

Luella's mother's voice broke into her contemplations, and she jumped to attention. "Sorry, Mom. I was deep in thought."

"Jah, I could tell." Mom leaned close to Luella. "From your expression, I'm guessing they weren't happy thoughts."

Luella sighed. "You're right, they weren't."

Mom gave Luella's shoulder a tender squeeze. "You need to move past this, daughter, and try to find some happiness again. Even if things don't work out between you and Eugene, someone else will come along. You'll see."

I'll always love Atlee, and no other. Luella

picked up the hand shovel and attacked an ugly weed. There was no point in saying anything more about this. Simply put, her mother did not understand.

That evening, as Esther got ready for bed, she reflected on the conversation she'd had with Luella earlier today. The poor girl was miserable and might never get over the love she felt for Atlee and his boy.

Esther turned to look at her husband, propped up in the bed, reading his Bible. "Do you think we may have been too hasty in refusing to give Atlee and Luella our blessing?"

Owen set the Bible aside. "Are you suggesting we should change our minds?"

Her face tightened. "I . . . I'm not sure what I'm suggesting. I only know that our daughter has been miserable since we refused to accept a relationship between her and Atlee."

"Jah, well, it was for her own good. And now that Atlee is selling his place and relocating, Luella will get over the silly notion that she's in love with him and move on. Why, by this time next year, she and Eugene will probably be married."

Esther took a seat on the end of the bed, pulling her hairbrush through the ends of her long hair. "I'm not so sure. Haven't you noticed Luella's expression when she's with Eugene? She's not in love with him, Owen."

"Well, maybe not now . . ."

"Luella's expression is one of pure joy when she simply speaks about Atlee. He was a good husband to Dena. I'm sure he would be good to our daughter as well."

Owen looked at Esther over the top of his reading glasses. "What about their age difference?"

"It might not matter in their marriage. Shouldn't we allow them the chance for happiness with a life together?"

Owen motioned for Esther to come closer. When she moved to sit beside him, he clasped her hand. "Let's pray about this and make our decision in the morning."

When Luella came down to breakfast the following day, she was surprised to see both of her parents at the table, drinking coffee. Normally Dad would be in the barn doing chores while Mom got breakfast ready.

Dad motioned to the chair across from him. "Luella, please take a seat. Your mamm and I have something we'd like to say to you before your sister and brother get up."

Luella did as he asked, curious to know what this was about. Her parents' expressions were so serious, making her wonder if she'd done something wrong.

Mom looked at Dad. "Do you want to tell her, Owen, or should I?"

"Why don't you go ahead?" He smiled and patted her arm.

Luella leaned forward, anxious to hear what her mother had to say.

Mom set her coffee cup on the table. "Your daed and I did some talking last night —"

"Praying, too," Dad interjected.

Mom nodded. "We've decided to give you and Atlee our blessing."

"Are you serious?" Luella clasped her hands under her chin.

They both nodded.

"So you're saying you wouldn't mind if Atlee and I got married?"

"That's right." Dad rapped his knuckles on the table. "It wasn't fair of us to try and keep you two apart. It might just be that God brought you together."

"Ach, my!" Luella squealed. "This is the happiest day of my life." She pushed her chair back and stood then raced for the back door.

"Where are you going?" Mom called.

"This can't wait. I need to see Atlee and tell him you and Dad have changed your mind and are giving us your blessing."

Before going out the door, Luella ran back and gave Mom and Dad a warm hug. "Danki. You don't know what this means to me."

Luella didn't take the time to hitch Dixie to a buggy, so she ran all the way to Atlee's house, eager to tell him the good news. It was a beautiful, summerlike day, but she barely noticed. She'd never expected Mom and Dad to change their minds and felt like pinching herself to see if she were dreaming.

I know Eugene will be disappointed, but he'll find someone more suited to him. I'm going to be Atlee's wife. I'm going to be Daryl's new mother. Luella felt like shouting the words. Just a little way to go and she would be there.

When Luella approached his house, she saw the FOR SALE sign on the front lawn, with the word SOLD pasted across it. *Oh, no. He can't move now. Atlee has to stay here in Bird-in-Hand.*

Luella dashed up the porch steps and knocked on the door. When no one responded, she knocked again, a little louder this time. Still no one came.

She stepped off the porch and ran out to

Atlee's shop. Finding the door locked, she peered in the window. No sign of Atlee inside, nor any of his woodworking equipment. Her heart pounded. *Oh, no. Surely he couldn't have moved already. Is it too late for us?*

The birds tweeted merrily from tree branches above, and blossoms waved lightly in the breeze. She barely noticed. Luella walked over to the porch steps and sat down. Her head hung low, and it was hard to swallow as tears gathered and threatened to spill over. One minute she'd been filled with happiness and hope. Now emptiness coursed through every fiber of her being. *Are Atlee and I not meant to be together?*

Luella looked around the yard, remembering the good times she'd had in this place. It seemed like only yesterday when the three of them had played in the snow. Her heart ached like never before as she raised her head and gazed toward the sky.

The *clippety-clop* of a horse's hooves caused Luella to look toward the road in front of Atlee's house. Her mouth went dry when the horse and buggy turned up the driveway and came to a halt in front of the hitching rail. Quickly she wiped her eyes.

A few seconds later, Atlee stepped out of the buggy and tied the horse to the rail.

Then he went around and helped Daryl down. The boy was the first to spot Luella. Waving excitedly, he ran across the yard. Luella bent down and scooped the child into her arms. Daryl wrapped his arms around her neck and gave it a squeeze. Oh, how she had missed those hugs.

Atlee strolled across the yard and joined them. "Luella, I'm surprised to see you. Do your folks know you're here?"

She stifled the laughter bubbling in her throat. "As a matter of fact, they do."

He blinked. "Really?"

"Jah, and they're okay with it. In fact, they've given us their blessing."

"That's *wunderbaar!*" A huge smile spread across Atlee's bearded face. "Does this mean you will marry me?"

Tears of joy welled in Luella's eyes, as she nodded her head.

Atlee took Daryl from Luella and set him on the ground. Then he pulled her into his arms. As he lowered his head, Luella unconsciously parted her lips. Atlee's kiss was tender but firm. Luella's pulse raced, and her knees felt so weak she could barely remain standing. Had it not been for Atlee's strong embrace, her legs might have given way.

"What about your house?" she murmured

against his chest.

"What about it?"

"The sign says SOLD."

He nodded. "A young Amish couple with three kinner are buying the place, and I'll be moving out over the next thirty days."

"But where will you go, and how will this affect us?"

"I'm ready to start over, and I found a place in Paradise that will work well for my needs." His cheeks reddened. "I mean *our* needs — yours, mine, and Daryl's." Atlee turned and picked the boy up. "Since Paradise is only a few miles from Bird-in-Hand, we can visit with your folks often."

Luella reached up and stroked Atlee's beard. No words were needed. Whatever the future held, their love for God and each other would see them through. She glanced up at the clear blue sky and smiled. *Dena, if you're watching, I hope you approve of how things turned out. When I made my promise to you, I didn't expect life would lead me to this. But be assured, for as long as I live, Atlee and Daryl will be deeply loved.*

EPILOGUE

Luella sat beside Atlee in the living room of
their new home, watching their son Daryl's
happy expression as he looked down at his
baby sister, Karen, lying in her father's
arms. Draped across Luella's lap was the
beloved quilt Dena had given her for Christmas a few weeks before she died.

Luella's heart swelled as she reached over
and stroked the baby's soft cheek. Someday,
when Karen got married, she would pass
the special quilt on to her. Until then, Dena's quilt would remain on Atlee and Luella's bed, as a reminder of the love Dena
had for her husband and son. She cared
about them so deeply that she wanted to
make sure their needs were met, even after
she was gone.

Luella lifted one corner of the quilt and
silently read the embroidered verse once

more. *"For thou art my rock and my fortress; therefore for thy name's sake lead me, and guide me"* — *Psalm 31:3.*

How thankful she was for the wisdom in God's Word, for He surely had led her to the right man — a man she would cherish for the rest of her life.

Luella's Shoofly Pie

Ingredients for Filling:
1 cup molasses
1 cup warm water
1 1/2 teaspoons baking soda

2 unbaked pie shells

Ingredients for Crumb Mixture:
2 cups flour
1 cup sugar
1 1/2 tablespoons butter
1 1/2 tablespoons shortening
1/2 teaspoon cinnamon
1/2 teaspoon nutmeg
1/2 teaspoon ginger
Pinch of salt

Preheat oven to 350°. In mixing bowl, combine molasses, water, and baking soda. Divide mixture equally into unbaked pie shells. Blend ingredients for crumb mixture and sprinkle evenly over top of both pies. Let stand for 10 minutes, then bake for 30 to 40 minutes or until done.

■ ■ ■ ■

Karen's Gift

BY JEAN BRUNSTETTER

■ ■ ■ ■

CHAPTER 1

Lykens, Pennsylvania

As Karen Allgyer rode home from church with her family, she gazed at the bundle of sweetness in her arms. The baby subtly stirred as Karen brushed against its soft, light, downy hair. Nancy Anne was three weeks old. Though the infant had arrived early and her birth weight was low, so far she appeared to be healthy.

The doctor had said there could be some problems, not only because of the baby's early birth, but also because Karen had contracted German measles during her pregnancy. Amish parents were not required to vaccinate their children if they attended a one-room Amish school, and given that there weren't any outbreaks of the disease when Karen was a child, her parents hadn't had her vaccinated.

Unfortunately during her fourth month of pregnancy Karen had a casual conversation with a person who was infected with German measles but didn't have any symptoms at the time. Two weeks later, Karen came down with the measles.

When Nancy Anne was born, Karen had felt so relieved that the doctor pronounced the baby normal. In follow-up appointments with the pediatrician, he reassured Karen and her husband, Seth, that he couldn't detect anything wrong with little Nancy Anne, but he reminded them to keep an eye on her and call if they noticed anything unusual. The next appointment wasn't for a while, and Karen was feeling more confident that her baby girl might not suffer any birth defects. Karen looked down at the sleeping child and smiled. *Nancy Anne is our special gift,* she thought. *A perfect baby from head to toe.*

Karen glanced over at Seth as he handled the reins. Usually he urged their buggy horse, Millie, to get moving because she poked along. But today he let Millie go at her own pace. He was quite handsome, this husband of hers — especially dressed in his Sunday best. Seth's deep blue eyes beamed with contentment, and the curl in his brown hair and beard framed his face nicely. Karen had to admit, Seth's good looks were what first attracted her to him.

Rounding the corner, Karen shielded her eyes from the bright afternoon sun shining through the front window of their closed-in buggy. Today had been her family's first real outing together since the baby arrived, and Karen would treasure every moment.

She looked over at Seth. "It's a beautiful day, especially for late March." She shifted on the unyielding seat. "It felt so good to be away from the house for a while, but all the activity left me tired."

"*Jah.* I like being out with my whole family, and I'm so glad you are doing well, my *fraa.*" He leaned close to Karen and peeked at the baby. "She sure is pretty, just like her mother." Seth smiled. "We'll be home soon, and then you can rest awhile."

"*Danki.*" Karen leaned against his shoulder, looking up at him.

Seth urged Millie to speed up as her plodding slowed. "It felt great to be in church today. I enjoyed the meal afterward and the chance to visit with some of the men. The women in our community sure know how to cook."

"I'm glad you had a nice time." Karen's mind trailed off to all of the church families who'd come by their home to welcome Nancy Anne. Some had brought food. Others had gifts for the baby and treats for Karen and Seth's two older girls.

Karen smiled, listening to Roseanna and Mary giggling behind them, as their rolling rig vibrated against the pavement. Roseanna was five years old. Mary, aka "the copycat," had recently turned three. Both girls had hair like their father's, and just as curly, too.

Karen glanced over her shoulder. Roseanna and Mary were peeking out the back window, waving at their grandparents, who followed in the open buggy Seth had loaned them. Karen's folks had been staying with them since the baby came, but it wouldn't last. They'd have to get back home to their own place in Lancaster County.

Sighing, Karen faced forward. *I can't believe we've been here in Lykens almost two years. I miss the familiarity of the town of Paradise. Most of all, I miss Mom, Dad, and the rest of my family.* Her shoulders slumped. *Why can't my parents live closer? Sure I have friends here, but it's not the same as being with the people I grew up with. I'd love to move back to the Lancaster area, even if my husband says it's become too commercialized.*

The buggy jarred against a rough patch in the road, causing Karen to jostle against the hard seat. Talking with Seth about where they lived was pointless. He wouldn't budge.

He liked it here and didn't want to move back home.

Snapping the reins, Seth coaxed the horse onward. "How's the *boppli* doing?"

"Still napping." Karen adjusted the infant's blanket.

"Nancy Anne sure grabbed the attention of all the ladies today. Did everyone get to hold her?"

"Not everyone, but a good many, I'd say. We even received a few more cards, as well as another present." Karen pointed at the gift bag by her feet. "A new blanket for the crib."

Seth smiled. "People in our community have been most generous."

"Jah." Karen appreciated the friends they'd made here in Dauphin County, and she'd tried to adjust and make the best of things. But hardly a day went by when she didn't think of Paradise, the place where she'd grown up. Was it the town or the people who lived there she longed for? Perhaps all of the above and more.

They were almost home, and Karen began to think about what they could have for their evening meal. Something grilled outdoors would be good, along with a potato dish and vegetables from last year's garden.

The buggy slowed and turned into the

driveway. Seth pulled into the yard, leaving room for her parents to pull in next to them. After he secured the horse, he came around and took Nancy Anne from Karen so that she could step out and help their other daughters climb down from the buggy. Her folks soon joined them.

Mom readjusted her shawl as she moved toward Karen. "It was a nice ride home. Roseanna and Mary were so cute waving from the back of your buggy."

"We have very special grandkids." Dad's brown eyes twinkled as he winked at Mom.

She smiled and nodded, pushing a wisp of faded blond hair back under her head covering.

"Grandpa, did you wink your eye?" Roseanna tugged on his jacket.

Holding on to her toy bunny, Mary came up to her sister and began to hop up and down. "Look, I'm a bunny. I'm a hop-hoppy bunny!" She giggled.

"I'm a bunny, too. Now follow me into the house." Roseanna began hopping along, looking back at Mary, who did as she was asked.

"They're busy *kinner* and full of energy." Karen reached into the buggy and grabbed her diaper bag and purse. "I wish you and Dad could stay here or we could be there with you in Paradise. It's easier when you're both around to help me through the re-adjustment of having a new baby." Karen kept her voice low.

Mom gave her a hug. "With the help of your church, I'm sure you'll get through this." She retrieved the gift bag with the crib blanket. "Maybe you can come visit us soon so the rest of the family can meet Nancy Anne. You're always welcome to stay at our place. We would love it."

"I'd enjoy coming so much, and the children would, too. I'll need to talk to Seth about it and find out when the right time would be. We may have to wait until this summer."

"There's plenty of time to think about it." Mom patted Karen's shoulder. "But for now we should go inside and get settled for the evening. We can put our supper plans together and do what needs to be done." She waited for Karen to go inside then closed the door behind them.

After supper that evening, everyone gathered in the living room to relax. Karen's dad slept on the couch, with her cherished Christmas quilt draped over his legs. Seth sat reading *The Budget,* looking for a buggy horse for sale. Karen and her mother relaxed in their respective recliners, enjoying the luxury of having their feet up. The baby lay in her bassinet, sleeping soundly. Mary and Roseanna had gone upstairs for a while but crept back down to play with their dolls on the coffee table. All was quiet until Karen's decorative seashell got bumped by Mary's elbow.

Karen gasped and leaped out of her chair when the shell toppled over and banged on the floor, startling everyone except the sleeping infant.

Mary began to sob. "I'm sorry, Mama. I didn't mean to knock over your shell."

Karen bent down and pulled her daughter into her arms. "It's all right, little one. It's so heavy it didn't break."

As Mary calmed down, Karen looked at her mother. "Isn't it strange the baby didn't wake up from that loud crash?"

"Many babies sleep through loud noises," Karen's mother replied.

Karen knew this was true, but she still wondered if this might be a sign that her baby had hearing problems — one of the most common complications from measles.

Dad sat up and yawned. "I wish it were me still sleeping like Nancy Anne."

Karen forced a smile. "We could have dessert now. All I need to do is get out the pies.

Is anyone hungry yet?"

"I have room for pie." Her father patted his stomach.

Seth set the newspaper aside. "I wouldn't mind some myself."

"I'm ready for a slice, and I'll help you get things out for it." Mom stood up and let out a yawn. "That little nap I got was nice."

When the women entered the kitchen, Mom pulled the pies out of the refrigerator. "They all look so yummy."

"I made our favorite lemon meringue and a custard one, too. The girls really like the sweet vanilla flavor." Karen unwrapped the pies and took a deep breath. "They smell good, too, if I do say so myself."

"I'm looking forward to having a slice of lemon pie with some hot tea." Mom grabbed the plates and utensils. "There's also plenty of coffee left to drink with our dessert."

"Okay. I'll heat some water, and there's milk for the girls." Karen carried the pies out to the dining-room table, and asked Roseanna to get down cups for her and Mary to use. Everything in place, they invited the men to join them.

Nancy Anne was awake, so Seth brought her out to the dining room. Everyone chatted and enjoyed their desserts, with the men going for seconds on the pies, along with more hot coffee.

"I'm going to miss the kinner when we have to leave on Tuesday." Mom sipped her hot tea.

"Same here. I'm done with my pie, so how about letting me hold my newest grandchild?" Dad looked over at Karen.

She got up and gave Nancy Anne to him. "She's awake for the moment, but who knows for how long?"

"That certainly brings back memories of you holding Karen when she was a baby." Sighing, Mom folded her hands in her lap.

"Nancy Anne is smaller than Karen was at this age, but in every way, she's just as cute." Dad beamed.

"He's not a proud grandpa, is he?" Mom left her seat and started to clear the dishes.

Karen followed suit. "I'll collect the pies."

When the men went back to the living room, Roseanna took her dirty dishes to the kitchen, and Mary quickly followed her big sister's example. Their grandmother put the plates and forks with the other dishes awaiting washing.

"Danki. You two did a good job eating all your custard pie." Mom's praise brought smiles to their faces.

"I love you, Grandma." Roseanna gave her

a big hug.

Not about to be outdone, Mary raced over to hug her grandma, too.

"Look at these precious girls." Mom leaned forward and hugged them back. "I'd take you two home with me and Grandpa, but your mom and dad would miss you both very much."

"You girls will need to get ready for bed in a little while, but you can play until then," Karen instructed.

Roseanna motioned to her little sister. "Let's go upstairs and play teachers, Mary. We can use our stuffed animals."

"Jah." Like her big sister, Mary hurried out of the room.

"Walk up the stairs girls — no running!" Seth's voiced boomed from the living room.

"We don't want you falling down the stairs," Karen's dad spoke up. "You could get hurt."

"Okay." Roseanna responded.

When they had finished the cleanup, Mom set the sponge by the sink. "Let's go relax in the living room."

"Sounds good. But first I'll go change Nancy Anne's *windel* and put her in a clean sleeper. Then I'll need to check on the girls."

They both headed for the living room. "Your father is still holding our granddaughter." Mom took a seat in the rocker.

"I'm going to take Nancy Anne from you for a while," Karen told her father. "She needs a clean windel."

"She's kept her eyes open most of the time. I've enjoyed our little visit." Dad handed Nancy Anne to her. "Nothing is as wonderful as a sweet little boppli."

"I'll be back soon." Karen took off with the baby.

Seth folded up the newspaper. "I think the local auction in two weeks might be worth checking out. Our buggy horse is okay, but she walks like a slug." He shook his head. "I appreciate my friend loaning us one of his horses for you to use while you're here."

"Jah. That horse did well today. I didn't have any problems with him." Atlee stood and stretched then ran his fingers through his salt-and-pepper hair.

"Next time you're here, I should have another horse to use."

"Maybe the horse you need will be at the auction coming up. Say, Luella, is there any more coffee?" Atlee asked.

"I believe so." The lines around her pale blue eyes crinkled as Karen's mother smiled over at him. "I wish we were going to be here for the auction. It sounds like it'll be fun."

"But we need to head back home. After almost a month, I'm sure the rest of our family would appreciate a break from taking care of both places." Dad picked up his mug and made his way to the kitchen.

As Seth started discussing auctions with his mother-in-law, a crash reverberated through the house.

CHAPTER 2

Karen carefully placed Nancy Anne in her crib then bolted from the nursery toward the loud noise. She hoped no one had gotten hurt.

"Luella!" Karen heard her dad's voice. "Don't come any closer in your stocking feet. There's broken glass and spilt coffee on the floor."

"Oh my! And you're wearing socks, too. You'll need to wait until one of us can clean the floor around you."

Karen halted in the kitchen doorway. "Are you okay, Dad?"

"My hand is burned a bit. Your *mamm* will need to take a look at it." Karen could see the red mark, but fortunately he wasn't cut.

"I'm wearing shoes, so hang on," Seth said. "I'll get the broom and dustpan." Stray shards crunched and crackled under his weight. He returned and started to sweep up the glass, while Karen held the dustpan

186

for him.

"Was is letz do?" Roseanna appeared at the doorway with her sister.

Seth paused and looked at his daughters. "What's wrong is that we had a little accident with the coffeepot. Your *grossdaadi* burned his hand, and we need to pick up the glass so nobody gets cut. You two go and play. Everything should be okay."

Roseanna looked at her dad. "I want to make sure Grandpa is all right." She stood with a delicate hand on her waist.

Mary copied her big sister and put a hand on her waist, too, while holding her toy bunny, Big Ears.

"I thought I'd set the pot in place," Karen's dad explained, "but it slid back out and dumped hot coffee all over my wrist. Then it crashed, leaving this mess on the floor." Grimacing, he shook his head.

"Don't worry girls, I'll take good care of your grandpa." Karen's mom gave them a reassuring smile.

Later, Karen's dad sat on the couch with Roseanna right by his side, along with Mary and her long-eared stuffed friend. His hand was now bandaged in gauze and secured with first-aid tape. Karen watched her family. Mom sat working on a fall-motif, needlepoint table runner, adding beautiful colors that added depth to the pattern. Seth's rocking became more inconsistent as his eyes grew heavy. Karen rocked Nancy Anne, while watching Roseanna being attentive to her grandfather. She couldn't help feeling pleased with how nurturing her oldest daughter had become at such a young age.

"Does your hand hurt now, Grandpa?" Roseanna looked up at him expectantly.

"Just a little. It feels better than it did." He patted her head. "I'll be good as new in a couple of days."

"When are you going to leave, Grandpa?" Roseanna leaned closer to him.

He tugged on his beard. "Tuesday morning after breakfast. Grandma and I will need to finish packing tomorrow night because our driver will arrive early to pick us up."

"I wish you'd stay longer, Grandpa." She hesitated, looking away from him. "I'll miss you and Grandma a lot." Her smile faded.

Karen's dad reached around Roseanna's waist and gave a hug. "We'll miss you and the whole family, but we'll come again to visit."

Roseanna clung to her grandpa, and Mary got off the couch to give him a hug. Her daughters seemed to drink up the time they could be around her parents. Karen would not be the only one to miss her folks when they left; her daughters would, too.

On Monday, Karen made another custard pie, as well as a shoofly pie — her dad's favorite — and everyone filled up with dinner and dessert. Later that evening the men went to the living room to relax, while Karen and her mother restored order to the kitchen. Karen had her daughters clean off the dining-room table. Glancing out to the living room, she saw Dad holding Nancy Anne in his arms. She stood for a moment, taking it in.

He looked up and grinned. "Nancy Anne's still awake and looking at her grandpa with them curious eyes."

Karen nodded and looked toward Roseanna and Mary. "Okay, girls, you can go play now." They quickly went upstairs to get their dolls.

As the last bits of cleaning were taken care of, Mom suggested gathering everyone together in the living room for singing. Karen got the baby and called up to the girls to join them. While they took turns singing everyone's favorite song, Karen watched her family closely, not wanting to miss anything. She wished this wonderful day would never end, but in the morning, her parents would be gone.

"Girls, it's time for you to go upstairs and get ready for bed." Karen stood up.

"Oh, Mom, I'm not ready yet. Can't we stay up longer?" Roseanna's tone sounded desperate.

"You need to get upstairs and brush your teeth. Come down when you're dressed and ready for bed." The girls scurried up the steps.

Seth sighed. "It was fun singing those songs with you both."

"Danki." Karen's mom picked up her water and took a sip. "Our grandkids sure like singing, don't they, Atlee?"

"All our grandkids enjoy singing together like this." He beamed.

When Roseanna and Mary came downstairs, Karen had already put Nancy Anne back in her crib. "Give me and your *daed* kisses and hugs." She held out her arms.

After the girls said their good-nights, Grandpa got up and took hold of their hands. He motioned toward the stairs with his head. "Luella, let's you and me head up with our granddaughters to tuck them in for the night."

"Wunderbaar," she replied.

The next morning, Karen put Nancy Anne into her playpen in the dining room. Her mother worked at the stove, browning potatoes in a large skillet. The aroma of butter and garlic mixed with a hint of bacon grease tickled her nose. A breakfast casserole Karen had made last night was already in the oven.

The table had been set, and her dad was still upstairs packing his bag. The timer went off, and Karen retrieved the casserole. She could hear the stairs squeak as someone descended.

"Is breakfast ready?" Her dad's deep voice hung in the air. "I heard something ding. Is it time to eat?"

"The potatoes are ready. I'll put them on the table alongside the hot breakfast casserole." Mom picked up the skillet, wearing a pair of oven mitts, and carried it out to the dining room.

Seth came into the house from feeding and watering the animals. "Something sure smells good for breakfast. I better wash up quick, so I can eat. Don't want to be late for work." He walked over to the kitchen sink. "The birds are going to town on the feeders right now. It's warming up nice this morning."

"Spring is my favorite time of year." Mom's voice sounded chipper. "Getting the garden planted with vegetables and watching them grow."

"I like spring, too, Grandma." Roseanna bounded into the room, waving around a bubble wand. "I like playing outside the best."

"Me, too." Mary tripped on the fringe of the throw rug, wearing her little pink clogs.

"Careful, sister. Don't fall," Roseanna warned as she placed her toy on the side table.

"Are you girls hungry this morning?" Karen smiled at them as she poured apple juice.

Her daughters both nodded and took their seats.

"I wish there was coffee this morning," Karen's dad commented.

"The teapot is ready for making hot chocolate, tea, or freeze-dried instant coffee." Mom waited by her seat.

Karen set the juice on the counter and placed platters of orange segments and apple slices on the table. "We have plenty to eat this morning, so don't be shy." She stood by her mother.

"I'll take some instant coffee." Seth smiled at Karen. "I've had it when I didn't want to fuss with making a whole pot."

Dad cleared his throat. "Make that two cups. I'll give it a try."

"I'll have to leave for work right after breakfast. I'm working on a big masonry job, and my foreman will be here soon." Seth slid his chair closer to the table.

"At least we can enjoy another meal together before we have to part ways." Dad sipped his apple juice.

Karen came back with cups of cocoa for her and Mom. Then she sat down and waited for her mom to join them.

"I would have liked to have had the time off while you both stayed with us. But I've been trying to save up some vacation days for this summer." Seth looked over at Karen and grinned.

"Don't give it another thought. We understand," Karen's dad said.

"Here's your coffee. I think it's time we eat before things get cold." Mom sat next to Karen.

All heads bowed for silent prayer, and then the food was passed around. Karen couldn't imagine anything more important than enjoying these last moments of her parents' visit. She'd soak in all the love and joy in hopes that these memories would comfort her when she felt so alone after they left.

Late that morning before lunch, Karen's

daughters colored at the kitchen table. Nancy Anne lay in her playpen napping. Her folks had left awhile ago, and Karen felt lost. Maybe going into the guest room they had used would help her feel closer to them. Closing the door behind her, Karen wrapped herself in the Christmas quilt and sat on the bed. *I wish Daed and Mamm could have stayed longer. It's hard not to be jealous of my friends like Rachelle who have most of their family around.*

Wrapping the quilt closer around her body, Karen gazed about the room until her eyes blurred with tears. *This house seems less busy already, and so void of my parents' love. I value their wisdom, and the girls blossom when their grandparents are around. Is it too much to ask that we be closer to them?*

Karen began to weep, burying her face in her mother's beloved Christmas quilt so that the girls wouldn't hear their mother bawling like a baby. Releasing her pent-up emotions seemed to lessen her pain, and gradually the tears stopped.

Karen looked at the verse so carefully embroidered on the quilt backing: *"For thou art my rock and my fortress; therefore for thy name's sake lead me, and guide me."* The words lodged deep within her soul.

Reluctantly, Karen put the quilt back in

194

place, dried her eyes with her apron, and decided to pray. *Lord, please give me the strength to get through this day, and help ease the pain I'm still feeling. Amen.*

A moment later, she was interrupted by a cooing sound drifting in from under the door. Getting up from the bed, Karen looked at herself in the mirror until satisfied that her tears were gone, then headed out toward Nancy Anne.

The baby let out a few more melodic coos.

"You sound happy, Nancy Anne." Karen leaned over, smiling down at her precious infant.

"She sure does, Mom," Roseanna called from the kitchen. "Where were you?"

"I was in Grandpa and Grandma's room to see if they'd forgotten anything." She didn't want her girls to know what had taken place behind that door.

"That's a new sound you are making for us." Karen gently scooped up her sweet baby. "It would've been neat if everyone could have heard you this morning." Karen cradled Nancy Anne while she stepped over by the girls to watch them color.

"How do you like my picture, Mom?" Roseanna slid her book close to Karen.

"It's looking good."

"Mamm, look." Mary pushed her book

195

over and hopped down to come stand close to her.

"Yours is nice, as well." Karen repositioned Nancy Anne in her arms. "Someday your baby sister will want to color, too."

Her daughters giggled, and Mary picked up her coloring book, taking her seat again.

"What would you like for lunch? Maybe peanut butter with chocolate nut spread?" Karen got up with Nancy Anne.

"Mmm, that sounds good." Roseanna's eyes twinkled as she looked at Mary and grinned.

When Mary repeated what Roseanna had just said, the girls looked at each other and giggled.

"Let me take care of your baby sister first. Then I'll start making our lunch." Karen left for the nursery.

That evening Seth held Nancy Anne in the rocking chair and stroked her silky blond hair. He thought how quickly his little ones were growing. It wouldn't be long before Roseanna started school, and Karen had said the other day that she needed to let down some hems on the girls' dresses. Seth hummed to Nancy Anne. When he'd gotten home from work, he'd checked the phone messages. One was from Karen's folks. Her father said the ride home went fine and that they had enjoyed their stay. Atlee also said they couldn't wait for them to come to Paradise this summer. Seth had passed the message on to Karen when she called him for supper.

His wife had seemed quiet since he'd gotten home. He'd let her know of the message from her father, and Karen had perked up a bit. She'd filled him in on the girls' day while they ate dinner, but her blue eyes held no sparkle. He wondered if taking Karen out for a meal with the girls, or just the two of them, would help her feel better.

Karen came into the room with the girls trailing in behind her, wearing their pajamas. "Good job getting ready for bed. Have you two brushed your teeth yet?" Seth asked.

"Jah." They both spoke at once.

Nancy Anne began fussing in Seth's arms. "I think someone needs her diaper changed." He wrinkled his nose.

The girls giggled. "Daddy, you're silly." Roseanna giggled some more.

Seth stood up and walked over to his wife. "Okay, girls, give your mom hugs before you head up for bed."

Karen hugged the girls then held out her arms for the baby. "Now it's time to hug your father good night."

Mary hopped next to him giggling, while clutching Big Ears. "*Gut nacht,* Daed."

Roseanna took her turn, and they headed up the stairs for bed.

"Well, I need to go get Nancy Anne fixed up with a fresh diaper and see if she's hungry."

"When you're finished with Nancy Anne, we could sit and have something to drink. Would you want anything?" Seth asked.

"Umm, sure, some sweet tea would be good, and we could have some cheese with crackers, if that appeals." She smiled.

"Sounds good." Seth watched his wife leave, noticing the slump of her slender shoulders. He hoped to bring her some happiness, but would his efforts be enough?

CHAPTER 3

In the weeks that followed, Karen grew more depressed. By the first Monday of May, the weather had been warming up nicely. Lykens was surrounded by evergreens and hills bursting with spring color. But nothing seemed to reach her heart.

Seth's folks were arriving that evening to visit for a week or so, but they wouldn't be staying as long as she'd like. Although she wasn't as close to Seth's mom as her own, Karen was hungry to see any family members — those people who had known her all her life and could understand her in a way friends she'd known for only two years could not.

Karen worked around the house, making sure the place was clean and ready for company. She watched the sheets blowing in the wind, while stirring a pot of soup warming on the propane burner. Making up the guest bed was one of the last details requiring her attention, but she couldn't do that until those sheets had completely dried.

Karen stirred the soup a few more minutes until it bubbled in the pot, and then turned off the heat.

"Okay, girls, go wash up for lunch. We'll be eating soon." She lifted the steaming soup off the stove and headed for the table.

"I'm hungry. Do we have crackers, too?" Roseanna called, as she went to wash her hands.

"We do. You can choose from a couple different types." Karen carefully ladled the soup and filled each bowl.

Setting the empty container in the sink and running water into it, her thoughts detoured. *How can I talk Seth into moving back? Doesn't he see how much I need family to depend on, and how I miss all the familiar surroundings I grew up in?*

"Mom, the water's running." Roseanna's voice intruded her thoughts.

"Oh dear, I was thinking about the home I grew up in." Karen shut off the faucet and joined her daughters at the table. "I'll tell you about it, if you'd like sometime. Let's go ahead and pray."

They bowed their heads in the quietness of the afternoon. Even with the wind getting rambunctious outside, things were peaceful and quaint within their cozy home.

When prayer was over, Karen noticed the wind was playing havoc with the clothes drying on the line. "I better go out and get the clothes off the line, before the wind does it for me." Karen pushed her chair back and sprang up. "Don't forget to blow on that hot soup," she reminded her daughters before bounding out the door with the basket to survey the damage.

Some casualties already lay on the ground. Heavier items were hanging by mere chance, as the wind twirled and waved them about. In short order, Karen collected what was left of the clothes on the line.

"Oh no." Karen spotted a couple of small towels that had ended up in the muddy flower bed. "Those will need to go right back into the wash," she pouted, carrying all the clothes back into the house.

Once indoors, she set the heaped basket off to one side of the back door and put the dirty things in a bag to deal with later.

"Hi, Mamm." Mary looked up at her.

"You have all the clothes." Roseanna's voice was sweet and cheerful.

"Jah, I brought them all in." Karen began to re-pin some hair that had come free from her head covering in the wind. "How's your homemade soup taste with the crackers?"

She washed her hands before returning to the table.

"I like the taste, Mom, and the crackers are good, too." Roseanna smacked her lips.

"Me, too! Me, too!" Mary sounded excited, taking a bite of one of her crackers.

Karen sipped her drink. "This evening your grandparents will be arriving for a nice visit." She grabbed some crackers and broke them over her soup. Karen watched the smiles grow on her daughters' faces. "Are you guys excited to see them?"

"I can't wait until Grandpa and Grandma Allgyer are here," Roseanna almost shouted.

"Yippee! Grossdaadi und *Grossmudder!*" Mary popped down from her seat and hopped about.

"Nancy Anne's awake in her playpen," Roseanna reported, after peering around the corner.

Karen took another spoon of soup before retrieving her baby girl. "Did you get enough nap time?" She lifted a yawning Nancy Anne into her arms. "I'm sorry we got so noisy, but we're just happy that's all. Your other grandparents are coming very soon to see all of us. Won't that be nice?" Karen cuddled close to her littlest one.

Nancy Anne offered a sweet smile. At her last visit, the pediatrician had told Karen such smiles were a sign of recognition and affection that she should expect to see, and Karen was happy to be able to check off another item that marked her baby as developing normally.

That evening, Karen had a roast with all the trimmings keeping warm while they waited for Seth to get home from work and his folks to arrive from Bird-in-Hand. The girls went upstairs to play and popped down a time or two to see if their grandparents were there yet.

Soon Karen heard the familiar rumbling of Mike's truck. One of Seth's coworkers, Mike, drove him to and from work.

"Hello, I'm home." Seth carried his lunch box into the kitchen, setting it on the counter.

"Hi, Seth. Did you have a good day?" Karen gave her husband a big hug.

He held her in his arms for several seconds. "It was good. I got enough done so tomorrow should go even better." Seth released her, stepping back and taking a seat.

Karen went through his lunch, taking out the used containers and throwing away the garbage. "You were pretty hungry. I gave you an extra sandwich and added more chips like you'd hinted about yesterday."

"Thank you for doing that." He stretched his arms over his head and let out a long yawn. "I'm tired this evening, and I have a *koppweh*."

About then, Roseanna and Mary bounded into the room with welcoming hugs for Dad.

"We were playing when we heard you come in, Daddy. Mary and I are waiting for Grandpa and Grandma." Roseanna's cheeks were flushed.

Karen looked over at her husband. "I hope you feel better soon." She wiped out his lunch box and set it aside.

"What's wrong with Daddy?" Roseanna's brows furrowed.

Mary came and sat on his lap with a doll tucked in her arms.

"Your father has a headache."

Karen stopped by the playpen to check on Nancy Anne. "She's growing so well. I'm happy her appointment the other day went well and she's right up there for her weight and length."

Seth bounced Mary on his knee then picked her up and set her on the floor. "You shouldn't worry about Nancy Anne. She looks and acts pretty healthy. I knew the doctor would say she is doing just fine." He grinned.

"I know. I'm like a veteran because Nancy Anne is my third baby, but I just don't want to get too self-confident and miss something." Karen's forehead wrinkled.

"You're doing a great job with our children." Seth untied his work shoes and slipped them off.

"Thank you." Karen opened the oven door to check on the roast. "So how's your appetite? Is the pain from your headache bothering your stomach?"

"No, it's fine. I've worked hard today, and I'm always ready for your tasty cookin'." He smiled, getting up and putting his work shoes by the kitchen door.

While Karen poked the roast with a fork, Seth disappeared and then returned holding Nancy Anne. "Have you been a good little girl today?" He spoke in a playful tone.

"Daddy, babies can't be bad." Roseanna giggled.

"They can't be bad?" Seth paused. "You're right, Roseanna, babies are good and a blessing to their family. Just like you and Mary have been and will continue to be."

All heads turned at the sound of a vehicle pulling up near the house. "Is it the folks?" Seth got up with Nancy Anne and peered out the kitchen window.

Karen joined him. "Jah, they are here!

Let's go welcome them."

"I'll put the baby in her crib and be right out." He left the room.

Karen led the way out the front door, the wind blowing against her dress. A white passenger van sat in the driveway, and Seth's folks got out, their faces beaming.

Karen hugged Paul and Emma, and the male driver helped unload their things. Like pinecones on a fir tree, the girls hung on to their grandparents.

Paul looked at Emma. "You have the money for our driver."

"I do. Let me get it out of my purse." Emma pulled out the cash. "Thank you so much, Bill, for driving us here today."

"Jah, thank you very much." Paul's usual rosy cheeks deepened as his booming voice cut right through the heavy breeze.

"Give me a call when you're ready for me to come back and pick you up," Bill reminded them.

"We'll do that, and thanks again." Emma waved to him and was about to pick up her suitcase when Seth rushed out of the house.

"Mom! Dad! It's so good to see you." He hugged them both then picked up her luggage, while Dad carried his own.

Everyone headed into the house, and Seth showed them to the guest room.

"You've done a nice job decorating this room, Karen." Emma's brown eyes twinkled.

"Jah, *des iss die gut schtubb.*" Roseanna placed her hand on the beautiful quilt draped on the bed.

"Danki, I've been working on making this 'the good room' for our guests." Karen's face heated. She hoped they didn't think she was prideful.

"Let's go see Nancy Anne," Grandpa Paul suggested, and they filed into Nancy Anne's room.

"She's a good baby," Seth whispered.

"I've been waiting for this moment." Seth's mom went up to Nancy Anne's crib and tilted her graying head, watching her newest granddaughter rest.

"She's trying to sleep." Seth's dad stood by his wife, grinning.

"Shh . . . We should step out until Nancy Anne is awake." Emma motioned to her husband. "I smell something good coming from the kitchen."

Karen closed the door to the nursery once everyone had made their way out. "We have roast tonight, and there should be plenty to eat, so don't be shy."

"I'm pretty hungry." Seth rubbed his midsection. "We poured a large patio at a residence today, and I'm hoping the customers will be pleased with it tomorrow."

"That's good, Son." Paul patted Seth's shoulder. "Your mamm is after me to make her patio larger to hold more chairs." He sighed. "I can see that our family is expanding and it would be a welcome addition."

"There's fresh coffee in the kitchen. Would anyone like some?" Karen asked.

The men both lit up to the idea and nodded. Seth and his dad walked to the living room.

"I'll bring you both some." Karen turned and hugged her mother-in-law. "It's so nice to have you both here. How about you, would you like some coffee, too?"

"That sounds good." Emma followed Karen into the kitchen.

"Do you need help with anything?" Emma fussed with her sleeve.

"I haven't set the table, and the potatoes are waiting to be mashed." Karen grabbed a cup from the cupboard, filled it with coffee, and passed it to Emma.

"I'll set the table; just point me to the plates and glasses." She took a sip of her coffee and placed it on the nearby counter. "Mmm . . . that's good."

Karen showed Emma where everything was and began mashing the potatoes. Her daughters followed their grandmother to the big table. "Grandma, what's in your bag on the floor, there?" Roseanna pointed at it.

"Oh, you saw that. Well, I brought some things for your family." Emma went back for silverware.

Mary came in behind her grandmother. *"Was inwendich?"*

"What's inside?" She reached into the utensil drawer. "I'm getting the forks, spoons, and knives out."

"No, Grandma." Roseanna let out a small giggle. "Mary meant what's inside the big bag you brought to our house."

"Well, Grandpa and I brought you each a small gift from home. You'll see after dinner when I give them out." Emma then headed for the table with her hands full of the needed silverware.

After dinner, the girls enjoyed their new books from their grandparents. Roseanna's paperback was a story about a kitten and a butterfly. Mary's book had animals with names by each picture. Karen and Seth received hardcover novels. They both enjoyed a good story. Grandma Allgyer had made a cloth book for Nancy Anne. It was cute, and Karen placed it in the nursery to share with her littlest one.

■ ■ ■ ■

Tuesday morning after breakfast, Seth announced that he was popping over to the neighbor's place. Not long afterward, Seth returned and came whistling into the kitchen. The girls were hanging out with Grandma and Karen. Clearing his throat, he announced, "Okay, Mel will be coming by about nine thirty this morning to pick everyone up in the van! We're going to the auction to find Millie a new friend."

"Yippee! Yippee!" Roseanna jumped with excitement.

"Yippee, yippee, yippee!" Mary mimicked her sister, hopping around in her lilac-colored dress. Her whole face smiled.

Roseanna put a hand on her little sister's shoulder. "Okay, Mary, you're getting too happy.

"Can a person really be too happy?" Grandpa's deep voice resonated.

"I'll get things put together for Nancy Anne and the girls to take along," Karen said as she finished wiping off the table.

"I'll get the dishes washed so you can get the girls' things ready," Emma volunteered.

"Thanks so much. That will help us be ready in plenty of time." Karen hurried off to the nursery.

The auction was a huge success. Roseanna and Mary enjoyed seeing other children, and when they noticed an English couple with their two older boys who were selling some cute bunnies, they asked if they could pick one out to take home. Seth found a horse that he felt would work well with his family.

The food servers grilled burgers and chicken that would whet anyone's appetite, along with warm rolls, fresh coleslaw, and fountain drinks. Seth chatted with a friend from their community. As they ate, Karen saw Rachelle Stoltzfus, a friend from their church district, and introduced Seth's folks to her. When the others finished eating, Karen stayed to visit with Rachelle a bit.

"It must be nice for you to have some family come visit." Rachelle put her hand on Karen's shoulder.

Karen nodded. "Even though I've made friends here in Lykens, I miss my family so much. We have always been very close, as most Amish families are, and they share memories of my childhood."

"I understand. I feel blessed to have my family living nearby now, but we've had times of living at a distance. It can be hard to focus on the other blessings we have."

The women chatted for a few more minutes, and then Karen caught up with Seth and his family.

Emma wanted to look at some quilts, and Karen was happy to go with her while the men agreed to stay behind with the children. As the afternoon reached an end, Seth and his dad took them all to get ice cream with their favorite toppings.

Karen was having a wonderful time with Seth's parents, but she already dreaded the day when they'd have to leave. Even though she had a loving husband and a friend like Rachelle, they couldn't be there for her all of the time. The bond she had with her mother and even Seth's mom was so tight that she felt like part of her was torn away whenever they went home. Would she ever move past this need? Maybe she needed to try focusing on her other blessings, like Rachelle had suggested.

CHAPTER 4

Seth heard his ride pull into the driveway for work. He dashed about putting on his shoes, getting lunch, and grabbing his commuter mug full of coffee. "Don't forget, you and I have a dinner date this evening." Seth hugged his wife good-bye for the day.

"I won't forget, Seth. I'm looking forward to a nice meal out with you." Karen gave him a hurried embrace. He kissed her quickly and ran out the door. Seth had wanted to take Karen out for a while, but here it was, the first week of June, and they hadn't found the time till now.

He certainly was looking forward to this evening. He'd be taking out the new buggy horse, Ash, a young, charcoal-gray gelding. Seth had taken him to be trained several weeks ago. He'd done some test-runs with the horse in the couple of days since Ash was brought home. What a difference from Millie! This new horse moved with fresh energy and a smooth transition between its gaits.

"Good morning, Mike." Seth climbed into his foreman's green pickup and set his drink down in order to put on his seat belt.

"It's a nice morning." Mike put the truck into gear. He seemed in a good mood. Seth felt that his foreman was more of a friend than a boss.

The sun was quickly raising the temperature, but a commuter mug full of hot coffee was still welcome. Mike's truck was an older vehicle that made various types of squeaking noises. Sometimes it could make a tired guy drift off.

Seth was eager for the day's work to end. He and Karen had agreed to go to the China House on Main Street in Lykens. Karen told him she'd arranged for her friend Rachelle to watch the kids this evening. He hoped Karen would enjoy the break. She'd been in the dumps since his folks left. Seth wanted his wife to be as happy as he was living here. He closed his eyes and prayed: *Lord, please help bring joy to Karen's heart. Show me how to be a good husband for her. Amen.*

"Did you get your brother's place painted all the way yet?" Seth asked Mike.

"Almost done, but we ran out of paint. So

we'll hit it hard this evening and should be finished with the living room. His kids' rooms will be next."

"It's nice to get projects finished around the house, but eventually they need attention all over again." Seth chuckled then gulped down a large swig of his drink.

"I gave this green beast a wash on the way to my brother's house yesterday. You probably couldn't tell since it's needing a new paint job." Mike slowed the truck to a crawl, before going around a horse-drawn buggy in front of him.

Seth waved at the Amish driver as they passed by. "Actually, it looks cleaner — I just hadn't had a chance to mention it yet."

"David and Roy are working on the fireplace. Hopefully that cabin house should be done in short order. David mentioned the homeowners are wanting to move in soon, and they come by about every day, checking out the progress." Mike glanced over at Seth.

"The patio turned out nice. It's a good-sized space for them to entertain in." He fiddled with his hat brim then set it back in place.

"If you've got the money, then you can add anything you want." Mike turned on his blinker.

As they pulled in to the job site, Seth noticed the new employee out by his car, finishing up a cigarette. Stan Ronald had started work last week. Mike had mentioned that Stan liked to talk about how much better he was than anyone else and that he didn't think much before opening his mouth.

This morning, first thing, was the shop safety meeting. Then the boss would send his crew out to various jobs for the day. The men gathered in the rather nice-sized break room. Everyone grabbed a seat except Stan, who stood back by the counter.

The boss came in and cleared his throat. "Good morning, everyone."

"Morning," most of the workers replied.

"Hope you're ready for this brief video I've got for you all. When it's finished, I'll read some more on this topic and try to answer any questions you may have." The boss started the video and dimmed the lights.

When the presentation was over, no one had any questions, so the boss gave the men their assignments for the day. Seth hadn't worked with Stan yet, but today it was his turn.

Seth filled up his coffee mug and headed for the truck. Stan followed. "How do you like working here so far?" Seth asked.

"It's not bad, but at my old job, the shop was twice the size of this one." Stan climbed in and started the vehicle.

"This masonry shop isn't the biggest, but we do keep very busy." Seth tugged at his collar.

"We also had newer trucks, not like this one with all the dents and scratches." He shut the door, pulled on his seat belt, and began backing out of the lot.

"I don't mind it, as long as it gets us there." Seth looked over at Stan.

"You're Amish, like a couple of the other men who work here." Stan looked at him with raised eyebrows. "Don't you wish you could drive and not rely on us English to do it for you?"

Seth rubbed his beard. "Not really. My transportation is horse drawn, and that suits me just fine." He then told Stan to take the next right.

"Horses aren't so tough. I rode them on the beach one year during a trip out to the Washington coast. Those horses hardly did anything. The only time it was exciting was on the way back when the horse finally moved like it wasn't half dead."

Seth bit his lip. Apparently Stan wasn't too impressed with Amish ways.

At the job site, Stan helped Mike set forms for the driveway. Then they had a curved front sidewalk to do that led up to the front door.

Seth and Ervin, another Amish employee, worked on the front of the house, adding bricks to accent the siding.

The boss had let them know the concrete truck would be there late this morning.

The time flew along, and soon the rumbling of the cement-filled rig came up the road.

Mike walked along the forms, checking them, making sure they'd hold. "Hey, Stan, these are still loose right here." He shook his head. "Get this fixed." Mike walked over to the concrete truck as it pulled in and stopped near the driveway.

Seth's foreman chatted, while Stan walked over and fiddled with the form. "I don't know why he's so worried about it. I could sure use a smoke right now," he mumbled.

Ervin stepped up to Seth with a dropped tone. *"Er iss net schpassich."*

Seth lowered his voice. "No, he's not funny."

The four men worked on the driveway pour, spreading then smoothing the concrete. Then Seth and Ervin went back to the brickwork. Mike supervised Stan with the walkway. Later on, they had their break and went back to finish what they could before the end of the day. Seth was relieved to learn Stan would be working at the cabin house next, so tomorrow Seth could relax and work like normal.

Karen had heated up some leftover chicken-and-rice casserole for her daughters. They were eating in the kitchen while Karen nursed Nancy Anne in the living room. As she sat in the rocker, she glanced at the clock hanging on the wall. Seth would be getting home in a half hour, and Rachelle would be here about the same time with her two kids. Roseanna and Mary were excited to have a "play date," as Karen had heard the English call it.

"I'm done with dinner and put my dishes in the sink." Roseanna traipsed into the living room, holding her book from Grandpa and Grandma Allgyer. "I really like this book a lot."

"I'm glad you do." Karen spoke soothingly.

Something hit against the kitchen floor. "I dropped my cup!" Mary shouted.

"I'll go see." Roseanna turned and hurried to the other room. "It's just a little spill, Mom. I'll get it clean."

Karen smiled as she carried the baby to the nursery. After she fed and changed Nancy Anne, she placed her in the crib. When the baby kicked her little feet, Karen reached in and tickled her toes. She was rewarded with giggles and the sweetest of smiles.

After Nancy Anne settled down, Karen went to her bedroom to get ready for her date with Seth. She couldn't wait to take Ash, the new horse, for the trip into town. Karen had just put on her prayer *kapp,* when she heard knocking. She opened the door to Rachelle and her two small children: six-year-old Melissa, and Tim, who was a month older than Mary. Roseanna and Mary were happy to see their company and wanted to head right upstairs to play.

"I'm not going to have a lot to do. Our children will be playing, and I'll be with Nancy Anne. That will be easy." Rachelle hung her sweater on the wall peg, along with her kids' outer garments.

"She shouldn't be a problem, and I put out snacks on the kitchen counter." Karen also showed Rachelle the drinks in the refrigerator.

As they waited for Seth to get home from work, Rachelle talked about how her mother and aunt had been working on a quilt project with her and had enjoyed a nice lunch together.

Seth walked in and smiled at Rachelle. "Would you like me to put your horse in the corral?" He sat his lunch pail on the counter and turned toward Karen's friend.

"That would be great." Rachelle stepped away from the fridge.

Seth came over and stood close to Karen. "We've got plenty of time. I'll get Ash ready, too. Then I'll come back in and get washed up before we leave." Seth grinned at Karen before walking out of the house.

Seth and Karen had a nice ride into town, enjoying their new buggy horse and the opportunity to talk without interruptions from the children.

Once they placed their order at the restaurant, they chatted over hot tea while waiting for their meals to arrive. The food looked and smelled wonderful. They both silently prayed before reaching for their forks. No way was Karen going to try eating with chopsticks. She would probably end up with more food on her lap than in her mouth.

"Mmm . . . This food is good." Karen rested the fork on the plate and reached for her cup of tea.

Seth nodded. "I wish we could do this

more often. I've been wanting to come here with you for weeks, but something always seemed to change our plans."

She looked across at her attractive husband. His stunning blue eyes were almost hypnotic.

"I'm glad we did this. It feels nice to come here, especially not having to cook this evening." Karen dabbed her mouth with her napkin. "Rachelle said this restaurant has been here for some time."

"I hope it continues to stay in business because their food is good." Seth took another bite of almond chicken.

The restaurant was busy, with the hum of conversation a constant in the background. They visited while they ate, but Seth wasn't as talkative as when they first sat down. He seemed preoccupied, looking out the window. Karen wondered what was up.

"The girls are enjoying the new bunny. We took it out again today and held it." Karen sipped her tea. "They named it Star, for the little mark on its head."

Seth chuckled, giving Karen his full attention. "I think we need to get a trampoline for our girls to play on."

"I would be tempted to climb up and give it a try." Karen sat back in her seat and sighed. "I'm full. I'll need a box for the rest of my food."

"Mine was good, but I've got nothing left on my plate." He patted his stomach.

Their waiter dropped off their check and a box for Karen's food. Karen scraped her leftovers into the container, while Seth paid the bill.

Soon they were walking out to the buggy, and Karen climbed in while Seth untied their horse. He backed up Ash and headed out of the parking lot.

"You haven't said much about your day at work. How did it go?" Karen asked.

"Not so good. The new guy is not easy to work with." Seth frowned.

"What did he do that caused problems?" She smoothed the folds in her rust-colored dress.

Seth urged Ash onward with a snap of the reins. "Well, Stan likes to put himself first, and he comes off like he knows everything."

Karen looked away. This was the first time she'd known her husband to be put off so quickly by someone. *I wonder if this problem will cause Seth to want to move back to Bird-in-Hand.*

"Tomorrow Stan should be working at another job, so that'll be okay." He kept a solid grip while driving the buggy horse. Seth leaned closer to her as he drove along.

"But enough about Stan. Did you know you are my favorite girl?"

She rested her head on his shoulder. "I love you, Seth. You are my world."

They soon pulled into the driveway and parked near the barn. Seth got out and tied the horse up to the hitching rail. She helped him get the horse and buggy put away. It was nice having two horses now. Karen hoped in time they'd get another buggy that would hold more people.

Coming into the house, Karen and Seth hung their jackets on the wall pegs. Roseanna and Mary came up and hugged them. Rachelle asked how their dinner went and reported that everything had gone well with the children.

"We should get together again just for a visit sometime soon," Karen said to her friend.

"That's a great idea," Rachelle agreed, "but I need to check my schedule. We have a few family birthdays coming up, and I want to make sure I don't create a conflict."

Karen smiled, but inside she envied Rachelle's closeness to her family. *Can I learn to be content, or will I always long for home?*

CHAPTER 5

Roseanna and Mary had offered to help Seth clean out the stalls one Saturday morning, and their eagerness to pitch in did his heart good. They took turns picking up the used hay and putting it into the wheelbarrow.

Seth glanced over at his tractor calendar hanging on the wall. "Hmm . . . I need to change the month on that." Seth stopped what he was doing and set his shovel off to the side.

"What Daddy?" Roseanna paused and looked up at him.

He moved toward the calendar. "It's not June anymore. It's the second week of July." He chuckled. "I don't know why I've missed it this long."

Roseanna giggled and, of course, Mary joined in.

As Seth pulled the calendar off the wall, a pigeon swooped down from the rafters near his head. He hollered, and the girls jumped. Roseanna dropped her shovel.

"That was a little unexpected." He chuckled and shook off the event. Seth pushed up his straw hat. "Well, girls, do you know what is coming up next month?" He knelt down to their level, smiling.

Roseanna came closer. "I don't know."

Mary copied her big sister and wrinkled her little nose.

"Well, your mamm and I have a little surprise for you both. We'll tell you all about it at lunch." He reached around the girls and hugged them.

Seth went back to shoveling out the other stall. "We need to get our work done. Then we'll head back into the house to see how your mommy is doing."

Karen headed to Nancy Anne's room to check on her. Her baby was wide awake this morning, looking up at Karen and holding her chubby arms out. Nancy Anne smiled wide while being lifted out of the crib. Karen carried her over to the changing table to put on a new diaper. "How are you doing this morning, my littlest one?" Karen slipped Nancy Anne into a fresh outfit then carried her to the kitchen, where she fixed some baby cereal.

Since Nancy Anne could topple over easily, Karen set her in a car seat whenever she fed her cereal. The pediatrician had said it was fine to supplement her breast milk, especially if her daughter appeared to still be hungry. Nancy Anne was fun to feed and would laugh if Karen made a funny face at her. After she was fed, Karen wiped her little round face and hands, then placed her in the playpen in the living room.

Seth, Roseanna, and Mary came in from the barn. "Hello, Nancy Anne." Her husband leaned over the railing where she sat. "Did your mommy just feed you?" Seth looked endearingly at his baby daughter then stood up, turning toward Karen. "There's one more stall to clean and we'll be done. We just came in to get something to drink."

"Sounds like you three are accomplishing a lot this morning." Karen brushed away some baby cereal on her brown dress.

"Guess what made us jump out in the barn, Momma?" Roseanna asked.

"Hinkel!" Mary blurted out, jumping up and down.

"Chicken?" Karen's eyebrows lifted. "We have no chickens, Mary."

"It wasn't a chicken. It was a pigeon." Roseanna patted her sister's arm.

Seth explained the quick story as they walked into the kitchen. He grabbed more coffee, and got Roseanna and Mary water to drink.

"I'm going to mop the kitchen first then see about the laundry." Karen stood by the sink, running water in a bucket.

"The girls and I will be heading back outside. Come on, ladies." Seth motioned to them. "See you in a while, Karen." He waved.

Her daughters waved, too, as they went out, shutting the door behind them.

Karen stepped over to the playpen and added some different toys from a box for Nancy Anne to play with. The baby stayed awake more these days, now that she was four months old.

After Karen got a load of laundry going in the wringer washer, she peeked in on Nancy Anne, who was gnawing on a plush toy. "Baby's like to explore their world. I'll need to remember to wash off your toys."

A buggy pulled into the yard. Karen glanced out the window and saw the bishop getting out. She quickly tidied up her kitchen and moved the mopping supplies into the corner. She looked out the window again as he finished tying his horse to the hitching rail. "Hmm . . . I wonder." Karen tightened her brown head scarf.

Seth came into the house with the bishop, and their daughters followed.

"Hi, Karen. How are you doing today?" Bishop John asked.

"We're fine. Would you like something to drink?" Karen smiled at him.

"That'd be nice. Do you have any coffee?" He pulled off his hat, revealing his thinning gray hair, and hung it on a peg.

"Yes, and why don't you have a seat?" she offered.

Her daughters went down the hall to the bathroom to wash their hands. Then Karen saw them go upstairs when she brought the coffee to the men. She grabbed a glass of water and joined the men in the living room. Nancy Anne was sound asleep with a light blanket Karen had draped over her.

"What brings you by today, Bishop?" Seth gave him his full attention.

"I'd like to put a nice wall in the back of my yard. Would you be able to do it?" Bishop John leaned forward in his chair.

"Ah, I see. You could contact my boss. I've got his number." Seth pulled out his wallet and handed him a business card.

"Thank you, Seth. I'm hoping to get this done in time. My wife and I are planning to take a trip to Florida." He took a big drink.

"That sound's good, John. Are you bringing anyone else with you?"

"We're going with my son and his wife and possibly another couple." The bishop finished his coffee.

"Trips are a nice bonus, aren't they?" Karen looked at her husband.

"I know, and I'm about due to take some time off. But we're still breaking in a new guy at work." Seth took a sip and set his cup aside.

"That shouldn't take too long. Besides, the other employees can help teach this person, jah?" John smiled at Seth.

Seth shook his head. "No, my boss is relying on me to do the training, and Stan's irritating behavior is making it difficult."

"As hard as it may be, if you keep a positive attitude, exercise patience, and try to be kind, perhaps in time your relationship with the new fellow will improve. You might even gain a friend."

"I appreciate your advice and will try to remember it the next time I'm dealing with Stan."

John pushed his chair aside and stood up. "I've got to get going now. I still have more stops to make before I go home. I'll keep you in my prayers, and if you need to talk again, let me know."

"Thanks so much," Seth replied. They all headed for the door.

"Thanks again for the business card," the bishop said. "I'll give your boss a call and see when there's time to start this project."

"Yes, call him. Hopefully my boss will get you lined up as soon as possible."

"All right then. See you both on Sunday." Bishop John waved and walked to his buggy.

"I'm gonna go out and throw some more straw in Ash's stall. I was almost through when the bishop pulled in." Seth grabbed his work hat from the wall peg.

"I'll finish mopping this floor, and then I can heat up the stew from last night." Karen looked out the window at the bird feeder. "I might need to add more food because the bird feeder is nearly empty."

"Would you like me to do it?" Seth picked up the used coffee mugs and headed for the kitchen with them. "I guess the girls will be staying in at this point until lunch."

"I'll send Roseanna out to get you when the meal is ready." Karen followed him. "I think I'll make some rolled biscuits to go with the stew." She grabbed the mop and set it in the bucket of soapy water.

"The lunch sounds good, Karen." Seth adjusted his hat. "I'd better get outside and get some work done." He hugged her and left.

Karen squeezed out the sudsy water, and pushed the mop around the floor. It picked up all kinds of grime. "I can't believe how filthy this floor is." She shook her head. With the demands of a baby and her two other children, she had so little time to get much else done. It was harder for her to catch up with her chores than it was for her sisters in Lancaster County. They had help from each other and their mamm.

Karen rinsed out her mop and went over the floor some more. Gratified that the room was in better shape, she cleaned the mop and bucket and put them away. Nancy Anne was making her usual sounds in the living room, so Karen went to watch her baby play with a rattle. "You are precious. What a blessing you are to us."

Nancy Anne dropped her toy and put up her pudgy little hands to Karen.

"How can I resist this?" She leaned over and picked up her sweet baby. Karen cuddled Nancy Anne with joy and tenderness. She whispered, "I'm looking forward to Seth and me sharing the surprise later."

Karen finished holding Nancy Anne and returned her to the blanket. "I need to get lunch started." She got out the ingredients for the biscuits and set them on the counter. The washer had quit running, so Karen went to get the laundry. "What is all this on the clothes?" She sniffed at it. "It's chewing gum, and the clothes all smell like mint." She sighed.

"What's wrong, Mom?" Roseanna came in from the living room.

"I'm going to have to rewash this load of clothes." Karen tried to pick out the gum in the washer.

"Whose gum is it?" She tilted her head to one side.

Mary entered the room with Big Ears, the bunny, and came over to stand by them.

"It's your daed's." Karen threw away more gray-looking pieces in the garbage.

"That gum looks icky." Roseanna wrinkled her nose.

"Gut net." Mary moved away, tossing Big Ears a couple of times.

Karen looked at Roseanna. "She's right, it's not good. This stuff is messy."

"Are you *zanke* daddy about this?"

Karen shook her head. "If I scolded him, he'd only get upset." Seth had been upset about a lot of things lately because of work, so there was no point in stirring the pot.

Soon the washer was running again, and Karen had checked on the baby, fed Nancy

Anne, and changed her diaper. The baby was in her crib, having dozed off after nursing. Karen crept out of the room and took the stew out to heat up. She prepped the biscuits and turned the stew on low to keep warm. Karen watched out the window and saw a pony cart ride by their place. *Someday my children will be old enough to do that.* Turning away from the window, Karen noticed the oven was ready for the biscuits, so she slipped them in.

When the biscuits were about done, Karen sent Roseanna out to fetch her dad and had Mary wash her hands.

Seth and Roseanna came in from outside and went down the hall to clean up. Mary dashed into the kitchen. "Mamm, can I have *millich?*"

"You may have milk with your stew." Karen grabbed bowls, cups, and spoons and took them to the table. When she returned, Mary had the refrigerator open and was lifting out the container of milk. Before Karen could help her, the jug slipped from the child's small hands and hit the floor. The lid popped off, and milk poured out. Mary gasped.

"Hang on, Mary." Karen knelt down and grabbed the jug. She held it up. "There's not much left."

"Sorry, Mamm." She leaned into Karen's shoulder and cried.

"It's okay, Mary." Karen patted her back. "There's no harm done." She hugged her little daughter for a moment. "Let's get this cleaned up."

"What's going on in here?" Seth came into the room.

"There was a little accident, but we're taking care of it." Karen grabbed a couple hand towels from the drawer, and she and Mary worked on the floor. Then everyone came to the table to eat lunch.

"Everything looks good. I've been thinking about eating this the whole time I was out working." Her husband smacked his lips. "Let's pray."

After prayers were offered and the food had been served, Roseanna brought up the surprise, wanting to know what it was.

Mary wiggled in her seat and looked at her father expectantly.

"So you both would like to know what the surprise is, huh?" He looked teasingly at them.

"Jah, Daddy, tell us what it is!" Roseanna's voice grew loud.

"What surprise, Daddy?" Mary jumped out of her seat and ran over to him.

"Take a seat Mary, and I'll share what it

is." Seth patted her shoulder, speaking calmly.

She sat in her chair, and Seth cleared his throat. "We'll be going to Bird-in-Hand and Paradise for a vacation next month to see both of your grandparents — the Allgyers and the Zooks."

"Yippee! Yippee!" Roseanna yelled then covered her mouth.

"Yippee! "Yippee!" Mary copycatted Roseanna.

"Mary, you are really happy. I am, too." Roseanna smiled brightly. "I love my Grandpa and Grandma Allgyer and Grandpa and Grandma Zook, too."

Mary bounced in her chair and squealed.

"We've got some time before we take this trip, and we can think about what we want to bring along." Karen looked at her family. Truth was, she felt very happy knowing they'd be going on this trip. She'd start to count the days as soon as the date was in stone.

CHAPTER 6

Karen tried to think good thoughts while waiting for Nancy Anne's doctor to return to his office. She reviewed how much she'd enjoyed their trip to Bird-in-Hand and Paradise. It'd been only a couple of days since they'd come home from staying with Karen's parents. Before that, they had visited Paul and Emma and the rest of Seth's family. There had been a big get-together at Seth's oldest brother's house. Because they had six children, Brad and Sarah lived in a home with all kinds of space for family gatherings. Karen's daughters seemed to enjoy playing with the younger cousins.

The second half of the trip was spent at her parents' home. Karen loved being around all her siblings again. Her mother had everyone over to their place for a big meal. No one walked away hungry — that was for sure. Karen wished she could freeze time, just so the need for her family around would be met. She wanted to chat with her parents one on one, but everyone wanted to talk about what was happening with their lives.

Karen decided she'd call her family more often. It might help her feel more connected. She liked the trip so much she longed for another one.

Pulling her thoughts aside, Karen bounced Nancy Anne on her knee as she waited impatiently for the doctor. The nurse had moved them from the examination room to his office thirty minutes ago, and Karen was anxious for his results of the tests. She could feel her heart rate climb, and her palms grew sweaty. *This is so weird. I wonder if something is wrong.*

Karen thought about how the doctor checked her daughter's eyes and then tested her hearing on a machine. Nancy Anne wore earphones on her head the whole time she was tested. The doctor's demeanor had become more serious as the exam continued. He'd asked Karen questions about Nancy Anne. Had she noticed anything strange in her reaction to things? Karen honestly didn't have an answer. Yes there had been a few times when Nancy Anne didn't react to loud noises or slept through them, but she thought that happened with most children at one time or another.

One thing was for sure: her joy from the trip to Paradise and Bird-in-Hand was being erased as the waiting wore on. Karen heard the doctor outside the door, talking to another person. Then he entered the room, holding a couple papers. "I'm not sure what the cause of the problem is yet, but Nancy Anne appears to be deaf."

Karen gasped. "What?"

"I've called a specialist to have her checked over. He's been testing infants and children at his clinic in Harrisburg for years. He'll give Nancy Anne good care."

"I can't believe this. How could this have happened?" Karen teared up, holding back a sob.

"The root of this is from the German measles you had during your pregnancy. Deafness is one of the most common complications of measles during pregnancy. If your daughter is non-hearing, then she'll need to learn sign language when she's old enough. Nancy Anne and your family members can learn it together. But until all the testing is final, we won't know which course to take for her." The doctor patted Nancy Anne's head. "It's good that we've caught this now. Maybe there's something the pediatric audiologist can do for your daughter."

He handed Karen a business card. "He's one of the best around. His office will contact you to set up an appointment for your daughter soon." He gave her more papers. "The rest of this is summaries of today's eye exam and her weight and height information. She's doing very well in those areas. Other than her hearing problem, she's a healthy baby and progressing well."

He stood up and moved to the door. "My receptionist will make you an appointment for Nancy Anne's next well-child checkup on your way out. Good evening."

"Thank you, Doctor." Karen clung to her daughter and stumbled out of his office.

As she moved down the hall toward the appointment desk, the news began to fully sink in. *My daughter is deaf. My precious little baby can't hear me.* She swallowed against the pain in her throat. *If only my folks had taken me to get vaccinated when I was young, this never would have happened.*

Karen was almost home and thankful the new driver seemed more focused on her job than on talking. She felt gutted, and the sensation was only getting worse. Karen wanted to gather her parents and the rest of her family so she could tell them what she'd just learned. But that wasn't possible. Maintaining her composure was next to impossible. How could this be happening? Why didn't she notice Nancy Anne's problem before?

When they arrived home, Karen got out of the van and pulled the car seat out with the baby inside. She thanked her driver and paid her for the service then half-stumbled down the walkway to the house, her vision blurred by tears she was trying to hold back.

Rachelle greeted them at the door. "Roseanna and Mary have been good. How did it go at the appointment?"

Karen couldn't hold it in any longer. Tears streamed down her face. "Oh my. This is not a good day."

"What happened?" Rachelle's brows furrowed with concern, and she led Karen and Nancy Anne to the rocker, where she took the baby from the car seat and placed her in her mother's arms. Karen silently rocked, clutching her daughter.

Rachelle sat on the sofa and waited silently.

Finally Karen found the strength to talk. She told her friend about the appointment and the results of the tests. Rachelle listened as Karen wiped at her tears and shared everything that had transpired.

"It sounds like your doctor moved quickly on this."

Karen managed a nod.

Her daughters came downstairs, and Roseanna touched Karen's arm. "Why are you crying, Momma?"

"I'll leave you to talk to your children." Rachelle got up from the couch.

"Thank you for watching my girls and letting me unburden my soul." Karen rose with the baby.

"That's what friends are for. I'll be praying about this." Rachelle wrapped Karen in a warm hug.

"Danki." Karen appreciated her friend's kindness and support. She knew some of the other women she'd gotten to know in Lykens would be equally compassionate.

After Rachelle left, Karen took a seat again and looked over at Roseanna and Mary.

"Momma, why are you so sad?" Roseanna asked.

"I'm sad because your baby sister can't hear." Karen teared even more.

"How do you know this?" Roseanna questioned.

"The doctor tested Nancy Anne with equipment earlier today and found out she can't hear." Karen struggled hard to keep her emotions in check.

"Can they make her hear again?" Roseanna held her baby sister's delicate hand. Mary placed her hand on top of Roseanna's.

"I'm not sure, but we'll all take good care of her, no matter what the outcome is." Karen tried to be brave and positive. "I'll tell your daed about Nancy Anne when he gets home later, so please don't say anything, okay?"

The girls nodded, their faces somber.

Karen dreaded talking with Seth about their baby's condition. How would he take this devastating news?

Karen threw a casserole together for supper and had it cooking in the oven. She looked up at the kitchen clock. How would she tell Seth, and when should she tell him? She was still in shock, yet it fell to her to break the news to so many others in a calm and rational manner.

The rumble of Mike's rig pulling in made her look out the window. Seth's normal day was about to be changed in a big way.

She went over to Nancy Anne and checked her diaper. It needed to be changed, so she picked her up and headed to the nursery.

The front door opened, and Seth announced he was home. Soon she heard the girls in the kitchen with their dad. Karen could hear him setting down his lunch box and sliding a chair out while talking to Roseanna and Mary.

She finished up with Nancy Anne and brought her out to the living room. Karen watched her husband come out and take a seat. "How long till dinner's ready?" he asked.

"About a half hour." Karen placed Nancy Anne on a blanket on the floor and then plopped down in the rocker.

"What a day." Seth groaned. "That Stan guy sure can get on one's nerves."

Karen sat and listened.

"I'd better go out and feed the animals, even though I'm beat," he grumbled.

"First, I need to talk to you." Karen licked her lips.

"Can it wait till I get done?" Seth tapped his foot.

"No. I need to tell you what happened at Nancy Anne's appointment."

"Okay." Seth sat up in his seat, giving her his complete attention.

"The doctor ran tests on her vision and hearing." Karen's voice broke.

"What's wrong?" He kept his eyes glued on her.

"It's not so good. After he tested her hearing, he seemed serious, but he didn't say why." She paused. "Then we had to wait in his office for the results."

"So what are the results?" Seth leaned forward.

"Well . . ." Karen hesitated when Mary stepped into the room.

Seth looked at her, then he got up. "Maybe we should talk later."

"Our girls already know about Nancy Anne." Karen rose and motioned for Mary to go back upstairs. She was pleased when her daughter did what she was told.

"What do they know about her?" His voice raised.

"If you will please sit down, I'll tell you."

Seth did as she asked.

"The results on our baby aren't good." She started to choke up.

"What's wrong with her. Just say it." His form grew rigid.

"Nancy Anne cannot hear."

His face turned red. "What do you mean, she can't hear?"

"Nancy Anne is deaf, and we'll need to learn sign language." Karen sat quietly, her vision blurred with tears.

"I can't believe this. I'm already having a difficult time at work. I've got a lot of chores around here to do." Seth stood up. "I don't want to learn sign language." He headed for the door.

"Where are you going?" Karen stood up.

"I need to take care of the animals."

"When you come back in, I'll have supper on the table." She stepped over to him and placed her hand gently on his arm.

"I'm not having anything to eat. I've lost my appetite." He turned away and went outside, slamming the door.

Feeling like she had been slapped, Karen hurried down the hall to the guest room. She closed the door, pulled the beloved heirloom quilt from the bed, and wrapped herself in it. She fell across the bed and sobbed deeply, muffling her cries in the bedding. The Christmas quilt seemed to bring her closer to Mom. Karen felt isolated from her husband. Seth seemed to be in denial and had pulled away from her. She looked for the embroidered scripture on the quilt backing and ran her finger over the raised stitching while reading it. Then, she prayed that God would heal her family. Whatever the outcome, she would accept His will.

Karen dried her eyes, remade the bed, and hurried out to the kitchen. Her daughters came into the room with downcast expressions. Karen had a feeling her girls had spoken about their baby sister to each other.

"I'm pulling the casserole out of the oven." She put on the hot mitts. "Could you two see how Nancy Anne is doing?"

"Yes, Mom." Roseanna grabbed Mary's hand, and they both darted out of the kitchen.

As Karen grabbed the wheat bread out of the refrigerator, she heard Roseanna in the other room talking to Nancy Anne. "It's okay if you can't hear me, baby sister. I love you."

"Me, too, sister," Mary chimed in.

Karen's heart ached, listening to her daughters. They were dealing with this sad news better than their own father.

She buttered the bread and set it on the table, wondering if she should remove her husband's plate. She hoped Seth would decide to eat, after all, so she left his plate as it was.

When supper was ready, she called her daughters in to eat. Karen made up some cereal for Nancy Anne. The baby sat perfectly in her highchair these days, and she waited patiently for her food.

"Is Dad coming?" Roseanna asked.

"He might join us, but he's outside working right now." Karen lowered her head. "Let's pray."

When they'd finished praying, she helped

dish Mary's food on her plate then set the casserole near Roseanna. Once Roseanna had dished up some casserole, Karen passed the bread to them.

The girls nibbled on their food, while Nancy Anne ate like a champ. Why shouldn't she? Her silent world hadn't changed at all.

"You are sure enjoying your cereal." Karen smiled at her daughter.

Nancy Anne smiled and wiggled her legs in her seat.

"She's happy, Momma. Look how she is eating." Roseanna picked up her slice of bread and took a big bite.

"I'm happy, too." Mary hopped down and came over to Karen.

Karen was about to tell her to sit back down, when she heard the back door open.

Mary dashed over and returned with her dad, holding his hand.

"You go back and sit down now." Seth nudged her toward the table.

"Come eat with us." Roseanna looked up at him.

"I don't feel like eating right now. I'll just grab some water." He sauntered over to the cupboard and pulled out a glass.

Mary sat back in her chair and looked at her dad as he was filling his glass at the sink.

"It's okay. Eat your dinner, Mary." Karen spoke in a calm tone as she fed Nancy Anne another spoonful of cereal.

Seth drank his glass of water and set it in the sink. Then he walked out of the room and headed toward the bathroom.

Karen tried to eat her meal along with the children, even though her appetite had disappeared.

After they'd all finished their food and cleared the table. Karen took Nancy Anne to the nursery. Seth had gone back outside to work. She wondered how the night would play out. He wasn't acting at all like his usual self, and of course with good reason. *Actually none of us are being our normal selves. The only exception is the baby.*

Karen changed Nancy Anne and laid her in the crib. The baby's eyes drooped. Her little one had had a busy day at the doctor's with all the shots and tests. Karen stood watching her daughter slip off to sleep. *What will Nancy Anne's life be like someday? Will everyone accept her the way she is? Can our daughter live a normal life?*

Later that evening when the children had gone to bed, Seth sat in the living room, his shoulders slumped in the chair. He stared blankly at the latest issue of *The Budget*.

"I'm tired." Karen yawned. "Maybe I'll get ready for bed."

Seth looked up at her briefly and nodded.

Karen got up and walked to their bedroom. She took her hair out of its bun and grabbed the brush on the dresser. Sitting on the edge of the bed, she began brushing her long hair. Karen continued for a bit then set the brush back in its spot. She grabbed her nightclothes and went into the bathroom to change.

She heard their bedroom door open, followed by the squeak of a dresser drawer. Karen continued flossing her teeth, hoping to find Seth in a better mood. She stepped out of the bathroom and saw Seth leaning against his dresser with his arms folded.

"I'll need to call my folks about Nancy Anne." Karen sighed.

"I'm not wanting to call my parents to tell them this news."

"You need to, and the sooner the better."

"I'm not going to call them." His face reddened.

Karen stiffened. "Seth, you need to accept this and deal with it."

"I don't want to talk anymore about this. I've got enough on my plate right now." He clasped his hands behind his back and dropped his gaze to the floor.

Karen began to cry. "You are being unreasonable." She choked on a sob. "I'm not sleeping in here. I just can't."

"Fine, have it your way!" He jerked the covers back.

She rushed out of the bedroom, straight for the guest room. *How can I deal with this myself if he's not willing to talk about it?*

CHAPTER 7

The early fall morning was cool and cloudy. After Karen placed her sleeping baby in the playpen, she walked outside, carrying a couple of small baskets. Her two young daughters followed along. She caught sight of Seth standing near the barn with his arms folded, watching her. His ride would be here soon, and he would be on his way.

Karen trudged through the thick grass to check on her garden. Roseanna and Mary stopped to watch a bumblebee on one of the roses.

Karen squatted next to the garden and was about to pick a tomato when Seth approached. "We need to talk."

She gave an impatient huff. "About what?"

"About us." He tapped his foot. "About you moving to the guest room. How long are you going to let this go on?"

"When you apologize for your lack of support and can accept our baby's disability."

"I have accepted it." Seth's voice rose. "What other choice do I have? You just expect too much of me, Karen. Nothing I say or do ever seems good enough."

Roseanna ran up to them, her chin trembling. "Daddy, why are you yelling at Momma?"

"I'm not yelling. We're having a discussion."

Mary came over to Karen with tears in her eyes. She, too, looked visibly shaken.

Mike's rig pulled into the yard, and Karen didn't think she'd ever been happier to see it. The sooner Seth left, the faster she could calm the girls.

"Good-bye," Seth mumbled. He sprinted to the truck.

When it left the yard, Karen hugged her daughters.

"Help me find all the red tomatoes. They can be hiding anywhere, so look carefully."

Mary crouched next to Karen. She held Big Ears in one hand.

"This is like a game," Roseanna commented.

Karen picked at the tomatoes, barely able to focus on the task. All she could think about was her argument with Seth. Why did he not see that he wasn't giving her the support she needed?

"Look, Mom, here's what I've picked." Roseanna showed her the pretty red fruit.

"Me, too! Me, too!" Mary had a couple green tomatoes resting in her cupped hands.

"Wait, Mary, those are green ones, and they aren't ready yet to eat. Just pick this color." Karen showed her the basket of red cherry tomatoes.

Mary nodded then reached out and pulled off an orange one from the bush. "Look, Mamm!"

"That's right, Mary." Karen patted her arm.

After they'd picked off all the ripened fruit, Karen stood for a moment, enjoying the view of her surroundings. The sun had finally broken through the clouds. Karen thought she saw something out of the corner of her eye. She shielded her vision with her hand but didn't see anything out of the ordinary. Roseanna and Mary stood beside her, watching a fuzzy caterpillar crawling through the grass.

Mary pointed. *"Hass."*

"Why don't you two go talk to Star, the bunny, while I peek in on Nancy Anne?"

They both nodded and dashed off.

Karen picked up both baskets and plodded back to the house. Once inside, she placed the tomatoes on the counter next to the sink. Karen turned and saw Nancy Anne move in her playpen, but she was simply stirring in her sleep. Karen tiptoed back outside and headed for her two older daughters.

Both of the girls came running toward her.

"The bunny is gone!" Roseanna's cheeks were flushed.

"Hass! Hass!" Mary tripped with Big Ears, nearly taking a spill.

"Star is missing?" Karen rested her hands on her hips. "We should take a good look around the yard."

"I'm going to keep looking near his cage." Roseanna turned around and headed back to the rabbit's area.

Mary stayed with Karen, and they walked together toward some thick shrubs.

"These plants and shrubs can make a good hiding spot for any rabbit," Karen commented.

A rustling came from some small, moving grasses. Star hopped out from behind a plant. Mary pointed and began to jump and squeal.

"Roseanna, we found Star. He's over here by us!" Karen yelled.

"Oh, good, he's been found." Roseanna ran over and bent down to pick up Star. "I'm so glad you're safe." She cuddled the silky-haired pet.

Mary reached out and petted the little fella. She looked up at Karen with her sweet smile.

"How about after lunch, the four of us ride into Lykens and go to the library?" Karen scratched behind the bunny's ears.

"That sounds like fun." Roseanna held Star up close to her face and nuzzled him.

"*Mir!* Mir!" Mary tried to get close.

"Let Mary see Star. When she says, 'Me, me,' she really wants to do the same thing." Karen rested her hand on Roseanna's shoulder.

After Mary was reassured about Star's well-being, Karen announced, "We should put Star away into his cage and go back to the house."

When they were back inside, Karen made lunch, and the girls washed up. She thought about how weeks ago, she'd talked to the receptionist about scheduling an appointment with the specialist for Nancy Anne. Adjusting to their youngest daughter's situation wasn't the easiest thing to do, and she and Seth were dealing with it in very different ways. He left her the job of contacting family and friends. She'd called her folks and left a message about Nancy Anne. She'd also called Seth's folks because he never followed through with them.

From everything she could discover, no one else in the area or from their hometowns had dealt with a child facing this condition, so there was no one whose experiences they could learn from. The whole situation was uncharted territory, but at least they had their families' promises that they'd keep Karen and Seth and little Nancy Anne in their prayers.

After Karen, Roseanna, and Mary ate their lunch and things were put away, Karen asked the girls to find their library books. She'd changed Nancy Anne and replenished the diaper bag for their trip into Lykens this afternoon. Karen went out to hitch up Millie.

They rode together in the closed buggy to town. Beautifully colored leaves fluttered down from the trees.

"I like to go to the library, Mom," Roseanna commented.

"I like to go to the library, Mom." Mary slipped the pink clog on that had fallen off her sock-covered foot.

"Stop repeating everything I say!" Roseanna shouted.

Mary whimpered. "You're not nice."

"You're not nice when you copycat all the time."

"Do not."

"Do so."

Karen glanced over her shoulder. "That's enough, you two." If you don't stop fussing at each other, I'll turn the horse and buggy around and go home."

The girls settled down.

"Remember, in the library we need to be quiet." Karen reminded them.

"Nancy Anne doesn't know what that means," Roseanna replied.

"Jah, but she shouldn't be too noisy there." Karen snapped the reins, getting Millie to move quicker.

Nancy Anne was wide awake, and she liked to have attention from her sisters. She'd play by putting her hand out for either Roseanna or Mary to hold.

They reached the library parking area and pulled up to the hitching rail. After Karen secured both the buggy and horse, she held the baby carrier while she helped the girls out with their books.

Once inside, they headed to the return desk to drop off their books. Then they went over to the children's section. In no time the girls were sitting and looking through their choices.

"Girls, can you stay right here and flip through the pages of the books you have?"

Karen asked.

They nodded.

"Okay, I won't be long." Karen toted Nancy Anne in the baby carrier over to a different section. She looked for another sign language book to learn what she could. *Someday I'll be glad that I studied signing, but only if Nancy Anne can't be helped by the specialists. Too bad Seth has no interest in learning. Is he just being stubborn, or is he still in denial?*

Karen came back to her girls. "Do you have some books picked out yet?" She looked at their choices.

"*Guck,* Mamm." Mary held the book out to Karen.

"I'll look at your book." She turned a few pages and gave it back. "This is a good one Mary."

"How about mine, Momma?" Roseanna's voice was quiet.

Karen thumbed through her choice and then looked up at the library clock. "I think yours is good, too. Let's go check out our books, and maybe we'll have time for one more stop."

"Where?" Roseanna tilted her head.

"You'll see." Karen set her books on the counter for the librarian. Her daughters did the same.

After they completed checking out the books, the four rode in the buggy. Karen pulled into the drive-in parking lot. "Would anyone like an ice-cream cone?"

"Yippee! Yippee!" Mary jumped off her seat.

"Yippee, Momma!" Roseanna shouted.

Karen was happy to treat her girls to something special. After the argument they'd witnessed between her and Seth this morning, the girls were feeling the tension. Since she'd moved to the guest room to sleep, she and Seth were barely speaking to each other. She was struggling with her faith right now. Normally Karen looked to Seth for help, but between the situation at work and his inability to cope with Nancy Anne's disability, he didn't seem to be dealing too well with his own issues.

Seth rode along after work with Mike. His old green truck had been leaking water from the front of the engine for days, and the noise was getting louder.

Mike pulled off to the side of the road and turned off the ignition. "I can't keep putting water into this radiator. I'm gonna call for a tow truck and have them drop it off at the garage for repair." Mike pulled out his cell phone, found the number, and called.

Seth got out of Mike's rig to take a look at it. "Yep, there's a good-sized puddle underneath the front, and it's still dripping."

Mike nodded at Seth but continued talking to the tow place. A few seconds later he stuck his head out the driver's side window. "They'll be here soon. I'm calling my wife now. She can pick us up, and then we'll drop you off at your place."

Seth smiled. "Okay." He leaned against the truck. It was nice working on Bishop John's new wall. The staggered blocks looked real nice, and Stan wasn't there. He shook his head. *But I'll be working with him tomorrow, and I'll try to do as the bishop suggested and be kinder to Stan.* Seth lumbered back into the truck and watched Mike as he looked through some paperwork.

Minutes later the tow truck pulled up, and Mike hopped out to talk to the driver. Not long after, a red minivan pulled up behind Mike's rig. Seth got out and chatted with the tow truck driver as he began setting things up. Mike called Seth over to meet his wife. The green truck was hoisted up onto the flatbed of the rig and hauled away.

Mike opened the side door to the minivan and moved a black cowboy hat to the backseat. "Here, Seth. Get in."

He climbed in and located the safety belt,

while Mike closed the door. Seth noticed the pink camo seat covers up front. Even the woman's fancy purse was in a camo print. The interior of the van reeked of perfume, but what could he do? Seth sure couldn't hold his breath the whole way home.

Mike's wife, Jane, drove down the road, humming to a country song playing on the radio. Mike hummed, too, for a moment. Then he turned to Seth. "Pheasant hunting will be coming up in a couple of months. Would you be interested in going with me?"

Seth grinned. "I'd like to go."

Mike looked over at his wife. "I'd like to do an overnight trip and would use the small trailer."

Jane patted her husband's arm. "You've been working so hard. You deserve some fun."

"How about it, Seth?" Mike turned toward him once more.

"I'll definitely give that some thought." Seth twiddled his thumbs.

They pulled into his driveway, and he said good-bye, closing the van door. Seth watched them turn around and leave. He liked how nice Jane was to Mike about the hunting trip and wished he and Karen could get along like that again. Seth had told Mike about his daughter's plight, but the conversation hadn't lifted his burden.

Seth came in through the kitchen door. "Hello, I'm home."

His daughters raced into the room with hugs for him. Karen came into the kitchen with Nancy Anne on her hip.

Seth put his lunch box on the counter and came over to Karen. "How's Nancy Anne doing?"

"She's doing okay." Karen shifted her weight. "Supper's almost on the table. Everything is ready."

"I'll go wash up, then." Seth moved away and headed for the bathroom.

When he returned, they prayed and ate their supper of roasted chicken and mashed potatoes. Karen kept looking at him, and it made Seth wonder what she was thinking.

"Whose van were you in?" Her brows furrowed.

"That minivan belongs to Mike's wife, and we were in it because his truck had an issue after work today. His green rig is at the garage for repairs on the water pump." Seth scooted up in his chair.

"Oh, that's too bad." Karen sipped her iced tea. "Otherwise, how are things at work?" She leaned a bit forward, setting down her glass.

"Tomorrow I'll be working with Stan again. Need I say more?" His face contorted.

"Sorry to hear that." Karen fed a spoonful of cereal to Nancy Anne.

"Why am I having to work with the guy?" Seth moaned.

His daughters looked over at him but kept eating their mashed potatoes.

Seth felt totally bummed and didn't even want to go to work in the morning. He ate the rest of his meal in silence then retreated to the living room.

Karen put the rest of the leftovers from supper away in the refrigerator. Nancy Anne sat in her carrier, smiling and playfully kicking about. "I haven't forgotten about you, baby girl." Karen started to fill the sink with hot water and added dish soap to it.

Roseanna stood by Mary and the baby.

Karen turned off the water. Then she handed her oldest daughter the rinsed-out sponge. "Please wipe the table off, Roseanna."

She complied, and Karen took Nancy Anne down to the nursery. When they returned, she noticed her daughters were in the living room. They were telling their daed about their day. Karen sat the baby in her playpen and went into the kitchen to do the dishes.

"I wish Dad would be happier," Roseanna whispered, having slipped in to stand next to Karen.

She nodded at her daughter and rinsed off a plate.

"I told him what fun we had today, but Dad still looks sad." Roseanna's voice trailed.

Karen sighed. "It'll get better around here, just give it more time."

"I'm gonna go upstairs and look at my books with Mary." Her daughter shrugged and left the room.

Karen heard Roseanna call Mary to join her up in their room.

I can't get over what I've just told my eldest daughter. "It'll get better around here, just give it more time." Karen blew out a breath. *It's been strenuous for weeks in this house between Seth and me.* She bowed her head. *Lord, help us tonight. I need my husband back, and we both need You to help us out. Thank You. Amen.*

When Karen was done praying, she felt a little better, knowing God was in control. She finished washing the dishes and left most of them to dry. Karen went out to the living room and took a seat in the rocking

265

chair. Her husband's shoulders drooped, and he sat quietly looking out the window. Karen looked away and watched Nancy Anne playing with a toy ball. The silence, as usual, was deafening, but she couldn't help feeling sorry for how distraught Seth was.

Karen cleared her throat. "Was supper all right this evening?"

"It was fine." He turned and looked at her. "I've just been thinking. When does Nancy Anne go in for that visit to the specialist?"

"I'll have to look on the calendar. It was a way's out. The ear specialist's secretary left a message about the doctor's vacation coming up. So that moved some of the patients' dates out, like our daughter's." Karen rocked in her chair.

"The date doesn't matter, because whenever it is, I'm going with you." His voice cracked. "I owe you an apology, Karen. When I saw how our girls reacted to me being so sad this evening, I realized I've been so caught up in my own problems, that I've neglected your needs as well as the children's. When we learned about Nancy Anne's problem, instead of working with you to deal with our difficulties, I turned inward and only thought about myself. Will you forgive me?"

Tears welled in her eyes. "Jah, I forgive

you Seth, and thank you so much for offering your support by coming with me to that appointment." She smiled and got up. "I'd like some coffee. How about you?"

Seth pulled her into his arms and gave her a hug. "I could use a cup after the day I've had."

She got them their hot drinks and went back to the living room. Karen handed Seth his coffee. "Tell me all about your day." She took her seat in the rocker.

They visited over an hour before tucking the children in bed. Tonight, Karen did not go to the guest room. She came into their bedroom and found comfort in her husband's arms. She would not return to the guest room again. Her place was here with Seth. Karen wondered if things from now on would improve, or was this just one night of joy and peace?

CHAPTER 8

Karen separated the clothes for washing. Seth's work pants and shirts smelled heavily of cigarette smoke. That could only mean her poor husband had worked around Stan again. She threw his dark items into a separate load in the washer and started the machine.

It was a crisp, sunny afternoon in November, and the girls were wearing jackets as they sat on the steps just outside, blowing bubbles. Karen heard them giggling and having a good time together. She grabbed her signing book off the kitchen table and found a page to practice from. Seth still wasn't interested in any of it, but at least he'd shown interest in going to their baby's first hearing appointment.

Weeks ago, they'd gone to the clinic together with Nancy Anne. The doctor had gone over the information from the baby's pediatrician. He'd asked them if their child had shown any other problems or symptoms since she had been born. Neither of them could come up with anything specific.

Karen held Nancy Anne in her lap during the checkup. Dr. Bulcan checked her ears with an instrument and a light for any wax buildup. Then a number of other tests were done on their baby girl, but none of them were painful, and the visit took about an hour. So far the specialist hadn't detected any signs of hearing.

Karen tried to be strong and didn't want to worry. It wouldn't help Nancy Anne get better. She stopped practicing, closed the book, and set it on top of the refrigerator.

Roseanna hurried in with Mary. "Momma, can we have some juice?"

"Jah, there's apple cider in the refrigerator." Karen stood and got her daughters their drinks.

"Mmm . . . this juice is good." Roseanna licked her lips.

Mary wiped her mouth with her dainty hand. "Das gut, Mamm."

"Apple juice is good, and it's healthy for you, too." Karen smiled and got Nancy Anne from the playpen.

Roseanna took another sip of her juice. "Momma, when can I go to school?"

"When you are six years old before school

starts again next fall." Karen sat down at the table with Nancy Anne. She playfully bounced the baby on her knee. "That's less than a year away." Karen shook her head. "Jah, Roseanna, you'll have fun learning new things."

She nodded.

"I talked to Rachelle yesterday. We'll be going over there today to visit." Karen looked at her daughters.

"I'd like to do that." Roseanna finished her drink.

Mary drank her juice then set the cup down. "Ash, *kumme?*"

"Sure, we can use our new horse Ash to come along today." Karen stood with the baby. "Let me take care of Nancy Anne first. You two can put your cups in the sink and bring in your bubble stuff. Then you'll need to get ready." She headed out of the kitchen.

Karen couldn't wait to go over to her friend's place. Seth wasn't going to be home this evening. He'd gone hunting with Mike and wouldn't be back until sometime tomorrow. Karen nursed Nancy Anne and put her in a fresh diaper. She made sure she had everything her daughters might need. Karen looked forward to a visit with Rachelle and knew their children would enjoy playing together.

■ ■ ■ ■

Seth was thrilled with Karen's positive attitude about him going hunting and getting out of the house. He needed some "guy time" that wasn't work related. Seth was geared up to go hunting with Mike and hoped he'd get his prize to bring home. They'd arrived after work and set up camp. Seth still had the issue of their baby's deafness to deal with, as well as Karen's occasional moodiness over missing her family, but he hoped to gain some perspective while he was here. Since Seth had Friday and Saturday off, he could enjoy this hunting break.

He and Mike walked into an area, watching and listening for signs of pheasant. They crouched, and Mike set his firearm down beside him. He put his hand in his jacket pocket and pulled out a small bag of jerky. "Would you like some?" He held the open end toward Seth.

"All right, I could use a snack." He grabbed a couple of pieces.

So far things were quiet, and the men talked low, hoping their prey would show themselves.

Seth stuck his hand into a deep front

pocket and pulled out a bottle of water. "I think this is a good way to spend a Friday after work."

"I can't argue with that." Mike took a drink from his canteen.

Seth stood up slowly and looked around the vast meadow. A small creek fed the area. He reached for the binoculars around his neck and looked through them for a while.

"I've gotten birds here before, and maybe we both will come home with something to show for our time today." Mike stood and glanced around, too. "Well, do you see anything?"

"So far I haven't." Seth continued to look through the binoculars.

Mike walked over and took a seat at the base of a tree. "I'm gonna take a load off."

"Go ahead. I might join you in a bit." He continued scanning the area, but eventually he joined Mike under the tree. Seth reached into another pocket and pulled out a bag full of popcorn. Mike worked on more jerky but took a handful after Seth offered it to him. They sat shooting the breeze and snacking.

"I hope those steaks I've got in the cooler will be good." Mike stared straight ahead.

"They will be. With the highs today in the fifties, the heat from the outdoor grill this evening will feel good."

"The meat will smell good, too." Mike folded up the jerky bag and crammed it in his pocket.

Minutes later, Seth heard the call of a pheasant and jumped up. Mike leaped to his feet, too.

"I hope there are a couple running together for us." Mike looked around.

Seth grabbed his binoculars again and began combing the landscape.

"Anything so far?" Mike's voice elevated. "I should've remembered to grab my field glasses from the trailer before we left camp."

"Nothing yet. I'll keep looking." Seth stepped forward. "I hope it shows itself soon."

Seth waited with patience as time ticked on. Then another call rang out from a different direction. Soon Seth saw movement out near a fir tree. He pointed and gave Mike his binoculars to take a look.

"I see it over there. Here's your field glasses back, Seth. I'm gonna try and get 'em." Mike pulled his firearm up close to line up the site. Then the shot echoed through the meadow.

Another bird scared out of hiding flew into the air. Seth took his turn and fired at it. The feathers flew when he hit his pheasant. The men looked at each other, smiling as they started walking toward their targets.

"Well, let's see how I did." Seth kept walking a ways. His shot had gone farther out, closer to the creek.

Mike walked and then stopped, glancing around for a moment. "Hey!" He held up his prize. "What do you think?"

"Very nice!" Seth shouted then started walking again. He'd reached the spot where he thought the bird had dropped. Puzzled, Seth walked around for a bit.

His friend, carrying his bird, walked toward Seth. Mike soon pointed to the ground. "Your pheasant's right here."

"You're kidding." Seth shook his head and chuckled. "In the excitement I lost my focus."

"It don't matter because you've caught a nice-sized pheasant." Mike laughed. "This one I'm holding might look good stuffed and sitting in my den at home."

"I might do that one of these days, but mine will be supper." He picked up his bird and looked at it. "Well, what do you think? Should we take these back to camp?"

"Might as well. I can fire up the heater in the trailer then get the grill started." Mike started strolling back to camp.

Seth walked along with him, glad he'd

come this weekend. He couldn't wait to eat and relax this evening.

When they got back to camp, Mike got things going. He started up the heater in the trailer and then set up the portable grill on his tailgate.

Seth grabbed the folding chairs from the truck bed and set them near the warming grill.

"I'm gonna give my wife a quick call before I start cooking the steaks." Mike slipped into the cab of his pickup, while Seth sat in one of the chairs, nibbling on the remainder of his popcorn.

Mike emerged a few minutes later, putting his cell phone back in his pocket. "After I was done talking to Jane my phone buzzed again. It was Stan. He's out here hunting, too."

"He is?" Seth froze.

"Yep. I invited him here for a steak and to chat. He'll be here pretty soon." Mike went to the cooler sitting by the trailer, pulled out the steaks, and prepped them for the grill.

Seth's lips pressed together in a slight grimace. Of all the people to be coming for supper. *I wish now I'd decided to keep quiet about coming back to camp so soon.* Fidgeting, he fisted his hands. *I shouldn't be think-*

ing such thoughts — especially after deciding I should respond to Stan in a more positive way.

While the steaks sizzled on the grill, Seth's appetite increased. Karen had made a huge macaroni salad the day before for Seth to take up camping. About twenty minutes later, a car pulled in. Sure enough, it was Stan dressed in hunting clothes.

Mike was grilling when Stan walked up and shook his hand. "Well, you made it."

"Yep. It wasn't difficult to find you. Your directions were easy." Stan came over and sat by Seth.

"How's it going out here?" Stan turned and glanced at Mike. Then he reached into his jacket and pulled out his pack of cigarettes. Soon he was puffing away.

Seth squirmed in his seat but remained quiet. He would not let Stan get under his skin this evening.

"Not bad, but the temperature is beginning to drop." Mike stayed by the grill. "How do you guys like your steaks cooked?"

Stan's smoke kept drifting over to Seth. Finally, he got up, went to the cooler, and lifted the lid. "I like mine with some pink in the middle."

Stan puffed on his cigarette. "I like mine

276

sort of rare, Mike. What's in the cooler, Seth?"

Seth reached in and pulled out bottled water for himself. "There's soda and bottled water. Which would you like?"

Stan rolled his eyes. "There's no beer in that cooler?"

"Nope." Seth grabbed the cold salad and took it over to the tailgate.

"I guess I'll have a soda." Stan rose and sauntered to the cooler.

"I'll get you a chair, Mike." Seth reached into the back of the pickup.

"That'll be great. Here's the utensils for eating and a spoon for the macaroni." Mike plopped a steak on a plate. "Here, Stan. This one is yours."

Stan finished his cigarette and put it out. Then he got his steak. "Thank you." He took his drink and food back to his chair.

"Ours will be ready in a few more minutes." Mike set the spatula down.

"So, how did you two do hunting today?" Stan cut a piece out of his steak.

"We each have a pheasant in that old cooler filled with ice." Mike pointed to it.

Stan forked some salad into his mouth. "I'll have to take a look at them before I go."

"How'd you do hunting?" Seth took a seat

in the chair he'd just set out.

"Well, I heard some pheasant, but I couldn't see them." Stan wolfed down his salad and got back up to spoon more onto his plate. "I should've had a pair of binoculars."

Mike picked up the spatula and flipped the steaks again. Grabbing a knife, he cut into one and looked at it. Then he did the same with the other steak. "Okay, Seth. Ours are ready to go." Mike put the meat on the plate.

Seth rose and got his food. "Thanks, Mike." After returning to his seat, he bowed his head for silent prayer.

When Seth opened his eyes, he caught Stan staring at him.

"Hey man, were you praying?"

"Yes, I always pray before meals."

Stan pushed his food around on his plate. "Each to his own, I guess." He finished the rest of his macaroni salad and got up for thirds. "I must say this salad is quite tasty."

"Yes, it is," Mike agreed. "Seth's wife made it."

Seth cut into the meat and forked a piece into his mouth. *I can't believe how the day turned out. I'd planned on enjoying this steak and my wife's salad then relaxing with a full stomach this evening. That doesn't look too promising.*

When they arrived at Rachelle's place, another buggy was there. Karen wondered who it belonged to as she got out and secured the horse. Then she helped the girls down and grabbed the diaper bag with her purse. Karen realized as she knocked on the front door that the rig belonged to Rachelle's mom, Doris.

When the door opened, Doris answered. "Come on in, Karen. Hello, girls. How are you?"

"We're fine." Roseanna smiled up at her.

Mary gave a sheepish grin, holding Big Ears close to her.

"Hi, Karen. Come on in." Rachelle gave her a hug. "By the way, I've made a big pot of chili for supper, and we've made plenty of corn bread batter. The pans are filled and ready to go into the oven when it's time."

"Oh, Karen, you and the children must stay for supper. We'll need help eating all this food," Doris insisted.

"Well, since Seth won't be home this evening due to his hunting trip, why not?"

"Good." Rachelle smiled. "Do you need help bringing in anything?"

"If you could take Nancy Anne for me, I'll go get her playpen."

"Okay." Rachelle held out her arms to take the baby.

Soon, Karen had brought in the playpen and set it up where Rachelle suggested. Then she went out to the buggy, unhooked Ash, and led him into the barn so he could eat and drink.

Karen hoped Seth was having a nice time hunting. He needed a break and deserved this time for himself. If he did get a pheasant on this trip, they'd take it in to their meat locker to store in the deep freezer.

Karen sat down to enjoy her visit with Rachelle and her mother.

"Rachelle told me about your daughter's condition," Doris said. "I know a Mennonite woman who used to teach signing at the public school. Her name's Pam Miller, and she doesn't live too far out of Dauphin County."

Rachelle looked at her. "You've mentioned going to quilting bees with her."

"Yes, that's right. The group meets twice a month. We sure can turn out some wonderful-looking bed throws." Doris put her foot up on a vacant kitchen chair.

"I've been trying to learn signing on my own by looking through library books and practicing here and there." Karen fiddled with a spoon lying on the table.

"Let me call her and get things rolling, if you'd like. I'd be happy to introduce you to her. Maybe something can be worked out where she could help you learn to sign." Doris smiled and pushed a hairpin back in place.

They visited for an hour, and then Rachelle suggested setting up a card table for the kids to sit at during supper. Once Karen and Rachelle got the table and folding chairs arranged, Doris quickly set the table. Rachelle popped the corn bread into the oven, and Karen cut some veggies. The big pot of chili smelled good as it simmered on the burner.

The *clip-clop* of a horse and buggy came up the driveway.

"That would be James." Rachelle gave the chili a stir and looked out the window.

Karen helped the ladies get the rest of the things on the table for supper. *I hope the Mennonite woman agrees to see me. But would she have the time to help or want to teach a stranger? And will Seth support my plan and get involved, too?*

CHAPTER 9

After breakfast Karen cleared the table and put Nancy Anne in her playpen. The little girl, now sitting up on her own, clasped a cloth doll in her chubby little hands.

A wave of nausea washed over Karen. She'd felt this way since she first got up and had barely eaten any of her cereal or toast. Swallowing against the bile rising in her throat, Karen grabbed an umbrella and went out the front door. She strode through the rain to the phone shack, needing to hear any messages that may have come in this morning. She'd been to her doctor over a week ago. He'd talked with Karen and checked her vitals, ruling out the flu. Then he'd sent her over for lab work to confirm a possible pregnancy. The nausea was continuing, and Karen was beginning to think the doctor could be right.

The rain fell harder, and the clap of thunder made her thankful for the shelter of the little cubical. Karen sat on the stool and rested her finger on the button to start the messages. *My world might be changing in a moment.* Karen fidgeted, while insecurities toyed with her nerves.

Gathering her courage, she pressed the button. The first message was a carpet-cleaning service. "Well, that won't do me any good." Karen let out a brief laugh, as the voice talked on. The next message was from the doctor's office. The receptionist said the pregnancy test was positive. "Congratulations to you and your husband. Call us if you have any questions. Have a nice day."

Karen's hand flew to her chest. Even the pelting of the rain on the metal shed wasn't registering. She sat trying to absorb the news. Opening the door, she stared at the rain drumming on the ground. "I better hurry and get the mail from the box." She slammed the door, dashed to retrieve the letters, and ran to the house. Once up on the porch, she shook the water off the mail.

Roseanna opened the front door for her. "I saw you running, Momma. You're wet."

Karen removed her soaked tennis shoes and placed the umbrella in its stand.

Mary sat on the bottom of the stairs looking through her picture book. "You're wet," she repeated.

"Thank you for watching out for me." Karen set the mail on the coffee table. "It's raining cats and dogs out there."

Mary jumped up and darted toward the front window. She climbed onto the couch and looked out. "Where are the *katze* and *hund?*"

"Just kidding, Mary. It's only a saying, little one, not real cats and dogs." Karen stood next to her and watched the rain falling. "I'm going to go change into a dry dress."

Before Karen left the room she looked at the playpen and saw that Nancy Anne was asleep. Her daughter's soothing, rhythmic breathing caused her to linger. She brought her hand up to the wet scarf and realized she still needed to change.

After putting on a clean dress, Karen felt driven by her unsettled emotions to find comfort in the guest room. Wrapping herself in her mother's quilt, she began to relax. *I'm going to have another baby. . . . How am I gonna make it work?* She lowered her head into her cupped hands and wept. *Oh, Momma, I need you so much.*

Karen drew in a deep breath and dried her eyes. Pam Miller, the Mennonite woman, and Doris would be dropping by today at one o'clock, so she needed to pull herself together. Karen still wanted to tidy the kitchen, since she'd left things on hold to check phone messages. She left the guest room and hurried down the hall.

As Karen stood at the sink rinsing bowls and cups, she heard Nancy Anne fussing. She dried her hands and went to the nursery. Nancy Anne held out her arms. "Let's check your diaper first." Karen peeked. "Jah, you need a change."

"Hi, Nancy Anne." Roseanna came in and stood by them.

"Boppli Anne." Mary followed her sister in.

"We wore diapers once." Roseanna looked up at her mom.

Mary nodded, smiling at her baby sister.

"Jah, you both used to wear windel. Now you are too big and growing up fast before my eyes." Karen finished with the diaper change and picked up the baby. "Let's go to the kitchen."

After the dishes were washed, dried, and put away, Karen heated some water on the stove for a cup of tea. She also clicked on the oven to bake some cookies for her guests. Her nausea had kicked up again, like at breakfast. Karen grabbed a peppermint tea bag and set it in her mug.

Roseanna sat at the table, drawing a picture of their buggy horses. Mary played with a few of her stuffed toys on the table. Karen sipped her tea, and Nancy Anne entertained herself with a toy dog, sitting up well in her playpen.

"I'm going to shake out the rugs here in the room, and I will need your help, Roseanna." Karen got up and motioned to her.

"Okay, Mom." Roseanna set her pencil aside and came over to Karen.

"Let's get these two." She grabbed one and her daughter grabbed the other.

They stepped outside in the drenched grass and shook out the rugs. Karen looked up and noticed the horses in the coral staring toward the pasture. Soon, she caught sight of what was going on. A lone coyote was running along the back of their field fence.

"Look, Roseanna, out by the farthest fence." Karen held the throw rug under her arm and pointed toward the animal.

"What's that?" Roseanna stared at it.

"It's a coyote, and normally you don't see them out much during the daytime. Usually they're shy or afraid to be seen." Karen watched the animal run, until it slipped under the wire fence and disappeared into the tall field grass.

"It looks like a dog." Roseanna turned to her.

Karen gave the rug another shake. "Yes, it does. Coyotes usually go after rodents and also wild rabbits. But they can be a nuisance to our small animals like chickens, cats, and bunnies, like our Star."

Roseanna gasped and looked toward the rabbit's cage. "I hope it doesn't get Star."

"We'll let your daed know about this when he gets home tonight." Karen motioned for her daughter to go back into the house.

They brought out two more kitchen rugs and then took care of the front-door runner. When they'd finished putting the mats back in place, Karen and Roseanna washed their hands.

"I'm going to get the cookies started." Karen got out the refrigerated chocolate chip dough that she'd made up last night.

Roseanna went back to drawing her picture. Mary played with her toys. Karen added more hot water to her peppermint tea. It seemed like this bout of nausea was stronger than when she was carrying Nancy Anne. Karen wished her mother was around to comfort her. The news of her pregnancy was bittersweet.

Karen sipped some tea then put cookie sheets, the dough, and a few spoons on the table by the girls. "Who'd like to help me bake cookies?"

Both girls nodded.

Karen stuck the teaspoon into the dough and lifted the desired amount onto her spoon. "We need about that much." She popped it on the sheet.

Roseanna gave it a try. She used her fingers to get it off the spoon and onto the pan.

"You're doing a good job. Keep going." Karen helped Mary scoop out the cold chocolate chip dough then tap the spoon on the tray.

"Mary, you're getting the hang of it. Soon you'll be doing this all by yourself." Karen patted her daughter's arm.

In no time, the pan went into the oven, and they filled another one. The girls went back to playing, while Karen sipped her tea. When the first pan of cookies came out, Roseanna and Mary each sampled a couple with a cup of milk. Once the cookies were all baked, Karen divided them in half, some to freeze, the others to eat.

She took care of Nancy Anne's needs and then rocked her for a little while before starting lunch. Karen thought about Seth and hoped he was having a good day. He'd sure been happy about bringing home a pheasant from his hunting trip, but his good mood didn't last. Seth was back to moping around the house again.

Karen glanced at the wall clock. It was time to get lunch. She set Nancy Anne in the playpen and got out the stuff for sandwiches. When everything was laid out on the table, Karen put Nancy Anne in her high chair, while Roseanna and Mary took their seats. When they'd finished silent praying, they began to eat.

Karen fed the baby and nibbled on the sandwich half she'd made for herself. *This nausea is awful. I wish it would let up. I'm eating more crackers these days than anything else. And tonight I'll have to tell Seth what the doctor's office reported.*

Shortly after the lunch dishes had been taken care of, a blue car pulled up to the house. Karen watched Doris climb out. A petite, gray-haired woman with glasses came around the car, and the women headed to the door.

Karen waited for a knock then opened the door to let them in. "Hello, Doris."

"Hi, Karen." Doris hugged her. "This is my dear friend Pam Miller."

"Hello." Pam smiled and hugged her, too. "Doris has filled me in on Nancy Anne. Is this the little girl?"

"Jah, this is her." She paused. "Let's go have a seat in the living room." Karen led the way.

Her daughters stood near the top of the steps.

Doris nudged Pam's arm and pointed up to the girls. "The oldest is Roseanna, and the younger one is her sister Mary. "Hello, girls, how are you doing today?"

Roseanna smiled. "We're fine."

Mary hung in close to her sister, not saying a word.

Karen held Nancy Anne in her lap, and the two ladies took their seats. "Would you like some tea?" she offered.

The women smiled and nodded.

Karen placed the baby on a blanket on the floor. A few minutes later, she brought out their tea and some fresh-baked cookies on a pretty floral tray. "Here are some napkins. Can I get you ladies anything else?"

The two women shook their heads.

Doris took a sip of her tea and set the cup down. "Pam and I have talked about Nancy Anne. She said she'd try and help you."

Pam cleared her throat. "Nancy Anne is a little young yet, as far as learning to sign, I mean. I can help you with questions you might have, however. Also, I'll leave you my number in case you think of more questions to ask."

Karen leaned forward. "I've been trying to teach myself some signing from the library books I checked out."

"That's good. It's important to be able to communicate with your daughter." She bit into a cookie.

"It's so overwhelming." Karen sighed.

"As your daughter gains finger dexterity, she'll be able to start learning the art of signing. I like to call it an art because it's like when the ladies hula dance in Hawaii. They, too, are speaking with their graceful hand movements, telling stories with music." Pam sipped her tea.

The ladies visited for a while, and when they left, Karen felt better. Now she had Pam to fall back on for help, along with the specialist in Harrisburg. She picked up Nancy Anne. "We've got a lot of ground to cover in your future, but I'll stick by you." Karen hugged her precious little girl. Maybe this was a sign that God could help her deal with these situations without her mom close by.

Seth rode home with Mike. The last two days, they'd been working a lot farther away on a big job. He felt exhausted and couldn't wait to get home. The squeaks and other sounds from Mike's truck made Seth feel like he could doze off. It cruised along for miles, and the sky was beginning to darken. A jackrabbit darted into the road, and Mike swerved to avoid it.

"Whoa!" Mike jerked the wheel back after missing the critter.

"Whew, that was close!" Seth rubbed his eyes. "I sometimes miss living in Bird-in-Hand."

"You do? That's the first time you've mentioned it to me."

"I've been thinking about it lately, that's all." Seth reached for his bottle of water and drank the rest of it.

"What has you missing your home?"

"Just some things right now." Seth opened his lunch box and put his empty bottle inside.

"It's okay if you don't want to give me details. But you've shared about your baby's problem with not hearing. At work I've noticed that you seem more frustrated working with Stan. But since you don't have seniority over anyone other than Stan, the boss will probably keep working you two together." Mike glanced in his direction.

Seth said nothing.

"But you are a levelheaded man from

292

what I've seen, and you'll work this out for the best."

After dinner, Seth took a cup of coffee out to the living room. He sat there rocking and mulling things over. Realizing he still hadn't fed and watered the animals, he took one more sip of his coffee then called Roseanna from the kitchen.

"What, Daed?" She dashed into the room and came over to him.

"Let's you and I go out and check on the animals. I'm pretty tired this evening, and I could use a good helper like you." Seth looked down at her.

Roseanna nodded.

Seth let Karen know what they were up to. First they went to the barn and checked on the horses. Millie and Ash both whinnied, stomping in their stalls. Seth grabbed hay, while his daughter brought over some sweet oats to put in with it. He watered the horses and watched Roseanna give the barn cats their food and water. It reminded him of when he was a boy helping his dad. He continued to observe as she sat on a bale of hay, stroking one of the cats. It meowed and rubbed its head under Roseanna's chin.

"I'm done watering the horses. Let's take care of your rabbit." Seth shut off the hose and adjusted his straw hat that had slipped into his eyes.

Roseanna got up and followed her dad to the cage.

Seth blinked. "That little stinker got out again. I can't believe it."

"Where is he?" Roseanna's eyes seeped with tears.

They both looked all around for Star but came up empty.

"I'm sorry he's missing." Seth knelt down and hugged his daughter.

"I'm afraid the coyote will get him," she cried.

"No, he's a smart rabbit, and Star is an escape artist who likes to explore." He wiped her tears.

"I hope he comes back."

"Praying about it will help," Seth replied.

A half hour later, they returned to the house and went to the bathroom to wash their hands. Seth noticed that Karen was staring off into space as she dried the dishes.

When he and Roseanna had cleaned up, they both went to the living room and sat on the sofa. Mary came downstairs and walked over to Nancy Anne's playpen. Seth and Roseanna watched the baby smile at her older sister. Mary made Big Ears dance up and down inside the playpen, and Nancy

Anne started laughing. Then she went into a deep belly laugh, and Seth couldn't help laughing, too. The baby's laughter was contagious. Even Karen came out and watched Mary playing with Nancy Anne. Everyone was laughing at the goings-on. *I wish there were more days like these.* He grinned. *Lord knows I could use more joy in my life.*

Seth looked at his wife as her smile faded. Then she retreated back into the kitchen.

"Why don't you girls go upstairs and play?" Seth grabbed his coffee cup. Once his daughters were headed upstairs, Seth joined Karen in the kitchen, where she sat at the table. He poured himself a fresh cup of coffee and took a seat across from her. "What's up? You've been acting funny since I got home."

Karen shifted in her seat and avoided his eyes. "I got news from the doctor's office this morning."

"Well . . . We know that you don't have the flu. So what were the results of the blood work?" Seth leaned forward.

"We're having another baby." Karen looked away.

"I kinda figured, the way you've been feeling lately." His jaw clenched as he shook his head. "I'm glad what you've been dealing with isn't something serious. But this isn't the right time for another baby." He heaved a heavy sigh. "You have no idea how bad things are for me at work. I can't deal with this right now."

Karen stood rigidly. "I'm sorry. I can't change this. We are going to have another Allgyer boy or girl. I guess I'm gonna have to be happy enough for the both of us." She bolted from the room.

Seth lowered his head and walked over to Nancy Anne. He picked her up and held her close. He missed his folks more than ever. Sighing, he walked down the hall to check on his wife. When he reached the closed door of their guest room, he could hear Karen inside crying. Seth closed his eyes. *Lord, please show me how to fix things.*

CHAPTER 10

Town City, Pennsylvania

Seth spent the morning working with Ervin on a new house, and because they were the only men on the job site, they could speak Pennsylvania Dutch freely. Seth helped Ervin get materials ready for installing the walkways around the house. He enjoyed working with Ervin, who'd been with this business for seven years.

An order of blocks was due to be delivered by truck before lunch. Seth got the wheelbarrow loads going for gravel to fill in empty and low areas. Ervin started up the gaspowered machine for packing down the small rock and made the job look easy. Seth's coworker also knew the design pattern for the pavers the homeowner wanted.

It was about lunchtime when Mike drove up. "Let's take a break," he called. "I'll take you men for lunch at that deli in town."

Ervin set his stuff aside and made sure

things were locked up. "I'm ready to go. How about you, Seth?" He waited by the front door.

Seth put his Thermos and his untouched lunch box in the truck. "Okay, now I'm ready."

After they'd gotten in, Mike turned to Seth. "I heard through the grapevine that it's your birthday. I'll be buying your lunch."

Seth wiped at his brow. "Thank you, Mike. That's great."

"What are your plans after work?" Mike started the truck.

"I'm looking forward to going out with my family for pizza." Seth grinned.

Ervin removed his hat to smooth back some wayward hair. "It's hard to believe that Thanksgiving will be coming up soon."

"Will your folks be in town today or tomorrow?" Mike pulled away from the job site.

"No, they can't make it." Seth's shoulders slumped, and he stared down at his hands. "I've gotten some nice cards from both my family and Karen's. I'll check the phone messages when I get home to see if my folks have called. I could sure use some cheer today. Maybe my gift to myself will make it better — when it gets here, that is."

■ ■ ■ ■

After lunch Mike told Seth he'd be working with Stan the rest of the day. Seth couldn't help wishing he was going back with Ervin to work, but Mike was only following the boss's orders. Seth wondered if Stan would ever be easier to deal with. Stan seemed to constantly challenge him and do things the way he thought they should be done, not how they were told to do them. This made it doubly hard for Seth to keep a positive attitude toward the man.

The afternoon went exactly how Seth expected it would. Stan insisted on doing everything his own way and carried on a nonstop conversation about things unrelated to the job. And of course Stan smoked one cigarette after the other.

Near the end of the day, Seth felt like he'd been through his wife's wringer washing machine. He was relieved to look at his pocket watch and see it was almost time to start picking things up.

As Stan was getting ready to come down from the scaffold, he leaned back against the safety rail. It gave way. The next thing Seth knew, his coworker was lying on the ground.

Instinct kicked in, and he ran over to Stan and dropped to his knees beside him. "Are you okay?"

Gasping for breath, Stan tried to sit up.

"Don't move. Just lie still." Seth placed his hand on Stan's shoulder. "I'll call for help."

Seth raced to the truck, grabbed Stan's cell phone, and called 911.

Minutes later, Mike came by in his own rig to pick up Seth. After quickly explaining what happened, Seth returned to Stan's side while they waited for the paramedics to arrive.

Lykens

As they approached his driveway, Seth asked Mike to pull up to the phone shed. He waved good-bye to Mike and took a seat in the shed. Seth listened to messages mostly from family leaving nice birthday wishes. When Seth listened to his parents' message, a lump formed in his throat. He called them back, letting the phone ring for a while, and was surprised when his dad picked up.

"Hello." His father paused.

"Hi, Dad. It's me, Seth. I'm glad you answered, but I didn't think you'd be right there in your phone shack."

Dad chuckled. "I bet you called to thank me and your mom for the birthday wishes."

"Uh, jah. Danki."

"You're welcome, son. Have you, Karen, and my grandchildren planned anything for the evening?" His dad's deep voice boomed through the receiver.

Seth let out a breath. "We're supposed to be going for pizza."

"That sounds real nice. Tell Karen and the children we miss you all."

"Thanks, Dad." Seth sat quiet for a moment.

"Are you still there, Seth?" his father inquired.

"Yes . . ."

"What's up, Son?"

"An accident occurred at work today. One of the guys fell when part of the scaffold gave way."

"Wow! Was he seriously hurt?"

"His lungs collapsed. He's receiving good care at the hospital, but he'll be off from work for several weeks." Seth shifted on the chair. "My boss and I stayed with Stan at the hospital until his wife arrived and we learned that his injury wasn't life threatening." He swallowed hard. "This is the same fellow that's been giving me so much trouble at work."

"Sounds like you did the right thing. I'm proud of you, Son." Dad cleared his throat. "How's everything else going?"

"With Karen being in a family way again, she seems pretty overwhelmed." Seth groaned. "I can't seem to help Karen enough, and we don't always communicate very well these days."

"Your mother and I have been through similar situations, and we came to realize the importance of good communication and supporting each other through difficult times rather than turning away and focusing on our own pain."

"You're right. I need to work on that, so thanks for the reminder."

"We'll be praying for you. Remember, Seth, the Lord only gives us what He thinks we can handle. He'll help you through this." Dad cleared his throat again. "Have you been reading the Word and praying, Seth?"

He closed his eyes tightly as a tear slipped out. "No. I . . . I've been neglecting to do those things."

"Oh, Seth, you need to make prayer a priority, Son. We've taught all you kids to pray each and every day," his dad reminded.

Seth sighed. "I'll try to."

"I'm glad that I could get to the phone in time when you called." Dad coughed. "You really needed to talk about this and be honest with yourself about what's happening."

"I'm happy that I could unburden my heart; thanks, Dad." Seth shifted in his chair.

"Just pray, Son, for the Lord's help and direction through this difficult time. I will talk to your mamm, too. She needs to know what's happening so we can both be praying for all of your needs."

"Thank you again, Dad." Seth sniffed. "I'll let you get back to what you were doing."

"Okay, have a nice time with your family, and don't eat too much." He chuckled. "Have a happy birthday. 'Bye, Son."

"All right. 'Bye, Dad." Seth clicked off the phone.

As he walked up to the house, he noticed a package on the front porch step. When he got to it, he found it was exactly what he thought. He'd ordered a fancy rifle for his birthday and hadn't said anything to Karen about the purchase.

He grabbed the package and sneaked out to the barn to keep it hidden, not wanting to get her upset. Seth looked over at where he and Roseanna had spotted Star this morning. They were relieved to catch the little escape artist and put the rabbit back into the cage. Roseanna had been excited that God had answered her prayers.

Seth pulled the buggy out of the barn and laid out Ash's harness gear. Then he picked up his lunch pail and Thermos before going back to the house. He still needed to get ready for their supper out. After speaking with his dad, his day was looking a bit better.

A few minutes later, Seth was ready to go and simply waiting for Karen and the two older girls to be ready to go. He smiled, watching Nancy Anne sitting on a throw rug, playing with some pots and pans. Seth leaned over, and scooping his growing daughter into his arms, he held her high over his head and made silly faces. Soon Nancy Anne was giggling at him, and Seth began laughing, too. He brought her down against his chest and noticed a couple of presents on the kitchen table. Seth wandered over to snoop. As he suspected, one was from his wife and another wrapped package was from his daughters.

"What are you up to, Seth?" Karen came into the kitchen.

"Mostly playing with Nancy Anne — making her laugh."

"I'm ready to go, and the girls should be soon. I asked them to change into their green dresses. I'll check the baby, and then we should be ready to go." Karen held out her hands to take Nancy Anne.

Seth passed the baby over. "I'll get Ash ready and pull the buggy over to the hitching rail."

Karen nodded and headed with Nancy Anne to the nursery.

When Karen and the girls exited the house, Seth and Ash were waiting for them. Karen placed Nancy Anne in her carrier next to the girls in the back of the buggy and helped Seth get the horse clipped to the forks. Then they climbed in and started for town.

"Not a bad day to get out of the house." He leaned closer to his wife.

"It's Daddy's birthday today!" Roseanna yelled.

"Yippee, Daed!" Mary shouted.

"Happy birthday, Husband." Karen leaned against his shoulder for a moment.

"Danki." Seth looked at his wife. "I'm glad I captured Star in the barn this morning. Actually, the sweet oats that spilled on the ground kept the little guy enticed. He was quite easy to catch. Right, Roseanna?" Seth turned his head in her direction.

"Jah, he let Dad get him. I'm glad we have Star back."

"Me, too! Me, too!" Mary shouted and

bounced, holding on to Big Ears.

"I talked to Mike today about maybe going wild turkey hunting this time. What do you think?" Seth shook the reins to speed up Ash. They passed some people from their church district out walking along the road and waved.

"If you'd like to go, that's fine with me. We still need to eat the pheasant in our meat locker. When deer hunting season starts, some venison would be nice to have for suppers this winter. Maybe we could give some to the folks, too."

"I'm sorry I didn't eat the food you prepared for me this morning," Seth said, "but Mike treated me for lunch since it's my birthday."

"That was nice of him. Where did he take you, and what did you have?" Karen gave the baby a bottle of water to tide her over.

"We went to the deli there in Town City and ate turkey sandwiches at one of their tables. They were good. I'd eat there again." Seth licked his lips.

A bit later, they pulled into the pizza parking lot, and Seth secured the horse. Then the entire family headed in for their supper. The aroma of baking pizza welcomed them and made Seth's stomach growl.

"Let's take these seats." Karen pointed to

a table for six.

"Looks good to me. Okay, girls, find a chair."

Karen held Nancy Anne in her lap. Roseanna sat by Seth, and Mary sat next to her mother. They ordered quickly, and when the pizza arrived, they bowed their heads for silent prayer. Seth passed slices to the girls and Karen. She'd brought baby food for Nancy Anne. It was nice to see his wife eating well and Seth fervently hoped her morning sickness was behind her. Seth wished he could help her to have better days.

Karen cleared her throat and wiped off her hand with the napkin. "Sometime in the near future we'll have to think about moving Nancy Anne in with her sisters."

Roseanna tilted her head. "Why, Mom?"

Karen looked over at Seth. "Because our family is growing."

"One of these days," Seth added, "when you're ready, Roseanna, you can have your own room." Seth took a bite of his pizza.

Her eyes grew big. "My own room someday? Hmmm . . ."

"It's something to think about, right?" He took a drink of his soda pop.

"Yes, Dad." Roseanna drank some cola.

■ ■ ■ ■

After supper when everyone was settled at home, Karen called them to the kitchen. The beautiful cake she had baked and decorated was ready for serving, complete with lit candles. Karen, Roseanna, and Mary sang "Happy Birthday," and Karen served slices of cake with ice cream. Everyone bowed their heads in prayer, and then they dove in.

"Mmm . . . Good cake, Karen." Seth took another bite. "I enjoy your German chocolate. It's my favorite."

Karen looked at Roseanna, delighting in her piece, while little Mary picked the cake away from the frosting. "I think someone doesn't embrace the coconut and pecan icing."

"It's okay, my mamm isn't into it, either, but my daed loves it like me." Seth spooned vanilla ice cream into his mouth.

It was nice seeing Seth looking happy. Too bad every day couldn't be this special. Karen rested her fork on her plate. "Are you ready for your gifts?"

"I sure am."

"Yay, Daddy." Roseanna took a bite of her ice cream.

Mary bounced in her seat with some cake on her spoon.

Seth reached over and grabbed the girls' presents. "Look at these. Who made the nice pictures?"

"It's Millie and Ash. I made it for you." Roseanna's eyes twinkled. "Mary drew a picture of Star."

Next Seth unwrapped a bag of candy. "What's this? Who remembered these are my particular favorite?"

"Mom did." Roseanna giggled, looking up at her dad.

Mary got out of her seat and climbed into Seth's lap.

"I forgot your favorite candy," Roseanna admitted. "Mom helped us."

"Thank you guys for my birthday gifts." Seth hugged his daughters. "Well, I still have another gift to open, don't I?"

Karen nodded. "Jah, it's my turn." She pushed the present toward him. "Open this one."

He set Mary on the floor. "Go take your seat and eat some of the ice-cream soup you now have." He looked over at Karen and winked.

Seth unwrapped the gift from her. It was a new western novel he'd mentioned he wanted. Then he looked inside the package again and found a couple of new shirts and trousers. "I've been needing these for sure. Thank you." Seth went over and hugged her.

"You're welcome." Karen rose. "It's time to put our dishes in the sink."

"Come on, Mary. Let's take care of our bowls." Roseanna waited for her sister to climb off her chair.

Nancy Anne was in the playpen in the living room, and Karen took a seat in the rocker and watched Seth light a fire for some added heat, since the evenings were cooling off. She enjoyed watching the fire grow brighter. Soon its brilliant glow and the dancing flames lit up the room.

"It's nice having the fireplace warming us up again." Karen rocked in her chair.

Seth took a seat. "The fire is pretty to watch, and it's relaxing. I wonder if the English ever stop to enjoy life's simple pleasures like this."

Soon the girls came bounding in and flopped onto the couch. They sat quietly with their toys, looking at the fire.

Seth pulled out his pocket watch then gestured to Roseanna and Mary. "It's getting late. You girls need to get ready for bed.

"After you put on your jammies, come back, and I'll help you brush your teeth," Karen interjected.

When the girls had gone upstairs, Seth faced Karen. "There's something I need to confess."

Karen tipped her head. "What is it?"

"I bought a new rifle for my birthday and was afraid to tell you about it." His voice lowered. "I hid the gun in the barn."

Karen's eyes widened. "If you wanted a new gun, why didn't you say so? We shouldn't have secrets from each other, Seth." She pressed her hands to her temples.

"You're right. What I did was wrong, and I'm sorry."

"Thank you for being honest. I forgive you." Karen clasped his hand. "Let's not have any more secrets between us. Okay?"

He nodded and gave Karen's fingers a gentle squeeze.

Karen snuggled closer to her husband, leaning her head on his shoulder. She felt pleased that things between her and Seth were improving.

CHAPTER 11

Karen couldn't wait to spend Thanksgiving with both her and Seth's families. She had made herself and the girls new dresses for the occasion. Nancy Anne looked cute in her new little dress that Karen had just tried on her. The sleeves needed to be hemmed, so while the baby wore the dress, she marked the spots with chalk. Then Karen slipped it off and went back to the sewing machine.

Mary entered the room. "Boppli Anne's *frack?*"

Karen turned toward her. "Jah, its baby Anne's dress. Come closer and watch me finish it."

Mary did, yawning.

"Are you getting hungry?" She ran the machine.

"Jah, Mamm." Mary looked up at Karen.

"I'm about done. Only one sleeve left to hem." She grabbed the scissors. "Then I'll get our lunch started." Karen snipped off the hanging threads. "How about we all have chocolate milk with our peanut butter and strawberry jam sandwiches?"

Mary nodded and let out another yawn.

As Karen worked, she thought about Seth's behavior — how happy he was to be going home for the holiday. He'd called the folks and lined up the driver days ago. The house was abuzz of excitement over tomorrow's trip.

Karen refocused, checking the dress over and liking the end result. "Nancy Anne's dress is done. Now, let me put some things away here, and then I'll get lunch started." Karen patted Mary's head.

As Karen went to the kitchen, she heard Roseanna singing upstairs. She got out the bread, peanut butter, and strawberry preserves.

Roseanna dashed into the room with Mary. "I'll help you, Mom."

"Thanks. Can you grab some napkins and find the chocolate syrup in the refrigerator?"

"Okay."

Karen smiled as she made up their sandwiches. She was pleased to see her daughter being so helpful at such a young age. Karen's stomach began to growl. She remembered they had some sliced cheese they could eat with crackers, so she quickly added that to the food on the table.

"I'm happy to go see my grandpas and grandmas." Roseanna's voice raised.

"Me, too! Me, too!" Mary hopped around, bumping into her sister's arm.

The unlidded new bottle of chocolate syrup Roseanna held hit the floor and bounced.

Mary looked at Karen with teary eyes. "*Ich leed,* Mamm."

"I know you are sorry, Mary. It was only an accident." Karen picked up the bottle and set it on the table. She hugged little Mary, and then they cleaned up the mess. Karen still had enough syrup for their chocolate milk.

Soon they were sitting at the table for silent prayer. When they finished, they started eating their sandwiches. Roseanna helped herself to the cheese. "When do we leave for Grandpa and Grandma's house?"

"We'll need to be ready by eight in the morning, and our suitcases need to be packed before bed this evening." Karen took a drink.

"I can't wait to go." Roseanna grinned.

Mary bounced in her chair, while Nancy Anne watched her, smiling.

Karen waited for the baby to look back, before spooning her some cereal with applesauce.

"I'll get some pecan pies going in the oven after lunch." Karen took a bite of her cheese and crackers.

Roseanna fiddled with her ponytail. "Will you make a custard pie, Mom?"

"We don't need a pie like that, do we?" Karen teased.

"Yes, you make good custard pies," Roseanna replied.

"Mmm . . . *boi.*" Mary squirmed in her seat.

"I can't say no to so much praise. I'll make a custard pie, too." She wiped Nancy Anne's face.

After lunch, Karen took care of the baby and placed her in the playpen, dropping in a bright pink teething ring and Nancy Anne's favorite light-up toy ball. She returned to the kitchen and set all the pie fixings on the counter. As she began work on the pecan pies, Roseanna wandered into the kitchen and watched her mom work.

Karen checked the time on the wall clock. "Where's Mary?"

Giggling, Roseanna confided, "She fell asleep on her bed."

"Well, she was up early this morning, and

Mary did let out a few yawns before she went upstairs."

"Can I help you, Mom? I'll dry some dishes for you." Roseanna got up and hugged her.

"That'd be very nice. There's a towel, Roseanna." Karen pointed, then filled the sink with hot, soapy water. "When I get these cleaned up, I'll start getting the custard pie ready. How does that sound?" Karen looked at Roseanna.

Her daughter nodded.

When they finished the dishes, Karen started in on the custard pie.

"I can't wait to have some when we are at Grandpa and Grandma's house," Roseanna said as she watched Karen.

"It will be nice to celebrate Thanksgiving together." She poured the custard mixture into the piecrust. Then Karen picked up the nutmeg and sprinkled it over the pie.

The timer went off and Karen checked the oven. "Mmm . . . These pecan pies look yummy." She pulled them out, setting the pie pans on hot pads.

Then Karen slid the custard pie into oven, closed the door, and set the timer again. "Now let's check on Mary, and I'll get some suitcases out of the spare bedroom for tonight's packing."

They went upstairs and found Mary still asleep on her bed. Karen grabbed a folded blanket from the foot of the bed and spread it over Mary.

Roseanna grabbed her crayon box and a couple coloring books to take to the living room. Karen stayed and picked up a few toys, then she went to the other room.

Karen brought the small suitcase in and set it on Roseanna's bed. She picked up the girls' dirty clothes from their basket and carted them to the washer. The pecan pies were still cooling on the counters, so Karen started a load of wash.

She peeked in on Nancy Anne, who was napping. The room was so comfy with the fire going. Karen decided to get a book out to read. Before opening the book, she recalled the dream she'd had that morning. Her family was still living in this house, and the dream took place on Roseanna's wedding day. Karen had walked up the stairs to present the beloved Christmas quilt to her daughter as one of Roseanna's gifts on the special day. Full of emotion, Karen had reached up to wipe at her tears. "It's yours now, Roseanna," she told the bride in her dream. "I'd like you to have it."

The book fell to the floor as Karen's thoughts returned to the present. Over the past year, her marriage had improved, their children had continued to be well-adjusted to their surroundings, and her friendships had been strengthened and provided her with important support. Suddenly Karen realized her place was with her husband right here in Lykens. Although she would always miss her parents and siblings, Lykens had become her home. Karen would wait for the right moment to tell Seth, but she no longer needed to move back to Lancaster County.

As Seth and Mike listened to the radio on the drive home, abruptly the Emergency Broadcast System came on, warning the public of approaching ice storms in the areas. The hairs on Seth's neck stood up as he continued listening to news of the impending storm.

"This isn't good to hear, but it's been so cold lately." Mike turned up the heater.

"A few drops of rain are hitting the windshield. If it starts raining more heavily, the streets will be a mess to drive on." Seth groaned. "I can't risk my family out on roads covered in sheets of ice."

"Boy, that's sure the truth. No one wants to slide into a ditch or into another driver." Mike turned on his signal and turned his truck into the driveway.

Seth opened the door and grabbed his stuff. "You have a warm, safe, and happy Thanksgiving."

"You folks have a good one, too." Mike smiled, handing Seth his Thermos.

Seth came into the kitchen, which was filled with delicious aromas. Karen sat at the table, folding napkins for supper.

"I've got a pizza casserole in the oven, green beans cooking, and a tossed salad made." Karen got up and gave him a hug.

Seth put down his lunch box and Thermos. "Hello, Karen."

"How was your day?" She smiled up at him.

"Well, it was good until I heard the weather warning for our area and up near Bird-in-Hand and Paradise." Seth frowned.

"That doesn't sound good. The girls and I have been filling our suitcases all day. I was still drying some clothes near the fireplace that I washed after lunch." Karen sighed.

"The ice storm warning is in effect starting later this evening and doesn't lift until late tomorrow. I don't think we should go." He looked out the window.

"Our daughters will be disappointed with the news. They're still upstairs getting ready." Karen popped open the oven to check on the casserole. She moved the foil away then set it back over the dish. "It's about done."

"I need to go out to the phone shed and make a few calls. First our driver, second your folks, and then my parents." Seth turned, going for a glass from the cupboard.

"I'll go upstairs and tell the girls we're staying home." Karen opened his lunch pail, pulling out a spoon and a used container.

He drank his water. "I'd better go take care of the phoning and then check on the animals."

"Okay, I'll keep dinner warming until you are back inside." Karen turned down the beans bubbling in the kettle.

When Seth headed out to the phone shed, he thought about his wife's reaction to the disappointing news. It surprised him that she had taken it so well. Was she merely putting on a brave front?

He shivered against the cold, pulling at the collar of his jacket. He dreaded making these calls. Seth wanted to go home, but the weather had changed their nice plans. He wondered how many other families were dealing with this same issue.

Seth sat in the phone shed, his head bowed in silent prayer. *Lord, give me clear direction.* He called his driver first. Mark said he was going to call Seth and suggest not making this trip because of the dangers. They agreed they should stay close to home this holiday. He called Karen's folks then his own. Both sets of parents told him to stay home, be safe, and to try to have a happy Thanksgiving.

Seth closed the shed door and lumbered to the barn as the rain sprinkled lightly. He went to the bunny's cage and opened the door. "Hey, Star, I hope you're keeping warm in this weather." Seth poured in food, topping it off.

The rabbit hopped out of the hutch within the cage and looked at him, twitching its pink nose.

"I'll be back with your water." He locked the cage door and went into the house.

Karen was holding Nancy Anne when he came through the door. The baby saw him and held out her chubby arms. "Someone misses her daed." She smiled.

Seth put the water container in the sink as he washed his hands. "I'm going to hold Nancy Anne before I go back out in the cold."

The baby held out her hands again, making little squeals of joy when he came over and took her from Karen. He heard the rumble of a buggy pulling into their driveway. Seth looked out the kitchen window, trying to see who it was.

"Who does it look like?" Karen joined him.

"It might be Rachelle's husband James by the hitching rail." Seth moved from the window and stood near the back door opening it for his friend.

James walked up to him.

"Hello," Seth greeted him. "Come in. What brings you out on a night like this?"

"Good evening to you both. I came by to invite your family over tomorrow afternoon for Thanksgiving supper." He pulled off his hat. "I figured with this storm, maybe you wouldn't try to go out of town."

Seth looked at his wife and noticed Karen's expression had brightened. "Actually, I canceled our trip after work today. It wasn't easy, but I needed to do it."

"Are you sure you have room for us tomorrow?" Karen asked. "We don't want to impose."

"We'll have plenty to eat. Rachelle and the relatives always make a lot of food." James chuckled.

"Well then, it's settled. We'll come over for Thanksgiving supper." Seth patted his friend's arm. "Thanks for inviting us."

James put on his straw hat. "Not a problem for good friends like yourselves."

"Let Rachelle know I'll bring pecan pies, and I've got a custard one, too." Karen spoke with enthusiasm.

Seth passed Nancy Anne to Karen and followed James out into the cold. "Take it easy going home. It's getting a little slippery."

James waved and untied the horse from the hitch rail. He climbed into his rig then backed out and waved again. "See you tomorrow!"

Seth came back into the house. "I need to get the rabbit's water then take care of the rest of the animals." He winked at Karen. "I'll try and hurry."

She nodded.

About a half hour later, Seth came into the warm kitchen and removed his dripping wet coat. "I'm glad to be back indoors. It's nasty out there. When I'm done washing my hands, I'll go get the girls and have them wash up, too." Seth took off his wet boots and hat then walked over to the sink.

"It was nice of James and Rachelle to think of us." Karen dumped the hot beans into a dish and set in a serving spoon.

"What thoughtful people we have in this community." After drying his hands, he headed out of the room and went upstairs.

"Hi, Daed." Mary hugged him.

Roseanna reached out with a hug, too. "Mom says we can't go see our grandpas and grandmas because the weather is bad."

"We all wanted to go for Thanksgiving, but it's not worth risking the danger out there." Seth motioned to them. "You both need to go wash your hands for supper."

Seth followed them downstairs then headed for the kitchen. Karen sat waiting at the table with the baby in her highchair.

"I haven't said anything to our daughters yet about the new supper plans." He kept his voice down.

"I hope they'll feel better, like I am right now." Karen smiled.

Their somber-faced daughters took their seats. "Let us bow our heads for prayer," Seth instructed.

When they'd finished, the food was passed around. Karen made sure everyone had a taste of everything. Then she began to feed Nancy Anne.

"I thought I'd share something with you, Roseanna and Mary." Seth looked at his two older daughters.

"What is it, Daddy?" his oldest spoke.

Mary gave him her full attention.

"We'll be eating turkey in Lykens but not

here." Seth took a bite of the steaming casserole.

Karen rolled her eyes at him. "What your daed is trying to tell you is we've been invited to James and Rachelle's tomorrow for Thanksgiving supper." She looked at their girls. "How's that sound?"

The girls' eyes grew wide with anticipation.

"That sounds like fun to me." Roseanna smiled at Mary.

Mary let out a squeal and hopped off her chair, grinning widely.

"Okay, Mary, we know you're excited." Karen laughed. "Please, sit down now and eat your supper." She forked some casserole into her mouth.

"You gotta admit, the Lord works in mysterious ways, but always for good." Seth took a bite of his green beans.

Karen drank her iced tea. "I can hear the rain."

"Yep, it's getting slippery out there." Seth grabbed a bottle of dressing for his salad. "I've been thinking about deer season. It starts after the holiday."

"We could use some venison for meals," Karen commented.

"Does this mean you don't mind if I go hunting for food?" He wiggled his eyebrows.

Roseanna laughed. "Daddy, what are you doing?"

Mary giggled at him.

He continued to wiggle his brows, and soon made Nancy Anne giggle, too.

"You may go, husband." Karen chuckled. "You wouldn't be happy if I said no."

When they'd finished eating Seth helped Karen clean up the kitchen. He went out to the living room and added more wood to the fireplace before relaxing in his favorite chair. As he thought about home and how much he missed it, Seth felt at peace with the decision he'd made. He'd grant Karen her wish and have the family move back to Paradise. But he would wait and tell her when the time was right.

CHAPTER 12

Paradise, Pennsylvania

Karen sat at her folk's smaller kitchen table with a cup of coffee in her hand, gazing about the warm kitchen and soaking in its familiarity. Her mother's old, well-used roasting pan sat ready for the holiday turkey. Karen never grew tired of seeing Mom's rustic-style upper and lower cabinets. She smiled at her folks, who were busily stuffing the bird.

Karen enjoyed being home, especially during Christmas with so many traditional pleasures: filling up with the mouthwatering foods at Dad and Mom's big table and then eating yummy pies and joining in Christmas songs with Seth's family.

"This is a nice-sized turkey. It will feed all of us." Dad cleared his throat. "Earlier this morning we got the pheasant ready that you and Seth brought. That's now in the spare refrigerator in the basement."

"I like making the dressing. It's your grandma Ebersol's recipe." Karen's mom smiled.

"The stuffing sure does smell good. The aroma of it drifted to the top of the stairs, and I smelled it as soon as I came out of the guest room." Karen sipped her coffee.

"You could?" Her mother held on to the turkey pan.

Karen rose and walked to the sink. "I'll do up these dishes for you first and then get out the items we'll need for breakfast."

"Turkey's stuffed!" Dad's brown eyes twinkled as he nudged Mom's arm with his elbow. "The bird is ready to go into the downstairs oven when you're ready. We will cook the pheasant in the oven up here." He carried the spoon he'd used to the sink with his messy hands.

Karen stepped aside to allow her father to wash up. When he was done, she finished the dishes.

"How about we have some flapjacks and cook up some eggs for breakfast?" Karen's mom molded some aluminum foil over the turkey.

"Sounds good to me." Dad grabbed a hand towel to dry off his hands. "I can't wait for supper later. It'll be nice to have all the family here."

"I've been waiting to come and see all of you, especially when we couldn't spend Thanksgiving here." Karen dried the dishes and put them away.

"We are glad and blessed to have everyone able to come today. I love our family being together. Seth's folks will be having you all to their place for dessert. That'll be nice, too." Mom lifted the bird off the counter and headed to the basement steps.

"I'll help you open the oven door when we get there," Dad said as he followed.

When they returned to the kitchen, Dad grabbed a coffee mug. "Since it's still a little early, I'm gonna go sit in the living room after I've stoked the fire." He poured some hot coffee into his mug and headed out of the room.

"Seth and the kids are sleeping well with all the noise we are making down here." Karen's mom took the sponge and cleaned off the counter.

"They sure are, but the sounds from down here don't carry that loudly to the guest rooms."

Just as the two started putting breakfast together, the patter of little feet came up behind Karen, and she turned. "Good morning and Merry Christmas, you guys."

Seth, holding Nancy Anne, and their girls

swooped in and wished Karen a good morning and Merry Christmas in return.

Karen's mother smiled and hugged them all. "There's coffee, Seth, if you're ready for it."

"Sounds good. Then the baby and I will go out to the living room with Karen's dad."

Seth held their baby in the rocker. Nancy Anne giggled when he tweaked her nose. Karen felt warm inside, seeing her husband continuing to take so much interest in Nancy Anne.

Soon breakfast was ready, and Karen called everyone to the dining-room table. They bowed their heads for silent prayer. Karen hoped the day would be filled with joy. She looked forward to telling Seth that she had decided to embrace living with him in Lykens.

Seth rocked the baby, ignoring Atlee's snores from across the room and thinking back on the days leading up to this morning. He had enjoyed going turkey hunting with Mike and catching two nice-sized birds. Seth had arranged to bring each set of parents a turkey for the holiday dinners, as well as the pheasant to eat here.

His workplace had a Christmas party at the boss's home this year. Seth was surprised when Stan didn't show up, but Mike told him Stan had gone out of town to spend the holidays with some family. Stan was back working again, and Seth's relationship with him was much better. The more he was kind toward Stan, the easier it was to get along with him. Stan had thanked Seth several times for staying with him the day of his accident and making sure he was taken care of. Although they might never become best friends, they had a mutual understanding of each other, as well as mutual respect.

Seth was happy the weather had been decent and Mark, their driver, was able to bring them yesterday. He'd been in better spirits, and thought today he would share his decision about moving to Paradise with Karen. He figured Christmas Day would be an appropriate time to share the good news.

Mary and Roseanna, still wearing their pajamas, rushed over to Seth.

"Remember those pretty dresses we were gonna wear for Thanksgiving?" Roseanna put her hand on his knee.

Mary also placed her dainty hand on Seth's knee. "Mama made *schnee* fracke."

Seth slapped his forehead. "How could I have let that slip my mind?" He laughed. "First we should head to the kitchen and see if breakfast is ready. When we're done eating, you girls can put on those pretty dresses."

Bird-in-Hand, Pennsylvania

Later in the evening, Karen sat at the dining-room table at Seth's parents' place. His whole family was there, eating pumpkin pie with whipped cream or vanilla ice cream. Everyone seemed to be enjoying their desserts and the opportunity to catch up with one another.

Both of Seth's parents stood, smiling at Karen and her husband. "Paul and I have an announcement to make." Seth's mom looked at his dad.

"Jah, we have prayed and feel led to put our house up for sale soon." His father looked at the family. "Our decision is to move to Lykens to be near Seth, Karen, and the children."

Karen's jaw dropped.

Seth gasped. "What? I — I mean really, I can't believe this!"

Karen looked at her husband with tears blurring her vision. "What a wonderful Christmas gift this is."

Paradise

Before turning in for the night, Karen sat

332

on her mother's guest-room bed. She felt ready to tell Seth about the decision she had made before leaving home.

He came into the room and closed the door behind him. "Our children seemed to enjoy being tucked into bed by their grandparents this evening." He sat on the bed and slipped off his socks. "This has truly been a blessed day."

"I agree with you." She shifted to face him. "I've needed to tell you something." Karen looked into his eyes. "Before we came here, I realized that, in spite of our families living at a distance from us, Lykens is my home. I have a dear husband and supportive friends who will help me through whatever the future brings."

Seth's eyes widened. "You're not going to believe what I'm about to say." He leaned close to her. "When I realized how much I missed having my dad nearby to talk to about difficult situations, I began to understand why being near family was so important to you. I was going to tell you that I was ready to move to Paradise so you could be near your folks."

Karen laughed. "Seriously?"

He chuckled. "Jah, it's the truth."

They held each other in a long embrace. This was a Christmas Day Karen would always remember, so full of cheer not only for her, but also for Seth.

EPILOGUE

One year later

Karen stood in their nursery, currently occupied by their son, Adam Seth. As she stroked the beloved Christmas quilt draped over the rocking chair, her gaze rested on the embroidered verse: *"For thou art my rock and my fortress; therefore for thy name's sake lead me, and guide me"* — *Psalm 31:3.* Her prayers for strength and healing had been answered, although not in the way she had expected.

Things were much easier now that Seth's parents were living in Lykens. The men in their community had helped build a small *daadi-haus* for Emma and Paul to live in on Seth and Karen's property. The cozy cottage stood just down the road, so both couples were available to help each other out at a moment's notice.

Seth's parents were creating special memories with their grandchildren, memories that wouldn't have been possible when they lived farther away. Karen treasured her friends, but she was thankful to God for the extra blessing of having family close by.

Peace filled Karen's heart. Someday her little Roseanna would marry, and on the first Christmas after her wedding day, Karen would give her the special Christmas quilt. She hoped it would be as meaningful to her daughter as it was to her. Each generation of her family might face different challenges, but God was faithful. His strength and guidance were always available to His children.

KAREN'S VANILLA CRUMB PIE

Filling
1 cup brown sugar
1 cup light corn syrup
2 cups water
2 tablespoons flour
2 eggs
1/2 teaspoon cream of tarter
1 teaspoon vanilla
1 teaspoon baking soda

3 (9-inch) unbaked pie shells

Preheat oven to 375°. In saucepan, combine brown sugar, light corn syrup, water, and flour. Bring to a boil for 1 minute. Set aside. In large bowl, beat eggs, cream of tartar, vanilla, and baking soda. Add to cooked mixture. Divide mixture equally into unbaked pie shells.

Crumb Mixture

2 cups flour
1 cup brown sugar
1/2 cup shortening or butter
1 teaspoon cream of tartar
1/2 teaspoon baking powder

Blend all ingredients until mixture forms crumbs. Divide crumbs and sprinkle evenly on top of filling in pie shells. Bake for 45 minutes.

■ ■ ■ ■

ROSEANNA'S GROOM

BY RICHELLE BRUNSTETTER

■ ■ ■ ■

CHAPTER 1

Lykens, Pennsylvania

Roseanna Allgyer breathed deeply as she eyed the nearest tree outside the dining-room window. The autumn leaves glimmered in the evening sunlight, almost matching the blending colors in the sky. The sight calmed her nerves, for a little while at least.

Her mother's African violet plants bloomed, revealing their own beauty as well, with the pinks and purples of the velvety petals. The house had brimmed with family when Grandpa and Grandma Zook arrived a couple of days ago. They'd been helping with some preparations and answered any questions that might arise about wedding etiquette.

Roseanna was on the threshold of change. Knowing this caused her throat to constrict. By the time tomorrow was over, Roseanna would no longer be a Miss. She would approach the bishop with her beloved, and they would be married. Her name would then be Mrs. John Beiler.

She wasn't sure if she was prepared for the life she was about to enter. She remembered when John first moved to the community a couple of years ago. At the time, she was twenty years old and wasn't being courted by anyone. She'd had a chance to be with her friend Mark, but Roseanna didn't have romantic feelings for him. Eventually, he and his family had moved to Perry County.

Back then, Roseanna had been focused on making her hobby into a living. While most Amish women were taught to sew at a young age, some of her friends weren't as skilled or as passionate about it as she was. She spent her days after school making dresses, not only for herself but for anyone who needed one. It had become a full-time job and a good way to make money. She hadn't seen herself getting involved in a serious relationship with anyone, but meeting John had changed all of that.

She had made a new dress for her friend Katie Glick and had been on her way to deliver it. That was the day she'd met John. . . .

■ ■ ■ ■

Roseanna guided her horse and buggy down the road, heading toward Katie's house. She was almost there, when she saw a young Amish man she didn't recognize, riding a scooter. Suddenly, he lost his balance and plummeted toward the asphalt.

Thinking he may have been hurt, Roseanna pulled back on the reins, got out of the buggy, and tied her horse to a branch of a nearby tree. "Are you okay?" she called, reaching her hand out to help him up.

"I . . . I'm fine." His blond hair brushed the side of his flushed face as he clasped her hand. "I recently moved here from Ohio. We ride bikes there, not scooters." He motioned to the object, still on the ground. "Guess it'll take me awhile to get the hang of things."

"It does take a certain kind of balance. If you need a ride to wherever you're going, you can put your scooter in my buggy and I'll give you a ride."

He looked down at his leg then stared off to the side. "No, that's all right. I can walk."

"Okay." Roseanna was on the verge of going back to her horse and buggy, when she noticed a tear in the knee of his trousers, where blood seeped out. "My friend Katie lives just down the road. If you want to follow me there, we can get you a bandage."

He hesitated at first but finally nodded. His genuine smile and twinkling blue eyes made him quite appealing. Roseanna had a hard time not staring.

Before she got in her buggy, he introduced himself as John Beiler. Roseanna told him her name. Then she headed for Katie's house, hoping he would follow.

Bringing her thoughts back to the present, Roseanna moved away from the window and took a seat at the dining-room table. Tugging on the ties of her head covering, she chuckled over the memory of Katie's reaction when she'd opened the door to Roseanna standing with a good-looking young man beside her. After Roseanna explained what had happened, Katie gave John a bandage and some antiseptic then showed him the way to the bathroom, where he could tend his knee in private. When Katie returned to the living room, she commented on how cute John was, and said she hoped they would see him again.

After that initial meeting, Roseanna found the prospect of settling down with someone to be surprisingly appealing. At first, she worried her friend would end up with John, but it hadn't turned out that way. Within a few months, she and John began courting. He'd mentioned once that he'd felt intimidated because Roseanna seemed so confident — an idea she thought preposterous.

I'm far from being confident. It may appear that way to other people, but I'm actually afraid. Roseanna clutched the corner of the table and squeezed her eyes shut. *I'm afraid of not being the perfect spouse for you, John. I'm afraid of how our lives might change after we're married. I'm not even sure if I'm ready for marriage.*

Roseanna had been astonished when John proposed to her. They'd been courting for two years, so it shouldn't have been a surprise. She'd eagerly accepted. Now here she was, about to become committed to a permanent relationship with a man she dearly loved.

From the open window, Roseanna heard a buggy come into the yard. "Oh, I bet it's Grandpa and Grandma Allgyer."

Her mom rushed past her. "I'll get the door, Roseanna. It looks like your other grandparents are here, too."

Roseanna watched as Grandpa and Grandma Zook, along with her father's parents, walked toward the house. When she heard her mother oohing over a chocolate cake one of the grandmas had made, Roseanna went out to the hall to greet them.

Grandma and Grandpa Zook, who'd traveled the farthest, hugged Roseanna. Then her other grandparents, who lived just down the road, greeted her with tender embraces.

They all moved into the dining room, and Grandpa Zook grinned as he tweaked the end of Roseanna's nose. "I can't believe my little granddaughter is all grown up and about to become a married woman. This makes me feel so old."

Grandma nudged him with her elbow. "No teasing, now, Atlee." She smiled at Roseanna. "Are you *naerfich?*"

"*Jah,* just a bit." Truth was, *a bit* didn't begin to describe her nerves.

Grandma Allgyer gave Roseanna's shoulder a squeeze. "It's normal for a bride to be nervous on the eve of her wedding day."

"Let's move into the living room," Mom suggested. "We can visit awhile, and if anyone's hungry, I'll fix a snack."

The grandparents followed Mom into the other room, but before Roseanna could join them, Adam walked into the dining room and gave her a hug. He had come home earlier from working a half day. "How are you doing, Sister?"

"Okay, but with everything going on

today, it's kind of hard to relax."

"You'll be fine tomorrow, Roseanna. My oldest sister will be the perfect bride." Adam gave her a reassuring smile.

"Thank you, Adam."

He looked toward the kitchen. "I heard that Mary and Nancy Anne have been busy making some sugar cookies, as well as shoofly and vanilla crumb pies." He thumped his stomach. "I'm lookin' forward to sampling those desserts. How about you, Roseanna?"

"I'm really not that hungry, but I might have something later." Roseanna took a seat at the dining-room table.

"Whatever you want to do." Adam moved near the doorway. "I'll be going to the living room to visit with the family. Are you coming?"

"I will pretty soon, but I need to look at my list and go over everything I should do before tomorrow."

"Okay."

After her brother left the room, Roseanna looked over her to-do list as she listened to the steady hum of conversation in the next room.

A sudden knock on the door brought Roseanna to her feet. Thinking it might be John, she hurried to answer it.

"Hello, my good friend!" Katie nearly tackled Roseanna to the floor with the force of her hug. "It sounds like you have a full house in there."

"Hello." She tried to laugh, but the strength of Katie's arms around her made it hard to breathe. "How are you doing?"

Katie let her go and placed her purse on the floor near the door. "I should be asking you that question. After all, you're the one getting married tomorrow."

Roseanna heaved a deep sigh, dropping her gaze to the floor. "I haven't forgotten. But let's take this conversation to my room."

"Okay, that sounds like a good idea."

Once inside, Roseanna closed the bedroom door, and they sat on the bed. She stared blindly out the window.

"Hey." Katie gently shook Roseanna's shoulder. "Are you all right? You're not acting like yourself."

"Jah, I'm okay." She sighed once more and turned away from her friend, pressing her hand against her chest as it tightened.

A knock sounded on the bedroom door. "Roseanna, are you busy?" her sister Mary called. "Mom sent me to let you know we are starting to get out the desserts. Are you coming soon?"

She got up and opened the door. "We'll

be out in a little bit to join you and the rest of the family." Roseanna patted her younger sister's shoulder and looked back at Katie.

"I wouldn't mind some dessert right now." Katie spoke with a cheerful voice.

"Okay, Roseanna, I'll let Mom know." Mary turned and headed down the stairs.

Roseanna closed the door and returned to the bed, fidgeting with her hands.

Katie edged closer and touched Roseanna's arm. "Are you having second thoughts about getting married?"

"Not intentionally, but I'm doubting whether this will work out."

"What do you mean?" Katie tipped her head. "You do love him, right?"

"Oh, jah. I love John so much, and I want to be with him, but . . ." Roseanna's words trailed off as her thoughts scattered all over the place. She wanted to be honest with her friend about how she felt, but the words weren't forming in her head correctly.

"Oh, I see what the problem is. This happens to almost every bride before their big day." Katie giggled.

Roseanna's stomach fluttered while she stared intently at her friend. "What are you talking about?"

"Cold feet. That's what you have right now." Katie put her hands on her hips. "It's normal for you to feel this way. It's all part of the experience."

"How would you know? You haven't gotten married yet."

Katie's hazel eyes widened but then narrowed. "I don't need to be married to know. I've heard stories of this happening. Well, these stories came mostly from my *mamm,* but you get what I mean. The point is, you have nothing to worry about." Katie clasped Roseanna's hand. "If you have any doubts, pray about it. I know God will get you through this, and I'll do whatever I can to help. You'll feel better after the wedding is over."

Even though Katie could sometimes be a little overbearing, Roseanna was grateful to have a friend like her. Katie always seemed so sure of herself. Roseanna wasn't the best at making decisions, which was something she needed to pray about.

Roseanna coughed and turned onto her side. The sheets wrapped around her felt hot against her skin. She sat up and stared out the window on the right side of the room. It was still dark. She'd gone to bed earlier than usual, hoping it would help her relax and knowing she needed to be well-rested for her big day. Turning on the flashlight and glancing at the clock beside her bed, she noticed she'd only been sleeping two hours.

Roseanna pulled the rest of the sheets aside. "Ouch!" She turned her head and felt strands of her long, curly hair caught on the bedpost. Roseanna always let her hair down when she went to bed, but this usually didn't happen. Careful as she was to unwind most of the strands, Roseanna felt a few of them pulling out of her scalp. She rubbed that part of her head and winced.

"Maybe a cup of warm chamomile tea would make me relax and feel more tired." She got out of bed and made her way to the door. The soles of her feet felt like they were sliding on ice.

Roseanna's vision blurred in the dim hallway as she lifted her foot over the top step. The next thing she knew, she was toppling down the stairs. Her head hit one of the steps near the bottom, but other than that, she wasn't seriously hurt. "Well, that was fun." She groaned, placing both hands on the bump.

She pulled herself up from the floor and crept quietly into the kitchen, hoping she hadn't wakened anyone.

After preparing the tea, Roseanna placed an ice pack on her head. Steam rose from the cup. Since it was getting colder outside, having something warm to hold was comforting.

"John," she whispered, rubbing her thumb against the cup. "I think I'm ready to be with you. I wouldn't have said yes if I didn't love you." She closed her eyes. *Dear Lord, please, give me the strength I need for tomorrow as I enter this long-term commitment with my groom.*

CHAPTER 2

Roseanna's eyes opened to the light shining on her face. She pulled the warm blankets off and placed her feet on the floor, stretching her arms toward the ceiling.

Today's already here. Roseanna walked over to her bedroom window. The sun peeked over the trees in the yard. Although today was her wedding day, Roseanna felt as relaxed as the colored leaves falling to the yellow-tinted blades of grass.

She pulled the window open and breathed in the chilled air, helping her to feel more awake. *I'm not hungry right now, but it would be good to eat something.* She lowered her head and patted her stomach. I don't want to pass out from a lack of energy.

Yawning, Roseanna went over to the door hanger where her wedding dress hung neatly and humbly. The garment matched the color of a bright blue sky and brought out the color of her eyes. She was glad she'd chosen that shade of fabric. Roseanna scooped up the dress and laid it on her bed, smoothing the folds. She glanced at a small stack of dresses sitting on a table across from her. She had been working on some orders and had finished a couple of navy-blue frocks just the other day.

These folded dresses were much more muted than her own wedding dress and reminded Roseanna that this was, indeed, a special day. She'd never worked so hard on an outfit as she had on the beautiful wedding dress waiting for her. Roseanna had made sure every seam was sewn with care.

Roseanna had pressed her *kapp* and apron to a pristine smoothness, and there was no doubt from all the positive comments Mom and her grandmas had made that they all appreciated the effort she'd made. She tried to picture John wearing his new suit for their wedding. He would certainly look handsome.

I kind of like the idea of moving in with John's parents after we're married. She rubbed her forehead. Since the rental Roseanna and John had looked at was no longer available, they had no choice but to live at one of their parents' homes until another rental became available. The owner of the house they both liked had backed out of their agreement because he had a relative who wanted to live there.

Roseanna smiled, thinking about the time she'd spent chatting with both sets of grandparents last night, as well as the driver who'd brought Grandma and Grandpa Zook up from their home in Paradise. The bishop and his wife were there for dessert, too. Even their English neighbors, the Thompsons and their children, visited for a while. They had been good friends to Roseanna's family over the years. Roseanna would often babysit for the Thompsons, and Mary would help sometimes, too.

Roseanna couldn't help but giggle, thinking how the previous night, Katie couldn't stop taking samples of nearly everything Mom had set out. There was no doubt about it — her best friend had a sweet tooth.

Roseanna had been happy when Mom said what a beautiful bride her eldest daughter would make, and Dad's eyes glistened as he agreed.

Glancing out the window toward the hills, Roseanna smiled. "Thank You, Lord, for calming my fears."

Karen grabbed the pastries from the counter and placed them on the kitchen table. Since everyone in the house needed to be up early today, and the cooks and waiters were outside, she figured a simple breakfast would be the best choice. She needed to go out soon and make sure everything was going smoothly.

Her muscles quivered as she grabbed a stack of plates from the cupboard. *I can't believe this is really happening. My first daughter is getting married. Oh my, where has the time gone? It seems like yesterday when Roseanna was a baby.*

"Good morning, Mom."

Karen knew who was behind her. A mother always recognized the voices of her children, even in the midst of a crowd. "Good morning, Roseanna. Why don't you sit down?" She joined Roseanna at the table. "How are you feeling? Did you sleep well?"

"As well as I could, I guess." Her daughter opened the container of pastries.

Karen clasped her hands as she observed Roseanna's demeanor. She didn't appear very nervous. Well, not as nervous as Karen had been when she married Seth. People took experiences in differently, but most women she knew were overly anxious on their wedding day.

Roseanna sat at the table with a cup of tea, and Karen stood behind the chair, massaging her daughter's shoulders. "It's all right to be open about how you're really feeling, Rosey."

"What? No, I am fine."

"You don't want to talk about it?"

Roseanna rubbed the left side of her cheek. "There's not much to say. I mean, I am slightly overwhelmed, but who wouldn't be?"

Karen watched in dismay as Roseanna scooted her chair away from the table and started out of the room.

"Are you sure you don't want anything else?" Karen asked. "There are plenty of pastries on the counter. Or I'd be happy to fix you some eggs."

"No, I'm not really hungry."

Adam entered the kitchen and bumped into Roseanna. "*Ach!* You should watch where you're going." Adam frowned.

"It takes two people, you know. You could've moved around me." Roseanna crossed her arms.

This teasing wasn't what Karen wanted to deal with. She had enough stress supervising the waiters and waitresses. Before anything escalated between Roseanna and Adam, she stepped between them. "Both of you, please stop this. I don't have time to deal with this right now, especially not today."

"Okay." Roseanna rolled her eyes and walked away from Adam. "I should go upstairs and get ready."

"Only because you know I would win."

"Adam, you also have some responsibilities today, as do your sisters. So please do not go around taunting them. I'm depending on you, so try to act your age and set a good example. Understood?"

He nodded. "Jah, Mom."

Nancy Anne came in and signed: "I'm glad I got the last shed power-washed yesterday. Dad said it looked good." She gave her brother a silly grin. "I slept good last night. I love being with my whole family."

"Thank you, Sister, for working so hard in my behalf." Roseanna signed then went over and gave Nancy Anne a hug. Once Roseanna pulled away, she noticed Mom smiling as she watched the two of them.

Nancy Anne paused to look at the pastries sitting on the counter, then she went to the refrigerator and took out the pitcher of apple juice. After filling her glass and placing it on the table, she signed: "The pastries look good. I'll try not to eat them all."

"We all need to remember to model good behavior," Karen both signed and spoke.

Roseanna nodded.

Adam combed his fingers through his dark curly hair. "Yes, Mom."

"I'd better start getting ready for the busy day ahead." Roseanna hurried from the room.

"I'll come up soon to see how you're doing," Karen called after her.

Seth came in from outside, with his father-in-law patting him on the shoulder. "Work is a snap with all the extra help out there this morning."

"There are plenty of pastries here and leftover pies in the refrigerator. Not to mention all the meals we will be eating later on, starting with the noon meal after the wedding."

Karen's mother walked in. "When all of this is done, if we complain today, of all days, that we are hungry, we have a big problem."

His brows raised, Karen's dad laughed. He removed his hat and hung it on the wall peg. "I'd best wash off my hands and break out that shoofly pie waiting to be eaten for breakfast."

"We'll have to all go on diets after today." Karen's mother chuckled.

Soon, everyone had grabbed a drink and something to eat and gone out into the dining room. Karen felt the excitement growing in the house as the wedding drew nearer.

After Adam headed out the door, Karen sat down at the table for a moment, resting her head on her hands as she prayed. Nancy Anne sat next to her and laid a hand on Karen's shoulder.

When she finished praying, Karen looked at her daughter and smiled. "You are a smart young lady and know how to make your mom feel good," Karen signed.

Roseanna's morning could have gone better. Yes, she was used to butting heads with Adam, but that didn't help the situation. Then while she was in her room getting dressed, Mom had come up to see how she was doing. Katie and Mary were there, too, which helped as Roseanna fussed with her dress, making sure everything was perfect, and they gave her the reassurance she needed.

Later, as she was going downstairs, she heard her father making a fuss over spilling coffee all over his white button-up shirt. Since her mother had to go back outside to see how things were progressing, Roseanna hurried into the kitchen and started treating his shirt while he went to grab another one. Grandma Zook came in and offered to soak the shirt in cold water. Dad wouldn't be wearing it today, but at least a good soaking should help keep it from staining.

Grandpa Zook carried his black dress hat and joined Roseanna in the kitchen. "Did someone's white shirt get ruined?"

"It's probably not ruined, but Grandma is going to soak it for Dad while he gets a fresh shirt out of the closet." Roseanna gazed at her grandfather. He looked so handsome and well dressed. Except for his completely white hair, one would never know he was sixteen years older than Grandma.

Grandma stood in front of the sink, running cold water on the stain. "Your son-in-law spilled coffee on his shirt, and his mother-in-law is trying to help out," she called over her shoulder.

"What man hasn't spilled his drink down the front of a white shirt at one time or another?" He laughed.

"I'm glad we don't have to wear white dresses," Roseanna said. "That would be a challenge for sure, even with our white church aprons to cover up the front."

Roseanna's dad hurried into the kitchen, adjusting the loose side of his suspender. "How do I look now? Does this shirt look okay?"

"Yes, it does. Now just be sure and keep it that way, Seth." Grandpa's voice boomed with a chuckle. "Look, here comes our groom."

John stepped into the kitchen.

Roseanna gazed at him. He looked as handsome as she'd dreamed.

"You look very nice, young man," Grandma said.

"Th–thank you." His voice appeared thin.

Roseanna watched her father slip on his black vest, followed by his new black jacket. He moved to the small mirror on the wall near the utility room and positioned his black dress hat. "I'd better get out there and see if Karen wants me for any last-minute help."

"We need to head to the tent, Luella." Grandpa tugged at his long beard. "By the way, you look nice today, dear."

"Thank you, Husband." Grandma blushed. "Let's go, my dear Atlee." She fussed with the sleeve of her new, deep gray dress on the way out the back door.

I guess Dad's spilled coffee could've been worse. Roseanna cupped her chin and leaned forward. *It could always be worse.*

"Are you ready, Roseanna?" John hummed in her ear.

"Jah, I believe so." She grasped his clammy hand and gave a gentle squeeze. Roseanna knew John loved her very much and was obviously just as nervous as she was.

The voices in the tent enclosed Roseanna like spiraling winds, as she waited with John on the bench near the entrance. Next to them sat their witnesses: Roseanna's friend Katie, her sister Mary, and John's friends Nate and Amos.

She shifted, trying to get as comfortable as she could. With a forced smile, Roseanna shook hands with the people from her community while they walked past. Her fingers and toes were frigid, which was ironic given what she and Katie had discussed before. Maybe her inward feelings reflected her outer physique, but she hoped that wasn't the case.

She gazed at her sister. Roseanna noticed Mary bouncing her leg up and down while tugging at her kapp ties. About a month ago, Mary had commented on how she would find someone soon who'd want to court her, and then she'd be the next to marry. But it didn't look like she was quite so matter-of-fact about it anymore. *Yes, Mary. Getting married isn't as simple as you thought, huh?*

As the first hymn began, Roseanna went with John to the house to be counseled by the ministers, while their witnesses waited in another room. Roseanna knew this was important to their marriage, but her eyes were heavy. If she'd had a better night's sleep, she would've been able to listen wholeheartedly to what was being said. But as it was, she had to suppress a few yawns.

Afterward as they walked outside, the reverberation of another hymn being sung from the tent caused Roseanna's mouth to quiver.

"It's uplifting, isn't it?" Roseanna whispered.

"Jah." She felt John's fingers tremble as he squeezed her arm.

Roseanna's heart began to race as they entered the tent and sat in their seats in front of everyone they knew. Everything felt surreal, making Roseanna wonder if she were dreaming that all of this was happening. But Katie's all-too-realistic coughing assured her that this was in fact happening. When Katie's bout continued as the bishop talked, Roseanna handed her a cough drop from a small plastic bag she'd placed under her chair, knowing her friend was going to need them since she'd come down with a cold overnight.

"Danki," Katie mouthed, with a faint whisper as she removed the purple wrapper.

"You're welcome."

When the bishop stood among everyone and spoke, Roseanna made sure to give him her full attention. She knew what was coming next. She was about to become a Mrs., bound together with her groom so they would spend the rest of their lives together. Eventually they would have a house of their own, gain new responsibilities, and someday raise children. Was she certain this was the right choice?

But she never got to ponder her question. Without warning, John got up from his chair and dashed out of the tent.

Roseanna's eyes widened. *John? Where is he going?*

CHAPTER 3

John's heart raced, and sweat beaded on his forehead as he paced. He rubbed his face, dragging his palms to his chin. "How did I get myself in this predicament again?" he muttered. "What was I thinking?"

John's breath caught in his chest. His mind raced through so much at once that he couldn't organize any of his thoughts. Why did he walk out of the tent? He loved Roseanna so much, so why did he leave her there in front of their friends and family?

"John!"

He turned toward the familiar voice. His fiancée stood a good distance away.

"Are you okay?"

"Yeah." He shook his head. "No." John didn't know what to do. Part of him wanted nothing more than to run up to Roseanna, hold her, and apologize for behaving as he had. He wished he could tell her how much he loved her. He wished he could say everything would be okay.

Roseanna, I thought this was the right choice. I was sure I could spend the rest of my life with you. I thought I was ready this time.

She rushed toward him.

"I can't marry you, Roseanna." John's legs seemed to move on their own as he took off in the direction of the field. He wasn't sure where he was heading, but he needed to get away from Roseanna. How could he begin to express the way he felt? She wouldn't take it too well; he knew that much. Truth was, he didn't understand it himself. All he could hear was his blood pumping through his ears and the faint sound of Roseanna calling out to him.

Roseanna had attended a few weddings throughout her life. She recalled the chatter of people and the hymns she'd heard plenty of times. Even as the vows were being said, it was never entirely silent. But at the moment, the voices from the tent no longer existed. Surely everyone must be as shocked as she was.

Although the sun lit the entire property, the cold breeze stung Roseanna's cheeks as she ran over to the rows of buggies lined up in their field. It was a literal maze as she neared the line of horses, spooking some as she ran past.

"Where is he?" Roseanna panted. "Where is John? I need to find out why he thinks we can't be married."

Suddenly, Roseanna's vision met the grass under her feet, and her nose rubbed the soil. She wasn't sure what she had tripped over, but as she clambered to her feet, she had no time to figure it out. When she noticed a white shirt out of the corner of her eye, she jerked her head in the direction of where her groom was running.

"John!" Roseanna bolted toward him faster than she'd ever run in her life. Although she was a fast runner, John had always been a smidge quicker than her. Tripping had slowed Roseanna down as well. But she was determined to catch up to him, so she breathed in heavy, cold air and rushed forward. She practically knocked John over when she bumped into his back.

The impact stopped him. He turned and looked at her with an unidentifiable expression. "Roseanna."

"Why did you leave the tent? Why would you run away from me, John?" Roseanna murmured, barely able to swallow. Her mouth was moist, yet it was dry in the back of her throat.

"I . . . I don't know." His voice cracked as he stared down at his feet.

"What do you mean you don't know? John, you left. Right before our vows."

"But that doesn't mean I don't love you."

"Then what does it mean?" Her throat felt like it was burning. Roseanna despised it when people were dishonest, and she could tell John was hiding something from her.

John looked away and rubbed his nose. He appeared disconnected from his surroundings. Kicking the ground a couple of times, he remained silent.

"John, why did you leave? Please tell me. I need to know."

He clasped her fingers and lifted her hand. "Roseanna. I am truly sorry, but I have to go." John squeezed her hand like he had done earlier, but then loosened his grip and turned away. "I can't do this. I was *dumm* for thinking so."

"Please, John. We need to talk about this." Roseanna trembled.

He walked away and didn't look back at her even once.

Roseanna considered running after John again, but she was too hurt to do anything. She sank to the ground and wrapped her arms around herself.

■ ■ ■ ■

Roseanna stood by the tent as she tried to take in what had happened. How was she going to tell everyone? She was stunned. Glancing down at the front of her dress, she grimaced at the soiled spots left from when she'd taken her spill.

This is the least of my worries. My major problem is that John left me and he isn't coming back. Roseanna, still in shock, closed her weary eyes and asked the Lord to give her the strength she needed to enter the tent. She silently quoted Mom's favorite verse: *"For thou art my rock and my fortress; therefore for thy name's sake lead me, and guide me."*

As Roseanna stumbled into the tent, she felt eyes upon her from every direction. Her face heated up as she made her way over to the men's side, where her father sat on a bench. She knelt down next to him. It was unusual for the men and women to intermingle during a church service or wedding, so she assumed a few questionable looks were being cast her way as she leaned close to her father.

"D–dad," she whispered.

He gazed at her with concern in his eyes.

"What is it, Roseanna? Where's John?"

Roseanna looked toward the exit of the tent and asked her father to come with her outside to talk privately. He nodded and stood up, following her out of the tent. She could hear the murmurs filtering out of the tent. Roseanna could only guess what her family and friends were thinking as they waited to find out what was going on.

She explained to him what had taken place between her and John. Dad's wide-eyed expression made Roseanna wish she could disappear. She was aware of how devastated everyone would be, especially John's parents. Roseanna was already humiliated by John leaving the tent, but the embarrassment could have been remedied if he'd come back with her and said their vows. But he didn't come back. And he'd made it clear he wasn't going to. She had to accept the fact that John was not going to be her groom.

Dad gave Roseanna a comforting hug. "I'm sorry, Daughter, for what has happened to you. I can only imagine how you're feeling right now." He patted her back.

"Thank you." Roseanna swallowed against the burning sensation in her throat.

Dad let his arms fall to his sides. "I'll take it from here, Roseanna." His deep voice had a reassuring tone, and it wrapped around her spirit in such a comforting manner. "I'll go back into the tent and tell the bishop this news." Dad lifted her chin. "Go back to the house, and wait for us there."

Roseanna barely managed to nod.

Curious, she peeked into the tent, watching as her father went over to the bishop. She saw his lips move and the bishop nodding slowly.

This is the worst day of my life. Roseanna grabbed the folds in her dress. She felt another flush of embarrassment after the bishop and her father stopped talking.

The bishop stood up, clearing his throat while pulling on his coat sleeve. "It is with great regret that I must tell all of you the wedding has been called off."

Gasps and murmurs drifted through the tent.

"At the parents' request, however, you are all invited to stay and partake of the afternoon meal."

Unable to bear the humiliation, Roseanna dashed across their lawn and headed straight for the back door, not once looking back to see if anyone had noticed her. At least she hadn't had to tell everyone, but Roseanna felt numb. Why her groom had left her with a broken heart was beyond comprehension.

Slamming the door of her room, Roseanna gritted her teeth to prevent herself from screaming. Tasting the salt of her tears, she picked up one of her pillows and threw it across the room. Then Roseanna flopped on the bed and curled up against the mattress. She wiped the tears from her face with the sleeve of her wedding dress. *To think I was worried that I might panic and run out on John.* Her thoughts were scrambled and disjointed, for she never would have done something like that. If Roseanna had changed her mind about marrying John, she would have said something before the wedding.

The door of her bedroom swung open with the *whoosh* of a hurricane. "Roseanna!" Katie yelled, but then was overtaken by a fit of coughing. "Roseanna, are you okay? Why was the wedding canceled? What happened between you and John?"

"Katie, I don't want to talk about it right now." Roseanna sat up on her bed. "Can I be left alone for a while?"

"No. I'm your friend, and I am here to comfort you in your time of need." Katie came over to the bed and sunk her weight into the mattress. "Even if you don't want to tell me anything, I still want to be here for my best friend." Katie leaned over and gasped. "Roseanna — your leg!"

My leg? Roseanna looked down and noticed a few drops of red on the wooden surface of the floor. Pressing her hand on her stocking and then lifting it, she realized there was blood on her palm.

"How did you hurt your leg?" Katie covered her mouth. "Did John do this to you?"

"Ach! No, Katie. It's not what you think." Roseanna pressed her hand back on her leg. "I tripped earlier, but I didn't know it was that bad."

"Should I call your mamm? It could be a serious cut!"

"I don't think so, Katie. But you could go to the bathroom and get me the first-aid kit, please."

"I'll be right back." Before Katie headed out of the room, she looked back at Roseanna. "Good thing I didn't leave like you asked, huh?"

"I guess you're right." Roseanna rubbed her eyes with her sleeve again. She laid down on the bed once more, holding her leg firmly with her hands. Roseanna felt how sore her leg was now. *How strange. I can't believe I didn't feel any pain after I tripped.*

Roseanna nearly choked on the bile rising in her throat. *What a mess this morning has turned out to be. I can't even begin to figure out what is going on in John's head. Why'd he do this to us?* Her brows furrowed. *I thought I knew him well enough to sense how he really felt about me. His parents seemed so happy and sure about us living with them after the wedding. Wouldn't they have noticed if anything seemed off to them?*

All the gifts people had brought to the wedding would have to be given back. For days — maybe even months — folks would talk about Roseanna's runaway groom. She'd be bombarded with questions, curious stares, and well-meaning sympathetic gestures. Roseanna didn't want any of that. She just wanted to be left alone to deal with her grief.

As she remained on her bed, Roseanna heard voices now and then from the open window. She knew the meal would begin around noon, and it was getting pretty close to that now. If things had gone as planned, she and John would be getting ready to dine as man and wife with everyone else.

She wondered how her parents were doing among all the guests. Roseanna felt bad, not only for them but for John's parents as well. John had done a rotten thing, backing out like this with no explanation whatsoever. He'd left many individuals to stay and carry out their promise to do the serving and the cleanup of the meals, yet it all went to waste. Tomorrow, they'd take down all of the tents and put all the benches on the church wagons. Roseanna doubted that John would come back here and help with cleaning up the remnants of their failed wedding day. She wasn't sure she would ever see him again.

Her soul felt broken, like one of Mom's delicate teacups that had shattered and could never be repaired. Would the pain ever end? Roseanna covered her face with her hands. *How will I handle the challenge of seeing everyone at church this Sunday?*

CHAPTER 4

A couple of days had passed since John ran away, and Roseanna wasn't feeling any better. Church was scheduled for tomorrow, and while she wished she could stay home, Roseanna knew she would be expected to attend. In all of her twenty years, she had only missed church twice, and both times she had been ill.

Heading into the bathroom, Roseanna lit the gas lamp near the sink and applied a fresh bandage to her leg. She'd hit a capillary when she tripped, which was why her leg had bled so much. The injury was now protected by a scab, and her skin wasn't as dark as it had been at first. *Thank goodness my leg is all right.* Roseanna exhaled and pressed on the wound. *It seems to be healing fine. But what did I trip over? A buggy wheel, maybe?*

Extinguishing the light, Rosanna walked out of the bathroom and went to the living room, taking a seat on the couch. She smelled the pungent aroma of her favorite tea.

"Here, Rosey." Her mother handed Roseanna a mug. "How are you feeling?"

Roseanna took a sip of tea and then placed it down on the side table. "My leg is still sore, but it has gotten better."

"That's good." Roseanna's mother sat in the rocking chair and leaned back. "But how are you feeling about what happened? Are you doing all right?"

"As well as I can." *How can I be all right? The person I loved dearly decided he no longer wants to be a part of my life — no explanation given.* Roseanna grasped her mug and sipped the warm liquid. Her heart still ached, but the tea was comforting.

"Roseanna."

"I'd rather not talk about it, Mamm. Not now, at least."

Mom patted her arm. "Okay. But I'm here for you when you're ready."

As Roseanna finished the rest of her tea, Nancy Anne walked into the living room and sat down. She raised her hands and said *good morning* in sign language.

Their mother got up from the rocking chair and walked over to Nancy Anne, patting her shoulder as she gave an earnest smile. Mom then signed to Nancy Anne, asking her if she slept all right and if she'd be interested in some tea to drink, as well.

Nancy Anne's nod was slow, like it often was when she was exhausted. She'd worked excessively hard the day before to clean up everything from the wedding. Not to mention all the things she'd done to help out for many days before the wedding.

Roseanna's heart warmed, knowing Nancy Anne had a spirit of helpfulness and a willingness to work, regardless of her disability. Her sister would be able to overcome any sort of obstacles that may come up in her future.

"Come on, Roseanna." Katie clipped a purple leash on the collar of her Pomeranian. "Walking is a great way to get your mind off of things. And I know that Ella certainly needs the exercise."

Roseanna lowered her gaze to the floor in Katie's kitchen, focusing on the petite canine. With all its white fluffy fur, the dog resembled a cloud with feet. She knelt down and combed her fingers through the soft hair. *"Gut hund."*

"Ella is a good dog, isn't she? She's also very s*chmaert.* Here, I'll show you." Katie got up and went over to the pantry. She reached in, pulled out a red box, and shook it. "Come here, girl! Come here!"

Ella's ears perked up and she galloped away from Roseanna toward Katie. Her tail whipped side to side as Katie continued to shake the box and then proceeded to pull out a bone-shaped treat.

Katie held the treat over the dog's head and pointed to the floor. "Sit, Ella. Sit. No. You've gotta sit if you want the treat. Sit!"

Ella attempted to jump up and snatch the treat from Katie rather than listen to her command.

Roseanna stifled a chuckle, admitting to herself that it was amusing to watch.

"Ach. You just like teasing me, don't you? Katie dropped the treat back in the box and set it on the countertop. "Now you're not getting a treat, you goofy cotton ball."

Roseanna turned her head toward the hallway, hearing steady footsteps coming closer. She stepped aside for Katie's mother to enter the kitchen.

"Hello, Roseanna. How are you doing?"

"I'm all right." Roseanna forced a smile.

"That's good to hear." Katie's mom gave Roseanna a hug and went over to the sink. "Katie, could you hand me the dish soap?"

"Jah, sure." As Katie hurriedly moved past the box of treats, it toppled over and landed on the floor. Ella ran to the open box and stuck her head in. "No!"

Roseanna couldn't contain her laughter. Ella wore the box on her head and didn't even try to shake it off. The sounds of crunching could be heard as Ella walked around with no sense of sight. The dog appeared perfectly content.

"Katie," Roseanna said with a snicker, "I thought she was a Pomeranian, not a boxer."

"Ha! Ha! Very funny." Katie crossed her arms, yet she giggled, too.

After Katie got the box off Ella's head, she and Roseanna said good-bye to Katie's mom.

"Are you sure you both don't want something to eat before you go?" She dried her hands. "I can bake some gingerbread cookies. Christmas is coming up pretty soon, so it might help get you in the Christmas spirit."

"It's okay, Mom. I'm sure Roseanna's already had something to eat for breakfast."

"But don't you want to sit down for a little bit and visit?"

Oh, great. I'll bet she wants to ask me questions about John. Roseanna tugged on her jacket. "No, that's fine. Ella ought to go for a walk. The dog needs to burn off all of those biscuits she ate."

Ella let out a loud yawn and lay down near Roseanna's feet. *Figures.* Roseanna reached down and petted the dog.

"Well, okay. Have a nice time on your walk, you two. Be safe."

Katie smiled. "Thank you, Mom. We will."

Katie led Ella and Roseanna out of the kitchen and over to the front door. "It's a bit chilly outside this morning." Katie turned the knob and opened the door a smidge. "But morning walks are the best. It's a great way to wake your body up."

Roseanna followed behind as they walked along the side of the road. Her shoulders shook from the chill, and her lips felt like sandpaper. December was inching closer, which meant snow might be covering every part of the county soon. It made everything appear pure and innocent, though. "I am looking forward to sledding again," she admitted.

"Me, too!" Katie stopped and turned around to hand the leash to Roseanna. "Why don't you walk her for a while? It must be getting boring walking without a little pal dragging you." She snickered. "Am I right?"

Roseanna shrugged her shoulders but accepted the leash. She turned her head quickly, noting Katie's teasing expression as she followed her. Roseanna could tell Katie was trying to make her feel better, but doing leisure activities only took her mind off John for a few moments. She wasn't willing to express how she felt to her best friend, either.

Ella barked at a vehicle speeding past them and jerked forward, tugging Roseanna's arm. "Calm down." She pulled Ella back to prevent her from being in the road.

Katie tapped on Roseanna's shoulder. "Hey, Roseanna. Can we stop for a second?"

"How come?" Roseanna continued walking.

"I want to talk with you about the wedding."

Roseanna quickly turned around, which caused her towering friend to jump. "Katie, there was no wedding, and I don't want to talk about it."

"But it's not good to bottle up your feelings, especially when you're still hurting."

"What makes you think I'm still hurting?" Roseanna's voice rose as she clenched her fingers around the leash. "John left me. So what? He couldn't marry me? So what? I don't care anymore." Roseanna's stomach tightened as she stood in front of her friend, shaking and unable to look at her. *This is my fault. I'm the reason John left. Who in their*

right mind would want to marry someone as
pathetic as me?

Katie stumbled back a step. "So John didn't say why he decided to leave?" Apparently, she was not about to let up.

"No, he didn't. Now, would you please stop asking me questions?" Roseanna covered her mouth, seized by remorse. It wasn't right to snap at Katie. "Sorry."

"No, I'm sorry." Katie lowered her chin. "I was only trying to help."

"I know." Roseanna's eyes darted to a large animal coming up behind Katie. It was another dog, but it was immense compared to a Pomeranian.

"What? What's wrong?" Katie looked over her shoulder and froze.

The big dog snarled as it approached. Roseanna held her breath, wanting to scream but refusing to allow instinct to betray her.

"Should we run?" Katie's voice cracked.

"No." Roseanna brought Ella close to her side. "We need to move quickly, but we can't run."

"Why?"

" 'Cause dogs run faster than humans. That's why." Roseanna gestured with her hand. "Come on. We gotta get Ella out of here."

Roseanna paced herself, not wanting to move too quickly, which might encourage the larger dog. Fortunately, Ella walked cooperatively. Otherwise she could've agitated the larger canine even more.

"It's still following us." Katie's voice quavered.

"As long as the hund's not charging at us, we're fine." Roseanna's skin tingled where sweat had formed. *We should've brought some of Ella's treats with us. We could have thrown some to the dog.*

"I have an idea."

"Wait, Katie. What are you —" Roseanna looked behind and saw Katie bending down to the ground and picking up a rock. "Katie, don't."

Katie threw the rock, and it landed in front of the dog's left paw. The mutt stopped, eyed the rock, and then growled, lowering its back legs.

"Run!" Roseanna pulled on the leash to make Ella move faster.

"You said running wasn't a good idea!"

"It is now!" Roseanna scooped up the dog. She and Katie took off running, and Roseanna was too afraid to look back. They ran several minutes, until Katie informed her the dog was no longer behind them.

Roseanna stopped running. Catching her

breath, she leaned against a wooden post. She could feel the warmth of Ella's breath against her neck.

Katie approached Roseanna and hugged her. "Are you okay?"

"Yes, I think so." Roseanna looked up. "Thank You, Lord."

"Amen." Katie patted her back and then let go. "I haven't run that fast in my entire life. I thought we were goners."

"Same here. I haven't run that fast since John . . ."

"Roseanna?"

"I need to go home." Roseanna handed Ella and her leash to Katie.

"Do you need me to walk back to your house with you?"

"No, that's okay. I'll be fine. Danki, Katie. I'll see you at church on Sunday." She reached out and rubbed Ella's stomach. "Good-bye, Ella. Be a good girl for Katie."

Roseanna waved to Katie as she walked away, clutching her arms against her stomach. *Katie can finish Ella's walk on her own, but am I being selfish? Am I a horrible friend?* She wiped the damp corner of her eye with her hand.

When Roseanna reached her house, a buggy occupied the hitching post. Her leg muscles tightened. *Oh, my goodness. That's*

John's buggy.

As Roseanna grabbed the front doorknob, a rush of adrenaline overpowered her. "What do I do?" she muttered. "I can't go in there. He humiliated me." Roseanna's hands were almost as purple as the leash for Katie's dog. She needed to go into the house and warm up. *I could use the back door and then decide what to do without freezing to death.* She headed around to the back of the house.

Roseanna put her hands in her jacket pockets and sat on the indoor steps, closing her eyes for a moment. *After what happened between Katie and me, I don't want my emotions to interfere with any future choices.*

"What are you doing, Roseanna?"

Roseanna's eyes snapped opened. She lifted her head and saw Mary looming over her. "I honestly don't know."

"How was the walk? Was Katie's dog as cute as ever?" Mary stepped down and sat next to her.

"Yeah, very cute. But the walk didn't go so great."

Mary leaned an elbow on her knee. "Did Ella bite you?"

"No, but another dog almost did." She explained what had happened.

"Well, I'm glad you're okay." Mary rubbed

her hands on her dark green dress and sighed. "Bigger dogs scare me."

"Me, too."

Mary clasped her sister's arm. "Oh, Roseanna, John's mother is here, and she wants to know how you are doing."

"Huh? John isn't here?" Roseanna looked upward, sighing. *Thank goodness for small blessings.*

"No, but if he were, I would sure give him a piece of my mind. It wasn't right for him to leave you. I mean, we cleaned up after a wedding that didn't even happen."

"Mary, you're not making me feel any better."

"I'm sorry. John's mother being here probably doesn't help either."

"No, it does not." Roseanna stood up and brushed off her dress. "Don't worry. I'll get through it."

She went up the steps and past the living room, hearing her mother's voice coming from the kitchen. Roseanna peered in, wondering if she should turn around and leave. But it was too late, Mom had already seen her.

"Hello, Rosey. Welcome home." Mom raised her mug and sipped.

"Thank you, Mamm."

John's mother, Linda, rose from the chair

and placed her mug on the table. "I'm so glad to see you." She went over and wrapped her arms around Roseanna.

"It's good to see you, too."

"Here. Have a seat, Roseanna." Mom got up and grabbed a mug. "Would you like some *kaffi*?"

Roseanna shook her head. "I'm not in the mood for coffee right now."

"All right. Let me know if you change your mind." Mom squeezed Roseanna's shoulder and left the kitchen.

Roseanna sat in the chair. She was hesitant to make conversation with John's mother but didn't want to be impolite. Roseanna asked Linda how she was doing, and they continued to talk casually for a few minutes.

"Roseanna, about John . . . I came here to let you know that he left Lykens the day after the wedding."

"He left?" Roseanna covered her mouth. She'd been too overwhelmed with her thoughts and emotions to go over to John's house, but Roseanna didn't think he would leave the area. She figured her betrothed only needed time to think things over.

Linda took a drink from her mug. "Jah. He went to where his uncle and aunt live in Ronks. At least, that's where he told me he was going, while packing his belongings."

Roseanna made a humming noise from her throat as her stomach sunk. *I chased him away. I chased John away.* Her eyes became wet, but Roseanna suppressed her emotions.

"Roseanna, I am very sorry for what happened a couple of days ago."

"You don't need to apologize on John's behalf. It's not your fault."

"He's my son. My only child even." John's mother covered her face with both hands. "I just can't believe he did this again."

"What?"

"I mean . . ." Linda jumped up. "Oh dear. I thought you knew."

"I don't understand. What do you mean by 'again'?" Roseanna pulled her arms against her chest.

Linda wiped her eyes. "A couple of years ago while we were living in Ohio, John —" She hitched a breath. "He was about to get married to another woman until he ran away from the wedding."

Roseanna sat stiffly in her chair, unable to respond.

CHAPTER 5

Ronks, Pennsylvania

John watched as snowflakes fell from the clouds, his body numb from the winter winds blowing against him. He gripped the wooden handle of the shovel with gloved hands, squeezing his eyes shut as another gust penetrated through to his skin.

I wonder what my folks are doing right now. John grabbed his handkerchief out to take care of his dripping nose. *If I had followed through and married Roseanna, I'd be home with her and my family right now, living a brand-new life.*

John felt his shoulders slump to match his mood. "What have I done?"

Christmas would be here in a few weeks, and the thought of that made his stomach tighten. *I promised Roseanna we would have the best first Christmas as a married couple.* He rubbed his gritty eyes before continuing to shovel the snow from his uncle's driveway. The shovel's blade grazed the gravel. "I was stupid, Roseanna. Very stupid. You're probably still angry with me." John bit his lower lip and looked at the tree closest to him. All the branches were bare. What gave the tree vividness was stripped away.

The snowflakes felt like needles jabbing John's skin as they landed on his face. "I can't go back to Lykens. I just can't." He scooped a heap of snow and carried it over to the large pile out of the path of the driveway.

After he wiped his nose with his handkerchief, he stuffed it into his jacket pocket and grabbed the snow shovel again. John hoped the flakes that were falling wouldn't amount to much. Then again, maybe he deserved to clean out snow all winter for reneging on their marriage and hurting his fiancée.

"John!" his aunt called from the house. "Come in for a bit and warm yourself up by the fire!"

He turned to her and saw she was standing on the edge of the porch with a steaming mug in her hands. "I'll take a break when I'm done," he replied. "I'm almost finished!"

A short time later, John stepped onto the porch. He stomped the snow off his boots and shook the moisture from his stocking cap then entered the house.

The aroma of hot chocolate drew him into the kitchen. It was good to be in the house. He noticed a plate of lemon bars and chocolate chip cookies sitting on the table. John slipped off his jacket, hanging it up on the wall peg, then he laid his gloves and stocking cap on the bench.

He walked to the sink and washed his hands. The warmth of the water felt good against his cold fingers, and when they were heated through, he dried them off with the towel lying near the sink.

Aunt Lena smiled and handed him a mug of cocoa. "Help yourself to something sweet, John." She grabbed a napkin for herself and picked out a couple of treats. "Did you get all of the driveway cleared off?"

"Jah." He took a napkin and looked at the tray of cookies in front of him.

"Why don't we go into the living room and warm up by the fire? From the looks of your crimson cheeks, I'd say you need to thaw out."

John followed her into the next room and took the seat closest to the fire. As he drank from his mug, John gazed at the luminous colors flickering in the rising flames.

"Do you want to talk about it, John?"

"Talk about what?" He picked up a lemon bar and took a bite.

"You have been here a few weeks now, yet you've been keeping some things to yourself." The rocker creaked as she gave her chair momentum. "I know you're hurting, but it's not good to keep things bottled up."

"I know you mean well, Aunt Lena, but I really don't want to talk about it." John looked away. His aunt fell silent as she continued to rock. *You wouldn't understand, Aunt Lena. No one would.*

Lykens

Roseanna stitched the long sleeve onto the bodice of her project, threading precisely as she normally would. *There we go. I can have this dress finished by tomorrow.* She gave the fabric a firm shake, admiring the deep red shade. As Roseanna stitched another part of the dress, she heard footsteps coming up the stairs.

"Roseanna, Mom needs you to help in the kitchen."

When Mary entered the room, Roseanna raised her head and nodded. "Hang on, Mary. I'll be down in a moment." She stood and laid the dress on the back of the chair. Roseanna went over to the window and noticed the snowflakes were subsiding and that Adam and Nancy Anne were throwing snowballs at each other. "Heh. Kids."

"Hey, Roseanna."

"Yes, Mary?"

"Who is that dress for?"

"Oh, the dress? Umm . . . it's for . . ."

Mary patted Roseanna's shoulder. "It's not for anyone, is it?"

"Well, not anyone specific." Roseanna's stomach tingled. She'd sewn more dresses than ever before after John's mother let that one secret slip out. Roseanna pretended to be fine after her talk with Linda, but she wasn't.

Oh, my goodness. Roseanna covered her face. Her hands were frigid against her warm cheeks. *John, how could you? Why did you keep that hidden from me this whole time? I would have known better, John. I would never have agreed to marry you.*

The sound of Mary speaking again broke through Roseanna's thoughts. She wiped her eyes with her hands as discreetly as she could and then faced her sister.

"I'd better go help Mom." Roseanna went over to the bed and grabbed the white prayer kapp to put on.

"Roseanna, do you need someone to talk to? You know I'm here for you." While Mary wrapped comforting arms around Rose-anna, they rested their heads on each other's shoulder. "I'm your sister. I'll always be here for you."

Roseanna's heartbeat seemed to stop as she rested in her sister's embrace, debating whether she should express to Mary how she really felt. She made up her mind as she squeezed her sister tighter. "I know, Mary, but don't worry. I'm all right."

"Hello, Rosey," Mom said when Roseanna entered the kitchen. "Could you please bake your delicious pumpkin pies for our Christ-mas dinner this week? You know how much your Grandma Zook enjoys them."

Roseanna walked over to the pantry and grabbed a can of baking powder and coco-nut sugar. "Jah. And I'd have to say I love the pumpkin pies I make, as well. But they're not as good as the apple cobbler you made last year, Mamm. Where did you get the recipe?"

"I can't recall, Roseanna." She went over to the fridge, carrying a foil-covered dish. "I believe I have everything prepared for when your grandparents show up. I still have to defrost the turkey, and your father will be helping me stuff the bird early on Christmas morning."

"Just like he does every year." Roseanna

chuckled. "And then he'll fall asleep from eating too much turkey."

"Your Grandpa Allgyer, too." Mom went over to Roseanna and rubbed her shoulders. "Do you need help with anything before I leave?"

"No, I've got it all under control." Roseanna opened the can of pumpkin and scooped it into the medium-sized bowl. Between baking pumpkin pies and sewing dresses, she had control over some things in her life at least.

Everyone gathered around the dining-room table, with tantalizing Christmas aromas enveloping Roseanna's senses. The ring of tableware echoed in her ears, and the voices of family warmed her heart.

Occasionally, Nancy Anne would ask something in sign language, and their father would translate so the grandparents would know what she was saying.

Roseanna was disappointed when she heard Grandpa and Grandma Zook had caught the flu. It was a rarity to have everyone here at one time, and she'd been looking forward to them being here, too. She hadn't seen them since the day of the wedding. Not only that, but her grandmother wouldn't be able to have any of the pumpkin pie she'd baked. Roseanna prayed for her grandparents before they began their meal, hoping she'd be able to visit them sometime next year.

After the meal, her father and his dad went to the living room, and Adam tagged along. Roseanna and Mary headed into the kitchen to help clean up the dishes for their mother, so she could talk with Grandma Allgyer.

Roseanna ran her fingers through warm water from the faucet and sighed. She never minded doing dishes. It was a comfort. She poured the liquid soap under the stream of running water, watching as the suds began to build up and spread to the edges of the sink. The bonus was the soothing lavender fragrance.

Nancy Anne and Adam went past as they pulled on their gloves and hats.

"Where do you think you two are going?" Mary asked, signing at the same time.

"We're gonna build the best snow fort ever." Adam grinned.

"Not without me." Mary left the room for a few moments and came back wearing a jacket, scarf, and mittens, while carrying her boots over to the door. "Roseanna, wanna join us?" Mary slipped her boots on and tapped them against the wooden floor.

"Think I'll stay in here where it's warm and wait for dessert." Roseanna smiled. "You guys have fun."

"Are you sure?" Adam blinked. "You love being out in the snow. We've all gone out together every year."

"I'm not feeling up to it."

"Okay, see you later, then." Adam followed Mary and Nancy Anne out the back door.

Roseanna finished drying the dishes and went to her room, closing the door behind her. She took off her kapp and unpinned her bun. Her long tresses fell down over her shoulders, and she ran her fingers through it as best as she could to break up any tangles.

She stood by her sewing area, eyeing all of the dresses she'd made in the course of a month. Only a third of them were for buyers. Roseanna covered her mouth, giving in to her unpredictable emotions. *John, you were dishonest with me the entire time we were courting.* Her vision of the dresses blurred. *You promised we would be together for Christmas. But now . . . I don't know whether to be angry or sad about what you did to me.*

A knock sounded on her door. "Rosey, could I come in, please?"

"Uh, Mom, now is not a good time." Roseanna rubbed a palm against her chest as she turned away from the dresses. "I don't want any dessert."

"That's not why I'm here, Roseanna. Please open your door."

Roseanna went over and opened the door a crack. "What is it?"

"You have to let me in so I can show you, Rosey."

She took in a deep breath before allowing her mother to enter. Roseanna sat down on the edge of the bed as her mother unfolded a quilt in front of her.

"This beautiful covering was given to me by my mother when I was around your age. It has comforted me through hard times throughout the years, especially when your *daed* and I were having difficulties with our marriage." Mom pressed her hand on the quilt and smiled. "Your grandma Zook gave me this quilt during Christmas the same year your father and I were married, and now I want to pass it down to you, Roseanna."

Roseanna stared down at her feet. *Is it right for me to take this quilt when I don't deserve it? I didn't get married.*

Squeezing her eyes shut, Roseanna shook

her head. "No, Mom. I don't want the quilt."

"What?"

"Mom, I don't need to have it because I'm the oldest. You have two other daughters who are so close to becoming adults themselves."

"But, Roseanna —"

"Give the quilt to Mary when she gets married."

"If that's what you want."

Roseanna opened her eyes as the weight of her mother was no longer on the bed.

"Are you sure you don't want any dessert? Not even the pie you made?"

"No, it's fine. I've lost my appetite."

Mom refolded the quilt and carried it out with her without saying another word. Roseanna didn't want to turn down her mother's thoughtful gift, but she didn't see herself as being worthy of it. The decision would be different if John were here holding her in his arms and saying how much he loved her and never wanted to leave. But some things in life didn't play out exactly how people wanted them to. Some things were not meant to be.

CHAPTER 6

Roseanna thumbed through the fabrics lined up on the shelf, deciding which colors she'd take home with her. Fortunately, it didn't take too long to set the fabrics she wanted into the shopping basket.

"Now I just need some thread," Roseanna murmured as she went over to another shelf and reached above her.

"Do you need help with that, miss?" The male employee stood at the end of the aisle.

Looking around the taller person behind her, she shook her head. "No, I'm good. Thank you anyway." Roseanna stood on the tips of her toes and grabbed the spool of thread.

After Roseanna was finished gathering her needed materials, she walked to the checkout counter at the front of the variety store. She noticed Catherine was up at the register working today. Sometimes, she worked on the floor, restocking. Roseanna wondered if working here and constantly walking by all those beautiful fabrics would make it too tempting not to keep buying them. Catherine was Amish but hadn't joined the church yet. She was about two years younger than Roseanna.

Only a couple of shoppers stood in front of her, and they each held only one item. Roseanna scrambled through her purse and pulled out her wallet, opening it to grab a couple of twenties. *This should be enough for everything.* Roseanna tugged on the neckline of her dress as she moved up in the line.

"Ah, Roseanna." The cashier smiled. "How are you and your family doing?"

"We're doing okay, despite this cold weather." Roseanna wove her fingers around the bills in her hand. With the number of times she'd walked into this store, she was quite familiar with some of the employees working here. "How are things going for you, Catherine?"

"Pretty good. My brother had the flu for a few days, but he's feeling better. So far, he's the only one at the house to have gotten it." She smiled. "And we're all grateful for that."

"Good to hear. I'll be praying no one else at your place gets it." Roseanna pressed her lips together.

Catherine nodded.

Roseanna wasn't sure her response had been adequate, but it was all she could think to say.

She stood silently as Catherine rang up the items in her basket, but then the clerk lifted one of the fabrics. "This is a great color. Burgundy is one of my personal favorites." Catherine placed the fabric into a plastic bag with the rest of Roseanna's items.

"It's one of my favorites, too. I'm making a dress for one of my neighbors with that material."

"Not until you've paid for it." Catherine winked. "Which neighbor, may I ask?"

Roseanna couldn't help but giggle at that remark. "The widow, May Yoder. With her arthritis acting up, she can't do much sewing." She handed Catherine the amount she owed and then grabbed the plastic bags. "I hope the rest of your day goes well."

"Thanks. You too, Roseanna."

Roseanna pushed on the door and stepped outside, grimacing as the cold stung her face. *At least March will be here in a few weeks. There's no point in having winter winds without any snow.* She gripped her scarf.

As Roseanna approached her horse and buggy, she smelled the enticing aroma of food and wondered if she should get something to eat before heading home.

Turning away from the buggy, Roseanna walked along the street as she bundled up in her jacket, keeping warm as best she could. As she headed in the direction of the restaurant, she bumped into someone who had been passing by. This caused her to lose her grip on the plastic bags she was carrying. "I'm so sorry." Her face heated while she bent down to pick up the bags.

"Why are you apologizing? I was the one who wasn't paying attention."

Roseanna gasped when she looked up. "Mark?"

"Roseanna? Is that you?" Mark stumbled back, his expression brightening. "Oh, wow. What are the chances?" He chuckled and then bent down. "Here, let me help you pick up your stuff."

"Oh, danki." Roseanna's heart beat a little bit quicker when he inched closer to her. *Why do I feel so nervous?* She reached for a spool that had fallen from its bag and wrapped up the loose thread.

After she grabbed one of the bags, Roseanna stood up, and Mark handed her the other bag, making slight contact with her hand. Her arm trembled, but she had the cold weather as an excuse for her awkward behavior.

"Thank you again, Mark. I appreciate the help."

"No problem." He rubbed his dimpled chin and grinned. "How have you been, Roseanna?"

"I should be asking you that question. It's been a couple of years since you moved away. Are you here visiting someone?"

"Well, no. I actually moved back here about two weeks ago."

"Really?"

"Jah. I was missing this place. And the people I grew up with, too."

Mark's steady gaze made Roseanna's face heat up in a matter of seconds. "I see." She looked down at her bags. "Well, it's nice seeing you again, Mark. I better get home and get some things done."

As she was about to walk away, he rested a hand on her shoulder. "Wait, Roseanna. I know we haven't talked in a long time, but I was wondering, maybe sometime — if you're free of course — we could get something to eat and catch up."

"Umm . . ." Roseanna bit her bottom lip. "Right now isn't a good time for me."

"But weren't you heading to that restaurant across the street?" Mark raised a brow.

"I had thought about it, but there's still

some leftovers in the fridge at home I was planning to eat."

Mark laughed and nudged her shoulder. "It's okay. I wasn't expecting you to drop what you were doing right now to have lunch with me. Like I said, whenever you're free to do it is fine."

"All right."

"Okay. But before you go . . ." Mark reached into his jacket pocket and removed a pen. "Do you happen to have the receipt for the items you bought? I want to give you my home address and I have nothing to write it on."

Roseanna's hand shook as she dug through the plastic bag to find the receipt. "Here you are."

Mark took the receipt and knelt to the ground, using one of his legs as a surface to write on. While doing so, he flipped over the receipt and then looked at Roseanna. "So I see you were buying material. Does that mean you make dresses for a living, like you'd once said you wanted to do?"

"Jah, I've been doing it for over a year now."

"That's good to know."

"It's nice to earn a little money while doing something you love." She put her hands into her jacket pockets. "Speaking of jobs, what have you been doing for work?"

"Blacksmith. Mostly with horseshoes."

"Ah. And how has that been going for you, Mark?"

"As good as I'd hoped." Mark stood and handed Roseanna the receipt. "There you go. Now you can come over whenever you're ready to talk a bit more. I would love to stand around right now like we've been doing, but it's a bit chilly out here."

"So true. It was nice talking with you again, Mark."

"Same here. See you soon, Roseanna."

Karen was glad Roseanna was out shopping today. She hoped it was a sign that Roseanna was doing better.

Nancy Anne deserves a break, too. By the time she'd gotten up, her youngest daughter was in the kitchen and had the coffee going. Nancy Anne had even swept the living-room floor.

Karen stood by the washer, ringing out some towels, when Nancy Anne came into the kitchen to sweep that floor next. Karen smiled, pausing to look out the window. "Oh boy, Ash is out in the front yard eating grass," she signed, setting the broom aside. "I'd better go put him back in the corral." She groaned. "Great, Coal is out, too."

"No problem; I'll get them both put away," Nancy Anne signed. She threw on a heavy sweater and dashed out, closing the door behind her.

Karen smiled. Her youngest daughter couldn't hear, but she was certainly her most helpful child.

Karen watched out the window, to be sure neither of their buggy horses decided to be uncooperative. To her relief, Nancy Anne led both horses together into the barn.

At least their other buggy horse, Cinnamon, was with Roseanna in town today. They'd had their old horse, Millie, for several years, but they'd ended up giving her to a struggling Amish couple in a different community several years ago.

The typical February cold and breezy weather only added to the discomfort of being outdoors, so Karen wasn't eager to hang out the clothes. She finished wringing out the whites and had them piled, ready to be hung outside, when she called Mary to help get the laundry to the clothesline.

"I'm not looking forward to going out into the cold." Mary slipped on her heavy sweater.

Karen closed up her daughter's black coat and held open the back door. "I know how you feel, Daughter. Stoking the warm fire would be more my choice of something to do on a day like this."

On Mary's way out, she ran her hand into the doorjamb and almost dropped the basket. "Ow. That didn't feel too good."

"How does it look, Mary? Did you break the skin?"

Mary turned her hand to inspect the spot. "It's red and it stings a little, but I'll be okay."

They both went outside, and while Mary hung the sheets, Karen pinned all the towels to the line. With the way the breeze was blowing, the laundry would be dry in no time. "I need to start another load," she told Mary. "The next one will be the sheets off Adam's bed."

Mary hung some hand towels. "You know, Mom, I'm still not happy about how John left my sister on their wedding day. I think about it a lot."

"I agree with you. It was heartbreaking to see something like that take place — especially to one of our family members." Karen's dress stirred in the breeze. "But things happen sometimes, and there's no simple way to fix them."

"My sister should stop thinking about John and find someone new to begin courting with again." Mary dropped a clothespin and retrieved it out of the grass. "Of course, only when Roseanna has healed from her pain and is ready to move on."

Karen shook out a towel and pinned it to the line. "I'm praying for your sister, Mary. I know the Lord has the right young man for Roseanna."

Mary picked up the empty clothes basket. "You're right, Mamm. My sister needs encouragement from her family and friends. I'll keep praying, too."

Karen looked over at her. "Is something else bothering you? You look like you have a problem."

Mary toed her black clog against the grass and fidgeted. "Why does Nancy Anne get to sit in the living room, doing nothing?"

Karen frowned. "Doing nothing? Why, Nancy Anne was up early and did several chores — including putting two loose buggy horses away."

"Really? I didn't know the horses had escaped." Mary looked a tad sheepish.

"Your sister helps out around here a lot, so she deserves to sit in the living room and read a book once in a while."

"You're right, Mom. I shouldn't have assumed my sister was getting special privileges." Mary walked back to the house with

Karen, holding on to the empty laundry basket.

"That's okay, it's easy to draw the wrong conclusions when we don't have all the facts." Karen closed the back door behind her and walked over to the wringer washer.

"I hope Roseanna is enjoying her time alone in town, doing some shopping."

"I'm glad to see her keeping busy again and getting out among our community." Karen grabbed Adam's sheets and placed them in the washer.

"I'm sure she feels a bit awkward yet, but who wouldn't? I'm trying not to be prideful of how well my sister is doing."

"We'll both try hard to be humble and praise the Lord for His continued healing of our family." Karen grabbed the detergent, measured out what she needed for the washer, and started up the machine.

"I'll help you with the sheets outside when that load is finished." Mary pulled off her jacket and draped it over the kitchen chair.

Karen removed her own outer garment and slipped it on a wall peg. "We have time for a break, so I'll heat some water for tea. Would you like some?"

"I wouldn't mind some hot chocolate." Mary smiled.

Karen took the kettle over to the sink and

filled it with water. "I'll see if Nancy Anne would like anything."

"Maybe some of those snickerdoodles we made yesterday would be good with our drinks." Mary slipped off her clogs by the back door.

"I think you're right. They would taste good." Karen set the kettle onto the propane burner that she'd just turned on. "I'll go see if Nancy Anne would like something hot along with some tasty cookies."

Karen strolled out to the living room and saw her daughter engrossed in her book. She approached her from the front so there was less chance of startling Nancy Anne. Karen noticed her daughter already had a half glass of water on the end table.

Nancy Anne looked up and smiled.

Karen took a seat in the chair closest to Nancy Anne and signed: "How's your book?"

She laid it upside down in her lap. "It's a good story, full of mystery and suspense."

Karen nodded, then asked if she wanted something hot to drink or some cookies.

Nancy Anne grinned, pointed to her water, and then signed: "I'll come to the kitchen and get some snickerdoodles soon."

"Okay, I'll let you get back to reading your story." Karen headed back into the kitchen to check on the kettle.

Once the hot beverages were ready and Mary had set out the cookies, they took seats at the table, where they were joined by Nancy Anne. Karen enjoyed times like these when the simple things they did together made her feel so good.

Roseanna opened the door to her house. Leaning against the wall, she slid all the way down to the floor. *Why did I have to bump into Mark of all people?* Standing back up, she peeled her jacket off and hung it on the coatrack. *I could tell he's interested in me, like he was before. But I'm not sure how I feel about him. I only saw Mark as a friend. Nothing more.*

She went past the stairs leading to her room and headed down the hallway that led to her parents' and Nancy Anne's rooms. Roseanna knocked on her sister's door. *Oh, wait. She wouldn't be able to hear that. What am I thinking?* She opened the door a little and peered into Nancy Anne's bedroom, where she saw her lying on the floor, reading a book.

Nancy Anne placed her book down and smiled, signing, "Hello, Roseanna. How are you?"

Roseanna came into the room and sat

down. She signed an explanation of her encounter with Mark. She did her best to express how she felt during those moments when she was interacting with him and he'd offered to take her out sometime.

"Is it too soon?" She spoke in unison with her hands. "It's only been a few months since John left, and I'm not even sure if I like Mark that way."

Nancy Anne raised her hands and signed, "You'll never know unless you give Mark a chance."

Her sister was right, but Roseanna still wasn't sure if starting something with Mark was a good idea. Then again, perhaps she was overthinking the situation. Maybe Mark only wanted to catch up with her in a platonic manner. She signed while speaking again. "Should I accept his offer, or should I decline?"

Nancy Anne clambered to her feet and clasped Roseanna's arm. Then she signed: "All I want is for you to be happy."

"Happy?" Roseanna mouthed.

Nancy Anne raised both hands. "You've been unhappy ever since John left. You have been less involved with all of us because of your unhappiness. I want to see you smiling again."

Roseanna nodded. "All right. I'll give Mark a chance."

CHAPTER 7

The sun peeked over the horizon with its alluring beauty cascading on the hills in the distance. Grass prickled Roseanna's arm as she rolled over to meet Mark's gaze. "The sunset looks beautiful," she murmured.

"It certainly does." Mark crossed his arms over his head and turned onto his back. "But we'll need to be heading home soon."

"That's true. You have to wake up early for work, and I have to wake up early for chores." Shaking the grass blades from her dress, Roseanna gathered the scraps from the snacks she'd brought and put them in the picnic basket. "It's a shame the days can't be longer."

"Well, there's always another day." Mark stood up and offered his hand.

"Thank you." Roseanna took his hand and stood up then leaned forward to grab the picnic blanket.

Mark went over to his buggy and hitched

his horse while Roseanna folded up the blanket. Then she climbed into the passenger side. As she waited, Roseanna looked again at the sun, which was disappearing behind the hills. *I've never been so disappointed to have a day end.*

As they headed down the road, Roseanna leaned back on the cushion and peered out the window, eyeing the numerous stars appearing in the clear sky. *To think that those stars are so much bigger than they seem.*

"The sky looks awfully nice tonight, don't it?" Mark nudged her arm.

"Certainly a lot nicer than when we went out last time." Roseanna chuckled. "We both got soaked from being caught in a downpour after we had been nice and dry inside that restaurant."

"You ended up outrunning me to my buggy. I don't think I've ever seen you run that fast."

"Oh, trust me." She sighed. "I've run faster than that before — on the day my wedding was canceled."

They grew quiet for a while. The only sounds were the *clip-clop* of the horse's hooves as it continued to lead the buggy home. Roseanna had already told Mark what happened to her about four months ago, but she didn't give all of the specifics

— only the little bit she was ready to discuss. Roseanna's heart ached whenever she talked about John leaving her, but every time she did it, a bit of weight lifted from her soul as some of her bottled-up emotions found release. Besides, if she hadn't told Mark what had happened, someone else would have.

Mark broke the silence. "I'm sorry you had to chase after John. It wasn't fair of him to do that to you, Roseanna."

"I know." Roseanna swallowed as she reached over and placed her hand on his. "But I'm kind of relieved things happened the way they did." The heat of Mark's fingers, wrapped around her own, surrounded Roseanna with comfort and care.

"Me, too, Roseanna." He squeezed her fingers and then turned to her with a grin. "Mostly because I would've been embarrassed if you were married when I invited you to have a date with me."

Roseanna poked his shoulder and laughed.

"The next time we're together, I hope to have worked on this rig of mine. I'm gonna be painting it and cleaning all the leather on the harnesses, as well as shining up the metal trim." Mark gave her a promising gaze.

"I'm sure it will look nice when you're

through with it."

"I've bought the necessary cleaners and oils to use for all of the tack. I have the paint and brushes all ready to start on my project." He pushed back his straw hat as the buggy lurched forward.

Mark seemed happy as he drove the horse along the country road. Roseanna watched him guide the animal as the evening sky darkened. She tried not to stare at his strong, tan arms. He looked rather nice in his light, yellow shirt.

When they pulled into her parents' driveway, Roseanna saw her father beneath the battery-operated porch light. He sat in the hickory rocking chair, no doubt, waiting for her. She waved to him as they headed to the hitching post. When the buggy came to a halt, Roseanna let go of Mark's hand and moved the picnic basket and blanket over to the side. "I had a wonderful time with you today, Mark. Danki." She climbed out of the buggy and grabbed her belongings.

"It's been my pleasure, Roseanna." He grinned down at her. "Thank you, as well."

"You're welcome." Roseanna looked toward her house and back at Mark. "Do you want to come in for a little bit? I mean, I know you have to be up early tomorrow, but you're welcome to, if you want."

"Sure. I don't see why not." He climbed down from the buggy and secured his horse.

To avoid any questions from Dad, Roseanna led Mark to the back of the house. She opened the door and held it for him as they entered. She sat down on the inside stairs to unfasten her shoes. "You don't need to take off your shoes since you won't be staying too long. But make sure you rub them against the throw rug in case you track anything in."

When Roseanna stepped into the hallway with Mark, she went over to Nancy Anne's slightly opened door and pressed on it.

"Why are we going to your deaf sister's room?"

"Shh . . . Mark."

"What? She can't hear us."

"Jah, but that's no excuse for you to say that." Roseanna walked in and went over to Nancy Anne, whose back was facing them. She nudged her sister's shoulder to get her attention.

Nancy Anne's expression changed from a look of contentment to one of excitement when she turned to Roseanna. Placing her book down, a soft noise came from her as she signed "Hello, sister."

"Hello, Nancy." Roseanna spoke and signed to her. "Did you have a good day?"

Nancy Anne signed, "Mamm and I baked some cookies."

"Oh, that's nice. May I have some later?"

She nodded and then looked past Roseanna, motioning with her hands.

"What did she say?" Mark came over and stood next to Roseanna.

"Nancy Anne said, 'You're welcome to have a cookie, too.' "

"Oh. Thank you, Nancy Anne."

Roseanna's sister nodded again. Nancy Anne could read lips fairly well, but it didn't work all the time when she communicated with people. Some words would appear similar when there was no sound to distinguish them.

"Wait, Roseanna." Mark touched her arm. "How do you sign those common greetings again? It's a bit confusing to me."

"Oh, okay. Let me show you a few of them. You can always ask me for reminders whenever you want."

Roseanna knew Mark wasn't fond of the idea of learning sign language, but she was relieved to know he was willing to try.

"Come on, Roseanna!" Katie yelled from the volleyball field at the local park the following day. "We need you on our team!"

Roseanna placed her belongings near the

pile. After unzipping her bag and enjoying a refreshing drink from her water bottle, she hurried over to Katie and the rest of the group.

"All right, I'm here." Roseanna rubbed a drop of sweat from her forehead. "But I don't see why you guys need me to play. I'm not very good at volleyball."

Samantha, another friend of Roseanna's, patted her on the back. "Ach. You're being too modest, like usual."

"Only being honest. Katie is a natural at it, though."

"Yeah, well . . ." Samantha wrapped one arm around her torso. "I suppose."

Katie ran over to Samantha and nearly tackled her. "You may not have done well this last match, Samantha, but I believe you can improve your overall technique."

"Katie, really? She did an okay job." One of the girls from the other side of the net spoke up. "It's just for fun."

"I know. I know." Katie let go of Samantha and raised her shoulders in a proud manner. "But I must do my best to improve our team as a functioning unit for better results. We must think as one to be able to succeed in winning, because failure is not fun."

A buggy pulled in and parked. Mark

jumped out and waved toward Roseanna. Katie eyed him tying his horse to the hitching post. "You've got company, my friend."

"You're right. There's Mark." Roseanna waved at him then looked back at her best friend. "Now, about our playing method here." She grabbed Katie's shoulders. "We are not doing that. No need to take this seriously when we all have other things more important to worry about."

"I didn't think he'd be here today since this was a girls' day out. He must really like you to drop by and see you here unannounced," Katie was quick to blurt out.

"I don't think so," Roseanna countered. "He probably was on his way somewhere nearby and decided to pop in and watch us play for a little bit."

Mark took a seat nearby. The girls played out the match and were getting ready to change sides, so Roseanna stopped to grab her water bottle. She strolled over to Mark and sat next to him.

"You remembered I'd be here playing today." She smiled.

"Yep. I'm on my way to take care of something and thought I'd stop and see you. Are you and the girls getting some exercise?" Mark laughed. "Now if it were all guys out there, you'd see some major game-playing going on."

"We've got a few good matches happening so far. Besides, we aren't out there to hurt one another. Only friendly games, like it should be."

Mark caressed her hand. "You should know we fellas play more roughly and strive to be the best at times."

"Okay, if you say so." Roseanna rolled her eyes but held on to his hand with tenderness.

Mark motioned toward his horse and buggy. "I've been touching up the black paint on my rig, and it's looking a lot better."

"You've mentioned that you might work on fixing it up." She also looked at his buggy.

"All of my horse's gear has been cleaned up, and my horse had a bath yesterday." Mark's tone sounded self-assured, and his expression seemed confident.

"Hey, Roseanna!" Katie yelled. "Are you playing or not?"

"I better get back to my errand." Mark let go of her hand and stood up.

"Thank you for dropping by and visiting with me." Roseanna grinned and moved toward her teammates. "Will I see you later?"

"You can bet on it. I'll be by soon, Roseanna." He waved and headed back to the hitching rail.

She watched him leave then walked back and rejoined her teammates. *I like that Mark came by just to see me. I wonder what the other girls are thinking about this.*

"Roseanna, are you ready to play?" Katie tapped her shoulder.

"Certainly, I am." She cheerfully stepped over to her spot.

After they played for another half hour, most everyone grabbed up their belongings and headed home. Before Roseanna finished drinking the rest of her water, Katie approached her with hesitation. "Hey, can I speak to you for a second?"

"If it's about my volleyball technique, then no," Roseanna teased.

"Actually, it's about Mark. I mean — oh, where do I even start?"

"What about Mark?" Roseanna's heartbeat quickened. "Did it bother you that he came by here to see me?"

Katie shook her head. "It's nothing like that. It's just . . . well, what if John comes back to Lykens? Should you be courting with Mark when John could still show up and decide to marry you?"

Roseanna couldn't believe what her friend had said. After speaking with Katie months ago about John running away from a previous chance at marriage, she should understand that he was not the right man for her.

"Are you saying I should be with someone who keeps secrets?" Roseanna leaned forward. "With someone who disregards my feelings for his own? Not even caring how I feel? Is that it?"

"No, but, Roseanna, I don't think Mark's suitable for you, either."

"Why not?"

"He seems a bit full of himself and you're nothing like that at all."

"Mark cares for me, and he makes me happy. And what would you know about who is more suitable for me anyway?"

"Roseanna . . ."

Clenching her teeth to avoid saying anything she'd regret, Roseanna grabbed her bag. Standing up straight, she looked at Katie one more time before heading to her buggy. *Why would Katie want me to be with someone who betrayed me for his own selfish reasons? Do I not deserve to be happy?*

CHAPTER 8

Roseanna sat on her bed as she finished sewing the hem, holding the dress up to look at her work. "See? That's how you properly stitch with a needle and thread."

"I still don't understand how you're able to put it together so quickly." Samantha reached over to touch it. "This is beautiful, Roseanna."

"Danki." Roseanna handed her the dress. "I enjoyed making it, so I hope you enjoy wearing it."

"Of course I will. It was made by a talented dressmaker." Samantha held it up to the window, and the color of the dress glistened like stained glass.

Roseanna laughed. "Okay, I don't need to be praised."

Samantha scooted off the bed and placed the blue dress in the bag she'd brought with her. After she grabbed her purse, Samantha unzipped an outside pocket and held out the amount of money she owed Roseanna.

"Danki, Samantha. But you don't need to pay me. You're my friend."

"No, no. I insist. This is what you're doing for a living, and I'd feel awful depriving you of your pay."

Swallowing, Roseanna glanced at the money, while her muscles tensed. She tentatively reached out and took the money, placing it on her nightstand. "Danki, Samantha." She stood up from the bed and picked up her purse. "We should probably get going."

"Jah. You'll want to be back here before Mark shows up for your date."

"That is true. Then again, Mark seems to get along with Adam pretty well, so maybe it wouldn't be too bad if I was late." Roseanna threaded her arm through her purse straps. "They have bonded quite well, which is surprising, since Adam was not so talkative around Mark before he moved away."

"Really?" Samantha crossed her arms. "That's a bit strange."

"I think it's because Adam had a difficult time communicating with people older than him. Now he seems to enjoy listening in on adult conversations. But he can still be immature at times."

Samantha sighed. "I see. Speaking of being immature, Katie still hasn't talked with you since we played volleyball together, has she?"

"No . . ." Roseanna's body felt weighed down when she recalled how she'd snapped at Katie. *I know it wasn't right for me to get mad at her, but I still don't understand why she would want me to wait for John.* She tugged on her ear. *Would she wait for someone who had dumped her?* It wasn't as if it was the first time he'd done it, either. John couldn't be trusted.

Samantha placed a hand on Roseanna's shoulder. "Will you and Katie be okay? You guys have been friends for more than eight years, haven't you?"

"About that long." Roseanna saw the concern in Samantha's smoky-gray eyes. She could tell Samantha wanted the best for Roseanna and Katie's friendship.

They both headed downstairs to the kitchen. Roseanna noticed the eggs she'd set out to boil for later. "I forgot about this little job."

"I guess we were up in your room longer than you'd anticipated." Samantha tied her bag closed. "Well, you can't leave a pot boiling on the burner, or the kitchen will burn down. So maybe you ought to put the eggs back in the refrigerator." After patting

Roseanna on the back, Samantha went over to the door. "Shall we get going to town?"

"Okay." Roseanna put the eggs away and followed her friend out the back door and down the stairs. She would have plenty to think about while they were out shopping.

Ronks

John climbed down from the ladder leading up to the roof, carefully placing his foot on the small steps.

"Careful, John. You don't want to hurt yourself."

"Don't worry. I do this for a living, Aunt Lena." John jumped down as soon as he was close enough to the ground. "Besides, I know that Uncle Harvey will be happy with it."

"I'm sure he will. But I still want you to be careful." She patted his shoulder. "It's about time for a lunch break, don't you think? You've been tearing at that roof for a couple of hours."

"I've gotten about half the roofing off so far, and I'll need to finish it up after lunch." John walked out a ways from the house to get a better look.

"There's a lot of mess on the lawn with the wayward shingles and those loose nails lying around." Aunt Lena daintily walked on the grass about halfway to him and turned, looking up at the roof. "I'm glad I don't have to be up there working." She looked over at John. "Especially with the way my balance is. I'd be on the ground, lickety-split."

"Well, you don't need to worry about helping me up there. I've got it covered." He smiled. "I'll get this stuff picked up and out of here in a day or two. Just be careful where you step until I get this all cleaned up out here." He strode up to his aunt.

"It will be nice not having to worry about a leaking roof for a long while." She stood with her arms crossed.

"I'm really ready for something to eat, and a big glass of water would be good, too." John stepped toward the porch. Feeling his stomach grumbling, he pulled off his work gloves and laid them on the railing. He inspected his hand for any blisters but didn't see any. Then he removed his tool belt and carried it with him into the house, putting it on the floor with his shoes. "I better wash these filthy hands of mine before I decide what to have for lunch."

"Do you want me to make you anything?" his aunt called from the kitchen.

"No, thank you. I'll make myself some-thing." John went right to the sink and turned on the faucet. After he dried his hands, he eyed the multiple cans in the wooden lazy Susan in the cupboard. "Would it be okay if I had some tomato soup for lunch?"

"Sure. Go right ahead, dear." His aunt opened one of the cabinet doors and pulled out a small pot, placing it on the propane stove.

"Danki."

John lit the stove and carefully stirred the soup to keep it from burning. The robust smell reminded him of his childhood. His mother made tomato soup frequently when he was attending school, and he always looked forward to the evenings where a warm bowl of soup waited for him.

After the soup was ready, John turned the stove off and served himself with a ladle his aunt provided. Carefully, he carried the full bowl over to the dining-room table.

"John, you could've carried the pot over with a pot holder and served yourself."

"I figured this would be easier, but I know what you mean." John placed no amount of force to the bowl when he set it on the table.

Aunt Lena sat across from him, chewing on a slice of salami. She had an assortment of snack items on her plate. "You know, you can't stay with your uncle and me forever."

John loosened his grip on the spoon, but was able to catch it before it landed in his bowl. "What are you saying?"

"Roseanna will not wait forever for you, John. She will find someone else to be with, and whether you return to her or not, is all up to you."

"Roseanna is better off without me." John slumped in the wooden chair. "How could I even approach her after what I did to her? I don't know if she could ever forgive me. Besides, I'm not ready for marriage and may never be."

Aunt Lena took a bite of one of the crackers. "You need to pray about what the best choice would be. Otherwise, you may end up regretting it."

He shifted in his seat. *I'm not good at praying right now.*

Lykens

"Is Mark already here?" Roseanna asked Mary when she walked into the living room.

"I don't think so. I would've noticed if he were."

"I need some help deciding which dress to wear before Mark gets here." Roseanna brought down three of her dresses from upstairs.

"I like the russet one you just set down on

the chair." Mary shuffled her feet on the wooden floor. "You appear to be putting some extra effort into this date tonight."

"Of course I am. Anyone should if she wants to make a good impression." Roseanna picked up the bluish-lavender dress. "Are you sure I wouldn't look better in this one?"

"You do look fine in that one, Sister." Mary giggled. "But that's the same dress you wore out last time, remember?"

"Oh, that's right." Roseanna shook her head. "What would I do without your help?"

"You'd wear the same dress over and over again, probably," Mary teased.

"Okay, that's good." Feeling a sudden sense of giddiness, Roseanna kept a hold of her head covering as she walked over to Mary. "It was windy most of the day while Samantha and I were shopping."

Mary's eyes trailed upward. "I can see that, Roseanna."

"I know. My kapp almost flew away from me. That's why I'm glad Mark isn't here yet. I can't go out with my hair so untidy." Roseanna picked up the dresses and hurried upstairs. *I hope I have enough time to slip into my sister's choice of garment and redo my bun.*

Fortunately, Roseanna was quick as she

changed her clothes, plucked the pins from her bun and brushed through her dark curls. As soon as she placed the covering over her bun and secured it, she stood up, making sure all was good, and hurried down the steps. Her stomach fluttered when she reached the bottom of the stairs. "Hi, Mark."

"Hello, Roseanna." He smiled, not taking his eyes off of her. "Can I talk to you for a second? Before we go on our date?"

That fluttering sensation was gone as instantly as when it first started. Her mouth felt parched. "What is it?"

"Come with me outside. It'll give us more privacy."

Roseanna tried to calm herself by controlling her breathing. *Does he want to end our relationship?* She didn't want Mark to be aware of her nervousness, so she stood upright to appear more confident. "All right."

Leading her outside, Mark held her hand more gently than he typically did. He turned to her when they were next to the garden in the backyard. "Roseanna, I know we've been with each other for only a few months, but I feel something has grown between us. We have a good thing going, and . . ."

"And what, Mark?"

He lowered his head and tightened his hold on her hand. "When I asked if I could court you a couple of years ago, you said you weren't interested in being in a committed relationship."

Rosanna nodded.

Mark raised his head slightly. "But even after I moved away, I couldn't stop thinking about you. I would close my eyes and remember your pretty eyes and wonderful smile."

"Mark . . ."

"Now that I have you, Roseanna, I never want to let you go." He paused. "I know it was bold of me to say those words to you." He looked into her eyes. "We can take this relationship between us slow. I'm willing to do that for you."

Her legs felt weak, but Roseanna continued to keep herself composed. "I —"

"It's okay, Roseanna." He reached for her other hand. "I know you've been through so much when I wasn't here, and you have every right to be leery. Just think about it, okay?"

She smiled and nodded.

Roseanna felt even colder than she did during the winter. Mark admitted how strongly he felt about her, yet Roseanna still wasn't sure how she fully felt about him.

Was it too soon for her to feel this way about another person when she was close to being married just a few months ago? At least Mark sounded willing to take things at the pace Roseanna would feel most comfortable.

He is up front with his feelings for me and doesn't seem to be the type to back out all of a sudden. Not like John . . .

Chapter 9

After everything from breakfast had been put away, Karen decided to take the bull by the horns and go work on a big overdue project. It would be a tad cooler in the basement, so she wrapped up in her shawl. The old, familiar steps creaked as she went down to the basement. Because their family had been accumulating possessions for years, she figured it was time to sort through them and give away the items they no longer had any use for. Knowing how many memories she would lose by doing that, Karen felt some regret, but it had to be done.

When she went over to the stockpile of household goods, her nose tickled from the light coat of dust. *I'll need to clean off these things before I can find them a good home.*

The first cardboard box was full of mismatched dishes. "Oh boy. That will need to go." She touched the bowl on top of the plates. *Why haven't I given this away or tried to let go of them through a yard sale?* Karen dove into another box. Her fingers felt something soft.

"What's this?" She lifted the fabric out of the box. "Oh, yeah. This is an old table covering we used before Mary was born." Karen cradled it close to her and squeezed it with her arms. "Now someone will have the chance to make memories with it."

After she placed the tablecloth down, Karen went through more of the family's belongings. She found some kitchen utensils and piled them on the cloth then stuck her hand in one of the other boxes. Karen had held off sorting their possessions, for the sake of sentimental value. It was her way of recollecting cherished memories.

A lot of time has passed since Seth and I moved to Lykens. So many things have happened. She grasped a book entitled *Beginner's Guide to Sign Language.* "Not all of the memories were positive, but the Lord can bring good from everything, even if we may not see the good at first."

After placing more items into a pile, Karen reached into another box and raised her eyebrows when her hands touched familiar material. She pulled it from the box, flipping it over to reveal its face. "Big Ears." She smiled. "Mary's toy rabbit."

Karen remembered when Mary toddled around the house with Roseanna, carrying Big Ears with her and hopping around like a rabbit. It was adorable. Of course all of her children had grown older, yet it was difficult to move past those memories. In some ways, Karen was relieved when John left a few weeks after he ran out on the wedding. If he and Roseanna had gotten married, Roseanna would be gone and Karen would've had to adapt to no longer having her eldest daughter in the house. Roseanna was an exceptional role model for her three younger siblings, especially to Nancy Anne. How would she be without her oldest sister living in the house anymore?

She picked up the stuffed animal and walked over to the staircase. "Mary! Are you up there?" Karen called.

"Jah!" Mary hurried down the stairs. "What is it, Mamm?"

"I have something to give you." Karen handed her the rabbit. "Do you remember this?"

"Big Ears!" Mary's eyes brightened.

"You used to carry him around with you all the time when you were younger."

Mary touched the rabbit's ears, closing her eyes. "Yes, I did. I had Big Ears with me whenever I was with Roseanna."

"That's right." Karen reached out, placing her hand on Mary's arm. "You looked up to Roseanna back then and wanted to be like her."

Mary opened her eyes. "I wasn't trying to be like Roseanna."

"Are you sure about that?"

"Mamm, do you like to *retze*?"

Karen chuckled. "I'm sorry, Mary. I won't tease you about it anymore. However, I need to ask something of you."

"Hmm?"

"I know you are closer to Roseanna than you are to Nancy Anne and Adam, but since Roseanna may not be living at this house much longer, I need you to encourage your younger siblings. Especially Nancy Anne."

"What? But I'm very encouraging to her. I talk to her through sign language all the time, and we are always together."

"Okay." Karen went over to the boxes. "Do you want to keep Big Ears? I'm sorting through some things and deciding what to give away."

Mary looked down at the stuffed animal. "I guess I'll keep him."

"All right, it's up to you." Karen reached into the box. "But some of this stuff doesn't belong to your dad and me. I need you to get your siblings down here to go through these boxes, too. Could you please do that for me?"

"I'll go get them, but shouldn't Daed be going through this stuff also?"

"Your father does enough around here, so don't worry about that, and focus on doing what I asked, please."

Mary went up the stairs, calling for Adam.

Karen sighed. *If Mark is right for Roseanna, then I'll have to prepare for my oldest daughter moving away all over again.* She gathered up some of the items and looked to the staircase. *Mary will have to prepare for that, too.*

Roseanna's hand shook when she prepared to knock on Katie's front door. She lowered it immediately. *I can't do this. Katie should be apologizing to me, not the other way around. I have every right to be upset with her.* Roseanna turned away and stepped down from the porch step. *I need more time to think this over.*

On the way back to her house, she stopped along the side of the road, and her throat thickened. *This . . . this is where I met John for the first time.* Roseanna pressed her fingernails into her palms and continued walking. *Why am I so bothered by this? John didn't love me — or did he?* She rubbed her forehead and quickened her pace, trying to get him out of her thoughts. Roseanna had Mark now, and he'd opened himself to her weeks ago, yet she still wasn't sure what to do. She'd had a difficult time trusting people before she met John, but what ability to trust she did have had evaporated after John ran from the wedding. Even her friendship with Katie had been affected by it. No wonder she didn't want to be hasty with her decisions anymore.

On her way home, she saw May Yoder at her mailbox. The older woman waved at her. "How are you doing today, Roseanna?"

"I'm okay. I was out walking this morning and getting some fresh air." Roseanna grinned. She didn't want to admit to the widow that she couldn't apologize first to a good friend. How long was it going to take for her to give in and do the proper thing to save a worthwhile friendship?

"Getting some exercise sounds like a good idea." Mary cleared her throat. "I've already worn the dress you sewed up that I ordered. You did a fine job. The garment fits well and is comfortable."

Roseanna smiled. "I'm glad you like it."

The older woman looked overhead at the blue sky. "If you take a minute to look around, you can really see the Lord's handiwork." She hesitated a spell, looking up toward her house. "I'm thankful for my family and all of the dear friends in my life. We shouldn't stay upset with any of them. I remind myself to always work toward resolving problems that come along." The widow looked at the mail in her hands. "Well, I best get up to the house and try to get some wash going. You have a good day now, Roseanna." She closed her mailbox.

"Thank you. You also have a nice day." Roseanna turned and started walking. *That was weird how she said those things to me, even though she has no idea what I've been going through. Maybe the Lord was speaking through her.*

Roseanna kicked her feet against the gravel in her parents' driveway, noticing Adam was near the shed messing with a pocketknife and a piece of wood. "You'd better be careful with that knife, kid. I don't want you to cut one of your fingers."

Adam looked up at her and frowned. "Don't worry about me. I'm not the clumsy one in this family. Besides, I'm not a kid."

"Okay, but don't say I didn't offer a warning if you hurt yourself." Roseanna walked over to Adam and patted him on the back. "You're my only brother, so I have to worry about you."

"Heh. Thanks." Adam's expression softened as he continued to slice the wood. "Same to you, Roseanna."

She smirked. "That I'm your only brother?"

"No, I mean — you get what I mean."

"I know. I'll let you get on with it." Roseanna rushed to the house.

Removing her shoes, she ran up to her room. Sewing for a while should give her a break from troubling thoughts. She rummaged through a plastic bag, took out her recently purchased supplies, and sat down next to the sewing table. "I better start making one of the children's dresses, since it uses less fabric."

Nancy Anne came bounding into the room where Roseanna sat. "Hi, Sister," she signed.

She scooted her chair away from the sewing table. "Hi. What's up? Come take a seat and visit with me."

Her sister did so but looked at her with a strange expression.

Nancy Anne is too intuitive about me. I feel a bit transparent with little ole smarty pants sitting next to me. Maybe I'll fool her this time, if I can keep up a good front.

Nancy Anne signed: "I was about to get the glass cleaner out to wipe down the windows. When I saw you come in from outdoors you seemed a little upset. What's up, Roseanna?"

She sat in her chair mulling over what to say. "I thought I'd go down to Katie's place this morning and apologize for the disagreement we had awhile back."

Nancy Anne sat looking intently at her and waited.

"But I didn't follow through on my task. I guess it turns out I'm not quite ready yet."

Roseanna's sister patted her shoulder. "You did try, so that's a start." Nancy Anne smiled as her hands expressed her thoughts. "My advice is to keep praying for strength. It should come to you in time, and then you'll be ready."

Roseanna mouthed, "Thank you, Nancy Anne." She got up and gave her youngest sister a hug. They visited a little while longer, and then Nancy Anne left to wash more windows. Roseanna got up and went to the window, stretching her arms out. She closed her eyes and quoted Psalm 31:3. *I know Mom repeats that verse often, but where did she get it from?*

As she was laying out material on the table, Roseanna couldn't stop thinking about Mark's willingness to wait for her to decide if she was ready to fully commit to their relationship.

The tempered wind swept into the room from the open window as she leaned forward and laid her head on her propped-up hand. *I am thankful to have Mark in my life. He has been nothing but good to me, even before we ended up together. He's always shown devotion to everything he does.* Roseanna closed her eyes, breathing softly through her mouth. *Could I ever return the love he has for me?*

Roseanna recalled the feelings she'd had before entering the tent that Thursday morning. The feelings of uncertainty. She'd been worried things might not work out between her and John. Yet she'd pushed her doubts aside. But with Mark, as strange as it was for Roseanna, she had no feelings of uncertainty. What held her back was the possibility of getting hurt a second time. Was she willing to risk being vulnerable again?

She got up from her sewing table. "I'm going to see Mark and tell him that I'm sure of our relationship now."

Walking with wide steps, Roseanna was at the back door in a matter of moments, stopping to slip on her shoes. *Mark will be relieved to know that I'm sure of myself now.* Roseanna twisted the doorknob. *Maybe we could do something together after I tell him that —*

"Roseanna! Are you going somewhere?"

The sound of her heartbeat thrashed through Roseanna's ears as she stood with the door hanging open, staring at her runaway groom. "J–John?"

CHAPTER 10

This cannot be happening right now. Roseanna shut the door in John's face, gulping air until she began to feel light-headed. *Why is he here?* John knocked again. It had been rude to close the door in his face, but she'd acted on impulse. She'd never expected to see him again — especially after all these months.

Trying to regain her composure, Roseanna grasped the knob. When she opened the door, she was surprised to find him still there.

John lowered his head. "Roseanna, I know that I'm probably the last person you'd want to speak to, but —"

"That's a bit of an understatement." Roseanna bit her tongue.

"Maybe this isn't a good time. I'll come back later."

"No." Her palms were damp as she held them against her hot cheeks. Roseanna lifted her chin, trying not to show how badly she was shaken. Keeping her tone steady and firm, she said, "You may as well tell me what you came here to say."

John's gaze trailed up to hers. "I don't know where to start, but I'm gonna try. Can I please come in?"

Roseanna shook her head. "I'd prefer if we didn't talk inside. Let's take this out somewhere in the yard where there are fewer interruptions."

"Okay." John stepped out of her way.

Roseanna's thoughts were jumbled as they walked along. She felt like screaming out her frustrations — reminding John of how much damage he'd done by running away from her. He'd thrown everything Roseanna thought she knew about him out the window and turned his back on her. But nothing was ever one sided. There were always explanations for a person's behavior, good or bad. John had first appeared to be an honest and upright person, who would never hurt someone intentionally, but she'd obviously misjudged him.

Taking a deep breath, Roseanna crossed her arms, waiting for John to speak.

"Roseanna, I'm sorry for everything. I made a huge mistake leaving you." Beads of sweat glistened on his forehead, and he reached up to swipe it away. "I just . . . I got scared. I regret what I did to you. I know I hurt you and . . . I wish I could take it all back."

Roseanna's throat tightened as she drew in a deep breath. "That's not all, John."

"W–what?" He stood near a shrub and pinched off a leaf in his nervousness.

"Your mom came over here to check up on me a couple of days after you left. She told me what happened with your previous girlfriend."

His face paled, and he took a step back, bumping against a tree. "I wish she hadn't told you that. It was my place to do the telling."

"Then why didn't you?" Roseanna kept her gaze locked on his.

"I — Well, it was too hard to admit. If you had known, you may not have agreed to marry me."

Roseanna bit the inside of her cheek. "What was her name? Do you still love her, John?"

"You think that's why I left?"

"I don't know. . . . Maybe."

He shook his head. "That wasn't the reason, Roseanna. I haven't spoken to Sara for several years."

"Then what, John?" She groaned. "Was it

because you had second thoughts about me? Did you suddenly decide you didn't love me anymore? Was that why you ran out in the middle of our wedding?" Roseanna's voice quavered.

"I . . . I . . ." He rubbed his eyes with his sleeve.

Roseanna heard a bird in the distance singing to its heart's content. The bird's cheerful tune was the only thing keeping her calm.

"Please, give me the chance to prove myself to you. I want you back, Roseanna. I want you to trust me again."

"John, I can't."

"I couldn't stop thinking about you. I still love you, Roseanna. Please. I'm so sorry." His voice cracked.

"It's too late for us. I'm with someone else now." Roseanna could not believe after all these months that John had just shown up. If he was going to come back, why couldn't it have been before she became involved with Mark?

As John walked away from the yard, he couldn't keep himself from looking over his shoulder. *This is what I deserve.* He clenched his fists, heat radiating throughout his shaking body. *I would be with her right now if I weren't such a coward.*

John headed to the hitching post, hoping no one else had noticed he was here. He didn't want to be approached by any of Roseanna's family. He'd come here hopeful that Roseanna would take him back, but he realized now there wasn't much chance for that ever happening.

"Hey!"

Mary? Oh, great. I better pick up the pace. John climbed into his buggy to make a quick getaway, but Mary came running up next to the back wheel.

"John, what are you doing here?"

"I came to apologize to your sister."

"Well, you're a little late." Mary stepped near the front of the buggy. "Months late."

"Jah . . ." He rubbed the back of his neck.

"You know, Roseanna might have taken you back if you had shown up before Mark began courting her. Not right away, of course, but I know how she felt about you. When you two were courting, she could never stop talking about you."

John looked away. What could he say? Mary wasn't wrong, and he certainly wasn't about to deny it.

"I told my family I was going to give you a piece of my mind if I ever saw you again, but you voluntarily showed up here to apologize to Roseanna, so I won't say anything more." Mary crossed her arms. "Just don't ruin my sister's happiness because of your mistake. She deserves to be happy after everything she's been through." She turned and walked away.

As John headed back to his folks' house, all he could think about was Roseanna and the mess he'd made of things. Was there a chance he could get her back, or was it too late for them now?

"I don't know what to do, Mom." Roseanna stumbled over her words. "I still can't believe John came back. It's too much for me to take in." She sniffed. "I don't even know what I want anymore."

Pulling Roseanna into an embrace, her mother rubbed her back tenderly. "It's okay, Rosey. It's going to be all right."

"Is it?" Roseanna's throat felt parched, and her sight had become hazy. She would've fallen to the floor if it weren't for her mother propping her up. "I need to sit down."

"That's fine." Mom led her to the living room. "Just try to relax for now."

"Danki." She slumped on the chair and closed her eyes. *Breathe, Roseanna. Breathe. You'll get through this somehow.* Roseanna's chest felt like it was weighed down by bricks.

"I'll make you some tea. Want something to snack on, too?"

"No, tea is fine. I'm not very hungry."

Why did she feel so conflicted about this situation? She'd been so sure of her feelings for Mark, but seeing John again brought back the familiarity she'd once had with him. And Roseanna now realized that she hadn't fully moved on from their relationship. How was she supposed to when John was back in Lykens and wanting her back? Did she want to move on?

"Here you go, Rosey. Some chamomile to help you relax." Her mother placed the mug down on the side table. "I hope it'll make you feel better."

She paused then brought up another point. "Now that John is back home, you'll probably be bumping into him here and there. What will you do?"

Roseanna pondered the question.

Her mom rocked slowly, sipping her tea and nibbling on a cookie. "If you don't feel comfortable being in Lykens right now, maybe you could stay with Grandpa and Grandma Zook in Paradise for a while. I'm sure they would love for you to come and hang out with them while you sort this all out, Roseanna."

She shifted in her seat and looked over at her mom. "I think that would be good. I'm confused about John being around again. It's strange. When he left and was away for so long, I adapted." Roseanna's hands rested in her lap. "Right after the wedding I wanted him back with me. But now my heart simply feels numb to him."

Her mother got up and gave Roseanna a hug. "You need to pray through this, Daughter, and the Lord will make things much clearer for you in His time. Then you can decide how to pursue this situation." Mom released Roseanna and smiled brightly. "I'll go out to the phone shed here in a few minutes and give Grandma Zook a call and line it up for you."

"Thanks so much." As her mother left, Roseanna sipped from her mug of tea and thought. While she was collecting herself, a knock sounded at the front door. Roseanna couldn't stop her heartbeat from quickening. *Please, don't let that be Mark.*

She went to open the door.

"Hi, Roseanna."

"Oh." Relieved it wasn't Mark, Roseanna still wasn't excited about her guest. "Hello, Katie."

"Could I come in? I need to talk to you." Katie's voice was unusually soft.

"I suppose." She moved from the doorway to allow Katie to come in. Roseanna then led her upstairs so they could have a private conversation. It was strange that her best friend felt almost like a stranger.

"I'm so sorry," Katie cried. "I shouldn't have said those things to you. I thought I was helping, and I didn't mean to make you upset."

Roseanna's heart plunged as she watched Katie's tears stream down her face. She didn't know how to respond. Awkwardly, Roseanna wrapped her arms around her friend.

Gasping for air, Katie continued. "Please forgive me. I don't want you to be mad because of what I said."

"I'm not mad about that anymore, Katie." Roseanna rubbed her back, the way Mom had rubbed hers earlier. "It's all right."

"No, it's not. I ruined our friendship."

"You didn't. We're still friends, Katie. We'll always be friends, no matter what." Roseanna tightened her arms and squeezed, hoping to reassure her. "I forgive you. I'm sorry for snapping at you."

"Roseanna, you had every right to." Katie sniffed. "But I forgive you, too."

"Every argument is two sided. Besides . . ." Roseanna let go of Katie, feeling heat rise to her forehead, "you were right."

Katie's eyes widened. "Did you and Mark break up?"

"Ach! Not that. No, but John was here earlier."

"Really? What happened?"

Roseanna briefly told her friend what had occurred. Even talking about it caused her to get a little riled up.

"Oh my word, Roseanna." Katie clasped her hand over her mouth. "What are you going to do?"

Roseanna took a seat on her bed and invited Katie to join her. "I have an idea. My mom is calling my grandmother in Paradise about me staying with her and Grandpa for a while. All I know is that I need some time to think." She went over to her closet and slid some of the dresses from the hangers. "I'll need to get my suitcase and start figuring out what I should bring with me for my long visit. I can't stay here with the possibility of Mark or John showing up."

"But, Roseanna, it's not good to run away from your problems."

"That's not what I'm doing." She pulled out her bag from the closet floor and stuffed the dresses inside. "I know I'll do something I'll regret if I simply react irrationally."

Roseanna gathered more of her belongings and laid them on her bed. Her friend sat there watching. "I'll miss you while you're gone. If you need me to help in some way or do anything for you, just let me know."

"Thank you, Katie. I'll give you my grandparent's phone number before you go home so we can chat. I will need a good friend like you to talk to."

She didn't want to leave without Mark knowing where she was going, but she had to do what she believed was best. *Maybe I wasn't ready to commit to you after all. I'm sorry, Mark.*

CHAPTER 11

Karen missed her oldest daughter already, and she could tell her other children did, too. Suppertime was different without Roseanna's presence at their table. Karen and Seth both wondered how long their daughter would be gone but knew what was most important was to pray for her.

Karen pulled an apple cake from the oven. She inhaled the sweet spicy aroma and decided to take a quick breather. She took some relaxing sips of her warm tea. Eyeing the washer, Karen set her drink down. First, she should get the clothes out on the line to dry.

I'm going to my bedroom to get a sweater. There's a slight chill in the air this morning.

Karen stood in front of her dresser and sifted through her choices. She picked out an old gray sweater that wouldn't be damaged by her housework. As she was leaving, her eye caught sight of the pretty box sitting in the corner of her room. *I wish my daughter had accepted the Christmas quilt. If only my Roseanna was happily married, instead of going through such turmoil.* Karen closed the bedroom door and proceeded back out to the kitchen.

Picking up the heavy laundry basket, she lumbered out to the clothesline. A buggy was coming up their lane. "That looks like Mark's rig, and he's pulling in here."

Nancy Anne came over, wearing a shawl, and stood by her. "I'm done with my chores, Mom. I thought I'd go for a walk." She spoke with her hands. "Mark's here. I wonder why."

"I'll be finding out soon. He's already securing his horse," Karen signed. "Enjoy your morning walk, Daughter."

Nancy Anne nodded and headed for the road, pausing briefly to wave at Mark.

"Good morning, Mrs. Allgyer. Is Roseanna around? I came by to see her."

"Hello, Mark." Karen hung up some socks. "Sorry, but Roseanna isn't here and won't be back until she works through some things."

"Roseanna left?" Mark pulled on his shirt collar. "When did she leave? Where did she go?"

"She left a few days ago to spend some

time with her grandparents down in Lancaster County." Karen shook out a pair of damp trousers and hung them on the clothesline.

"Why would she go there without telling me? I had no idea she planned to go anywhere." Mark drew a quick breath. "Business has been overwhelming this week, and I've been too busy to even come by or ask her on a date."

Karen bit her lip. "You know how Roseanna mentioned to you that her groom ran from their wedding last year?"

"Jah, but what does that have to do with anything?"

"Well, apparently John is back. Roseanna said he came to see her, and she was quite upset." Once the basket was empty, Karen picked it up and moved toward the house.

"Please, can you tell me where her grandparents live?" His voice faltered as he followed her. "I need to talk with her about this."

Karen tensed, and she turned to face him. *Would it be right to tell him? If Mark visited her, maybe his presence would help Roseanna sort through things. But that would be meddling.* Karen wanted Roseanna to rely on the Lord and trust in His plan for her life. Karen hoped everything would work out for her daughter in the end, just as it had for her. She'd gone through so much when she moved to Lykens with Seth and their girls. Karen and Seth had drifted from each other for a time, and Karen hadn't known what to do. Although she got caught up in all of the events that affected their family, she was reassured when she remembered a line of scripture she held deeply in her heart. In the end, the situations resolved themselves, and she and Seth had decided to stay in the Lykens Valley.

She shook her head. "I'm sorry, Mark. I know you have plenty to say to Roseanna, but I don't think it's the best idea right now. You need to give her some time to think and pray about things."

"I guess you're right." Mark clasped his hands. "I've been patient with her so far, and I'll continue to do so."

After Mark said good-bye, Karen watched his horse and buggy head down the driveway. Obviously Mark wasn't thrilled about John showing up here, but at least he'd agreed not to pressure Roseanna. Karen felt sure her daughter would make the right decision. God was watching over her family and would continue to do so, no matter what happened.

"Mamm." Mary peered out through the

open window. "I got all my chores done. Can I go hang out with my friends?"

Karen looked over her shoulder. "Even cleaning the bathroom?"

"I'll be right back." Mary slid the window shut.

Looking out to the field, Karen smiled as she saw Adam cropping in the distance. It looked like a good hay harvest. *Lord, thank You for watching over my family and for keeping us safe.*

Paradise, Pennsylvania

Roseanna sat on one of the couches in her grandparents' living room. She had been staying at Grandma and Grandpa Zook's home for almost a week but still hadn't figured out what she would do when she returned to Lykens.

I wonder if Mark knows that I'm no longer at home. I should have let him know that I'd be leaving for a while. Roseanna stuffed a throw pillow behind her head. *Maybe I'll give Katie a call and visit with her in a day or two.*

She'd been focusing more on working on another dress and was fortunate that her grandmother had some supplies she was able to borrow. But Roseanna couldn't stay with her grandparents forever, and she didn't want to overstay her welcome, even though she knew they enjoyed her company.

Roseanna was on the verge of resting her eyes for a bit, when she heard footsteps coming from the hallway.

"How's my lovely granddaughter this morning?" Her grandfather's wrinkles were defined by his pleasant expression.

"I'm doing okay." She eyed the coffee mug he held. "I see you're having your boost of energy for today."

"Jah." Grandpa took a long sip. "But only one cup of coffee per day. It's all I need to stay awake." He sat down in his recliner and pulled the lever to elevate his feet. "I could brew you a cup once I finish mine if you want, Roseanna."

"That's okay, Grandpa. I'm not much of a coffee drinker."

Coming from the kitchen, Roseanna's grandmother entered the living room. Her blue eyes twinkled as her gaze went to the front door. "It's nice out this morning. Why don't you join me on the porch and take in God's beauty for a while?"

"Sure." Roseanna stood from the couch. "Would you like to join us, Grandpa?"

"Nah. I've been outside for most of the morning anyway. I'll be fine in here."

When Roseanna stepped outside with Grandma, the breeze from the morning air brushed the fine hairs on her arms, creating a tickling sensation. She and Grandma shared a seat on the porch swing and talked about several things, like how Roseanna felt when she created the dresses her neighbors requested — especially the dimples that formed on little girls' faces when they got pretty new outfits. But Roseanna's thoughts still centered on the larger issues she was facing.

Once her grandmother paused to look out to the yard, and since they were alone on the porch, Roseanna figured it would be the perfect opportunity to confide in her grandma about what was really going on.

"Grandma, I need to confess something to you." Roseanna fumbled with her fingers. "I didn't come here for a simple visit. I actually came here to give myself time to think over a huge problem. But I haven't been able to come up with a proper solution."

"You're being a little vague."

Roseanna lifted her head. "I know. I'm sorry."

"It's okay, dear." Grandma leaned forward to make the swing rock. "Whenever you're ready to tell me, I'll be here to listen."

Sitting in silence, Roseanna intertwined her fingers as she tapped her feet. She trusted her maternal grandmother to give her some encouragement. Even though she didn't see her grandparents as often as she would like, they'd always done their best to be there for her.

Roseanna sighed and then told Grandma about John and how he apologized to her. She expressed her conflicting feelings and said she hadn't stopped thinking about him, even after he first left. She sighed. "Mark made me happy while I was trying to move on. He gave me a sense of hope to commit to a relationship again."

Roseanna paused. "But when I saw John standing there . . . Well, I wanted to tell him to leave and that I never wanted to see him again." Roseanna felt cold, and she knew it wasn't from being outside. "Yet I knew that I would've been lying. To him and to myself. When I saw him, part of me felt happy."

"Hmm . . ." Her grandmother leaned forward, concentrating on Roseanna. "You know, I was in a similar predicament before I married your grandfather."

"What?" Her heartbeat quickened. "What do you mean, Grandma? Grandpa ran from your wedding?"

Her grandmother giggled and patted Roseanna's shoulder. "No, dear. But there was another man who was determined to have me. And for a time, I even considered that option."

Roseanna slapped a hand against her cheek. "You mean you almost didn't marry Grandpa? But what made you decide he was the one?"

"It was not a difficult choice to make, because I loved him very much." She brushed Roseanna's shoulder and smiled. "But my folks didn't approve of our relationship because Grandpa was sixteen years older than me. All I could do was pray about it and rely on God to give me a sense of peace. Of course, in the end my parents gave us their blessing, and we've been happily married ever since." Grandma patted Roseann's arm. "When you ask the Lord for guidance, He will surely have an answer for you."

She shook her head. "Grandma, I have prayed about it, and I still don't know what to do."

"Answers don't always come right away, Roseanna. Everything happens in God's time, but it will all work out when you have faith in the path He has for you."

Roseanna fiddled with her sleeve, feeling her muscles tense up. *I know I need to continue to pray, but I need an answer now. I can't wait any longer. If I do, then I may not have the chance to be with John or Mark.*

"I also refer to a verse that has been with me throughout my long life."

"What is the verse, Grandma?" Roseanna swallowed. "Maybe it could help me, too."

Her grandmother sighed with contentment. " 'For thou art my rock and my fortress; therefore for thy name's sake lead me, and guide me.' "

"Where is that verse found in the Bible?"

"Psalm 31:3." Grandma closed her eyes as she kept the swing moving. "I am surprised you aren't familiar with the verse."

"What do you mean? Should I have memorized it?"

"I would suggest you memorize many verses from the Bible. We all need to be reminded that God is always there to guide us through even the most difficult times. That constant reminder will be what you need to get through your decision."

Leaning back in her chair, Roseanna noticed how some of the leaves were beginning to drift away from the branches of the sugar maple tree. *Fall is just around the corner.* Roseanna took in a deep breath. *Please, Lord. I know everything happens in Your time, but I hope You'll answer my prayers soon. Please give me a sense of direction.*

CHAPTER 12

Lykens

December started snowy and cold. Roseanna compacted the cold powder in her hands, trying to form a snowball, but it crumbled away. "Looks like we can't have a snowball fight, after all."

"Again?" Adam's shoulders slumped. "Why can't it be the good kind of snow? It would make the cold weather better if it was."

She rubbed her hands together, quickly enough for them to ignite with warmth. "Hey, Adam. You know that one hillside we go to every year?"

His mouth stretched wider than taffy. "Are you suggesting we go sledding, Roseanna?"

"Maybe. Why don't you go and fetch Mary and Nancy Anne, while I get the sleds?"

"Can do."

As Adam took off to the house, Roseanna

hurried to the shed and flung the door open. *Maybe we could invite Mark on the way there.* She giggled as her face heated up. When she'd returned to Lykens over a month ago, Roseanna had decided she wouldn't let John influence how she felt toward Mark, so she continued to turn him down regardless of his persistence.

Roseanna realized it was best to move on, but John had yet to give up on her. He stopped over to see Roseanna several times a week, saying he'd changed, and always with the promise that he would never hurt her again. Roseanna couldn't find it in her heart to trust him. He'd hurt her deeply, and she couldn't let it happen again.

Her lips pressed together in a slight grimace. *It would be much easier for me to move on if John would, too. Having him around makes me think about what we once had.*

"We're ready to go, Roseanna!" Mary called.

"Okay." Roseanna pulled two of the sleds out of the shed. "Could you help me carry these to my buggy?"

"Of course." Mary scooped up her sled, and Roseanna took Nancy Anne's. Then they headed to the buggy.

As they turned onto the road, not far away

from where they lived, Roseanna directed the horse to Mark's home. She pulled into his driveway, and after halting the buggy, she climbed out and hurried to the front door. The snowflakes slowed, and it seemed as if time had almost stopped.

"Do you have a sled, Mark?" Roseanna called when he came out of the house.

"I do."

"Good to hear. Would you like to go sledding with us?"

"Think I'd rather watch you enjoy the snow, so I don't need to bring my sled along."

"Oh, okay." Roseanna couldn't hide her disappointment.

Mark leaned over and planted a kiss on her forehead. "Don't lose that beautiful smile of yours."

Even though her face felt numb from the cold, the heat traveling to her cheeks seemed to remedy the feeling. Mark had a way with words, and she couldn't help but smile whenever he said something nice about her.

Mark climbed into the buggy with them, and when they reached their destination, Roseanna's siblings were quick to get out of the buggy and run up to the top of the hill, hollering all the way.

"So this is where you guys sled every

year?" Mark helped Roseanna down and picked up her sled for her.

"Thank you. And yes, some of the other people from our community come here, too, this time of year. It's kind of our designated place to sled."

They walked up the hill together, giggling and bumping one another's arm as their feet sank in the fresh-fallen snow. When they reached the top, a handful of people were already sliding down the hill to the edge of the road.

"Roseanna!" Samantha ran over, waving her arms above her head. "How are you doing today?"

"I wanted to do some sledding. Now that we're here, I'm doing okay."

"I can see that." Samantha glanced at Mark and smiled. "How have you been, Mark?"

"Work has been keeping me busy. Fortunately, I'm able to make horseshoes quicker than most blacksmiths, so I take enjoyment from it." Mark looked at Roseanna. "But I'm never too busy to see her."

Roseanna gazed at him, noticing how the soft strands of black hair lying across Mark's forehead contrasted with the pure white snowflakes. The way he laughed made Roseanna feel like there was nothing to worry about, that nothing else mattered.

I felt this way about John, too, didn't I? Roseanna looked away from Mark. *What is it going to take for me to move on? Why did John have to come back and mess with my emotions?*

Her vision began to rock, like the time she went fishing with John on one of their first dates. Roseanna had bet him that she could stand while he paddled the boat back to the dock, but she ended up losing her balance and toppling over into the pond. When she surfaced, Roseanna started laughing, and John joined in as he pulled her out of the water.

"Roseanna? Are you okay?" Mark's thick eyebrows drew together. "You're awfully quiet, all of a sudden."

"I'm fine, Mark. Really. Don't worry about it." Roseanna knocked her knuckles against the sled. "But I am going to need this if I want to go down the hill."

Samantha snickered. "Good, because I was wondering how long you two lovebirds were going to stare at each other with adoration in your eyes. I'm feeling kinda envious."

Roseanna's face heated in a matter of seconds. "I'm sorry, Samantha. We'll avoid doing that from now on."

"No promises." Mark winked.

Samantha told them she wanted to stay longer but needed to head home soon to go to a family gathering at her uncle's place.

Once Samantha left, Roseanna took Mark's gloved hand and hurried in the direction of where her siblings had gone. The ice from the ground cut into her arm a couple of times as she rode her sled down the hill. When Roseanna rolled up the sleeve to check her arm, she had only minor scrapes. It was hard to tell when most of her body was numb from the cold.

Roseanna headed up the hill, massaging the tender spot on her arm. She could see Mark near the top, his hands stuffed in his jacket pockets.

"What's wrong with your arm, Roseanna? Did you hurt yourself?"

"No, I'm fine. I just —"

"Nancy Anne!"

As soon as she heard Mary's shrill voice on the other side of the hill, Roseanna lunged forward, adrenaline rushing throughout her body. Nancy Anne was at the bottom of the hill with a vehicle heading straight toward her.

Roseanna shouted out to her, forgetting for the moment that Nancy Anne couldn't hear anything. By the time Roseanna slid down the hill, it was too late. It all happened in a matter of moments, yet it seemed like everything around her had slowed down. Holding back the scream building in her throat, Roseanna fell to her knees beside her youngest sister.

"Nancy Anne, please, say something. Please." Roseanna placed her hand on Nancy Anne's forehead. Mary crouched beside her, shaking uncontrollably.

Adam came over and knelt next to Mary. "Oh no." He looked at Roseanna with teary eyes.

"Is she okay, Roseanna? Please tell me she'll be okay."

Roseanna turned to Mary and glared. "Why?"

"Huh?"

"Why did you just stand there? You could've done something, Mary! Why weren't you watching out for her?"

Adam stayed right where he was. "Let's calm down, you guys. Our sister doesn't need this right now."

"I didn't mean to! I just yelled, and . . . I . . ." Mary covered her face with her hands. "I'm so stupid."

"No, you're not." Adam rested his gloved hand on Mary's shoulder. "When the ambulance gets here, I'll rush home with the buggy and let Mom and Dad know right away about Nancy Anne."

"That would be a good idea." Mary smiled briefly with tears clinging to her lashes. "Thank you, Adam."

He nodded.

Roseanna wiped her cheeks with the collar of her jacket. As much as she fought the urge to sob, the tears kept trailing down her cheeks. "You're not stupid, Mary." She forced those words out, not wanting to upset her sister even more. Roseanna reminded herself that she had made many mistakes in the past. She'd always assumed she would be prepared for the worst. Obviously she wasn't.

Nancy Anne's petite body lay motionless, like a faceless doll. Roseanna was beyond keeping any sort of composure, yet she refused to let the sadness seep through. All she felt was anger toward herself for failing to protect Nancy Anne.

"An ambulance should arrive soon." The person who owned the van approached. "I'm so sorry. I tried to stop, but the roads were slick, and the sled came out of nowhere."

Roseanna said nothing. If she spoke, she might say something she would later regret.

"It isn't your fault, Miss," Mark spoke up.

"She may have gotten out of the road faster if she'd heard you. You see, the girl you hit is deaf, so that's why she didn't realize your van was heading her way."

"Oh, that makes sense. I hit my horn, but she didn't respond." The woman's voice trembled.

"Jah, and honestly, people like her shouldn't be doing activities like this, anyway."

The faint sound of a siren could be heard in the distance. Roseanna noticed Mary and Adam's dissatisfied looks at Mark after his unjust comment.

Roseanna's muscles quivered as she rose from the ground. "What are you saying, Mark?"

"I'm saying this wouldn't have happened if your sister weren't sledding in the first place — especially when she can't hear anything."

"Are you implying that she shouldn't have a normal life?" Heat flashed through Roseanna's body. At other times Mark had made negative comments about Nancy Anne's disability, but because he'd shown a willingness to learn sign language, Roseanna had seen his critical comments simply as minor teasing.

"She has been causing you nothing but

grief with her constant reliance on you, hasn't she? What happened here is an example of that. Your sister could've stayed home and would have been safer there."

"Nancy Anne does not cause us grief!" Roseanna's voice shook. "She has done the opposite of that. She is encouraging, endearing, and courteous. Qualities that you seem to lack!"

Mark's eyes flashed. "I'm not courteous? Do you not remember the many dates we went on? How much of a gentleman I was?" His nostrils flared. "I even learned sign language to communicate with her."

"But you weren't doing those things to be kind, were you?"

"What do you mean?"

"You were only trying to appease me the whole time. None of it was for her."

"Roseanna —"

"I don't want to hear your excuses, Mark." She drew in a long breath.

Their quarreling ended because of the arrival of the ambulance. Roseanna was relieved when the EMTs on scene began checking Nancy Anne's vitals. They asked Roseanna some questions about her injured sister and wanted her to come along for the support. Roseanna could help with communicating to Nancy Anne if she became conscious.

The paramedics told the siblings which hospital they'd be taking their sister to. Roseanna and Mary talked with Adam. He said he'd drop off Mark on his way back home to tell Dad and Mom. The EMTs loaded Nancy Anne into the ambulance, and Roseanna and Mary climbed in afterward. Roseanna noticed that Mark had walked away moments after they'd joined Nancy Anne in the ambulance. But she wasn't worried about him. Roseanna was only concerned about Nancy Anne's condition.

She grasped her sister's hand, so cold to the touch. All Roseanna could do for Nancy Anne now was to pray she would be all right.

CHAPTER 13

Harrisburg, Pennsylvania

Roseanna and Mary sat in the waiting-room chairs near the main doors of the hospital. Mary wanted to go into the room with their sister, but Roseanna informed her that the doctor and nurses needed time to diagnosis her. As soon as they had entered the building, Roseanna had wondered if her folks knew about the accident. Adam should be home by now and have given their parents the bad news. Roseanna's dad and mom would be arranging a driver to take them to the hospital.

Mary grasped Roseanna's arm, parting her lips, but nothing came out as she looked past the check-in counter.

"Mary?" Roseanna placed a hand on top of her sister's hand. "Mary, she'll be okay. We need to pray and think positive thoughts."

"But what if she . . ." Mary covered her

mouth as if to stop the words. Tears formed in her eyes.

"Don't say it. You don't know for sure."

"You don't know, either, Roseanna." Mary's eyes reddened, and her cheeks were stained with tears. "She wouldn't even need help if it wasn't for me. I should have been watching her more closely."

Roseanna couldn't blame her sister for feeling guilty. She felt the same guilt, even though neither one of them could have done anything to stop the van from hitting Nancy Anne.

But I could've suggested for us to head home sooner. Roseanna bit her lip.

A passenger van pulled up to the entrance with Roseanna's parents, Adam, and Grandpa and Grandma Allgyer. While Roseanna and her family waited to hear about Nancy's condition, John appeared. He'd heard about Nancy's accident from his parents' driver, who had taken Roseanna's parents to the hospital. With her sister's condition unclear, and feeling betrayed by Mark, Roseanna didn't know what to do.

The doors opened and a doctor approached the family. Roseanna could barely breathe. After confirming their identities, the doctor explained that Nancy Anne had received a minor concussion and a broken arm but would be okay.

The family's relief was tangible. The doctor went on to explain that they'd keep Nancy Anne in the hospital overnight for further observation because of the concussion. They were also going to set the break in her arm and would need to wait until the swelling went down before putting it in a cast.

Roseanna's parents went back with the doctor to see their daughter and explain to her what would be happening.

Roseanna leaned back in her chair, thanking the Lord for protecting Nancy Anne during the accident. She looked over at John, glad he'd come. Her family needed all the support they could get.

Lykens

After a few days had passed and Nancy Anne was back home, recovering from her injuries, Roseanna decided to make a trip into town to get more sewing supplies.

"How is your sister, Roseanna?" Catherine asked as she rang up the remaining items. "I heard about what happened to her, and I've been concerned."

"She's doing better, even with her arm hurting and in a cast. Nancy Anne just needs some time to heal."

"That's a relief. I hope she'll get better soon."

Roseanna smiled. "Thank you. I appreciate your concern."

Waving good-bye to Catherine, she went out the door and walked right into a light snowfall. Roseanna looked at the gray sky. It mirrored her overall mood. She hugged her bag of new sewing supplies close in an attempt to keep them dry as she headed toward her buggy.

I'll surprise Nancy Anne with a new dress. I'm glad she's home and not still at the hospital. But the night of the accident could've been a lot worse. She snugged up her scarf around her shoulders.

After having released most of her pent-up emotions over the past few days, Roseanna still struggled with guilt and frustration — especially toward Mark.

"Roseanna?"

Her shoulders jerked when she realized who was behind her. "Mark."

"Hey. I'm sorry for startling you." His eyes shifted to the side.

She waited.

Mark looked back at her. "I'm sorry I wasn't there at the hospital. After you got mad at me, I assumed you wouldn't want me there." He lowered his head. "Adam gave me a ride home. That was nice of him, considering how I was behaving."

Roseanna swallowed hard. She knew Mark cared about her. He had brought joy to her life, after the emotional upheaval she'd experienced from being jilted by John. But one thing was certain: they needed to address a few issues.

"I forgive you, Mark."

"Thank you." He slid his hand down the side of his trousers. "So, do you want to continue where we left off?"

"Mark, I know you mean well, but I —"

"Roseanna, I upset you, but things can go back to the way they were. We could be happy again. Please give me the chance to make it up to you."

"Mark, I don't think —"

"Please." He clutched her arm. "Don't do this."

Roseanna swallowed against the lump forming in her throat. "I'm sorry. I don't think it's destined for us to be together."

Despite Mark's pleas, Roseanna held firm. Even though he had apologized for not going to the hospital to see Nancy Anne, he had not apologized for the things he'd said about her being deaf. That's what hurt Roseanna the most.

"You'll find someone else, Mark, and I

wish you well."

"Does this mean you're going back to John?"

She shook her head. "I can't be with anyone right now."

Roseanna hurried away. It was over for them, and at that moment, she saw faithfulness in God's plan. There was hope for her to continue to grow from the troubles she had faced, and the best thing to do was to move forward, even though her future was uncertain.

Mark isn't the right person for me, and neither is John, since he can't commit to marriage. Roseanna climbed into her buggy.

John paced around his parents' home, attempting to clear his head. He wanted to confess to Roseanna why he hadn't been able to commit to their relationship before and explain why he was ready to do so now. Yet how was he supposed to approach the issue in a way that she would understand? *What about Mark? Is Roseanna committed to him now? Does she love Mark more than she loved me?*

"I need to do something," John mumbled. "I need to talk to her and sort this out."

John headed out the door, but a few minutes in the cold sent him back inside to get his hat and jacket.

Even though the ground was covered with almost a foot of snow, he decided not to take his buggy. John stumbled a bit as he lifted his feet while walking. *I hope you'll be able to understand, Roseanna. Understand why I left.*

When he reached her home, John breathed deeply, hoping to get his nerves to calm. He wasn't sure how Roseanna would respond to everything he was about to tell her, but she needed to know the truth. Maybe then, she would be willing to give him another chance.

John knocked on the back door and waited. As he stood there, looking up, snowflakes landed on his face.

The door opened. "John?" Roseanna's fingers touched her parted lips. "What are you doing here?"

He clasped his hands together. "I was just wondering. . . . Would you mind taking a walk with me? I need to talk with you."

She cleared her throat. "Okay. I'll go get my jacket."

Roseanna closed the door, leaving him waiting. He let out a soft breath. *I'm glad she didn't reject my offer.*

Roseanna returned, bundled up in her jacket, and closed the door behind her.

"Lead the way, John." Her blue eyes looked even more vivid with the snowflakes landing on her long lashes.

They walked from the house, side by side. As much as John tried to hide it, he was pretty sure Roseanna could sense his nervousness as they neared the frozen pond by her home. If he was courting Roseanna again, he would suggest they come here to ice skate.

Hesitantly, John took Roseanna's gloved hand and was relieved when she didn't pull away. "Roseanna, I know you are still with Mark, but I have to get this off my chest."

"No, John." She looked down at her feet. "I'm not with him anymore."

John blinked rapidly. "But, I thought you'd —"

"Worked things out? Well, we did, and we're not a couple anymore." Roseanna lifted her head. "But that doesn't mean you can swoop back in and expect that I'll take you back. It doesn't work like that."

John let go of her hand. He would do whatever he could to have Roseanna back in his life, even if it meant falling to his knees and begging for another chance to prove himself. But he couldn't do that and expect Roseanna to change her mind.

He sighed. "At least let me explain why I

left. Why I left the first wedding, too. You deserve to know that much."

"All right."

Sitting down on a log near the frozen pond, John prepared to speak. "Remember when you met my grandfather who lives not far from here?"

"Jah. I remember." Roseanna sat down next to him.

"You also know that my grandmother passed away when I was younger."

She nodded.

John shuffled his feet against the bottom of the log, attempting to process his thoughts. "He did live in Ohio with the rest of us at one point. We were all together as a family. Being an only child and having just a few friends, I would visit my grandparents fairly often."

John shifted on the uncomfortable log. "My grandparents were nice people. They looked after me and made every single moment I had with them enjoyable. But like most folks, they weren't perfect. They argued with each other over the smallest things. Sometimes those arguments would escalate to the point where I couldn't bear hearing them yell at one another."

He fiddled with the buttons on his jacket, struggling to keep his words on track. "The problem was both of them thought they were always right. It was a challenge for them to admit when they were wrong or that they'd spoken too rashly over something so minuscule. So they were left with a lot of unresolved issues that complicated their marriage."

"I didn't know that." Roseanna looked intently at him. "Your grandfather seems laid back and willing to hear someone else's point of view."

"Jah. He's more like that now than he used to be." John bit his lip. "Grandma and Grandpa got into an immense argument one time. I don't even remember what it was about. I think I was six or seven then."

"Didn't your grandmother pass away when you were around that age?"

John nodded. "My grandmother passed away a few weeks after that big argument, but she and my grandfather had never apologized to each other or resolved their issues." He looked away from Roseanna and stared at the pond. "My grandfather regretted not resolving their marital issues, and regrets it to this day. Part of him is still stuck in the past, unable to move on."

"So you thought the same thing would happen if you got married?"

"Jah. I've been afraid of marriage ever since."

"But you're nothing like your grandfather, and I'm not your grandmother. I can't really say much about the first person you were going to marry, but you can't determine how our marriage would've been based on what your grandparents went through. Not all marriages are that way."

"Roseanna, throughout my life, people have told me how much I resemble my grandfather. Especially when I got upset and wouldn't back down from an argument." His shoulders shook. "Just look at how much I've hurt you."

"You only hurt me because you left." Her voice cracked. "I thought it was my fault. I thought you didn't think I was suitable. And the truth is, I was afraid to commit, too. But I was certain we would be okay until the moment you ran out of that tent."

"I know. I made a terrible choice, Roseanna." John rubbed at his chin. "When I was courting Sara, we argued a lot. But we somehow believed we were ready to get married. When I ran out on that wedding and then met you, I thought I'd made the right choice."

"Then why?" Roseanna looked away from him, her voice more quiet. "Why did you leave me, John?"

John's chin dipped to his chest. Guilt cut through him like a knife. He'd been worried he would hurt Rosanna by marrying her, yet he had hurt her more by leaving.

Swallowing hard, he forced himself to look at her. "I didn't want either of us to regret not being able to resolve our problems. I didn't know if I could commit to being a good husband to you and be happy with our marriage." John's voice tightened and his vision blurred, as he struggled to keep his emotions at bay. "To be a good father. To be a good role model. I have no experience in that, Rosanna. You're the one who's suitable for marriage. Not me."

Roseanna looked at him through the increasing snowfall. "I've been listening to what you have said, John. Your faith is suffering the most from what I can tell. Your grandparents may have had problems with their relationship, but you can move on from it."

John gazed at her and nodded.

"I have seen the other side of a marriage with my folks and two sets of grandparents." Roseanna paused. "They interact most of the time with respectful accord."

John lifted a gloved hand to shake snow

from his hat. "I understand that not all families have problems with getting along. I was worried more how we — or more myself — would handle conflicts when they arose."

"But you didn't give us a chance to find out how we'd deal with difficulties." Roseanna shifted her weight. "Anyway, that wasn't a good enough reason to take off on our wedding day."

"I know it wasn't, and I am truly sorry for putting you through all of that." His tone was sincere. "If you will give me another chance, I promise not to let you down."

"John, I would like to pray about this." She moved away from him. "I'm going to head inside. I am getting cold sitting out here, and you probably are, too."

"Thank you, Roseanna, for hearing me out." John gave her a quick wave and headed to his buggy.

Once inside, Roseanna removed her outer garments, went up to her bedroom, and closed the door. Roseanna lay on her bed and grabbed the Bible on the nightstand. She turned to Proverbs 16:20 and read out loud: " 'He that handleth a matter wisely shall find good: and whoso trusteth in the Lord, happy is he.' "

Roseanna felt a strong confidence that she

could trust the Lord. During her visit with Grandma and Grandpa Zook, Grandma had said Roseanna should follow what her heart told her to do and follow God's leading.

She stared up at the ceiling. Roseanna was thankful for the time she'd spent with her grandparents. She appreciated their advice and enjoyed being with them. She prayed that God would give her wisdom about her relationship with John.

As she continued to lie there with the Bible in her hands, she tried to think of the verse embroidered on the back of Mom's beloved Christmas quilt. Roseanna remembered it was from a psalm, but which one? She began skimming through the book of Psalms, trying to find it. While she searched, Roseanna reached a conclusion: in the morning, she would speak to John and give their relationship another chance. She would trust God to make clear to her if John was the man He wanted her to spend the rest of her life with.

CHAPTER 14

Eight Months Later

Waking up to the light shining through the crack in her window shade, Roseanna sat up in bed and unraveled the covers. She could hear the early risers visiting downstairs.

Today feels vaguely familiar. She laughed nervously. It had been more than eight months since John had begun courting her again. She honestly didn't know what today had in store for her, but she wanted to be optimistic about it.

Roseanna went to the window. The leaves were showing signs of autumn, with the summer colors fading away, offering reassurance of her special day. It was the second time she and John had arranged to be married.

She walked over to her closet. Although she still had her original wedding dress, Roseanna had sewed another one for this occasion. She used a blue fabric again, but it had a hint of iris to the shade. Her blue eyes stood out as she looked at herself in front of the mirror, holding the dress.

"I made a good choice with this fabric color," she mused.

A knock sounded on her door. "Roseanna, are you coming down for breakfast?" Mary asked.

"Jah. I'll be down in a minute." She laid the dress on the bed. *I better hurry and get ready once I finish eating.* Roseanna opened her bedroom door. The aromas of familiar and favorite foods drifted in, causing her stomach to growl. *I can't wait to sample breakfast this morning. Hopefully I'll be able to control how much I eat.*

Roseanna met her father at the bottom of the stairs. "Good morning, Daughter. Did you sleep well?"

"Good morning." She tucked a stray strand of hair behind her ear. "For the most part, but I kept hoping I didn't forget to do something."

"Your list should help you with that, right?" He motioned her to lead the way.

"It's pretty much checked off as of now." She smiled at him then walked to the kitchen.

"How's my daughter and the soon-to-be-wife this morning?" Mom gave her a hug.

"I'm doing fine." She returned the embrace and took a seat at the table.

Everyone was all smiles. Roseanna watched her mother buzzing around the kitchen. Her dad poured himself some coffee and offered to get anyone else some. Grandpa Zook's voice boomed his need for a cup.

Grandma added, "I'd like a hot cup too, Seth."

As Roseanna sat eating breakfast with her family, she could barely focus on the conversation. It felt like she was reliving the past. Well, at least Dad hadn't spilled his coffee this time. And everyone seemed extra chipper. Soon Katie would arrive to help Roseanna prepare for her big day.

Mom and Grandma had made a couple of breakfast casseroles, as well as a bowl of fresh berries and cut-up fruit with yogurt and homemade granola mixed in it. Roseanna liked everything, but her nerves were challenging her appetite. After silent prayer, everyone dished up their breakfast, clearly enjoying their choices.

Roseanna took small portions of the fruit and a good spoonful of the casserole. "This is definitely one of my favorites. Thank you for making it," she said to her sisters, Mom, and Grandma, signing it as well.

"You're welcome," they responded in unison, with Nancy Anne signing the same words.

Nancy Anne sat next to Roseanna and signed: "How are you doing this morning? Any butterflies?"

"I'm doing well, so far." She smiled, placing one hand on her stomach. "My butterflies are doing good, too." Roseanna talked with her hands.

Nancy Anne laughed along with her whole family.

"My daughter will do just fine today." Mom beamed, and her eyes twinkled.

"You're right about that," Dad added.

"We're so happy for you, granddaughter. What an extraordinary day this is." Grandma reached over and patted Roseanna's hand.

Roseanna watched Adam spooning more casserole on his plate. Her brother could put away huge portions of food, and it hardly showed on him. He looked over at Roseanna. "Since you aren't eating much, I'll eat enough for the both of us."

"Just wait until it's your turn," Dad said. "Getting married can make anyone nervous."

"I remember your father on our wedding

day. He worried about whether his hair was sticking up," Mom teased.

"I didn't do that." He looked at his wife and then her folks.

Their heads nodded as they chuckled over the memory.

"See, Adam. That just proved my point. Even I was a bit nervous on my wedding day." Dad leaned back in the chair and brought his coffee cup up to his lips.

Roseanna finished the food on her plate. It was nice to have all her family here. Before noon today, she would be married and known as Mrs. John Beiler. She took a sip of her apple juice, staring out at a finch on the feeder.

"Rosey." Her mother's voice intruded. "Did you get enough to eat?" Mom got up from the table and put some of the food back into the pantry.

"Plenty." Roseanna carried her dish and glass over to the sink. "I hope I didn't eat too much. Otherwise I won't be able to eat any of the meal after the wedding."

Grandma Zook giggled. "We can't have that now, can we?"

Roseanna rinsed her dishes and placed them in the pan of warm sudsy water.

"Don't worry about the dishes." Mom enveloped Roseanna in a warm hug. "You need to finish getting ready for the wedding."

A knock sounded at the front door, so Roseanna went to see who it was. Katie stood there with her own dress. "Good morning, Roseanna."

"Hi. Come on in. Are you hungry? There's some food in the kitchen," Roseanna offered her good friend.

"Katie, is that you?" Roseanna's mother called. "If you're hungry, come on in here and we can take care of you."

"Well, okay. I barely ate a slice of toast this morning," Katie admitted.

Roseanna took Katie's dress and held on to it for her friend.

"Here's a plate for you. We can't have you passing out due to lack of energy," Mom teased.

Roseanna watched Katie dish up a nice amount of casserole and heap fruit on her plate. "Should I eat right here?"

"No, take it upstairs with you so I can start getting ready." Roseanna nudged Katie's arm. *I wish I had her appetite.*

"Okay, thank you for this meal." Katie smiled at Roseanna's mom.

"You're very welcome."

"Let's go up." Roseanna hurried from the room, with Katie trailing along.

■ ■ ■ ■

Leaves huddled around the outside of the tent and some skittered across the gravel, as Roseanna followed John. She couldn't fight the urge to shiver when the breeze whirled through. *It's a lot colder than it was last year.* Roseanna rubbed her arms to take off the chill.

"Are you nervous, Roseanna?" John sat down on the bench near the opening of the tent. Leaning slightly forward with one hand on his knee, he looked up at her.

"No. Well, yes." Her face heated. "It was just a chill. It's not exactly the warmest of days."

"Yeah, true."

Roseanna sat beside him. Her fingers tingled as she heard guests coming into the tent. "Are you nervous?"

"Very much." He reached for her hand. "But I know I can get through it because I have you."

Roseanna's heart fluttered. It felt like butterflies were dancing in her stomach. The first hymn had begun, which meant it was time for her and John to be counseled by the ministers, so they got up and headed toward the house. *John and I will make it through this.* She looked over at him. *I sure hope we can.*

It seemed to take hours to finish the counseling. Her mind wandered into possible outcomes of the wedding. Either she would become John's wife and have a future with him, or she was going to be disappointed again. Roseanna could see how her fiancé was different this time around. She could also see how much he cared for her, yet her fears still battled her hopes.

Roseanna tugged on her dress. *I don't want you to leave me again. I don't want you to hurt me again. I couldn't bear it.*

She scolded herself. *Is this the way someone of faith should think or feel about the one they love?*

After the counseling ended, it was time to reenter the tent and sit down in front of everyone. Roseanna was nervous about who was watching and what they might say about her and John. Fortunately, most of the people in her community were caring and supportive. Rosanna prayed everything would go according to the Lord's plan. Discreetly, she glanced over at John.

He scooted his chair forward, which caused a wave of anticipation to wash over Roseanna. She wished she could get his attention, and felt relieved when he relaxed against the back of his seat. *Oh. He was just repositioning himself.* She clasped her fingers together. *I'm being too paranoid.* Closing her eyes briefly, she prayed, *Lord, I ask for Your perfect peace to wrap around me and John. Amen.*

John's eyes shifted to Roseanna, noticing how uneasy she looked. *Roseanna probably thinks I'm about to run out on her like I did before. I understand why she would.* He lowered his head. *There's no excuse for what I did to her. Don't worry, Roseanna. I'm done running. I am committed to sharing our new life together.* He closed his eyes. *Lord, please allow my thoughts to concentrate on Your spiritual principles in the messages about marriage that will be given this morning, and let me remember these words of wisdom. Amen.*

John's jaw had been sore from being clenched, but he began to relax as he focused on the message one of the ministers was giving about the importance of honesty, communication, and commitment in marriage. The sacrament of marriage was not to be taken lightly.

When the first minister finished, there was a period of silent prayer. All those present turned around and knelt, facing their bench.

After the prayer was over, the congregation stood, but still did not turn around. A deacon read a passage of scripture from the Gospel of Matthew. The congregation sat down.

As the bishop stood up to speak, John glanced at his betrothed. Her genuine smile removed all fear.

When the bishop finished his message, he announced: "We have two people who have agreed to enter the state of matrimony, John Beiler and Roseanna Allgyer."

Roseanna and John rose from their seats, walked forward, and stood before the bishop.

The bishop looked at John. "Can you confess, brother, that you accept this, our sister, as your wife, and that you will not leave her until death separates you? And do you believe that this is from the Lord and that you have come thus far by your faith and prayers?"

John answered without hesitation: "Yes."

After that, the bishop directed his words to Roseanna. "Can you confess, sister, that you accept this, our brother, as your husband, and that you will not leave him until death separates you? And do you believe that this is from the Lord and that you have come thus far by your faith and prayers?"

"Yes," Roseanna replied with confidence.

After another quote from the bishop, he took Roseanna's right hand and placed it in John's right hand. Putting his own hands above and beneath their hands, he continued with a blessing. "The God of Abraham, the God of Isaac, and the God of Jacob be with you together and give His rich blessing upon you and be merciful to you. To this I wish you the blessings of God for a good beginning and a steadfast middle time, and may you hold out until a blessed end. This all in and through Jesus Christ. Amen."

At the name of Christ, all three bowed their knees.

"Go forth in the name of the Lord. You are now man and wife."

As Roseanna and John returned to their chairs, she felt blissful and knew they would do their best to live according to God's biblical plan for marriage. With every passing day and night, they would be together as one mind, one body, and one soul.

EPILOGUE

One year later

On the day for exchanging Christmas gifts, the snow had been falling lightly. Roseanna was surrounded by her family at her and John's new home. They'd had a nice turkey dinner along with some tasty trimmings. The women had cleaned and put away all the dishes. Then they joined the men in the living room, where a warm fire burned in the fireplace. Adam had been chosen to pass out the gifts to the family members.

Roseanna and John had lived with his parents the first months of their marriage, putting money away toward a home of their own, which they had recently purchased. During the months that had passed since their wedding, Roseanna could see positive changes in John as his faith grew. She was excited to be living in the older home they'd bought, with all the new things they had added to it. Today's gathering was a testament to how well everything was working out for Roseanna and John.

While exchanging gifts, Adam handed Roseanna a familiar package from her mother. Opening the pretty box, she pulled out the Christmas quilt she had refused to take when she'd been jilted by John. Roseanna looked up. "Mom, why didn't you save the quilt for Mary?"

Mom smiled. "You're the eldest daughter, so it goes to you. I have other special mementos for Mary and Nancy Anne when their times come."

Feeling grateful for the family God had given her, and especially for John, Roseanna accepted the beloved Christmas quilt.

After all the gifts had been given out, the ladies went to the kitchen to get the desserts. There was plenty to eat and a couple of new things to try. About the time they'd finished their pies and cakes, everyone was ready to do some singing. What fun it was to be together enjoying one another's company.

That evening after all the family had left and the house stood quiet as the soft falling snow outside, Roseanna examined the quilt, realizing the verse Grandma Zook had shared with her was the same one embroidered on the quilt backing. She read the verse silently. *"For thou art my rock and my fortress; therefore for thy name's sake lead me, and guide me"* — *Psalm 31:3.*

As she held it tenderly in her arms, Roseanna looked forward to someday passing both this special Christmas quilt and the promise it contained on to her own daughter.

ROSEANNA'S PUMPKIN PIE

Ingredients:
1 cup pumpkin, cooked
1 1/2 cups coconut sugar
1 teaspoon salt
1/2 teaspoon cloves
1/2 teaspoon allspice
1 teaspoon cinnamon
4 tablespoons coconut flour
4 egg yolks
4 cups milk
1 teaspoon vanilla
4 egg whites, beaten until stiff
1 (9 inch) unbaked pastry shell

Preheat oven to 375°. In mixing bowl, combine pumpkin, coconut sugar, salt, cloves, allspice, cinnamon, and flour. Add egg yolks, milk, and vanilla to the dry ingredients, stirring until mixed well. Fold in stiff egg whites. Pour into unbaked pastry shell. Bake 1 hour or until knife inserted in pie comes out clean.

ABOUT THE AUTHORS

New York Times bestselling and award-winning author **Wanda E. Brunstetter** is one of the founders of the Amish fiction genre. She has written close to ninety books translated in four languages. With over 10 million copies sold, Wanda's stories consistently earn spots on the nation's most prestigious bestseller lists and have received numerous awards.

Wanda's ancestors were part of the Anabaptist faith, and her novels are based on personal research intended to accurately portray the Amish way of life. Her books are well read and trusted by many Amish, who credit her for giving readers a deeper understanding of the people and their customs.

When Wanda visits her Amish friends, she finds herself drawn to their peaceful lifestyle, sincerity, and close family ties. Wanda enjoys photography, ventriloquism, gardening, bird-watching, beachcombing, and spending time with her family. She and her husband, Richard, have been blessed with two grown children, six grandchildren, and two great-grandchildren. To learn more about Wanda, visit her website at www .wandabrunstetter.com.

Jean Brunstetter became fascinated with the Amish when she first went to Pennsylvania to visit her father-in-law's family. Since that time, Jean has become friends with several Amish families and enjoys writing about their way of life. She also likes to put some of the simple practices followed by the Amish into her daily routine. Jean lives in Washington State with her husband, Richard Jr., and their three children, but takes every opportunity to visit Amish communities in several states. In addition to writing, Jean enjoys boating, gardening, and spending time on the beach. To learn more about Jean's books, visit her website: www .jeanbrunstetter.com.

Richelle Brunstetter lives in the Pacific Northwest and developed a desire to write when she took creative writing in high school. After enrolling in college classes, her overall experience enticed her to become a writer, and she wants to implement what she's learned into her stories. Just starting her writing career, her first published story appears in *The Beloved Christmas Quilt* beside her grandmother, Wanda E. Brunstetter, and her mother, Jean. Richelle enjoys traveling to different places, her favorite being Kauai, Hawaii.

The employees of Thorndike Press hope you have enjoyed this Large Print book. All our Thorndike, Wheeler, and Kennebec Large Print titles are designed for easy reading, and all our books are made to last. Other Thorndike Press Large Print books are available at your library, through selected bookstores, or directly from us.

For information about titles, please call:
(800) 223-1244

or visit our website at:
gale.com/thorndike

To share your comments, please write:
Publisher
Thorndike Press
10 Water St., Suite 310
Waterville, ME 04901